THE EVENING HOUR

D1070139

THE
EVENING HOUR

a novel

CARTER SICKELS

B L O O M S B U R Y
New York Berlin London Sydney

Copyright © 2012 by Carter Sickels

All rights reserved. No part of this book may be used or reproduced in
any manner whatsoever without written permission from the publisher except
in the case of brief quotations embodied in critical articles or
reviews. For information address Bloomsbury USA, 175 Fifth Avenue,
New York, NY 10010.

Published by Bloomsbury USA, New York

All papers used by Bloomsbury USA are natural, recyclable products made
from wood grown in well-managed forests. The manufacturing processes
conform to the environmental regulations of the country of origin.

LIBRARY OF CONGRESS CATALOGING-IN-PUBLICATION DATA

Sickels, Carter.
The evening hour : a novel / Carter Sickels.—1st U.S. ed.
p. cm.
ISBN: 978-1-60819-597-8
ISBN-10: 1-60819-597-X
1. Mountain people—West Virginia—Fiction.   2. Working poor—Fiction.
3. Mountain life—Fiction.   4. Mountaintop removal mining—Fiction.
5. Choice (Psychology)—Fiction.   6. Appalachian Region—Fiction.
7. Domestic fiction.   I. Title.
PS3619.I27E94 2011
813'.6—dc22
2010053034

First U.S. Edition 2012

1 3 5 7 9 10 8 6 4 2

Typeset by Westchester Book Group
Printed in the U.S.A. by Quad/Graphics, Fairfield, Pennsylvania

For Yukiko Yamagata

And it shall come to pass in the last days, saith God, I will pour out of my Spirit upon all flesh: and your sons and your daughters shall prophesy, and your young men shall see visions, and your old men shall dream dreams.

—ACTS 2:17

The mountains shall bring peace to the people.

—PSALMS 72:3

PART ONE

CHAPTER 1

COLE DOUBLE-LOCKED THE TRAILER DOOR behind him, then stood on the top rickety step for a moment, still waking up. Gunmetal sky, with the faintest hint of light rippling at the edges. There was a tight chill in the air on this early April morning, and he shuddered, rubbing his bare arms. The air smelled like sulfur and scorched earth.

He started his pickup, let it warm up a minute. He'd just bought the Chevy off his twin cousins. Piece of shit. Busted taillight. A rusted-out hole in the floor of the passenger side that he covered with cardboard, so that dust and gravel didn't shoot up into the cab.

Instead of heading out, he drove up to his grandparents'. The lights were on, blazing yellow squares beckoning him. He knew his grandmother would be up. She didn't sleep much; Cole was the same way. He saw her looking out the kitchen window, her pale moony face always worried.

The house was warm and smelled like frying bacon. Cole wiped his feet on the welcome mat and tightened the drawstring waist of his scrubs, which were too big for him, the cuffs spilling over his black hightops. He glanced at himself in the mirror by the front door. It had been a late night, and he looked rough. Three-day-old beard, beak of a nose, thick lips. Goat eyes small and sleepy. His scruffy, bleached-out hair made him look like somebody else.

"I've got breakfast ready," his grandmother greeted him.

"I can't stay. I got to get to work."

In pictures from her youth, his grandmother was thin and willowy, but he'd only ever known her as stout, with sausage-link fingers and doughy flesh. Her hair, in a bun, was the color of gravel. This morning she wore a button-down denim shirt pulled over a thin housecoat and mint green slippers, her white-as-bone ankles thick and swollen like they'd been injected with something.

"Pshaw," she protested, pinching his arm. "You set and eat, put some meat on those bones."

"Grandma, I just stopped in for a minute."

She was studying him. "Well, I see you did that foolishness to your hair again."

"It'll grow back." He added defiantly, "Anyway, I like it."

"I don't know why you'd want to mess with its natural color. If God wanted you to have blond hair, he would have given it to you."

"Well, anyway. I just come by to check on Granddaddy." Yesterday she had called to tell him that his grandfather was throwing a fit; Cole hadn't listened to the message until he rolled in at three a.m. "Sorry I couldn't get over here last night," he added.

"You're hard to get a hold of."

"You could call my cell when I'm not at home."

"I thought you said it doesn't work."

"Doesn't, most of the time." Cole glanced at the clock on the wall. He should have just gone straight to work. "Well, is he okay? How is he?"

"He's all right now. Rebecca and Larry came over last night to help get him settled down." She shook her head. "It was the blasting. Lord, he thought it was the end of the world, you never heard such carrying on," she said angrily. "You smell the sulfur?"

"Yeah, I figured."

Whenever the coal company blasted the mountain, the walls of Cole's trailer trembled, the floors vibrated. His friends told him to take the money and run. The other day he'd found rocks the size of basketballs in his yard.

His grandmother's eyes darkened behind the thick lenses of her glasses. "You look at what they've done."

He followed her through the sparsely decorated house. Nothing hung on the walls save a few family pictures and framed Bible inscriptions. Cole's grandfather believed that austerity led to a clean, healthy soul.

In the hallway she pointed out the jagged cracks.

"Maybe I can patch that up," Cole said.

"You can't patch nothing up. It's not just the walls. They've done ruined the foundation. This house is sinking."

His grandmother logged the time and details of every blast in a legal pad, the chart now a dozen pages long. This seemed to give her some kind of satisfaction and hope, even if it was a waste of time, just like all the calls she'd made to government agencies.

Cole traced the cracks in the wall. They ran up from the floor, broke off, then spread near the ceiling, splintered and spidery like the lines in his own hands. "It's nothing that can't be fixed," he said.

His grandfather was asleep in the La-Z-Boy, one side of his face frozen from a stroke a few years ago. He'd also had what the doctor called "mini strokes," which did not alter his face but ate away at his brain like acid. Every day he said fewer words. "Dementia, similar to Alzheimer's," said the slick doctor in Charleston, who would not look Cole or his grandmother in the eyes.

"When you look at him sleeping like that, he almost looks gentle, don't he?"

Cole agreed that he did and touched his grandfather's cool waxy brow, but he did not stir, breathing in kittenlike breaths.

His thin hair lay in streaks as if painted on. On the stand next to his chair was the King James with its cracked spine, delicate pages. His grandfather no longer read, but sometimes he still opened the Bible and stared at it. He used to quiz Cole on Bible verses. It was the only thing his granddaddy wanted him to learn. Fortunately, Cole was good at memorizing. The verses stayed with him, even now.

"But he wasn't so gentle yesterday," his grandmother added.

The fits were getting worse. A couple of weeks ago, after a blast went off, he had hurled pots and pans, flipped over furniture. His grandmother had locked herself in the bathroom and called Cole at work. By the time he arrived, the old man was curled up under the kitchen table, shaking like a dog.

"I wish you'd take him off that waiting list," Cole said. "If he goes into the nursing home, it'll be the end of him."

"You'll be there with him. You'll take care of him."

"He can't go in there."

She looked away. "Come on and get a bite to eat."

"I gotta go," he said.

"At least let me make you a plate."

Cole followed her into the kitchen. She filled a plate with strips of bacon, scrambled eggs, and biscuits, and poured coffee into a thermos. It was black and steaming. Cole's granddaddy didn't even drink coffee, that's how pure he was.

She handed him the plate, covered in tinfoil, and he thanked her. But before he could head out the door, she stopped him. "Rebecca and me talked last night. She wants me to move in with her and Larry." She took off her glasses and cleaned the lenses on her shirttail. "It's something I've got to consider."

He tried to read her expression. About a year ago, when he had asked if she wanted to take the coal company's latest offer, she said, "There's nowhere else that is home." He wasn't surprised about his aunt Rebecca. All three of his aunts had been talking to him about it, but he stood behind his grandmother. Now he said, "You're backing out."

"I ain't," she snapped. Then, softer, "But things are changing. I got a bad feeling about the land. I been having dreams."

Cole gulped the coffee, burning his mouth. He did not want to hear about her dreams and prophecies, all her worry. The only good thing he'd ever done was to stick by the land and the couple who had raised him. Two years ago, his aunts sold off their parcels of land, one by one, and when Cole had said, "Well, I'm staying," his grandfather just looked up at the sky, like he didn't even hear him.

"I'm running late."

"Can you take me to church tomorrow?"

He shook his head. "I can't."

"Well, come out for dinner," she said. "You can bring that girl if you like."

"I'm working."

"You know what your granddaddy would say about that, working on Sunday."

Cole backed out of the driveway, the thermos of coffee resting between his legs. There was only one road that ran through Rockcamp, and his grandparents' property, tucked in a hillside, was at the end of it, where the rutted asphalt turned to dirt and cleared land gave way to forest. The twenty acres, now whittled down to fourteen, had originally belonged to Cole's great-great-grandfather. For over two hundred years the Freemans had been on this land. Cole's grandparents still lived in the same house where they'd been all of their married lives; his aunts and uncles and cousins used to live on the small plots around them, but they had moved away, spread out across West Virginia and beyond.

Cole lived on a slivered portion of land that would have gone to his mother, if she was around. He drove past his single-wide, which sat close to the road, the hills looming behind it; sometimes when they blasted, the trailer was engulfed in a cloud of dust. The Heritage mining operation up above them had grown to 1,800 acres. It wasn't like the old days of sending men underground. Now, to get to the layers of coal seams, they blew the tops off the mountains, bringing them down hundreds of feet, and then pushed the rubble into the valleys. It was impossible to grasp the enormity of 1,800 acres. That was almost 1,800 football fields. He'd never seen the site; it was guarded and blocked off, and from here, it looked as if the mountain was still standing. Behind the ridge, it was a different story.

He wondered what his grandmother had seen in her dreams. The Holiness said God gave his people gifts. *To another the working of miracles; to another prophecy; to another discerning of spirits; to another divers kinds of tongues; to another the interpretation of tongues.* Cole did not have a gift. He did not speak in tongues or handle snakes or see the future. His grandmother said he needed to open himself up to the Holy Ghost. He'd grown up knowing that there was another world beyond this one; there was more than a person could see with just his eyes.

The folds of forested hills, with newly budded trees, rose like giant steeples behind abandoned homes. At the mouth of the holler sat a few trailers where the miners lived. Most everyone else had moved away—pushed out by the blasting, the dust, the flash floods. One old-timer, Floyd Mitchell, still lived in a shotgun shack, him and his toothless dog Sugar.

He approached Route 16, the main road that ran along Dove Creek. The only road that led him out. Turn right, he'd pass by the processing plant, where the coal was cleaned and shipped out across the country. The leftover waste was then pumped into a basin on the mountain and held back by a giant dam. The sludge dam. Out of sight, out of mind. Turn left, he would head in the direction of Stillwell, the only real town in the area; eventually, that way, Route 16 would connect to other roads, which led to highways, which could take him far away from West Virginia.

He turned left. The sky was lighter, a glowing pink in the east, the air warmer. He drove down the mountain with his elbow resting out the open window, his hand lightly guiding the wheel. The craggy land rose up all around him, pressing in on both sides of the road. Plumes of mist spiraled up from the dips and valleys, the ghosts of the Cherokee and mountaineers, his grandmother would say.

He rounded sharp curves and switchbacks, occasionally looking down into a hollow where the houses huddled together like scared children. He drove by dilapidated clapboard homes, deserted churches, shot-up road signs, and little white crosses with plastic flowers commemorating the dead. All of it was as familiar to him as his own skin. Cole had lived here for all of his twenty-seven years, except for a few months after graduation, when he'd moved to Charleston. He used to dream about leaving for good; in high school, he and Terry Rose made up plans to run away and never come back. All of that seemed like a long time ago.

An overloaded coal truck barreled around the bend, coming at him from the opposite direction and sending up sprays of dust, and he quickly rolled up the window and clung to the right side of the road. As they passed each other, the trucker waved, but Cole did not.

He clicked on the radio, sang along with the Eagles' "Desperado," which the classic rock station played about a dozen times a day. His mouth felt limber, words alert on the tip of his tongue. When he was a boy, his grandfather had prayed for his stuttering to disappear. For the most part, it had, but sometimes when he was tired or nervous, it returned like memory, twisted his tongue in rippled knots.

Just outside of Stillwell he let up on the gas, coasting through the shell of a town, crossing the bridge where Dove Creek spilled into the Cherokee. A hand-painted sign outside of a Freewill Baptist church said "Walk by faith, not by sight." He passed a general store that also advertised a special on tanning, a beauty shop in a double-wide, and an abandoned gas station spray-painted in red: "Miners, All It Takes Is Unity," and "Best Wise Up if You Want to Keep a Standard of Living."

Cole pulled into the parking lot and cut the engine. He ate a bite of bacon, but his stomach clutched—too early—and he washed it down with coffee. The T-shaped, low-slung building looked as if it had been dropped there by mistake. No landscaping around it, save the strips of scrubby grass, a few trees. He sighed and tossed his burning cigarette. He was already ten minutes late and didn't need Linda's shit this early. He went in through the back door. Clocked in. Poured coffee into a small foam cup. Flipped through schedules and charts.

In the lounge the old people were watching cartoons. A superhero that Cole didn't recognize flew above a sparkling city.

"Hey y'all," he said, but only Hazel Lewis looked up.

"Cole, Cole, Cole, it's so dang hot." She tugged on her sleeves as if they were heavy chains, the pink cotton shirt pushed up, exposing her stomach. His first day on the job, he'd walked in on Hazel stark naked, her cowlike body unfurled on the bed. Powder-white flesh, sagging breasts. Cole had snapped a sheet over her like she was a corpse, then called for one of the female aides.

But now he adjusted her shirt, smoothing it over her jiggling belly.

"Cole, Cole, Cole."

"That's my name, don't wear it out."

He spent the early hours emptying bedpans, brushing teeth and dentures, and giving sponge baths. Sometimes when he woke the old people, they started like frightened deer, or talked to him as if they were still dreaming. Others, wide awake, demanded sweet rolls and coffee. He helped two ladies into the cafeteria, which smelled like eggs and lemon disinfectant, and then loaded trays onto the breakfast cart. He would like to sit and talk with a few of his favorite residents, but there was little time for breaks. He needed a smoke. But he kept moving.

In the hallway, Linda stopped him. "You need to get to room ten. Fletcher, the new guy. He hasn't eaten yet."

"I'm going," he said.

Linda was the head nurse. She had been working at the home for fifteen years and couldn't wait until she retired. She was a large woman, taller than Cole, with wrestler arms and wide shoulders; she always looked angry.

"Well, get on it," she snapped.

Ellen, a new nurse on staff, was watching, and when Cole rolled his eyes, she smiled. He stopped the cart in front of her. Ellen was his age. She was upbeat and gentle, and had learned all of the residents' names within a couple of days. Pretty, a little chubby. Chin-length red hair, gray-blue eyes, and enormous tits. She wore pink scrubs printed with teddy bears.

"What's going on?"

"The usual bullshit."

"You staying out of trouble, Cole?"

"Trying to."

"I'll just bet you are," she said, laughing.

He grinned, watched her go. Unlike the aides, the nurses were respected. They dispensed meds, drew blood, and gave orders; they did not change diapers or clean up vomit. Cole would like to be a nurse. But a nursing degree required at least two years of schooling, and the nearest program was a hundred miles away. Even if it were closer, he knew he wouldn't go.

Larry Potts was parked in a wheelchair, twiddling his thumbs. He had thick meaty hands, but his thumbs twirled like little jewelry-box ballerinas. Scenes like this still managed to stop Cole in his tracks. He put his hands over Larry's, felt his thumbs buzz against his palms like insect wings. Larry used to work the deep mines, crawling around on his hands and knees in the dark. "It's okay, Larry," he said, wheeling him into the cafeteria.

The new resident, Warren Fletcher, with gleaming bald head and tongue lolling, looked like a wrinkled baby. He'd arrived yesterday. A bed had opened up after Raymond Willis died on the way to the hospital. There was a long waiting list, and when the old people were brought in, most of the time, they never went back home.

"Hey there," Cole said loudly. Warren opened his eyes, startled. Cole spent much of his day shouting, so even when he was not at work, he occasionally caught himself talking to people as if they were half deaf.

Warren pulled his tongue back in his mouth like a lizard. "What's your name, son?"

"I'm Cole."

"Who's your people?"

"Freemans, up in Rockcamp. My granddaddy is Preacher Clyde Freeman."

Warren didn't say if he knew his family or not. His hands were shaking too badly to hold the spoon, so Cole sat beside him and fed him the lukewarm oatmeal, dabbing at the corners of his mouth with a paper napkin. After a few bites, the old man's eyes closed, and Cole pulled the blanket up to his chin and watched him. He looked harmless and near dead, hollowed out by too many years.

As Warren slept, Cole peeked out into the hall. Nobody was coming. He closed the door partway. Then he opened each dresser drawer, sifting through neatly folded underwear, T-shirts, dress pants, and plaid shirts, all of which Warren would never wear again. This is what he found:

Silver wristwatch, ticking, which he slipped in his shirt pocket.

Worn brown leather wallet with twenty bucks, a driver's license, and a faded picture of a woman, all of which he put back, intact.

In the bottom drawer, under a stack of threadbare undershirts, a knotted hunting sock.

Bingo.

He untied the thick knots and pulled out a roll of fifties. He stared at the money for a second, then returned it to the sock. Two aides walked by. Cole froze in the shadows. He waited until their voices died out, then he tucked the sock under the waistband of his jockeys and wheeled the breakfast cart out of the room.

As he drove around the county, his headlights reflected on the scarred places where trees had been cleared for mining, like giant razor gashes across the land. He sold most of what he had in a couple of hours, then went to the Eagle. Drank a couple of beers, watched a fight break out in the parking lot, and lost a game of pool. He was on the lookout for Charlotte Carson. A couple of months ago at a party, he'd found himself nibbling on her tiny ear. "Ohh, I like that," she'd said.

When she didn't show, he drove to her place in Pineyville. The Carson family had been smart and sold their land early on to the coal company, when the offer was still good. Charlotte lived with her three older brothers, large, sloe-eyed, dimwitted boys with reputations for short tempers and heavy fists. Their parents had been killed in a car accident a few years ago, so it was just the four of them. They lived in a double-wide up on a hill. Although they talked about building a house, all they had done so far was dig a pit for the foundation, which was filled with rainwater.

He felt relieved that Charlotte's piece-of-crap Neon was the only car in the driveway. He knocked once, then let himself in. A Rebel flag hung over the door, and framed family pictures and curling posters of beer ads were tacked to the walls. A new-looking big-screen TV sat on a low stand made from a pine board and cinder blocks, with various video games, mostly sports stuff, scattered on the floor around it. He called out over the shrieking music, and Charlotte yelled that she was in her room. A jumble of clothes and dirty glasses and CD jewel cases. She was perched on the bed in the midst of the mess like a mother spider on her web.

"What are you doing here?"

"Looking for you."

"You making a special delivery?"

"If you're lucky."

She wore faded, shredded-up jeans and a tight baby tee, her peroxide-dyed hair shooting out like toxic weeds. A few weeks ago, she'd convinced Cole to bleach his hair too, and when he looked in the mirror, he'd been startled by the towheaded reflection: "God-damn, I look like an albino." By now he was used to it, even if his grandmother wasn't, and didn't think he'd ever go back. With their fiery blond hair, they looked like brother and sister.

Cole snapped off the stereo. "That shit you listen to gives me a headache."

"Sometimes you're such an old man."

He knocked the lacy black bras and mismatched socks onto the floor, and reached for Charlotte. He touched her slightly moist underarms, breathed in the baby-powder scent of her. Laughing, she pushed him away. "You bring me something or not?"

She looked at him with cola brown eyes and pursed her lips until they crinkled like crepe paper. She was not exactly pretty. Freckles swarmed over her face like red ants, and she had a hard boyish face. But when she looked at him in this way, he felt as if he were floating along a river, and he liked the thrill of the currents and unexpected drops. He searched his pockets, handed her twenty milligrams of Oxy, not much. She licked the tablet, crushed it, and put her nose to the mirror like she was giving it a kiss. Then she came up smiling, the entire twelve hours of pain relief shooting to her bloodstream all at once.

"What do I owe you?"

"I'll think of something," he said, scooting closer.

But she told him she had to leave for work soon. She had just started at the Walmart in Zion.

"What kind of hours are those?"

"On the night shift, I can get as lit as I want to, nobody's around to notice."

"That's something," he agreed.

"Guess who's one of the new managers?"

"Who?"

"Your old buddy, Terry Rose."

Cole looked up.

"You didn't know he was back?"

The last he'd heard about Terry was that he was still in Kentucky with his wife and kid, working at an RC warehouse. Cole lit a cigarette, playing down his surprise. "Walmart? What a fuckin' loser."

"Well, we all got to make money."

"I guess."

Charlotte reached up and took the cigarette out of his mouth. "Maybe I've got time for a quickie."

She shucked her jeans and red panties, stripped off her T-shirt, her body adorned in an assortment of tattoos. She unbuckled his belt. Her breath was hot, and the sharp points of her hair tickled his thighs. It suddenly seemed too quiet, just the noisy sound of her mouth on him. He pushed her face away. "Where do you want me then?" He got behind her and watched the inky dreamcatcher on her lower back arch up, then flatten beneath him. He squeezed his eyes shut, disappearing, and yet was still here, inside of her. She moved against him, and he grabbed on to her hips as if to keep himself anchored, finding that secret place beyond everything else. Right before he came, he pulled out, heard himself whimper. When he opened his eyes, Charlotte was smiling at him.

15

"That was nice," she said.

"Yeah." He reached over and flipped the light switch. Although he never stayed the night, he liked to lie beside her and look up at the plastic glow-in-the-dark stars clustered all over the ceiling. He never worried about falling asleep; he survived on very little of it. Charlotte said it was like he had his own special kind of speed.

"You make me feel good," she said.

"You're just high."

"You could be too."

But Cole rarely used the drugs he sold, and when he did, he was more likely to drop a Xanax than to snort Oxy, which frightened him with its bright blue promises. Anything that felt that good would only lead to trouble.

Charlotte tapped his chest. "What are you thinking?"

"Nothing," he said, but he was still mulling over the news that Terry Rose was back in town. And he sure as hell didn't want to be thinking of him. Instead, he tried calling up Bible verses. It was a game he played. He never forgot the scripture his granddaddy drilled and seared into him, and it was times like this, in the darkness and quiet, that the words sometimes returned, ghostly and pale like the Indian pipes hidden in the woods.

"You're so quiet."

"It's just how I am. You know that."

All his years of stuttering had taught him something about silence. He spent most of his childhood too terrified to speak. Kids laughed, teachers looked at him with pity. He learned to bite down on his tongue until people forgot he was there—and he heard everything that way. But he couldn't play that trick with his granddaddy, who demanded he speak, and whenever Cole stuttered, his grandfather's eyes brightened with a mix of fury and satisfaction: *It's your mother, her sins led God to cursing you.* The praying, the Bible lessons, all of it was supposed to heal Cole's twisted tongue, but did he deserve such light, such healing? For the most part, he'd lost the stutter—but it had nothing to do with God.

Charlotte rested her head on his chest. "I can hear your heart. You hear it?"

He used to believe what his grandfather said, that the stuttering was a punishment from God, but around twelve or thirteen, he began to secretly reassure himself with the story of Moses, *but I am slow of speech, and of a slow tongue,* whose brother Aaron spoke for him to lead his people out of Egypt. Except that Cole was an only child and the closest he ever came to having a brother was Terry Rose.

"No," he said, rolling over. "No, I don't hear nothing."

CHAPTER 2

COLE DROVE UP to Devil's Pike, a mess of old strip mines, with a few trailers stranded there like lost ships. Orange acid water trickled like Kool-Aid out of a mountainside; probably an old underground mine had blown out. He parked in front of Harley McClain's. The front yard was overrun by plastic and ceramic animals, like some kind of cracked-out cartoon world. Harley's wife had collected the lawn ornaments, and now that she was dead, Harley couldn't bring himself to get rid of them. They gave Cole the creeps. He walked up to the front door, careful not to bump into any of the geese or deer or wide-eyed kittens. The mountains cast a dark shadow over the property. He would have to be quick. He did not like to be in the old people's homes after dark, when they were more likely to get nervous or confused.

Harley, a World War II vet who collected disability, invited Cole in. He wore stained gray sweatpants and a T-shirt that said "Awesome" in glittery letters. He poured grape pop from a two-liter into a plastic cup for Cole, then drew himself a glass of water.

"I told you, you ought not to drink that water."

"Oh, it won't kill me." Harley beckoned Cole. "I got something to show you."

All over the house sat models of churches and houses that Harley had constructed out of Popsicle sticks. He showed Cole the latest. "Look here. This is a cathedral I saw when I was flying over Italy." Harley had been a pilot in World War II. Some days he liked to tell stories about the war, but other times he'd clam up and not say a word, his eyes wild with memory.

It looked like all of the other models, but Cole said, "It looks like a castle."

"Yes, that's what it looked like, a castle."

Harley was lonely, so Cole stayed for a while, shooting the shit. Before he left, he sniffed the milk to make sure it wasn't spoiled, checked the bread for spots of mold. What divided the old people who still lived on their own from the ones at the nursing home was a thin, slippery slope.

"Make sure you eat something," Cole said. "And stop drinking that water."

Harley handed him a brown paper bag, clicking his dentures as Cole rummaged through the goods. OxyContin, Xanax, and nerve pills, all prescribed from a quack VA doctor.

He took the cash out of his back pocket. "You did good, Harley." The old man smiled, grabbed the green.

Cole got in his truck and locked the bag in the glove compartment, then headed out to make a few more transactions. He felt satisfied, pleased. It was almost too easy. When he had first heard about the nursing home's outreach program, where they delivered toiletries and food to the elderly and homebound, he knew he'd hit gold. Except for the occasional stray bottle, he never took meds from the nursing home—too risky. But this was different. Easy. Although the program had since been shut down because of funding, he didn't stop making visits. He'd met the majority of his suppliers this way; others he'd known through his granddaddy's church, or they were friends of residents. Almost all of them were poor and lonely and living out in the hills.

But now some of them made over a couple grand a month. They used what Cole gave them to pay their bills—*I need heat more than I do that old medicine*—or to buy big-screen TVs or gifts for their grandchildren. They never asked Cole what he did with the medication; they liked to pretend that he was giving it to the sick and needy. But looking closely into their quiet faces, Cole thought most of them knew the truth. Just as they didn't ask him what he was doing with the pills, Cole rarely asked them how they could go without them. He knew that some of the more savvy ones went to different doctors to get multiple prescriptions of the same drug. Others tried to get by on a substitute that was cheaper, less potent. Sometimes they sold him the Oxy in order to pay for their other meds, or they kept half for themselves and sold him half. Cole believed that he would be able to detect any signs of suffering. If they were in too much pain, then he would not make the deal. This was what he told himself. But it was better not to ask. It was better not to look too closely, or to think about it for too long.

Cole moved his clothes from the washer to the dryer and dropped in a handful of quarters. Though his grandmother had a washing machine at home, the water turned his whites shit-yellow. He didn't like to feel dirty. While his clothes were drying, he went next door to the Wigwam and ordered a coffee and a slice of butterscotch pie from a pretty blonde. It was quiet, nobody around except a cop smoking at the counter, and an old codger guarding his plate like a dog.

The pie was sweet and gummy, and Cole ate slowly, taking small, even bites and following each one with a sip of coffee. He glanced out the window and watched a pickup pass by. Nothing else happened. He did not mind. Charlotte, who hated the dullness, had told him he was crazy to stay. After graduation, she'd moved to Cleveland, where she had lived until just a few months ago. Came back broke and a little broken. Already she was talking about leaving again.

The waitress refilled his coffee. Sharp, foxlike face, crystalline eyes. Her hair was long and honey-colored, twisted in a complicated swirl on the top of her head.

"I've seen you before," she said. "What's your name?"

He told her, and she said, "I was away for a few years, lost track of people." She smiled. "I'm Lacy."

"Lacy what?"

"Lacy," she said. "Lacy Cooper."

"Cooper. You Denny's wife?"

"Was," she said, raising an eyebrow. Cole had never met Denny Cooper, but he knew who he was, everybody did. Years ago he led the high school basketball team to the state championship, and people still talked about his three-pointers and record assists. Cole had never played on any team. He didn't possess the skills or desire, and anyway, his grandfather thought sports were a waste of time.

When the bells on the door jingled, he looked up, then slid down in his seat, pretending to study the laminated menu, the words a blur. He kept his head lowered as Terry Rose passed by with his wife and kid. He hoped they'd continue walking to the back, but they sat in the booth directly behind him. Cole's mouth went dry, and it felt like pins were jabbing his chest. He quickly took a few dollars out of his wallet, slid them under the saucer, and started to get up.

But Terry stood at his table, grinning. "Cole, I thought that was you." He wore a starchy Walmart uniform with a manager button pinned to the collar. "It's been a long time," he said, sliding into the booth so they were facing each other. He folded his arms over his chest, looking him over. "I ought not to recognize you with those goldilocks."

Cole touched his hair. "It's a good disguise."

"I guess it is, if you're in the need of hiding."

Terry had always had a stocky, muscular build, but now he was twiggy, with a thin face, hollow cheeks. He'd lost his boyishness, and the expression on his face was a mixture of resentment and resignation, no baby fat left to soften the bitter lines. Cole wiped his palms on his pants and tried to act like running into Terry Rose was something that happened every day.

"What are you? Some kind of doctor?"

"What?" Cole remembered that he was also wearing a uniform. He told Terry what he did.

"Nursing home? No shit?"

"No shit."

"I guess it pays the bills. Hell, look at what I do." Terry pointed to his vest. "I was laid off in Kentucky, and came back here a few months ago."

"I didn't know you'd been back that long."

"Yeah, I've been around."

Cole fumbled with his cigarettes and asked if he wanted a smoke, but Terry said he'd quit. "Wife don't like it." He ran a hand through his hair. It was still curly and dark, but was cut shorter than he used to wear it.

As Lacy walked by, Terry said, "How about bringing me a coffee?"

"It's coming."

He watched her walk away and said in a low voice, "I'd like to get me some of that." Behind them, the boy asked who his daddy was talking to, and Kathy told him to hush.

Lacy poured Terry a coffee, and he said, "Thank you, sweetie," and she smiled in a forced way.

"I work with some real dumb fucks," Terry told Cole, stirring milk into his coffee with a butter knife. "But a few of them are cool. As a matter of fact, Charlotte Carson . . . I heard that you two have got something going on." He set down the knife. "That true?"

"It's nothing serious."

Terry's dimples appeared in each cheek when he smiled: so he hadn't lost all of his boyishness. "Me and Charlotte saw each other a few times back in high school. Remember?"

"Yeah."

"She still wild?"

Cole shrugged. The restaurant was starting to get crowded and noisy. People talking and forks scraping plates and the crackling of the deep fryer. A popular country song about small-town love played over the speakers. Terry seemed eager to keep talking, to pretend like everything was the same. How long were they going to sit here like this? Cole started to ask Terry about where he lived, but stammered, stopped. Terry didn't notice the stutter, never had. He seemed to intuitively understand the question; he told Cole that he'd sold the family land a few years ago, after his mother died. Now he and Kathy lived in a house with a big bathroom and a two-car garage on land where they didn't have to worry about drainage seeping into the well.

The door opened again, bells jingling, and Cole looked up to see a woman waving at him.

"Hell, is that Jody Hampton?" Terry looked at Cole. "What's she want?"

"Hold on." Cole made his way over to Jody and took her by the elbow, steering her to the door. He told her he'd be out in a minute, and on his way back to the table, he glanced at the cop. Nothing to worry about. The guy had his nose buried in a newspaper, didn't have a clue.

"Listen, I gotta go."

"You got something on the side with Jody?" Terry grinned. "Don't worry, I won't say nothing. But before you rush off, I want you to meet my son. And say hi to Kathy."

Kathy, still pretty and aloof, hooked her blond hair behind her ear and looked up at him with steely eyes. "Hi, Cole."

"Hey."

The boy's name was Terry also. Same curly dark hair and dimples and squinty eyes as his daddy. He must have been eight years old by now.

"Hey, little man."

"This is my old friend Cole. Say hi."

"I hate mashed potatoes," the kid said. "I want McDonald's."

Cole again said that he had to be going. "I'll see you around."

"Hell yes," Terry said enthusiastically. "Let's get together one of these nights."

Jody was sitting on a slatted bench outside, chewing the ends of her hair. Cole motioned for her to follow him to his pickup.

"What in the hell are you doing?"

"I saw your truck—"

"You know how it works. If you don't like it, go to someone else."

She looked like she was about to cry, and he reached over and pushed her greasy hair out of her eyes. Jody Hampton had been a couple of years behind Cole and Terry in school, the kind of girl that the boys went to when they were sad or afraid, or just plain horny. Not one of those boys had stayed by her side. Instead she'd married a drunk from Bucks County who ran out on her a couple of years ago. Now here she was, hair unwashed and a line of blackheads risen across her forehead like bug bites. She still had pretty blue eyes.

She handed Cole a sweaty wad of cash and he gave her a few Oxys that were wrapped in foil and she smiled and said he was a good man. Then she got in her banged-up Buick and turned down the road that would take her to her hamlet. Cole didn't go anywhere. Not yet. He sat in his pickup and watched rain clouds roll across the land. He and Terry used to think that they would leave here one day too—Charlotte wasn't the only one. They had talked about Texas or Florida, someplace where they could get to the ocean. But they were just teenagers, didn't know anything. The sun disappeared behind sky the color of wet cement; he could smell the oncoming rain. He watched from his truck as Terry Rose and his family came out of the Wigwam. They crossed the street, the boy running ahead. Kathy reached for Terry's hand. At his wedding, Terry had grabbed Cole's hand and said he was like a brother, and this was both the truth and a lie. Now he watched his old friend get in his truck and drive away to his house with the big bathroom and double-car garage, his wife next to him, his son with his face pressed to the rear window, waving good-bye.

Cole punched in the lighter and turned down a street in Stillwell known as Blacklung Block; on bad days, the entire neighborhood turned gray with coal dust. Tonight the streets were quiet. Yellow light shone from a row of old coal camp houses, and through the windows he could see flickering TVs and silhouettes of people who stayed home, who lived happy, good lives. Families in front of the TV, eating popcorn, playing Old Maid. Like Terry Rose and his family, maybe.

He parked in front of the duplex and lit a cigarette. Knowing all along that this was where he would end up. He stopped by a few times a month on business, and he guessed by now that he also considered Reese Campbell a friend. But he could never shake the underlying feeling of dread that he carried with him whenever he came over here. Not alarm, just a low humming in his gut, like a slight fever he couldn't shake. At least tonight there were no cars in the driveway, except for the antique ice blue '61 Cadillac that was always there, like an anchored boat.

Cigarette butts and crushed beer cans littered a patch of dead roses. Though Reese rarely left his house—living like a shut-in, just like Ruthie, the owner who lived on the other side of the duplex—he was famous for his parties. A three-legged cat was perched on the porch steps, meowing. "Hey Gimp." Cole lifted it under his arm like a football and rapped on the door. When there was no answer, he let himself in. The house was pitch-black, and he hit the light switch. Nothing happened. He set down the purring cat.

"Who the fuck is in my house?"

Cole ran into something with a sharp edge and yelled out. Reese's laughter broke through the shadows.

"It's me," Cole said, massaging his thigh. "What's wrong with the light?"

"Turn on the one by the chair."

Cole stumbled around until his hand touched a slender floor lamp. A dim yellow light fell over the room, and Cole blinked. It looked the way it usually did, Ruthie's antiquated furniture (pale rose sofa, old-fashioned table lamps) mixed in with what Reese and his friends left behind (overfilled ashtrays, crumpled cigarette packs, empty bottles of Jack Daniel's).

"This place is wrecked."

"Had a few guests last night. Fuckin' slobs."

Reese was sprawled on the sofa with a flimsy throw over his lap. His thick dark hair was matted and slept-on, and there were heavy rings under his eyes.

"What were you doing in the dark?"

"Trying to sleep. What in the hell do you think I was doing? Just settin' here thinking?"

"You want me to go?"

"I'm up now." He rubbed his eyes. "I hope to Jesus you got a cigarette for me, blondie."

Cole lit two, handed one to Reese. "Got any beer?"

"Should be some left."

In the short time it took Cole to walk into the kitchen and back, Reese had already dozed off. His T-shirt hung off him, a couple of sizes too big. Too much speed, Cole thought. He removed the lit cigarette from Reese's hand. A jagged scar zipped across his cheek, a souvenir from jail, and his nose was permanently crooked after being broken so many times. Still, he was not ugly. High cheek-bones like an Indian, pale blue eyes. He was thirty-six, but could pass for twenty-six.

The cat had nosed open a box of old pizza and ate quickly, tugging on the cold, rubbery cheese. A kitchen timer beeped, and Reese opened his eyes. "Time for Ruthie's medicine."

"How is she?"

"Still dying."

Ruthie Roberts, a childless widow, had taken in Reese after his parents and little brother were killed in a car crash. Rumor had it that eight-year-old Reese had crawled out of the burning hunk of metal without a scratch, and that Ruthie was the only one in Dove Creek who wanted him. But it wasn't anything that Reese talked about.

"What are you going to do with her?"

"Same thing I've been doing. I ain't sticking her in no hospital, and I'm sure as hell not putting her in that dump where you work." Reese hitched up his jeans. "If any riffraff shows up, don't let their asses in."

He sauntered across the room to the shared door that led to Ruthie's side. By now Cole was used to Reese's queeny walk, but the first time he saw it, he'd been shocked, his face hot with shame, or maybe fear. He'd never seen a man move like that before. Cole still didn't care for Reese's homo ways, but usually now, whenever he saw him swing his hips or flick a wrist, he looked the other way, his mouth no longer filling with disgust. Still, it was difficult to understand, a fairy living in Dove Creek. How he did not get himself killed.

He'd been hearing about Reese Campbell for a long time, but didn't meet him until a couple of years ago at a party. Cole knew it was him by the web of tattoos that wound over his arms and hands—it was well known that Reese had been locked up several times and that with each release, he'd come out with more ink and more meanness. Later in the night, while Cole was fishing a beer out of a tub of ice, Reese had come up behind him.

"Hey handsome."

Cole had quickly turned, clutching the beer to his chest like a bouquet. Reese grinned. "You're a nervous Nelly."

He told Cole he was looking to get high. At the time, Cole had been dabbling in pot, selling to a few high school students, a couple of old hippies. When Cole named his price, Reese said, "I'll give you half that."

"For an ounce?" Cole had scoffed. "No way."

Reese had stared at him, still grinning, but as he stepped toward Cole, the grin vanished. Cole had backed up and stumbled against the tub, melted ice sloshing all over his shoes.

"All right, all right," he'd said, the stutter rising like a fever.

Then Reese had suddenly laughed, startling Cole.

"I was just fucking with you, son."

Since that night, Cole had watched Reese pull the same act with others, tough country boys moving out of the way for his sashaying sissy hips. Sometimes it backfired, especially when he was high. He'd get too brave, too mouthy. Flirting or spilling secrets about which rednecks had followed him out to the bushes, wanting what their wives wouldn't give them. On more than one occasion, Cole had shown up to find Reese bloodied and busted up. Though Reese had friends all over Dove Creek—roughnecks who hated queers but partied with him—they would never call Reese one of their own.

Now he tossed Cole a prescription bottle. "I got a couple of 'scripts filled. One for Ruthie, one for you."

Cole read the label. "Hundred and sixty milligrams."

"Terminal cancer. You're getting the cream of the crop, son."

Cole handed over the envelope of cash. He had started dealing as a way to help pay his grandparents' medical bills, but now he felt like he could not stop. It was the same with the stealing. He'd palmed a couple of wedding rings, a little cash, from the old people for no reason at all, other than for a quick thrill. But now it was a part of him. Who he'd become, or who'd he'd always been.

"God bless the pillheads," Reese said.

"Amen," Cole echoed.

He paid Reese more than he did the old people, but this was fair since it was Reese who had actually pointed out what a gold mine Cole was working in. Reese used to deal coke, but now was too scared of getting sent back to the pen; he said he did not care about the money anymore, as long as could keep Ruthie medicated and himself well stoned. He taught Cole how much the pills went for on the street, told him who was looking to buy.

"You look like you haven't slept in days."

"It's been a while." Reese yawned. "You ought to think about changing your line of products. You'd make a hell of a lot more with meth."

"I only sell what's doctor-prescribed and FDA-approved."

"For fuck's sake," Reese said, rolling his eyes.

Cole did not try to explain that he actually liked the old people, and that he did not want to be mixing up chemicals and dealing with paranoid tweakers. Explaining all of that was like explaining why he didn't use drugs in the first place. "You're about the only dealer I know who doesn't use," Reese had pointed out before. "I find that strange, son." Cole had tried just about everything, but he liked reading about the drugs more than he liked taking them. Learning about their components, side effects, dosages. His mind retained the information easily, the way it did with scripture.

They cracked open beers and clinked the cans together, though they did not say what they were toasting to. Reese turned on the stereo and Johnny Cash confessed that he had fallen into a burning ring of fire. They talked about people they knew, who'd been busted and who was getting divorced and who'd been laid off.

Reese asked after Charlotte.

"She's all right."

"Better keep an eye on that one. I expect she's got a little taste for her own kind."

Cole had heard it before. When Charlotte returned to Dove Creek, a swarm of rumors followed her, including that she'd been a stripper at a lesbian club up in Cleveland. Cole didn't pry. Charlotte said what she liked best about him was that he knew how to keep his trap shut. She told him that she had worked in a tattoo shop and played drums in a band, and he didn't ask questions.

"She ain't no bulldyke."

Reese looked at him like he was slow in the head. "There's more than one kind."

"She likes what I give her," Cole said testily. It was like this every time. He didn't know what he was doing here, drinking beer with an ex-con faggot, who as sure as they were sitting here would one day fall into his own burning ring of fire.

"All right, simmer down." Reese lit another cigarette. "What else is going on? Your granddaddy still living at home?"

"For now. The family is itching to put him in the nursing home. I don't think my grandma wants to, but she won't stand up to them." He hesitated. "I wonder if I'm doing him wrong, if I should move in and take care of him all the time, like you do Ruthie."

"That's a bad idea."

"How come?"

"Ruthie ain't a mean old preacher. Anyway, you better be moving them out of there instead of you moving in."

"What for?"

"Before that coal company blasts y'all out."

"Hell, you'd think nobody ever mined coal before in West Virginia, the way everybody's carrying on."

"Well, from what they say . . . You better go 'fore you catch cancer or something."

"I think this'll do me in first," Cole said, indicating the cigarette.

"Let me tell you something. I see the way Ruthie's doing, and I don't ever want to go like that. Remember that for me. If I don't go quick and easy, you shoot me dead. All right?"

"Please. I ain't going to jail for your ass," Cole quipped. Reese waited a beat, then burst into his loud, horsy laugh. Cole grinned uneasily. He could never predict how Reese would react, that was the thing. Couldn't figure out which of them held the power. With everyone else Cole did business with, there was no confusion, no uncertainty: they wanted something from him, and he gave it to them. It wasn't a bad thing, what he did. People needed him, counted on him. He gave them what they asked for. He made this life for himself. It was his.

CHAPTER 3

COLE CARRIED TWO COFFEES into the bedroom, one with milk and three spoonfuls of sugar, one black and unsweetened, and set the mugs on the plastic milk crate next to the bed. He pushed open the window, heard the trilling of field sparrows. Charlotte was sleeping, tangled up in the sheets. He leaned over her and lightly traced her tattoos, the eagle feather on her shoulder, moving down along her pale arm where a thin snake slithered, around to her stomach, where a lightning cloud twitched. Though she descended from the Scots-Irish like just about everyone else around here, Charlotte liked to think she was connected to the old Indian ways.

She blinked.

"Morning," he said.

She brightened when she saw the coffee and held the mug in both hands like a little kid. "That's a nice thing to wake up to."

"It's about all I can do. I don't have much else."

"Cigarettes and coffee, that's all I need."

Last night, she'd shown up around two a.m., doped up and wanting to get laid, still wearing her Walmart vest. Now she looked like she wasn't exactly sure how she'd ended up here.

"What time is it?"

"Almost eleven."

"Let's spend the day in bed."

"Can't. I'm going to my grandma's for dinner."

"Saturday dinner?"

"Nobody could go tomorrow. Anyway, it's nothing big. It's just that my cousin's gonna be there. You want to come?"

Charlotte just looked at him. "Please. I've heard enough about Preacher Clyde Freeman to know a girl like me isn't welcome."

"Oh, he don't say much now. He's too far gone for that."

But she said that she was going to call in to work instead, to see if she could pick up any extra hours. "I been fighting them tooth and nail to get twenty hours a week. Terry Rose is talking to them for me."

"He's got that much pull?"

She looked at Cole like she'd just remembered something.

"What?"

"Last night Terry was asking where he could score. I told him you could hook him up."

"What did you tell him that for?"

"Why not? That's what you do."

"You don't need to be telling everybody."

"It's just Terry Rose."

"I ain't selling to him."

"Why not?"

"I just ain't."

"I'd like to know what happened between you two."

"Nothing happened. I just don't trust him, that's all. I'm not selling him anything."

"Okay, whatever."

"Is that who you got high with last night?"

"Jealous?" She stared at him, smoke rising around her face, the sheets bunched up around her legs. Her bare breasts were small and pink.

33

"I just don't want to see you get hooked," he said, walking off to the shower.

He stood for a few seconds under the icy spray and then adjusted the knobs until the water steamed. He did not like the idea of Charlotte getting high with Terry Rose. He'd thought that Terry was living the straight life, with wife and kid. But what did he know? He still couldn't even believe that Terry was back. One time, when they were sixteen or seventeen, they'd gone to a party in the woods, and Charlotte was there, hanging on to Terry, laughing loudly at his jokes. Cole was quiet, watching; Terry would tell a girl anything she wanted to hear. The next morning, he called to say that Charlotte Carson was a sweet piece of ass. He said maybe Cole could get with her next, he'd set them up. Or maybe they could take her together. But like most things with Terry, it was all talk. Back then, Charlotte had never even looked Cole's way.

After he slipped on jeans and a T-shirt, Cole made the bed with the sheets pulled tight, hospital corners, the way he did at the old folks' home. He straightened his room and tossed yesterday's clothes into the laundry basket. Then he walked through the trailer, drying his head with a towel. None of his relationships ever lasted more than a few weeks, and he'd never expected this one to.

"Charlotte, where you at?"

He found her around back.

She took a long drag on her cigarette. Cole sat next to her in the grass. They stared at the trees, the folds of hills. It was impossible to see out across the land. Nothing was flat. You could only look up. Patches of sky.

"I don't know why you stay here. It's just one big wasteland."

"It don't look like a wasteland to me."

"But you know it is." She sighed. "I don't know why I came back. I've got to get out of here."

"That's what you keep saying."

"Back to Cleveland. Or maybe New York City. One of my friends in Ohio moved to Brooklyn. She said I could stay with her."

He tried to imagine her outside of these mountains and valleys, outside of this state. All he knew of big cities was what he saw on TV: sparkling skyscrapers where queers and rich people lived, or housing projects overrun by foreigners and gangs. This was all he knew, all he'd really ever known. There was a time, after high school, that he'd tried to leave. He'd lived in the state capital for a few months and hated everything about it, the strangers, the noise, the buildings pressing in from all sides. He felt cut off from the land and from himself. He came back here, feeling like he'd failed, and the old man had met him at the door. "You come back to get saved?" he asked. But Cole just wanted his mother's land. His grandfather practically spat at him: "I ain't stopping you." When he was a little kid, Cole used to dream of running away with his mother, and then later, he and Terry made plans to bust out of here, until one spring day all of that burned up in Cole's hands.

He stretched out on the ground, and Charlotte lay down next to him.

"You could come with me."

"What?"

"You've got money. Then I wouldn't have to wait. We could go now. We could get us a nice little apartment."

"I like it here."

"It's a wasteland."

"Yeah, you said that."

"There's another world out there."

Cole closed his eyes. The sun was so bright that he could see the orange flesh of his eyelids. He smelled the grass and dirt. He felt her stand up, the shadow of her falling over him like a cape, then she was walking away and he did not call her back. He could stay here all afternoon, just him and the land. She slammed the car door, and then he heard the rattle of the engine. She was gone. He still didn't open his eyes. He used to hunt, fish. When he was a kid he and his grandfather would hike up the mountain, digging ginseng roots, picking mushrooms. His grandfather used to go up there to get closer to God. Fasting, praying. When he'd come back down, his face would be shining with love. The times that he took Cole with him, he was unusually soft-spoken and kind. They sat next to each other in the rising light of the sun, and his grandfather told him that God was all things good. Cole hadn't been up there in a long time. The mining site now sprawled across some of those places where he used to hike and hunt. The sludge dam too. But he couldn't see any of that from here. There was one time that he had started to go up to get a closer look, but the forest floor was so cracked and eroded that he stopped halfway, didn't want to see anymore.

He pulled the bed out about a foot from the wall so he could reach the safe that was bolted to the floor. He ran the combination and popped it open. Warren's fifties, the ticking wristwatch, and a few stray Percocet. A bottle of OxyContin. More pills divided into plastic baggies. Pictures, a strand of pearls, an emerald ring, stacks of greenbacks. Although he deposited his measly work check into a bank account, whatever else he earned he squirreled away like the old folks who'd lived through the Depression and hid their money all over until they eventually forgot about it, people like Warren Fletcher, who didn't trust banks and thought that old socks would keep their money safe. Cole counted out six hundred bucks and slipped the bills into an envelope.

Then he walked up to his grandparents', his boots clacking along the cracked dirt road. From the high weeds, a rabbit peered at him, its eyes so placid and deep, they looked to be without color. The animal twitched, scampered away. Cole stopped at the footbridge to finish his cigarette and gazed at his grandparents' clapboard house. It used to be bright yellow, but now it was dull and dreary, the color of dried cornhusk. The paint was peeling away, and the front porch sagged on one side. But the tall sugar maples and pignuts were blooming, little buds like eyes, and the daffodils leaned toward the sun. Maybe he should turn around. He'd thought that only his cousin Kay and aunt Naomi were coming over, but Rebecca and Larry's truck was here too. He glanced at the shallow creek, the strange silvery sheen. There were no fish in it anymore. He wondered if anyone had seen him. Could he just walk away?

But his grandmother was counting on him, and it had been a while since he'd seen anyone else in the family.

She was in the kitchen, laying out slices of Colby cheese on a plate. A basket of sandwich buns. Country ham. A large bowl of yellow potato salad. "I thought you weren't going to turn this into a big deal," Cole said.

"It's not much. Just sandwiches."

"Where is everyone?"

"In there with Clyde, I think."

"Larry and Rebecca are here too?"

"Just Rebecca." She added, "Esther was supposed to come, but she's sick with a cough-cold."

Cole glanced behind him. "Here." He withdrew the envelope from his back pocket.

"You sure?" she asked, then took it and hid it away somewhere inside her dress just as his aunts walked in.

"Would you look at that hair," said Naomi.

"I've never seen a Freeman with hair like that," added Rebecca, the oldest of the sisters. She was only in her fifties, but sometimes looked as old as his grandmother, her flat pancake face etched with worry lines.

Naomi patted her own disheveled mane. "I kind of would like to try going blond myself."

"You'd have more fun," Cole said.

She laughed, gave him a hug. Naomi had always been his favorite aunt. The one closest to his mother, she had tried to look out for him when he was a kid, whereas Rebecca was overly stern and Aunt Esther was too busy taking care of her brood to pay attention to Cole. The aunts didn't hold strictly to the old ways, like their father did, and occasionally Cole would sneak over to Naomi's to watch reruns of *The A-Team* or *MacGyver*.

Each of his aunts had between three and nine kids, giving Cole a heap of cousins, and now several of them had babies of their own. He was the odd one, without parents, siblings, or offspring.

Four daughters, no sons. Cole's grandfather had named the first three after women in the Bible, but his grandmother had picked out the name for Cole's mother. It was one of the few times she stood up to her husband. And maybe feeling defeated that he'd been given yet another girl, he relented, allowed his youngest to be called a secular name. *Ruby.* The color of blood. A jewel hidden deep in the earth in foreign parts of the world. Cole's grandmother had taken the name from a country song that she heard on the radio, listening when her husband wasn't home.

"I reckon it's time to eat," she said. "Go get your granddad, Cole."

His grandfather was in the recliner. Next to him on the floor sat Kay, reading a book. She wore her hair in a ponytail, and her face, dotted with freckles, looked serious and still. She was Naomi's youngest, and the only one of his cousins that he truly felt close to. In the fall she would be the first in the family to go to college.

"Hey girl."

"Long time no see." She grinned. "You go out drinking last night? You look like you tied one on."

"For your information, I stayed in. Reading." He winked. "Help me with Granddaddy?"

She looked at him skeptically. "What do we have to do?"

"Get him up." Cole leaned over his grandfather. "It's time to eat,

Granddaddy. Grandma wants you in the kitchen." The old man stared. "Come on, now." Cole held him by the arm and motioned for Kay to get the other one, and they helped him stand. Once he was up, he shook his arms free and walked, baby steps, into the kitchen.

Cole felt relieved that none of his uncles or other cousins had shown up. When he was younger, they had big Sunday dinners and crowds of kids were always around, and even then, he felt like an outsider. Though his cousins lived on the same land that he did, he was, in a way, his grandfather's child, the weird kid who didn't play sports, who rattled off Bible verses.

They crowded around the Formica table, and Cole sat between Kay and his grandfather.

"Cole, you say the prayer," his grandmother instructed.

This was tradition; the man of the house said the blessing. But this was not Cole. He looked at his grandfather. His mouth hung open like a child waiting to be fed. Then his eyebrows knitted together, and he glared at Cole. His grandfather wouldn't speak, but he still held the scripture inside of him, as hard and brittle as bone.

"No, I'm not good at it. You say it."

His grandmother sighed. "Now, Cole—"

"I'll do it," Kay spoke up. "Granddaddy's just going to have to suffer and listen to a woman."

Their grandmother didn't argue. They bowed their heads and Kay said a quick prayer, and then they passed the food and filled their plates. Cole wondered how many times he had sat here at this table, in this very spot. Night after night, the heavy King James opened before him and his granddaddy pacing behind him. Cole would turn the thin pages, and when he got to the right place, he'd lick his lips and try to recite without stuttering. His grandfather taught him early on what to fear. Once a soul fell into outer darkness, there was no hope. No light, no peace.

Sometimes he would call out a passage to be recited from

memory. That came easy for Cole, and his granddaddy, occasionally pleased, called him a quick study. It was the speaking that gave him trouble. The lessons went on for at least an hour, and the later it got, the worse his stuttering. Finally, his grandmother would remind his grandfather that Cole had schoolwork, and so he would let him go, although Clyde Freeman didn't think much of book learning. Cole didn't either. Instead, he'd go to his room and hide under the covers and look at the postcards from his mother, the faraway and foreign places.

"Rebecca, you heard anything from Ricky?" his grandmother asked.

She said she'd been able to talk to him the other day. "He says he's fine." But her eyes flickered with uncertainty.

Cole thought his younger cousin was crazy to sign up for the army, especially when he knew he'd just be shipped over to Iraq or Afghanistan. His grandmother said he was patriotic; Kay said it was his only way out. There's got to be other ways, Cole had argued, but then couldn't come up with any.

"Oh, I worry," his grandmother said. "I pray for him every day."

Naomi got up for a glass of water, and Cole reminded her to get it from the plastic jug on the counter. The water that came out of the faucet was sometimes black, sometimes orange. They didn't drink it, but they bathed with it. "We're likely all to be poisoned," his grandmother said.

This got Naomi started on why she should sell the land, and Rebecca asked her if she'd given any more thought to moving in with her and Larry.

Cole looked up, caught eyes with his grandmother.

"I don't want to go anywhere yet," she said.

Rebecca and Naomi argued with her, explaining why their father needed to go into a nursing home, why she shouldn't be living here. "Mama, we live too far away to drive over here whenever he acts up or whenever something goes wrong," Naomi said.

"I'll do it," Cole said. "I help, don't I, Grandma?"

"Yes." She added, "But I wish you'd come over here more." She sounded tired. "Your granddaddy would like that. You could read scripture to him. On Sundays, since you don't go to church—"

"You know I usually work—"

"You could come over here instead of that running around you do."

A hotness sprang to Cole's cheeks like he'd been slapped. He looked at his grandmother, and she didn't blink. He felt shaken, even betrayed. Everyone was quiet. Then Naomi changed the subject to her kids, and Rebecca joined in, trying to smooth things over. His grandmother looked away, and then she looked at him again.

"Would you hand me the salt?"

He shouldn't have come over. Maybe it was her daughters pestering her that caused her to snap at him. She looked worn down. Even her dress was frayed at the neckline. Cole wished his aunts would leave her alone. He handed her the salt shaker, then reached over to help his grandfather, who was having trouble keeping his sandwich together. He was making a mess of his plate. Cole peeled the sliced ham off the bread, and cut it up into small pieces for him.

As he was trying to think of something else to say, something that would make his grandmother happy and make the aunts back off, the warning siren sounded.

"Oh, Lord," his grandmother said.

A moment later, a blast from the mountain ripped through the silence like the reports of a million rifles. Bigger than that. Bombs. Cole dropped his butter knife. The house vibrated, windows rattled. The water glasses shivered, and Aunt Rebecca let out a shriek. Then the sound rolled on down the valley, its echo calling back to them, taunting.

Nobody said anything at first. They all had to catch their

breath. Straighten the plates. Swallow hard. Wait and make sure it was over. Nervously, Cole turned his eyes to his grandfather. They were all looking at him, and he glared at them like he was about to hand down a judgment from God. Gunky potato salad all over his face. They waited. He picked up another slice of cheese.

"See, this is what we're talking about, Mama," Rebecca spoke up. "I don't know how you and Cole stand it. My nerves are rattled to pieces."

His grandmother left the table and returned with her notebook. "Look at this," she said, flipping the pages.

"You should sue," Kay said.

His grandmother had already dragged Cole with her to an office in Charleston, where a lawyer, a woman, was friendly and sympathetic, and offered to represent them. But they couldn't afford it; they'd need to pay for engineers and surveyors and who knew what else. Even if they could afford it, the case would be tied up for years, and would probably be settled out of court, the land already ruined.

"No, you shouldn't sue. Mama, you've got to let go," Rebecca said. "You've got grandsons and son-in-laws that work for Heritage. You can't be messing with their jobs."

"She's right," Naomi agreed. "I just heard where Tom Wallace got fired from Heritage. Now why do you think? Because his cousin is Janey Burfield, and she's been trying to sue and cause a ruckus." She shook her head. "You best just think about moving."

"That old Satan," his grandfather suddenly cried. He slapped his hand on the table hard. His voice was loud, slow. "That old Satan."

"Clyde?"

He pushed back his chair and stood and stumbled, and everyone jumped up as if to catch him. He waved them away, his hands batting at them like they were a swarm of gnats. Then he shuffled out of the kitchen, his wife behind him. Cole and Kay and his aunts looked at each other.

"Good Lord," said Rebecca.

They followed them into the living room. His grandfather sat in the recliner, his grandmother next to him. Cole looked at them in their house that he knew so well and could not imagine them in any other place. As a little boy, he used to sit between them at the dinner table. It was always the three of them.

His grandmother whispered something in the old man's ear, and he held her hand and they looked up. Husband and wife, hands entwined like a twisted, deformed vine, staring at their children and grandchildren, and on their faces was the same look Cole saw on the folks at the home every day. They knew it, all old people did: they'd been abandoned and betrayed.

His grandmother's eyes filled with sudden tears. "I don't think he's gonna remember who any of us are much longer."

"That won't happen," Cole told her, but it would, he saw it all of the time at the nursing home.

Rebecca and Naomi went over to comfort her, and Kay tugged on Cole's arm.

"Come on."

He followed her outside. The air tasted hot and thick and bitter. They sat on the steps and looked up toward the ridge, dust raining down and swirling in silver clouds. Cole's eyes burned and itched. He ran his finger through the sticky coal dust that clung to the house no matter how often his grandmother swept.

"I can't wait to get out of here." Kay looked at him. "You just gonna stay here forever? Granddaddy being the way he is, the whole goddamn mountain falling on your head? Look at that shit. I can taste it. It's in my teeth."

Cole thought about Charlotte asking him to leave with her. *There is another world out there.* She didn't really mean it.

"I don't know what I'll do," he said.

"You ever seen the sludge dam?" she asked. "You ever go up to the mining site?"

"No. You can't get up there. Anyway, I don't want to see any of it." He stared at the smoke coming from the mountain. "It's just the way it is. You live with it."

"You don't have to."

"Granddaddy never wanted to sell."

"It's over now, Cole."

He remembered the first time the coal men had come to the house. His grandfather had invited them in for coffee and pie, but before they could say a word, he started preaching, and they didn't know how to respond when he said, "It is easier for a camel to go through the eye of a needle, than for a rich man to enter into the kingdom of God." The men had offered to help him relocate, far away from the coalfields, and he'd just laughed: "Why would I want to live on land that my people never walked on?"

Cole shook his head. "He'll never last if he goes in the nursing home."

"He's not supposed to last forever."

They each lit a cigarette, then Kay rested her head on his shoulder. "Cole, you ever wonder where your mom is?"

"No, not anymore. Why?"

"I don't know, I just wondered." She hesitated. "When I was little, I used to wish I had a mom like that. It seemed cool, her being out there, traveling."

"Better to have one that sticks around."

Cole's mother was sixteen when she got pregnant and ran off. She came back only once. He was ten years old and she blew into town for a week and showered him with junky gifts. Sea monkeys, candy cigarettes, baseball cards, Shrinky Dinks, and cheap T-shirts that were too small, as if she'd picked them out for a four-year-old. But Cole didn't care. He stretched the shirts over his chest and arms, making them fit and wearing them until his grandfather threw them away.

"You ought to get out," Kay said. "Like she did."

"What do you expect me to do out there?"

"What you've been talking about."

"What's that?"

"Be a nurse."

"Shit."

"Why not? Get away from all this. You could come up to college with me."

"Don't you think I'm a little old?"

"This is something you want."

He stood up and brushed off the seat of his jeans. He thought of his grandmother accusing him of running around. Did she really think that the money he gave her came from working at a nursing home?

"It's all talk," he said. "I couldn't never get in."

"You don't know."

"Oh, yes I do know. I know."

Cole walked over to the land where his aunts and uncles had once lived. The air was still heavy with dust. It smelled of chemicals. He coughed, spat. The aunts' houses used to be hidden from each other by towering oaks and hemlocks, but Heritage had burned the trees and demolished the houses, leaving behind a mess of upturned earth and monstrous bulldozer tracks with pools of black, brackish water collecting in the ruts. The gardens were torn out. The henhouse was gone too, so was the barn that had once housed the milk cow and goats. It was hard to remember the way the land used to look. A valley, a little stream. Gone, buried.

Most of the mining land had already been swindled from the people more than a hundred years ago, but the coal companies always wanted more. After Heritage pressured the widow Shirley Scott, who lived at the head of the holler, into selling, then it was easy enough to get rid of everyone else, either by buying them out or making their lives hell. The first thing they did was clear-cut the forests. Bulldoze the trees, burn them. Oaks, hickories, everything. Then they drilled giant holes into the earth and filled them with explosives, and after they blasted, they dumped the rocks and rubble into the valleys. One day, not long after Heritage got its first permit, Cole was driving to town, and as he crested a hill he looked over and saw the felled trees covering the hillside like graves and he knew then that what was coming was too big to stop.

He walked through the tall weeds over to the path that they'd always called Church Lane. A black slickness rose up in certain places where he stepped, and he went carefully as if the land was rigged with mines. *Wasteland*. The church was still standing, but barely. Last year a flash flood had rushed down from the barren hillside and smashed into it. Cole had helped his grandmother fill out FEMA forms, and they collected about half of what they needed, using the money for bills instead of rebuilding. Up behind the church was a little family cemetery on a half acre that the coal company wanted but would never get. Cole thought about the little cemeteries all over the mountains and hollows, protected by law from the coal companies. Maybe in the end it would be the dead that saved the land.

The church was once a sturdy, box-shaped building without stained glass or a fancy altar, nothing like the churches on TV, or the ones his aunts now went to. This was just a bare room with aisles big enough for the ladies to fall down into fits of passion. Until he was seventeen, Cole went to church every Sunday, and usually Monday and Wednesday nights as well. His grandfather had preached his last service two years ago. Cole was not there, but his grandmother told him that his granddaddy had grabbed the sides of the pulpit as if he was afraid of falling, and, confused, had asked, "Who are you?"

Cole pushed a pile of branches out of the way and walked through the vine-strangled doorway. The roof was partly caved in, the walls warped and stained yellow, the windows shattered. The church had been stripped of its pictures of the Last Supper and of Jesus on the cross. Even the mismatched folding chairs, which they had used instead of pews, were gone. Squirrels scurried along the rafters. He walked to the front, his boots crunching shards of glass and twigs. The pulpit was still in its place. Cole stood behind it and faced an invisible congregation.

When his grandfather preached, he often went on for hours. He talked more fire and brimstone than most Holiness preachers, and his strict, dour ways, combined with his quick temper, also set him apart from the more joyous types. Cole had once overheard a churchgoer describe his grandfather as Holiness with a strong dose of Baptist. He was the old-timey gaspy kind of preacher, sucking in and spouting out air, ending practically every line with an inflection. "It's a glorious day-ah for those who have felt the Holy Ghost-ah, I'm saying the Holy Ghost-ah." On special occasions, snakes were kept next to the pulpit. Sometimes they were quiet; sometimes they rattled their cages. The scripture they followed was a simple verse: *They shall take up serpents.* Bites were rare, but his grandfather's wrist had been grazed, and Uncle Larry had lost a couple of fingertips. The rattlers would kill.

His grandfather never touched a snake unless he was anointed, which meant that God was moving through him. Then he could do anything. He would reach into the hissing, slithering pile as if in a trance and hold a snake above his head and shout. At first, the congregation would hush, a quivering silence falling over them, and then a collective rush of sound would follow—gasps, praises to God. Some would go forward and pass the serpents hand to hand. Cole had seen them draped around a person's neck like jewelry. People shouted, wept, danced. Once he watched an old man drink strychnine and never blink.

"Your mama used to handle serpents," his grandfather told him. "Before she turned into a harlot."

What Cole knew of his mother was a mix of his grandmother's soft words and his grandfather's judgments. A few stories from his aunts, a single faded photograph. Mostly he learned about her from the family silence, the quiet that was wrapped around her name. His grandfather said she was a whore who turned her back on God, but there was another time, a time when he had adored her. Ruby had started preaching at eleven years old. She went to baptisms and revivals, and at school, she proselytized. Unlike her own child, Ruby had no trouble speaking, and people loved to hear her, her little-girl voice puncturing something deep and frozen within them.

One time, when he was a little kid, Cole had looked up at the pulpit to see his grandfather glaring down on him, a copperhead in his hands, and before he could stop it, a prayer rushed through him. *Bite him*, he'd thought, the words wild and fevered. The snake had opened its mouth, revealing its set of fangs, but then his grandfather smiled, a victorious, gloating smile, and dropped the snake back in its cage. His grandfather was waiting for the day that Cole would rise to the challenge, the way years ago his youngest daughter, who had never been afraid, lifted a serpent and gave herself to God. "What happened to my little girl?" he would ask, tears in his eyes. "How did she get so poisoned, what was it, Lord, that took her away?"

Cole looked around at the dirt and dust and torn-up walls. He gave the pulpit a gentle kick, and it clanged against the floor and a part of the top broke off. He flicked his lighter. It would all burn so easily. The sun was setting and shadows loomed across the shell of a building. The wood squeaked, settled. Chills tickled the back of his neck. He didn't want to be here anymore. He shoved the lighter in his pocket and quickly walked away, his eyes not lifting from the path in front of him.

CHAPTER 4

THE ENGINE WOULDN'T turn over.

"Damn it," Cole muttered.

Charlotte rested her motorcycle boots on the dash. "Why do you drive this piece of shit?"

"I like it."

"I bet you've got money to buy a new one."

"I ain't gonna spend all my money on a truck."

"Why not?"

"You must think I'm a millionaire."

"You got more than I do, that's for sure."

"Have you ever thought I don't want to draw attention to myself? 'Course, you've already told just about everybody about what I do."

Cole tried again, pumping the gas. What was between them now felt different. Charlotte still talked about leaving, but did not say anything about him going with her. They did not see much of each other anymore. It was the beginning of summer. A lightness filled the air.

On the fourth try the engine started. He took the curves fast, and Charlotte leaned out the window and yelled. He smiled, watching her. He still liked how wild she was, how unhinged.

The lot at the Eagle was full, so he parked along the dirt road. From the dark woods, a chorus of tree frogs called out steadily, a familiar hum that for a second made him feel strangely homesick.

"How about we party?" Charlotte said.

"I just feel like getting drunk."

"I wish once you'd get high with me."

"Seems to me like you want me to be somebody else altogether."

He gave her twenty milligrams, but she wanted more. He searched the bottles and found a forty, and she crushed the tablet on her compact and leaned her face to it and then opened her eyes wide. The moonlight shone over her; she looked pretty and fearless. She wore a little midriff shirt and hip-hugging jeans; her hair was pushed up and spiked out.

"I can't go in just yet," she said, lighting a cigarette.

They sat on the bed of the pickup. Two women they'd gone to school with walked by and said hey, voices loud with drink. After they were far enough away, Charlotte said, "Nobody ever leaves this place."

"That ain't true."

"People around here don't know how to think big," she said. "Me and Terry were talking about it. That's why he left in the first place. Nobody around here has any dreams."

Cole rolled his eyes. "Terry Rose went to Kentucky. And now he works at Walmart. Is that thinking big?"

"He's not planning on doing that forever."

"Then why don't you take him up there with you to New York."

"You don't think I'll really go," she said in a small voice.

"I don't know what you'll do."

The Eagle was one big room, with the bar at the front, and a small dance floor and pool tables in the back. It was smoky and crowded, and he trailed behind Charlotte, who pushed her way through, all elbows, not caring whose feet she stepped on. While she was in the bathroom, Cole waited at the bar. The bartender stood at the cash register, her back to him, and when she turned around, they both smiled. It was the waitress from the Wigwam. Lacy Cooper.

"I didn't know you worked here," he said.

"Just started last week."

"You quit the Wigwam?"

"Working both places." She asked him what he wanted, and he ordered two beers. "So," she said, "I finally figured out who you are."

"Oh yeah? Who?"

"You're one of the preacher's grandsons. Rockcamp."

"That's me."

"I grew up on Thorny Creek," she said. "Right above you."

She told him that her mother had gone to his grandfather's church a few times before she got too sick. "Too fat, actually."

"Oh yeah? I think I remember her."

She laughed. "She was always trying to get me to go, but I didn't want any part of that fire, brimstone crap. I bet it wasn't easy growing up with him, was it?"

"No, not what I would call easy."

"Y'all really mess with snakes?"

Before he could answer, Charlotte came back and threw her arms around him. "Whoo," she yelled. Attempting to steady her, Cole gave Lacy a little smile.

"Looks like you got your hands full."

"I better go find her a place to sit down."

"Yeah, you better."

They took a table near the dance floor. A few women were line dancing, laughing and turning in unison, while the men stood around watching them and drinking beer. Cole kept an eye out for customers. Another dealer, Dave D., a heavyset guy with a stiff crew cut and a soul patch, stood in the far corner. Dave D. dealt weed and dabbled in pills. He usually didn't come into the Eagle, which Cole thought of as his territory. When Dave D. nodded in his direction, Cole barely raised his chin.

Then Charlotte called out, "Yo, brothers."

The three brothers, big and mulish, were moving toward them in a pack. "Try to act sober, would you?" Cole said, but her face was lit up, shining, and they noticed right away: "Char, you on something?" She laughed, slid farther down the chair. They looked at Cole. "What the fuck did you give her?"

He was afraid of talking, the words bunching up in his mouth. Almost every weekend a fight broke out in the Eagle. Busted bottles, tipped-over tables. Cole had not been in a fight since high school, when some guys went after Terry Rose for sleeping with one of their girls. Cole came out of it with a bloody mouth and an aching jaw, but also feeling like he was a part of something.

He looked around, wondering how he could escape. Then he saw his twin cousins. He lifted his hand, and they headed over.

"Hey, blondie," said Dell, still just as bucktoothed as he'd been as a kid. "How's that old Chevy running?"

"All right."

"Didn't I tell you?"

Charlotte's brothers glanced at each other. Although his cousins had pounded on him when he was a kid, when it came to fighting, a person could usually count on kin. Cole was not sure what would happen next. He clenched his hand into a fist. But then Lyle suddenly let out a coyote-yelp, startling everyone; seconds later, a slow song came on the jukebox. The men stood there, all glaring at each other. Then one of the brothers said he was going to play pool, and the other two trailed after him. The twins looked at each other and laughed.

When they were kids, Cole had tried to stay clear of them. "Spit it out, retard," Dell would say, thumping him on the head, while his brother laughed wildly. Lyle was borderline crazy; even his grandmother said he was a little bit touched. Tonight, they had washed the motor grease from their hands and faces, and wore clean jeans and button-down shirts. "Y'all clean up good."

"We're celebrating a week of work," Dell said. "Justin got us on at that new site. He's up there at the bar."

"What are y'all drinking?"

"Whatever you want to buy." Dell laughed.

Cole still felt pumped with adrenaline. Jumpy. He watched Lacy pour out four shots. "How old are you, Cole?"

"Twenty-seven."

"Oh, you're just a baby. I'm an old woman compared to you."

"You ain't old."

"Thirty-six," she said. "And I got an eleven-year-old kid. What do you think of that?"

He carefully balanced the shot glasses. "That ain't old," he said again.

Back at the table, Cole and his cousins and Charlotte downed their shots in unison. Justin had joined them. He wore a camou-flaged cap backward, and his gigantic T-shirt and jeans hung loosely from his linebacker frame. All of his cousins, the men any-way, were taller and stronger than Cole. It had always been this way.

"Cole, you should've applied for a job at that new site in Bucks County," Justin slurred. "I could've gotten you on. I got the twins on."

"I already got a job."

"You could be making double what you earn now." Justin shook his head. "I don't know how you stand to be around those stink-ing old folks all day."

"You get used to it." But Cole knew what they thought of his job. The men in the family, of those who were actually employed, worked in the mines or construction, jobs like that. He'd never wanted to work for the coal companies; he couldn't gut the moun-tains the way they were doing and feel right about himself.

Charlotte's face was shiny with sweat. She grabbed Cole's hand. "Dance with me."

"You know I ain't one for dancing."

She moved her hips seductively. "Come on."

"No, I said."

"This is what I'm saying," she accused. "You're happy just sitting there doing nothing." Cole stared through her, lit a cigarette. "I guess I'll have to find someone else," she said, and turned to the twins, tugging on their meaty arms, but they just laughed. Charlotte finally gave up. She flipped all of them off and walked away, disappearing in the dark.

After a while, Justin complained he had the spins, and stumbled out of the Eagle. The twins said they better go after him. "All right," Cole said, but they just stood there, like they were thinking hard. "There's something else—," Dell started, but then Lyle, who rarely spoke, interrupted: "Cole, you got any Ritalin?"

"What?"

"Some guys at the site were asking," Dell explained. "I told them I could probably get it."

Cole shook his head. He didn't know how much his cousins knew about what he did. "I don't know what you're talking about."

"Ritalin, Adderall, whatever. Something to keep us up, you know. It would be a nice chunk of change for you."

Cole hesitated, and the twins looked at him eagerly. But he'd always promised himself that he would not sell to family. Family complicated things.

"No, I don't have anything."

Dell and Lyle looked at each other. "All right, that's cool," Dell finally said. "If you hear of anyone—"

"I'll let you know."

After they left, Cole studied the room, also keeping an eye out for Charlotte's brothers. But now his game felt thrown off, and he wondered if he should give up and go home. Everything felt too small, too close. He wanted it to be simple, the give-and-take, the little ball of power. A couple of regulars walked in. He made a few quick deals, then went out to the parking lot. The Oxy went fast, and he also sold a few tablets of the Adderall that his cousins had wanted. With his pockets stuffed with cash, his mind felt clearer. He considered bailing on Charlotte. It would be the easy thing to do.

Instead he went back in. He maneuvered his way through the crowd, and then stopped at the edge of the dance floor. There was Charlotte, her arms around a tall hatchet-faced guy. He looked at least twenty years older than her, maybe more. A slow song came on the jukebox, and Charlotte's eyes were half closed and the man had his hands on her hips. Just a few hours ago she'd been on her back on Cole's sofa. He stood there and watched, then she opened her eyes and saw him. She looked sad and tired. She stopped dancing and stepped away from the man and stood with one hand on her hip, as if she was waiting for the music to change. He thought she would come to him. She would come to him and he would dance with her, he would dance and dance. He wanted her to know that he was a dreamer too, that he grew up in a house where dreams and prophecies were as real as the food on their table. But the man leaned over and said something to her, and she followed him up to the bar.

The cigarette in his mouth burned down to nothing.

"Hey, Cole."

He turned and tried not to show his surprise. He guessed that he was going to have to get used to running into Terry Rose. This time he looked more like himself, or at least the way Cole remembered him, wearing jeans, T-shirt, and boots.

"Let me get you a beer," Terry offered.

"Nah, I'm heading out."

Terry saw where Cole was looking: Charlotte at the bar, leaning against a man old enough to be her father. "Oh, shit."

Cole started to go, but Terry asked him to wait. "You got an extra smoke?"

"I thought you quit."

"Only when my wife's around." He lit the cigarette with a match. "You and Charlotte broke up or something?"

He sounded sincere and fake at the same time. Did he sound like that when he was getting high with Charlotte, talking to her about New York and big dreams and other stupid shit?

"Don't worry about it," Cole snapped, but Terry was unfazed.

"Ain't this the shit, bro? Running into each other again?"

"It's not that big of a place."

"We ought to get wasted together, like the old days."

"I gotta go."

"Wait." Terry leaned in close. "You got anything on you?"

The goddamn question of the day. "No. I don't know what you're talking about."

"But Charlotte—"

"She doesn't know anything."

"I'll take whatever. Even Xanax, I don't care." Terry grinned. "Come on, look who you're talking to. I know you must get some good shit at that nursing home."

"Man, didn't you hear what I said?"

"Wait. Wait, Cole."

But he walked out the back door, and Terry didn't come after him. His pickup started on the first try, and he drove home in a drunken haze. His heart was pounding. He stood outside. Everything spinning. Several pieces of brick-size flyrock were scattered on his lawn, blasted down from the mountain, and he picked them up one at a time and hurled them into the road. "Fuck," he yelled. "Fuck, fuck."

He went in and flung his jacket across the room. He paced the trailer and then sat down, holding his head. Everything was still spinning. He reached for the remote and turned on the TV, just to have something in the room with him. Only three stations came in, all fuzzy. A late-night talk show and a zombie movie and an Irish man talking about sheep shearing. He flipped back to the zombie movie and watched the dead dig themselves out of their graves. A Heritage commercial interrupted. The camera panned on happy miners and their wives and their kids wearing Heritage ball caps. *Responsible to coal miners, to West Virginia, and to the environment.* The commercial ended with a view of a big green mountain, then zoomed in on a herd of deer and a chickadee perched on a tree limb.

"Fuck you," Cole said.

He snapped off the TV and pressed the blinking red light on his answering machine and listened to his grandmother: "Cole, honey, I need to talk to you." She'd been calling all week. He was tired of being the one she expected to fix everything. Didn't want to hear about how he should go to church with her, didn't want to hear about her prophecies or talk about giving up the land. He erased her voice. Then he stripped down to his underwear and stretched out on the sofa and thumbed through the pill book, a drug dealer's bible, but there wasn't anything that he didn't already know.

He went in his room and took out the safe and counted the money he'd made today, though he knew exactly how much was there. The bills felt soft in his hands, and he brought the green up to his nose, breathing in the inky smell. He had a little over twenty-five grand, more dough than his grandparents had ever had. Aside from what he gave to his grandmother and what went to his granddaddy's doctor bills, Cole rarely spent the money. Charlotte was right to say that he had it. He didn't know what he was saving for, but he liked knowing it was there.

He added today's earnings, pushing aside old-lady jewelry. It always surprised Cole how the residents, and their families, forgot to lock up their valuables. He didn't worry about getting caught. If anyone actually noticed something was missing, which they never did, it would be easy enough to blame it on the Alzheimer's patients, who were always wandering into other residents' rooms and stealing family photos, eyeglasses. Once he'd discovered a half dozen pairs of dentures hidden in a closet.

He leaned over his bed and took out an old Christmas cookie tin. He used to store the money in here, until Reese said, "Are you completely stupid?" and told him to buy a safe. Now Cole was extra careful. He never left his trailer or his truck unlocked. The junkies around here wouldn't stop for anything, even if they had to pull a job way out in the hills. It was also why he didn't sell out of his home.

He pried the lid off and dug out the postcards, worn by years of handling. The first one arrived when Cole was three years old, and after that, they came sporadically—sometimes five in a month, sometimes one a year, but always another one. Las Vegas, Dallas, small towns in Michigan, Ohio. Cities and states he learned about in school, but to him were as far away as the North Pole. As a kid, he had looked at the postcards nearly every night, tracing a pencil over his mother's slanted, loopy scrawl, mimicking the handwriting until it became his own.

The trees in California are a lot bigger than the trees in Dove Creek. They almost touch the clouds. They are big enough to stand inside of. xoxox, Ruby

The messages were all like that, short, simple, random. Never a return address. If his granddaddy had known about them, he would have burned them, the way he did her pictures. But Cole and his grandmother always retrieved the mail. The last postcard came when he was fifteen. There was never another.

Under the postcards were a few photographs. One of Cole with his grandparents on his tenth birthday, the same year his mother had visited. The single picture of her that his grandmother had salvaged from the flames. He set them aside and picked up one of him and Terry Rose. They were at a party, a bonfire. Their arms slung over each other's shoulders. Terry stood a head taller than Cole, his black curly hair cut in a mullet, the back trailing almost to his shoulders. They didn't look like brothers, but when they were thirteen, they opened their skin with Terry's pocketknife and smashed their hands together.

Before Terry, Cole didn't have many friends. The stutter ostracized him as soon as he opened his mouth, and belonging to a crazy snake-handling church didn't win him any friends either. But mostly it was his voice. If he was called on at school, he would mumble inaudibly in order to cover up the stutter, an annoying habit that he never completely kicked. While in his mind he constructed sentences and stories seamlessly, eloquently, whenever he opened his mouth to speak, the words came out mangled. Ugly.

Spit it out, retard.

Over time, as the stuttering faded, his teachers thought he'd outgrown it and his grandfather believed that God had cured him. But Cole credited Terry Rose, who talked so much that his words infiltrated Cole's speech and he began to sound like a boy instead of a stuttering preacher, losing the strange speech patterns that had been derived from the convoluted style of his granddaddy's sermons and verses of the King James.

Cole had met Terry Rose the summer he was thirteen, on a day that Cole had sneaked away to go fishing. He had just cast his line when a voice rang out: "Is there anything to do in this shit-hole?"

The voice belonged to a boy who was smoking a cigarette. He wore a baseball hat that said "Indy 500," and told Cole that he used to live in Indianapolis. "You like cars?" he asked, his voice flat, nasally.

Cole shrugged.

"My dad was a race car driver," Terry said. "He got killed in an accident." Now he and his mother were living with his aunt in Rockcamp.

Terry told Cole that he had a brother in Texas and a sister in Florida, and as he talked about the places he'd been to, many of which were the same places that the postcards had come from, Cole felt a warmth blossoming inside him, a combination of wonder and familiarity, as if this boy was the missing link to his mother. Terry bragged that he knew how to take apart a carburetor and put it back together. He said he was going to be a race car driver like his dad. He claimed that he'd already had several girlfriends. Cole had no reason to disbelieve anything the curly-haired boy told him. He had never met a city-dweller before: he wondered if they all talked this much. When Cole went back the next day, Terry wasn't there, and Cole felt disappointed, wondering if he had been real or if he was one of the restless spirits that his grandmother said walked the mountains. But a couple of days later, he was back. Terry never seemed to notice Cole's stutter, and eventually Cole also learned to ignore it, so much that it began to disappear.

Once he'd overheard his granddaddy complain that Cole had been a pretty good boy until Terry Rose came along. But Cole had never felt like a good boy. When he closed his eyes, he saw Charlotte dancing with the man at the Eagle. He saw Terry Rose, his toothy grin. He wished they would both disappear. He felt drunk and mixed up and far from God.

When he woke up, his head was pounding. He showered, ate several aspirin, and poured black coffee into a thermos. He was heading out the door when the phone rang.

"What are you doing?"

"I'm on my way to work."

"Well, I thought you would already know by now."

"What?"

"I got a call a few days ago." His grandmother's voice sounded thin and tight. "There's a space for your granddad."

Cole's skull felt like it was going to explode. "No, I didn't know."

"I thought they would have told you."

"It's a mess down there. Nobody knows what's going on." He tried to think of which space was open, then remembered Otis Smith, his grown children standing over his cold body. "You sure you want to do this?"

She took a breath. "I don't see what else we can do. The other night, he grabbed the fire poker, scared me to death. Larry and Rebecca have been coming over here almost every day, it's too much."

"I've been busy," Cole said defensively. "Working all the time."

"Oh, honey. Listen, over there he'll get the care he needs." She sounded like she was trying to convince herself. "I'll visit him every day. It'll be nice."

Cole looked out the window at the thick fog lifting across the back field. "You want me to take him in?"

"He's sleeping now. We'll bring him in later." Before she hung up, she added, "The only reason I feel okay about this is 'cause you'll be there."

As usual they were short-staffed. Cole, with his head still screaming, spent the first hour changing diapers and sheets. The old miner John Hill, suffocating with black lung, couldn't get out of bed, and Cole maneuvered around him, carefully turning him as he rolled on the new sheet. As soon as Cole finished, John let loose, peeing all over the sheet he'd just put down. "Fucking hell," Cole said.

He stepped outside for a smoke, joining Ellen. "It's going to be weird," he admitted. "Working in the same place where my grand-dad will be."

"Don't you pretty much just take care of him anyway?"

"I guess so," he said, feeling a sharp pang of guilt.

Ellen patted his arm, said everything would be okay. He liked Ellen. He could talk to her about nursing school, and she did not seem surprised that a guy like him would consider it. He used to entertain the thought of asking her out, but she was engaged. To a cop, of all people. He looked at her hand on his arm and Charlotte flashed in his head. Why hadn't he done anything, instead of just standing there, watching her put her arms around someone else?

Cole walked by the room that his grandfather would be moving into, still pulsing with the most recent death. Stripped bed, bare walls. He tried to imagine his grandfather among these people, Larry Potts twiddling his thumbs and Hazel Lewis trying to take off her shirt. The truth was, he'd probably fit right in.

Mabel Johnson was sitting in a rocker with a ball of blood-red yarn on her lap, looking dressed for church: blue belted dress, strand of plastic pearls, stockings the color of sand. She barely hit five foot, but wasn't frail; she looked like she could walk for miles. Mabel was ninety-five years old and had the memory of an elephant. She was the only black resident in the home, and a few of the patients refused to room with her.

He handed her a can of apple juice with a bendable straw poked through the top, and set down a bowl of tapioca pudding.

"You got anything else?"

"Just for you." He dropped several chalky peppermints into her wrinkled hand. She popped one in her mouth and for a second it sat, a bright pink medallion on her fleshy tongue, then her lips smacked and it was gone. "Mmm," she said. "I like those candies." One time Mabel had walked in on Cole as he was searching her dresser, the closest he'd ever come to getting busted. He pretended that he'd lost something, a ring, he muttered, and she narrowed her eyes: *I never knew you to wear no ring.* After that he had avoided her, until one day she put her hands on his: *I don't hold grudges.* To this day he wasn't sure what she knew.

He asked what she was knitting.

"A scarf."

"Who for?"

"One of the grandchildrens, I 'spect." She motioned for him to lean forward and her icy fingers grazed his neck. "Or maybe I'll give it to you. I can see this color kindly favors you."

Cole said he'd be proud to wear such a scarf. Mabel's children had fled the coalfields long ago and rarely visited, but she didn't complain: "I reckon they're busy." Now she looked at him, and her eyes were dark and velvety and filled with stories. The old people clung to the past. They could go on and on; usually he liked hearing them talk, but today he was preoccupied.

"You know they whipped my brother, Cole."

She told him this story nearly every time she saw him.

"In nineteen hundred and eighteen, before we got the union," she started, and she told how her brother had wandered over to the white section of the coal camp, and they accused him of watching their women. "They said the next one who came over to their side would be hung—" She held onto the arm of the chair like she was afraid of falling off. "I'll never forget those men's faces. They all dead now, but I can still trace their kin. I look at everyone here and know exactly who they come from, what kind of people they are."

"I know it," he said.

"But you come from good stock."

"Crazy stock."

"Your granddad is a good man."

Although Mabel, a Baptist, told Cole that she did not like that Pentecostal gibber-jabber, she respected his grandfather and believed he was a man of God. She'd told Cole stories that he'd never heard before. How his granddaddy delivered sweets to the poor on Christmas. How one time the town pharmacist put up a sign that said Whites Only, and his grandfather had escorted Mabel in and told the man that he would burn in hell if he didn't take down that sign. He took it down.

"Well, I'm glad you like him, because you're going to be seeing an awful lot of him."

She titled her head. "Explain yourself."

"He's moving in."

She showed no expression, and he wondered if she'd heard him. Then she looked down at the yarn in her hands. "Sometimes I see things," she said mysteriously.

He waited, but she said nothing else. Quietly, he eased out of the room.

As he headed down the hallway, Ellen stopped him. "Cole, he's here."

"Where?"

"At the door. Won't come in."

Cole jogged down the hall and nearly ran over Delphia Slone—hunchbacked and gray like some kind of creature from the dinosaur days, struggling to push her walker. "Watch where you're going," she yelled.

"Sorry."

At the front doors, his grandmother, Rebecca, and Uncle Larry were trying to coax his grandfather inside. Linda was waiting with a wheelchair, saying, "Come on Mr. Freeman," using her baby-talk voice, but Cole caught the undertone of impatience.

"I'll take care of it," he told her, and she looked relieved.

His grandfather stood stiff and hunched in the doorway, refusing to take another step. Cole's grandmother said, "Maybe he'll listen to you."

"To me?"

"Try," she insisted.

Aunt Rebecca had tears in her eyes, and Uncle Larry, in his Heritage security guard uniform, looked annoyed. "You take one arm and I'll take the other," he told Cole. "We'll carry him in."

More than once, Cole had overheard Larry talking to the other uncles, calling his grandfather a stubborn old fool.

"Don't touch him," Cole said sharply.

"What did you say?" he started, but Rebecca put her hand on his arm.

"Let Cole do it," she said.

He approached his grandfather cautiously, as if he were a wild dog.

"Devil won't leave me alone," his grandfather muttered.

"The devil won't bother you here," Cole said. "This is a good place."

A long silence, then the old man stepped forward. They parted for him. He probably hadn't understood Cole, but he'd listened to his voice and, for some complicated reason, trusted him. He held his grandfather's elbow and led him down the hallway, but felt as if he were leading him to his grave, remembering the scripture his granddaddy used to say, *My flesh and my skin hath he made old: he hath broken my bones.*

CHAPTER 5

HE THOUGHT EVERYTHING would change, but it didn't. Not much, anyway.

Today the cafeteria was decorated with crepe paper and American flags, and a volunteer from the Wives of the Veterans auxiliary group played "Yankee Doodle Dandy" on the upright piano. A few residents sang along, others looked startled. At the center table was a cake frosted with stars and stripes that Ellen was cutting into squares.

"Cole, help me pass these out," she said.

His grandfather sat at a table with five of the liveliest patients in the nursing home, all women. There were always more women than men. They were stronger, maybe just more stubborn.

"Granddad, you want a piece of cake?"

He chewed his bottom lip, eyes burning like a prophet's. Cole now knew him in ways he'd never wanted to. Wrinkles, bruises, smells of his old body. He had sponge-bathed him and tucked his flaccid penis into his pants. Cleaned up his piss and shit and spit. He did not think that his grandfather recognized him: Would he have tolerated his grandson undressing him, rubbing lotion onto his cracked skin, wiping his behind? He'd touched him more in the last month than he had his entire life.

"Here's Grandma."

The old man raised his eyes. She was the only person he still seemed to consistently recognize.

"How'd you get here?" Cole asked her.

"Erik."

"He couldn't come in?"

"Well, he had to get to work." She smiled apologetically. "It's hard for some of your cousins to see him like this. It's different for you, Cole."

"If you say so."

His grandfather did not take his eyes off her. Everyone at the nursing home figured he was mute, but Cole liked to think that his granddaddy was still talking inside his head, building a tower of words that one day would be knocked loose. A final, furious sermon spilling out of him.

"This is a real nice party," his grandmother said.

Wanda Woods rolled up in her wheelchair and took Cole's hand in hers. "Jamey, what are you doing here? You didn't tell me you were coming today."

Wanda always confused Cole with her son who'd been killed in a car accident fifty-some years ago. The first time it happened, he tried to explain who he was, but now he just played along, turning into a ghost for her, a smooth-talking seventeen-year-old with a girl named Penny.

Wanda smiled and laughed, but her eyes flickered. How many of the old people knew more than they let on? Did they see past this childish sing-along, the crumbling cake? Were they as dazed as they appeared? Cole looked around the room. He knew all of them. If they had family or not. What ailed them. If they were lonely, or confused. He knew what he'd taken from their rooms.

What they'd been prescribed. How much their meds went for on the street.

On his break, he walked over to the Wigwam, hoping Lacy Cooper would be there. He'd been stopping in a few times a week; if it wasn't busy, she would sit with him over pie and coffee, and they'd talk about their families and how funny it was that they grew up a couple of miles from each other but had never met until now. Cole's grandmother said things used to be different, there was a time when everyone knew everyone.

She was waiting on a couple of coal miners who were flirting shamelessly with her. Cole could see why. The top three buttons on the canary yellow dress were undone, and her hair was pinned back, showing off her long neck.

She saw Cole and waved. "Be with you in a minute."

He took an empty stool at the counter. The man next to him glanced over and smiled, then turned his attention back to the old woman on the other side of him. Cole had never seen either of them before. The old woman had a leathery face, and her hair was dirty gray and disheveled, her dull blue housedress frayed at the sleeves. "They're spilling sludge into my water, trying to run me out," she said, her voice gruff. She was from the hills, probably didn't get out much. But the man wasn't from around here. He spoke in a clipped songless voice: "Did anyone from the DEP come out to investigate?" He looked to be in his thirties. Short tapered hair, a black T-shirt, jeans, Buddy Holly–style glasses. Stubble. Small and fit. *Faggot.* The word jumped out at Cole, and he quickly looked away.

Helen poured Cole a cup of coffee. It sloshed over the sides. "You want anything else, hon?"

"No thanks."

"Anytime." Helen had been working at the Wigwam since it opened twenty years ago. She was a two-time widow, with brassy hair and basset-hound eyes. She turned to the old woman. "You want a refill, hon? Anything else?"

"A piece of that apple pie. You want a piece?" she asked the man, but he shook his head.

"Just a refill please."

Cole sipped the greasy black coffee, lit a cigarette. He stared ahead, watching the cook grill burgers and a bored teenager slop dishes into the double sink. He had the feeling that he was being watched. He looked over.

"Sorry. I was just wondering—do you think I could bum one of your cigarettes?" The man smiled apologetically.

Cole shook out a cigarette. The old lady wasn't in her seat, and then he saw her, shuffling toward the bathroom. He held out the cigarette, and the man took it.

"Thanks. It's nice to be able to smoke in a restaurant," he said.

Cole wished that Lacy would hurry up. Maybe this guy was a government man. Or an activist. He didn't want to be seen talking to him.

"I'm Michael Brody." He looked at Cole expectantly.

"Name's Cole."

"Thanks again, Cole."

"It's just a cigarette."

"Are you a doctor? A nurse?"

"No. Aide."

Cole felt relieved when Lacy waved him over to an empty booth. He drained the coffee and dropped a worn bill next to the saucer.

"Nice to meet you," Michael called out.

Cole sat across from Lacy in the back of the restaurant. She had faint circles under her eyes, but when she blinked, he saw the lids were brushed with a greenish-gray eye shadow, her lashes long and dark. "I need a vacation," she said.

"Shit, what's a vacation?"

"If you went on one, where would you go?" She didn't wait for him to answer. "I'd go somewhere far. Real far. Like Italy or France or something."

"Hell, I was just thinking Kentucky, maybe North Carolina."

She laughed, and he liked the sound of it. Then the bell on the door jingled and a little girl walked in, sweaty-faced, brown as an acorn. Lacy called to her. "Back here, hon."

She tousled the girl's sun-streaked hair. "This is Sara Jean. Hon, this is Cole Freeman."

"Hey, Sara Jean."

The girl barely glanced at him. "Hi." She was thin and small, sharp-elbowed, knobby-kneed. Cole wasn't used to being around kids, didn't particularly like them. This one looked part animal, bright eyes, messy hair.

"She looks like you," he said to Lacy.

"No, not really."

"I look like my dad," the girl asserted. "Hey, can Blue come to the fireworks with us tonight?"

"Sure. Ask her if she wants to come. You want to come too, Cole?"

He caught the disappointment in Sara Jean's eyes. "I don't think so. I'm not one for fireworks."

"Where is Blue, anyway?" Sara Jean asked. "Is she here yet?"

"She was sitting up there, talking to that fellow from New York," Lacy said. "I think she went to the bathroom. Why don't you go on up there? Ask Helen to make you a shake."

As the kid climbed onto the stool where Cole had been sitting, Lacy said, "All this has been real hard on her. Her dad gone, me working so much."

"Where is he, anyway? You never told me."

"Goddamn Wyoming. Working for a coal company out there. I don't want to talk about that son of a bitch." She glared at Cole.

"You know who came to see me the other day? Denny's dad. Gundy. You know about him?"

Cole shook his head.

"Vietnam vet, crazy as all hell. He took off when Denny was a kid, after his mom died. I only met him once. Lives way out in the middle of nowhere, but somehow he heard about Denny leaving. Comes by here, and gives me two hundred bucks. Sorry for what he done, he tells me."

"Does Denny send you money?"

"Once in a blue moon." She took a deep breath. "I don't miss that son of a bitch anymore. I just feel sorry for Sara Jean. Between him gone and then what's happening to the mountains, it's too much. When I'm at work, she stays with my parents. They live just a couple of blocks from here. But she wants to be up on the land all the time. She loves the woods."

The old woman had returned to her seat. She, Sara Jean, and Michael were talking to each other like old friends.

"Who is that guy?"

"A writer from New York. He came down here to do a story on mountaintop removal."

"A story?"

"I think it's going to be in the *New York Times Magazine*. Something like that."

Cole looked at her skeptically. "Why do they care?"

"People care."

"So he's an environmentalist?" The word sounded forced on his lips.

"I guess, I don't know."

Cole didn't think he looked like one. He used to see them in Charleston from time to time, holding rallies and protests outside the capital. Most of them were hippies. Young, raggedy.

"I'll tell you what, Sara Jean is caught up," Lacy said.

"What about you?"

71

"The more I find out, the more pissed off I get. Sometimes Sara Jean gets me on the computer . . . it's scary. I mean, if there's some kind of accident, all hell could break loose. It could be another Buffalo Creek. You know about that, don't you?"

"I ain't stupid."

"Well, you know about the big sludge dam?"

"I heard about it."

"Two billion gallons sitting right up above our heads. Right above where I live. If that dam breaks, it would probably get you too, if it comes down the ridge the right way." She paused like she needed to catch her breath. "Sometimes I wish I would have sold when they first came knocking. Now the sons of bitches cut their offer in half. It wouldn't be enough to move anywhere, except some trashy trailer park."

Cole gulped the last of the coffee. "Sorry," she said. "Sometimes I get worked up."

"It's all right. I like listening."

She smiled. "I'm glad."

After his shift ended, Cole drove his grandmother home, going slowly and glancing up at the mountain. "Grandma, what was it that happened at Buffalo Creek?"

"Don't you know? Dam broke. That was in '72, I think it was. Coal slurry. Killed a hundred and twenty-five people. My cousin Susie's husband was killed. It was sad. Just terrible. Just about everybody lost their homes." She paused. "Well, you coming in? I was going to make that chicken dish you like."

"Can't tonight."

"There's gonna be a good movie on," she said. "A two-parter."

He told her he'd be over tomorrow. "I'll catch the second part."

It didn't surprise Cole that his grandmother had turned into a TV-watcher, but he was surprised by just how much she liked it. A couple of weeks after his grandfather had gone into the nursing home, she had shown Cole a flyer from Walmart advertising televisions. "I reckon I wouldn't mind having one of those," she'd said.

Instead of heading directly to Stillwell, Cole went the opposite direction, turning right onto Route 16. He rarely went this way, and sometimes forgot the processing plant was even here. He passed under a conveyor belt that ran from the plant up to a mining site, crossing above the road and disappearing behind the trees like some kind of strange carnival ride. The plant was lit up like a tiny city. He pulled over. A tall fence ran around the property; locked gates; a guard post; cameras. He saw a few Heritage workers, in brown uniforms, walking toward the office. There were metal beams and platforms, he didn't know what they were used for. Pipes and conveyor belts. One led to an enormous silo. He was so used to seeing this kind of equipment and coal mining operations all around the county that it didn't leave much of an impression, everything a part of the landscape now, like the old coal tipples that still dotted the county like the shells of giant locusts. He couldn't see the sludge dam from here, but Lacy said the face of the dam itself was three hundred feet. After the coal was cleaned, the chemicals and water were sent up there. A lake of toxins, Lacy said. Two billion gallons. Mercury and a bunch of other stuff. The trees hid everything. Cole sat there until a worker started in his direction. He shifted gears, headed the other way.

He had long night of deliveries ahead of him—holidays were always good for business. First he went to see Reese Campbell. He pressed the bell a few times, until the door on Ruthie's side flung open. "Is there a goddamn fire or what?"

"You're the one who called me."

Reese wore a pair of denim cutoffs, nothing else. He was about the only guy in Dove Creek who wasn't afraid to wear shorts; most, like Cole, would rather sweat in jeans. His torso was webbed with tattoos: his name in baroque letters across his chest, the word *Fearless* scratched underneath, snakes, flames. Most of them were prison jobs, rugged scars and inky smudges, but wound across his stomach was a vine of yellow flowers that didn't look like any flowers Cole had ever seen. He thought of the tattoos on Charlotte, designs he'd brought his mouth against, then glanced away, blushing.

"You thinking of getting a tat, church boy?"

"Just wondering why everyone wants to have one of a snake," he said. "I bet you never even seen a snake up close."

"I've seen plenty of snakes. Just maybe not the kind you're speaking of."

"You're fuckin' sick, man."

Cole followed him inside, checking to make sure he wasn't leaving any dirt on the dusty rose carpet. Instead of stale cigarette smoke, Ruthie's side smelled distinctly of things gone old. The downstairs an unlived-in space. Furniture that had not been sat upon for years. Christmas catalogs collecting dust. A candy dish holding a gluey mass of lemon drops.

"I got an AC in Ruthie's room. One of the perks of living with an old lady on her deathbed."

The TV was insanely loud, just like in the old folks' home, drowning out the humming air conditioner. Also in the room were an air filter, a vaporizer shooting out clouds of cold air, and an oxygen concentrator. Equipment for the dying. None of this was new to Reese. In prison he'd helped out on the AIDS ward, he told Cole, "I seen the toughest boys wasted down to nothing." But Cole wondered how long Reese would be able to keep this up. He looked like he hadn't slept in days, and Ruthie was skeleton-skinny, her mouth pulled back in a wide, harrowing grimace, her jawbones practically visible through the skin. Cole took her hand in his, felt nothing but bone, but she looked at him with alert eyes. The first time she'd met him, she said she had no use for Bible thumpers, then Reese had told her, "He ain't like his granddaddy," and she'd softened.

Now she said, "He's handsome, Reese."

"He ain't my type, you should know that by now," Reese said, laughing.

Cole started to remind her of who he was, but she closed her eyes.

Reese turned down the TV. "You got any Oxy?"

"You don't have any for me? Ain't that the way it usually works?"

"Something's screwed up with Ruthie's Medicaid." He added, "I'll pay you, buddy. She needs it."

Cole hesitated, then tossed him a bottle. Reese woke Ruthie up long enough to place a tablet on her tongue, holding a plastic cup to her mouth. A few drops of water dribbled down her chin, which he wiped away with his thumb. He shook out another one for himself. "I been all speedy," he explained.

"My wig." Ruthie's eyelids fluttered. "I can't let this handsome feller see me like this."

"Who do you want to be?" Reese asked.

"You pick."

Reese dropped an armload of wigs on the bed and chose one with blond hair and soup-can-size curls. He adjusted it on Ruthie's nearly bald head and held up a hand mirror for her. "Nice to meet you, Miss Marilyn."

Ruthie's throaty laugh turned into a coughing spell. "I look a fright," she managed to say, gasping. Cole silently agreed. With the wig perched crookedly on her skull and the curls cascading around her wrinkled face, she looked like a demented clown, like Norman Bates.

After Ruthie drifted off again, Reese turned to Cole. "Saw your ex the other day," he said.

"I thought maybe she'd run off to New York by now." Cole had seen Charlotte a couple of times since that night at the Eagle, but they didn't have much to say to each other. There were some days he missed her, but also long stretches of time that she never even crossed his mind.

Reese snorted. "That girl ain't going anywhere. She was on the Oxy hunt." He twisted open a bottle of bright pink nail polish and started to paint Ruthie's fingernails. "I also met your buddy Terry Rose," he added. "That motherfucker is about to go over the edge."

"What do you mean?"

"He was all speeded up, talking to me about how he wanted to start cooking his own. Trying to hook me up. He ain't a narc or anything, is he?"

"Nah, he's all right."

"Well, he talks too much." Reese blew lightly on Ruthie's fingers. "Listen, till I get this Medicaid shit worked out, I might not have anything for you. I got morphine, but I'm holding on to that for when things get bad." He looked up. "I ain't gonna let her suffer."

Cole nodded in sympathy, but his mind raced with numbers and figures, what he stood to lose if Reese stopped supplying him with Ruthie's cancer cash-crop. He didn't think that Reese was selling, so he must have been using the Oxy harder than Cole thought, a way to come down from all the speed he was shoving up his nose. Asshole. Maybe it wouldn't hurt his business too much, since he already overpaid Reese. He didn't know why he was making all this money anyway.

He was on the road when the fireworks started. He heard them from his truck but couldn't see them, only a few flashes of light. Once, when he was a kid, his grandfather had begrudgingly taken him and his grandmother to see the show. She'd been so excited, oohing and ahhing every time another one hit the sky, but his granddaddy complained about the crowd and made them leave before the finale. Cole thought about his grandmother, in front of the TV, alone, worrying. I should have taken her to see them tonight, he thought, I should have done that for her.

Instead he turned up Muddy Ridge and pulled in front of Taylor Jones's single-wide. Taylor was a twenty-five-year-old

Marine who was up to 160 milligrams a day. Cole rapped on the door, and Taylor yelled for him to come in.

"Happy fucking Fourth of July."

He'd grown a bristly mustache and his shaved head gleamed. He wore a pair of camos cut off at the knees and no shirt. He looked scary. He was sloppy and overweight. Cole had never seen him eat anything other than red licorice and Snickers. A sweet freak like most Oxyheads. Taylor collected disability for getting his hand blown off in Iraq, but his VA doctor would not prescribe the higher dosage. "Fucking asshole," he raged. "Does he know what pain is, motherfucker?"

They were blasting not far from Taylor's, which was making him even crazier. Sometimes he talked nonstop. He described how it was over there, the dust and heat, how he'd seen strange body parts and splattered brain; other times he was as silent as a rock. Tonight was one of those nights, and Cole was glad. He spoke only to ask about Cole's cousin Ricky, the one in Afghanistan.

"Haven't heard anything lately."

Taylor took the tablets from Cole and washed one down with grape Gatorade. He didn't snort like most of Cole's customers. Taylor legitimately needed the Oxy for his pain. But he was still an addict.

"It's a fucking mess over there," he said.

"That's what I hear," Cole said. Wasn't the whole damn world a mess? He waited another minute, but there wasn't anything else to say. He told Taylor he'd catch him later and let himself out. The door banged behind him. As Cole was getting in his truck, Taylor leaned out a window, waving his stump arm. "Here too," he yelled.

"What?"

"Over here. It's a fucking mess over here too."

Cole looked at Taylor, stoned and fat and screaming out the window, and did not know what to say except, "Yes it is, man, it's a fucking mess."

On his drive, as he crested a hill, a spray of red and blue scattered in the sky, pretty and far away. Lacy and her kid were watching from the fairgrounds, and Ellen was probably there too with her fiancé. But if Cole went, he'd be behind the bleachers with all the burnouts and pillheads and glue-huffers and speed freaks and fuckups. What do I have? he thought. Pain pills, stashed cash, and jewelry he'd stolen from old doddering ladies. A stack of postcards. And a thousand useless Bible verses.

CHAPTER 6

T HE FIRST OF THE MONTH was always a busy time. Disability and Social Security checks arrived, prescriptions got filled. Cole loaded up his truck with groceries and headed toward Stinkweed Hollow, at the end of the county line. Even speeding, it took him forty-five minutes to get there. After he passed the last shack on the right he went up a one-lane dirt road for two miles, trying to avoid giant ruts and potholes that the coal trucks had left behind. Low-hanging branches scratched the sides of his pickup. He rolled up his window to keep out the dust. It was August, thick and sticky.

Like his grandfather, Cole knew all the back roads. For thirty years his granddaddy had worked for the electric company, carrying a paperback King James in his tool belt. "There's only two kinds of people," he liked to say. "The saved and the unsaved. Ain't no in between." When he occasionally took Cole with him, Cole would watch his grandfather scurry up an electrical pole that looked like the cross that Jesus died on. He pretended his grandfather was magical. He was like God—he gave people light. Even better, he gave them television. After he left his job to preach full-time, they sometimes went without heat because he believed

79

nobody should make money off the word of God. He preached the Gospel to the homebound and the unsaved. He brought plates of food wrapped in foil that he left on front porches, telling Cole, "Never make a man feel below his worth."

When Cole reached the dilapidated four-room house where Tiny Williams had lived for nearly all of his eighty-three years, a pack of mongrel dogs ran out and surrounded the pickup. Tiny came out and called off the dogs. He was reed-thin and stood about six-four. He'd started working in the deep mines when he was sixteen years old. His wife, Lottie, not much over five foot, stood next to him, waving.

"It's good to see you, son."

"How y'all doing?"

"We're okay, right, Ma?" Tiny said, grinning, mostly toothless.

"We're hanging on." Lottie wore a crumpled fedora, her face weathered and tough. "Except now the doctor tells me I got the sugar."

"Diabetes?"

"Yup."

"You taking insulin?"

"Yes. I hate a needle. But Tiny here, he's real gentle. He gives me the shots."

They hardly ever left their home except for occasional trips to the doctor. Cole brought them food, jugs of water, twenty-four-packs of toilet paper, cigarettes, and back copies of the paper because they liked to work the crossword.

As Cole and Tiny unloaded the groceries, the dogs ran underfoot. Lottie, smoking a menthol, looked at Cole with appreciation. "I don't know what we'd do without you."

"I like coming up here."

"You're a good boy," Tiny said.

The house was neat and sparse. Pictures of Bobby Kennedy and John Lewis the union leader hung prominently in the kitchen.

Many of the homes Cole went into had the same pictures. His grandmother said Bobby Kennedy was the only politician who made it to heaven, even if he was a Catholic. He was one of the only ones who ever stepped foot in Appalachia, who talked to the people.

After the groceries were put away, they spent the afternoon on the front porch. Lottie brought out iced tea and ham salad sandwiches. The maples and oaks shaded them from the heat, but sunlight trickled through to shine on the hundreds of tin cans that were arranged on fence posts and suspended from the clothesline. Lottie liked trumpery. From the fruit trees she hung ornaments made out of foil and bottle caps and glass that shimmered and twirled whenever there was a breeze.

"How's Clyde?"

"Still hanging on."

"What about Dorothy? Don't she get lonesome?"

"I guess sometimes."

Lottie and Tiny said they did not think they could stand to be without the other. They told stories about the old days. They talked about their children and the hard times they'd faced. At Cole's urging, they sang an old death ballad, their voices taut and sweet.

Before he left, he pointed to the porch's loose boards. "I could fix that for you."

"Oh, it ain't no trouble."

The coal company had been blasting the ridge behind them for the past year. Already, their well had dried up twice, and a piece of flyrock had busted their kitchen window. But the worst part was the valley fill, a two-hundred-foot wall of rock and rubble towering over them. There were no trees or roots left on the mountainsides to stop the rain, which ran down the face of the valley fill and into the holding pond below it and then flooded their land.

"They'll get out of here pretty soon," Tiny said.

"They offer to buy you out?" Cole asked.

"I told them there are some things that just ain't for sale."

"I could do without that blasting. It's ashaking the house. The pictures fall off the walls, the doors don't close right." Lottie continued, "They ain't gonna pay for no damages either, and you might as well forget about the government helping you out."

"That's true," Tiny said. "And I do sometimes worry about that fill sliding."

"I tell you what," said Lottie, "there's a lot of politicians that one day are gonna bust hell wide open."

Tiny said this was also true. He leaned back in his chair. "Don't worry, they'll get out of here before you know it."

But the coal company didn't look like they planned on going anywhere. It seemed like just about every peak and valley had some kind of mining operation going on. Eventually, maybe the sites would connect like one long flattened roadway. Cole did not know what to tell them. He did not know the answer.

Though the sun had descended, the heat was still thick, and he considered going to the Eagle for a cold beer. Maybe Lacy was working tonight. But instead he drove home, parked in front of his grandmother's. Through the windows he could see the glow of the TV.

"Didn't expect to see you," she said.

He hung up his ball cap. "Thought I'd stay over here tonight."

"You hungry?"

"Starving."

She looked pleased. "I haven't eaten yet either."

While she busied herself in the kitchen, Cole went upstairs. His childhood room had barely changed over the years, the same plain furniture, the same lake blue walls. A bookshelf with the King James and a couple of model cars. On top of the dresser, a few trinkets: an owl's feather, a piece of quartz, an arrowhead, a snail shell, all taken from the land. He lifted the quartz, its cool, jagged edges pressed into his skin. He used to have more of the same, feathers, rocks, bones. When he was a kid, he was always picking things up.

In the bathroom, he studied himself in the mirror. He was gaunt and pale, and his hair resembled the color of mouse fur. He pinched his cheeks hard until blood rose to his skin. He looked at his face until he saw what it would look like without flesh, saw himself without eyes or lips or nose, the jutting bones and the skeletal outline of his face, saw beyond his reflection. Then he stepped into the tub under the cool stream of water, forgetting everything.

After he dried off, he pulled on a pair of raggedy cutoff sweatpants, which he would not be caught dead wearing in front of anyone other than his grandmother. On the shelf that was reserved for him, his deodorant and shaving cream and hair gel, he found a kit of dye. He mixed up the chemicals and, wearing a pair of latex gloves, fingered and combed in the gooey mix, the way Charlotte had taught him.

His grandmother had the TV trays set up. She was eating a small helping of spaghetti, and she'd served him an enormous bowl, along with store bread, salad, and a glass of milk. The twenty-four-inch screen TV wasn't the only thing that had changed about the room. She'd also added prints of flowers, tiny porcelain animals, and needlepoint wall hangings. For years she'd been waiting to decorate the house her way, without having to listen to her husband grumble about it. Now she had her chance.

"What do you got that plastic bag on your head for?"

"Bleached my hair."

"I don't know why you've taken a liking to that towheadedness."

He started to respond, but she shushed him. A rerun of *ER* was starting. The satellite TV gave her a couple hundred channels. At first she had watched indiscriminately, but now she mostly stuck with hospital dramas and a number of cop shows that Cole never would have imagined her liking.

On commercial break, she looked at him. "You reckon your hair's done?"

"Maybe."

"You still seeing that girl?"

"Nah, we broke up a couple of months ago."

"Well, for goodness sakes, you should have told me." She hesitated. "You all right?"

"Yeah, I'm all right."

She dabbed at the beads of sweat on her brow with a washcloth, and they talked about the stifling heat until her program came back on, then Cole went out for a cigarette. He listened to the trickling creek. The thrum of night crickets. He looked for the moon, couldn't find it past the hills and trees. When he was a teenager, he spent many nights sneaking out and wandering the woods with Terry Rose, smoking pot, sipping whiskey, making plans about leaving. It had taken Cole a while to figure out that Terry had never been to the places he'd bragged about, not Florida or Texas or California, but he still acted like he'd been everywhere, and soon they began talking about going places. Places where they could get away from Bible verses and rules, and ghosts of runaway mothers and dead fathers. When they were fourteen they studied a map of the country, tracing their fingers along rivers and state lines, until they reached the giant spaces of blue. At seventeen, they'd still been talking about it.

Cole took the plastic bag off his head. His grandmother was in the kitchen, washing dishes. When she turned, he saw that her eyes were red and puffy.

"Why, it's so light. You look like a ghost."

"You know it'll grow back."

"I didn't say I didn't like it."

"What's wrong?" he asked. "You look like you've been crying."

She went back to her scrubbing. Then she said, in an even voice,

"I don't believe he would have ever done the same to me. He would not have stuck me in such a place."

She was right. As terrible as he could be, he would not have put his wife in a nursing home—he would have fought off his daughters and the doctors to the very end. But Cole told her, "You did the best thing for him."

"Till death do us part, that's what marriage is."

"Well, you're still married to him. Unless you're planning on getting a divorce."

"Why do you say such things?"

They carried bowls of butter pecan ice cream into the family room. This time when Cole sat down, he noticed that on top of the TV, along with the familiar family photographs, were a few that he'd never seen before.

"Is that Aunt Naomi?"

"No."

"Who is it?"

"It's Ruby."

He picked up the framed photograph. "How old was she?"

"Ten years old in that picture, I do believe. You see how you got her eyes."

"They don't look the same to me."

"Oh, yes. Hers changed color too, the way yours do." She sighed. "I been praying for her. One of these days she'll hear me, she'll come back."

He held the picture up to the light. His mother was in the backyard, in front of the forest, and the sun shone on her face and she was smiling and looked like she never wanted to leave that spot. Orange poppies and daylilies shot up all around her. She had not known fear nor sadness, not yet; she was still the apple of her father's eye. Six years later, when Cole was born, she named him before she ran off. No biblical name, no middle name, no lineage of his unknown father. Instead she named him for the black gold in these mountains that caused everyone so much grief. "You surely are your mother's child," his granddaddy would say when he was angry. "You surely are her child."

Somebody was knocking. Cole groggily looked out the window and saw a red SUV. The coal men. He yawned and let the curtain fall from his fingers and reached for his cigarettes. He'd stayed at his grandmother's last night, and he liked waking up in his childhood bed, the smell of the freshly laundered sheets, the openness of the room.

He pulled on Levi's. It was blazing hot, already felt like it was over a hundred. He padded down the creaky stairs, caught a glimpse of his white hair in the hallway mirror and stopped for a second, looking at someone who was not quite himself.

"Grandma," he called, then remembered it was Sunday. One of the aunts usually drove her to church. She'd been trying out different churches, couldn't decide on which one she liked best. She told Cole she didn't care for the churches that her daughters now attended, which were some sort of Pentecostal or another, but that wasn't the same thing as the old Holiness way.

He walked out, surprising the man who'd been spying through the window, soft hands cupped around his face. Jeans and a crisp tucked-in polo shirt. Clean-shaven, hair parted to the side. He wore work boots, which meant he wanted to walk around the property. Cole looked to see if there were any others, but the man had come alone. The nice one. They sent different types, usually two at a time—friendly, wheedling, menacing. Lacy told him he was lucky they even wanted to buy; they usually only bothered buying out whoever lived at the head. "You must be sitting on a heap of coal," she explained.

The man was smiling too much, but his eyes, nearly hidden under thick eyebrows, were mean, and Cole focused on them.

"How you doing, son? Joe Tuling, I work for Heritage."

"My grandma's not here. She's at church."

"You must be her grandson?" Smiling pleasantly. Eyes like a snake.

He told the man his name. Didn't offer him coffee or a cigarette. The man looked tired and hot, but Cole did not offer him a place to sit.

"Good to finally meet you," he said, holding out his hand, wedding ring shining. His grip was firm. "It's a hot one," he said. "Brother, is it hot."

Cole let him go on a while longer about the heat. He was glad his grandmother wasn't here; she might feel pressured to invite him in for coffee. Cole and his grandmother did not talk anymore about it, if they should sell or stay, but the questions and worry lingered, underneath everything, like the land itself.

"I've talked to your grandma a few times. Your aunts, uncles. Everyone but you."

"Well, they sent other guys around," Cole said. "My answer is still the same."

"Once your grandmother sells, it'll just be you."

"She ain't gonna."

"Now, son."

Joe's voice deepened, a business voice. He talked about the benefits of coal mining. He talked in figures—they were willing to pay thousands more than what the land was worth, he'd have more money than he'd ever imagined. He gave Cole the spin on helping his community, providing jobs and a steady income. All lies. Cole lit his second cigarette this morning. He just wanted to be left alone. Needed coffee. Sleep. To get laid. Cool air.

"I know you gotta do what you gotta do. But I'm not leaving. That's all I got to say."

Joe smiled, then seemed to check himself, and pulled a more somber face. "Listen to me, what I'm offering you is a chance you

CARTER SICKELS

don't want to pass up. This is an opportunity. And believe me, there won't be many more after this. This may be our last offer, Cole. It's a gift. Don't refuse a gift. You'll regret it later."

"Been nice talking to you," Cole said, thinking, This ain't no kind of gift.

He sat on the dusty porch steps and watched the SUV back out onto the road. How much longer he could hang on, how long could any of them? He breathed deeply. Closed his eyes. It's fight or flight, he'd heard one of the activists say on TV. He didn't want either one. Just wanted to be.

"How much longer you think he's got? Will he last through the night?"

The aunts surrounded Cole, wanting him to do something. Two days ago, his grandfather had been rushed to the hospital where he was expected to die, but he held on and was transferred back to the home. It was that way with most of them—desperately clinging, even the ones who'd talked with joy about meeting the Lord.

"Y'all should go on home," he said. "You must be exhausted. I know I am." Cole was pulling a double. It was almost midnight.

"I had a vision." His grandmother said she'd seen her husband standing on the crest of a hill, with a beautiful golden light shining on him. "It spread out in front of him, like a river, like a path going right up to heaven," she said. She squeezed Cole's hands. "I think he'll be all right till morning, don't you?"

"Probably."

"I'll be at Esther's. Make sure you call me when he gets close."

"Sometimes things happen. He might just go."

"I already said my good-bye." She looked at him. "But you need to make your peace."

The room smelled like death. Where was the divine healing? Once, at a revival, Cole had watched a little crippled boy walk down the aisle, and a few years ago, after a spot had been detected

88

on Rebecca's lung, the people in the church had put their hands on her, and the next time she went to the doctor, the spot was gone. Cole stared at his grandfather's sunken eyes, his face no longer a face but a skull with skin. He had always expected his grand-daddy to leave this world in a dramatic, fiery way. Not this linger-ing between worlds, this wasting away. His grandfather stirred, blinked his eyes open. He looked at Cole, and could see every-thing that was wrong with him. Cole's heart raced, and it was as if he'd lost all ability to speak. But his mind was sharp with scrip-ture. *Walk while ye have the light, lest darkness come upon you: for he that walketh in darkness knoweth not whither he goeth.* His grandfa-ther was thin and light and rising to heaven.

But Cole was heavy, and he sat in the chair next to the bed and switched on the lamp and turned it toward him so that a yellow beam of light fell over the crinkled pages of the King James and illuminated the words that he and his grandfather knew so well. He summoned his voice and read quietly, without stuttering. His grandmother had wanted him to do this months ago. He turned the pages of Acts and read the part when Paul leaves for Jerusa-lem and tells his followers good-bye: *And they all wept sore, and fell on Paul's neck, and kissed him, Sorrowing most of all for the words which he spake, that they should see his face no more.* His grandfather's breaths were shallow and ragged. He moaned until a shot of mor-phine dripped into his veins.

His grandfather did not fear death, but he worried that his grandson was one of the many who would burn up in a lake of fire. Bastard child punished for his mother's sins. No devil horns or six-fingered hands or clubbed feet; instead, God forked his tongue. His grandfather believed in fire the way he did the ser-pents. He said the world would be destroyed by fire. "It's not going to be the bomb or war or anything else man-made. God made this world, and He'll end it. You better be ready," he'd say with delight, "he's fixing to burn it all up."

At the end of his shift, Cole filled a plastic bucket with warm soapy water. He pulled the blankets down from his grandfather's withered body, and gently moved him so that his feet hung over the bed. The first red glow of dawn peeked through the window. When Cole unpeeled the little socks from his grandfather's feet, he showed no response. Cole felt queasy. He had never liked this part of the service. Men washed men's feet, women washed women's. Cole did not like touching anyone's feet, especially his grandfather's, which were callused and horny like hooves.

Now they had shrunk and softened, soft like a baby's, but the toenails were yellow and hard like they'd always been. The ankles were as white as teeth, the skin corded with wrinkles. His grandfather had never cared about the flesh: *For if ye live after the flesh, ye shall die.* Cole took a breath, holding the icy feet. What was it he wanted? Did he believe his grandfather would lay his hands upon him and give him salvation? Was it forgiveness he was after? Love? Once when he was a little kid, he and his grandfather had sat on a ridge overlooking a misty valley and his granddaddy told him to listen. *God talks to you, but He don't talk to your ears, he talks to your heart.* Cole wanted his grandfather to tell him that he was not alone.

He trickled water over the ankles and toes, and the old feet tightened and Cole looked up from where he kneeled on the floor and saw his grandfather watching him. This was his moment to say good-bye. He was afraid.

The wheezing grew louder, harsher. The old man's mouth began to work itself in some strange, ugly way, half paralyzed and without any teeth, gumming and spitting, his tongue pushed out over his bottom lip like a worm.

"Ruby," he gasped.

Cole jerked his hands away and his grandfather's feet flopped in the water like bloated frogs. The old man shuddered, said her name again, his eyes open and radiant with love. Said her name a third time, not with venom, but like some kind of prayer. The color in his face disappeared, but his eyes stayed open, gazing into some other world. The rising sun shone over him and the light looked just like his grandmother said it would look.

CHAPTER 7

I T WAS A BEAUTIFUL September day, blue skies, sunshine.
Cole's aunts sniffled and wiped their eyes, but his grandmother
stood dry-eyed, her arms crossed over her chest. It was a strangely
rigid and quiet funeral. Usually there was more wailing, more
swaying, but it was as if they were waiting for his granddaddy to
tell them what to do. When the preacher spoke the last words,
everyone hung their heads and said amen. There was no fancy casket or tombstone; the old man would have disdained such fanfare.
"We're gonna do this as cheap as we can," his grandmother had
said, shocked by the funeral costs. Cole paid for most of it, told her
not to worry.

Two nights ago had been the viewing, shaking hands with
family and strangers, *Thanks for coming, good to see you.* For a moment Cole had stupidly thought that maybe Charlotte, Reese, or
even Terry would stop by. Who were his friends? Old people, drug
addicts. But then Lacy Cooper had walked in, wearing her Wigwam uniform, and she kissed Cole's cheek and told him she was
sorry and he could hardly talk, but when she left, he stood for a
long time at the window gazing in the direction where she'd gone.

After the service, everyone headed to the house, but Cole still stood there, alone, in the little family cemetery, not far behind the wrecked church. A few weeks ago, the roof had finally collapsed, and now it was nothing but a pile of cinder block and rubble. The aunts and uncles had argued about burying him in such a precarious spot, but his grandmother wouldn't budge. It's what he wanted, she said with finality. Cole looked around at the mildewed, crumbling tombstones, the fading family names that could be traced to the living. *Everything's a fucking mess,* Taylor Jones had said, and this was true. One day there would be nothing left but upturned earth and black sludge and broken remnants of their family.

A four-wheel-drive pickup with a shovel attached to the front pulled up near the gravesite, and two guys, friends of the twins, jumped out. They wore work pants and dirty shirts; they were waiting for him to leave.

Someone tapped him from behind.

"You're jittery," Kay said. "How are you holding up?"

"Okay." He handed her a cigarette, lit one for himself. Smoking in front of his granddaddy's casket. The old man had said everything counted. Tobacco, alcohol, dances, ball games, all of these were worldly things. He had preached on it: "I ask myself, would Jesus be watching that old TV, or would he be off helping the less fortunate?" Cole exhaled smoke. What did it matter anymore?

"You look nice."

"I'm about the only one in a suit," he complained. All the cousins had worn jeans or khakis, short-sleeve polo shirts. He tugged at his tie, felt like he was being strangled.

"Yeah, and you're the only one who looks like you got any sense."

"So how's college?"

"It's different," she said. "There's a lot of drinking and whatnot."

"You can get that right here in Dove Creek."

She exhaled smoke. "You were with him?"

"Yeah."

"Was he in pain?"

"I think so."

"Did he know you?"

"I don't know," he said shortly. "I don't know what he knew."

People gathered in the backyard, sticking close to the food. There was plenty of it: fried chicken, honey-baked ham, green bean casserole, pickled eggs, glazed carrots, baked beans, and macaroni salad. Another table displayed the desserts: rhubarb-strawberry pie, banana pudding, Jell-O salad, chocolate cake, and Oreo cookies crushed up in Cool Whip. As Cole fished a Mellow Yellow out of the galvanized tub of ice, a woman with fluffy red hair called him over. It was Connie Wilson, one of his aunts' many cousins. Thin and freckled, she wore a wild dress with black and green swirls, like something from the disco era. She threw her arms around him like he was her lost son, then stepped back, beaming. Her teeth were some of the whitest he'd ever seen.

"You look just like your mom," she said.

He swallowed, didn't know what to say.

"You remember me, hon?" An old woman with dyed black hair smothered him in a cloud of gardenia perfume. His grandmother's sister, his great-aunt Pearl. "Lord, I know this don't sound right, but it feels like a family reunion, don't it?"

"Almost," Cole said.

"Doesn't he look like Ruby, Mom?" Connie asked.

"He sure does." Pearl sized him up. "Just like her, even with those goldilocks."

Cole faked a smile, but he felt queasy. He wished everyone would leave, or that he could disappear, go lay down somewhere. But as the day wore on, people grew comfortable and settled in to stay. Shirt sleeves rolled up, shoes shucked. Cole peeled off his socks, and the grass felt cool and slippery between his toes.

He went behind the shed with his cousins and took a few nips of the twins' whiskey. They hadn't said anything else to him about buying pills since that night at the Eagle, but from their jittery hands and dilated eyes, he'd guessed they had found themselves another dealer.

"You were with him when he died?" his cousin Erik asked.

Cole nodded.

"That sucks."

Erik was the oldest cousin. He'd fought in the first Gulf War and was always telling Cole that the army would do him good. Cole was not about to risk getting blown up. Most of Erik's friends were guys who were half crazy or missing body parts, guys like Taylor Jones.

His cousins talked jobs, football, hunting, the kind of talk that had been passed down from their fathers. They were even beginning to look like their old men, receding hairlines, ballooning drum-tight Dove Creek guts. Cole leaned against the shed, where his grandfather used to store the snakes. He would catch them in the mountains during the summer and cage them in flat boxes. Every year there were fewer and fewer serpent handlers. Most of the churches had given it up.

One time his cousins had threatened to lock Cole in the shed. He'd kicked and thrashed, his shrieks echoing down the hillside until his grandfather came upon them like a lion. He took a thin whip of a hickory and made the cousins line up; they pressed their small hands against the shed, faces squinted in dreaded anticipation, and one by one he whipped them and he did not stop until all of them were crying, even Lyle. *Withhold not correction from the child: for if thou beatest him with the rod, he shall not die. Thou shalt beat him with the rod, and shalt deliver his soul from hell.* Then his grandfather had led Cole back to the house and with unexpected gentleness, said, "Don't weep child, do not weep."

When Uncle Larry came around to the shed, Justin hid the canning jar behind his back, but Larry saw. "If your mothers find out," he said. Then, "Here, give me a nip."

Justin, grinning, handed him the jar. Larry took a swallow.

"Whoo," he said after. "Burns." He passed it to Cole. "How you holding up?"

"All right."

"I wish you'd talk some sense into your grandma about selling this place. Especially now that she's all alone."

"She's not alone."

Larry held his gaze for a second, then turned to Erik. "I heard you're gonna start working security at Heritage."

"That's right. Maybe we'll be at the same site."

"It's a good job." Larry looked again at Cole. "'Course, Cole here seems to be doing all right being a nurse." When Larry grinned, his mustache curled like a limp caterpillar. "Maybe I should look into that. You're doing real well there." .

"Larry the nurse," Erik said, and snorted.

They all laughed, and Cole squinted at Larry. How much did he suspect? Did they all know? He would have to be more careful, and remind his grandmother to keep quiet about the money. "It pays all right," he said evenly.

When he went up to the table for more food, his grandmother waved him over. She and the aunts, and other family and church members, were gathered in a circle of lawn chairs, passing around photo albums. More comfortable here, he pulled a chair up next to his aunt Esther, who was wiping away tears.

"I always loved to watch Daddy preach," she said. "The way he'd roll those sleeves up, like he was about to get in a fight."

Rebecca agreed. "It was like he was bigger than just a man."

Cole's grandmother was at the center of things. Her silver hair, which she usually pinned in a tight bun, hung freely, flowing past her shoulders.

"That's how I first met him," she said. "He was preaching all around West Virginia, the coal camps and what not." Cole knew the story well, could hear it in his grandfather's voice: *Dogs chased me and guns were pointed at me, but I was walking with the Lord.*

His grandmother continued, "He came up to Wolf Run and set up a tent revival. People was suspicious. Religion wasn't real big in that holler, was it, Pearl?"

Pearl exhaled a stream of smoke. She chain-smoked thin brown cigarettes, which her husband, Walter, lit for her with a plastic NASCAR lighter. She looked relaxed and happy in the sagging striped lawn chair, as if she were lounging at a pool. As she talked, she rested her hand on her Walter's knee. Cole wasn't used to seeing old people touch each other like that.

"Oh, no, it wasn't a real religious holler," Pearl agreed. "But we were curious about this revival. Good God, all that tongue speaking, and Clyde up there hollering. I was scared, but Dorothy was taken with him."

"Well, he baptized me." His grandmother looked at Pearl, who must have tried to convince her sister not to run off with this strange preacher man, but she married him anyway and he took her back to his family's place, where together they built a church.

"You didn't get touched by the Holy Ghost then, did you?" a church member asked.

She shook her head. "That happened later. I was feeling so empty inside. We were flat-broke and Clyde was laid off, and I had nowhere to turn. I was right over there." She pointed to a pile of dirt. "That's where the garden used to be, and I was staking tomatoes, then I just got this feeling. I dropped to my knees and started praying. Next thing I knowed I was speaking another language."

"We all thought Clyde was crazy," Myrtle interrupted.

His grandfather's sister, silent up until now, sat on a rocker that Cole had carried out from the house, and she looked like she'd already died and been dug up from the earth. Cole had never met her before today. She had brought several of her children and grandchildren with her, the men in faded jeans, T-shirts, work boots, and the women's dresses frayed with holes. Cole noticed their dirty hands. His grandfather rarely spoke of his kin except to say that he came from a family of unbelievers and Baptists. As Myrtle talked in a low, muffled voice, everyone leaned forward. She was missing several teeth, and her severe brow bone made her eyes look even more craterlike. They were the same blue as his grandfather's.

"Clyde went to the Baptist church with Grandma where he was baptized early on. He used to tell me I was going to rot in hell, so finally I got dunked too. But when he went to that holy-roller revival, he changed. He used to be a hard worker, but after he said he'd seen God's light, he didn't lift nary a finger to help on the farm. I reckon he was struggling with something—"

"The call to preach," Esther explained, the others nodding in agreement.

Myrtle wasn't through. "Clyde left us high and dry. We moved to Kentucky after Daddy lost his job at the mines, and I didn't see my brother for many years after that." She smacked her lips. "Maybe he was struggling with his calling. But I tell you what, God took him from our family."

"Well, he thought of you often," Cole's grandmother said softly.

"You think he would have come to my funeral?" Myrtle snorted. "It would have been a cold day in hell."

There was an awkward silence, then Esther started talking about how good the food was and the others chimed in, as if Myrtle hadn't said a word. Cole admired the old woman for speaking up. He stretched out his legs and felt the sun on his face. Then he heard his name.

"I don't know what I would have done without Cole. When Clyde was sick, Cole took care of him."

He opened his eyes, sat up. "I didn't do much."

"You did."

"Not enough."

Everyone was looking at him, and he thought they could see the truth. He made up an excuse about getting more food, and everyone encouraged this, they liked to see him eat, he was too thin, they said. But his stomach felt tight as he stood in front of the spread. He thought of Connie saying that he looked like his mother. Nobody else had mentioned her.

Naomi came up next to him and sprinkled a handful of potato chips on her plate. Her hands shook. "Here goes my diet."

"You okay?"

She paused, looked down at her hands. "Just a little nervous." She set her eyes on him. "You look peaked. You better not do any more drinking."

"What drinking?"

"Please, I know what goes on behind that shed." She clucked her tongue. "Lord knows how I raised such heathens."

"Well, you got a girl in college, that's pretty good."

"That's true." She smiled, but her eyes were searching him.

"You look like you want to say something," he ventured.

She hesitated, then shook her head. "No, just thinking. Go on now, get you some more to eat."

At the end of the day, as acquaintances and church members trailed out one after another, the quiet mood gave way to something wilder and unhinged. Kay said to Cole, "Granddaddy must be rolling over in his grave." Dell vomited, and Erik and Justin looked awfully pale. The next time the jar was passed to Cole, he turned it down. They should have been hanging their heads and weeping. The last glimmer of sunlight vanished and Cole looked up at the blanket of stars and wondered if his grandfather was up there somewhere.

Inside, he found his grandmother alone in the family room. He'd been surprised by how talkative she'd been, telling stories, laughing. Describing his grandfather in ways Cole didn't know—as gentle and kind, playful even. Now she looked sad and tired and old.

"I just want to set here for a while."

He told her he was sorry for all the drinking that was going on. "In the morning, the Lord'll be talking to them."

"That's true," he said. He wasn't sure if she knew he'd been drinking or not.

"You go out and visit some more. I'd like to be alone for a little bit."

"You sure?"

She nodded. At the doorway, he turned back, saw her staring at her hands, the way his grandfather used to do.

On the front porch, the women were laughing, wiping their eyes. Aunt Esther lifted a jelly jar to her lips. At first he thought nothing of it, then he realized. "You all drunk?"

Connie laughed. "Oh, we're just taking a little sup."

"Aunt Esther," he said. "I can't believe it."

"I just had a swallow, don't look so shocked." She glanced at Naomi and Rebecca. "My sisters don't approve, it's just me. Tonight, I'm the backslider."

"We're just talking about old times, Cole," Connie said. "Jawing the night away, laughing and a-crying."

"Telling stories on each other," added Pearl.

This set them off again into a fit of laughter. Cole didn't know what to say. He'd never seen a woman as old as Pearl drunk before. He started back in, but Connie told him to stay. He sat on the top step and listened to them tell stories about their husbands and kids; he took a nip when the booze was passed to him. A pair of headlights cut through the night. For a moment everyone was quiet and still like a herd of deer.

"Who could that be?" Rebecca asked.

"Somebody running late," Pearl offered.

A little car, chugging and spitting smoke, pulled in next to Pearl and Walter's RV. The driver cut the engine and the headlights went dim. Naomi stood, clasping her hands together like she was praying. Then a figure stepped out of the car, a woman, and she was waving and walking toward them. Someone hit the porch light; suddenly everything was too bright.

"Who in the world?" wondered Pearl, her smoke curling in the air like a tiny snake.

Slowly, Cole stood, backing up until he was against the door, knowing but not knowing.

"Oh my Lord," whispered Rebecca. "Oh my Lord."

As she stepped into the light, she looked the same and yet different. She wore a skirt and a black shirt that was cut low and Cole blushed, he hadn't remembered her looking like that, breasts spilling out, but then he saw her face and it was not changed: wide brow, strong cheekbones, and furious, lovely eyes.

"God heard my prayers."

Cole turned. His grandmother stood at the screen door, the hall light shining behind her. He'd never seen so much love and pain twisted into a person's face at once. She came outside and stood next to him and held his hand. Cole's tongue thick and hurting with words never spoken.

"You made it, sis," Naomi said. Cole looked sharply at his aunt—the only one who was not surprised. She'd known all along.

Suddenly, the spell broke: Connie nearly jumped on top of Ruby, laughing, and then all of the sisters hugged her and looked her over as if they wanted to make sure she was real. Only Cole and his grandmother stayed back.

"I thought I would get here in time," Ruby said.

When she spoke, Cole's grandmother squeezed his hand, and he understood: hearing her voice made him feel like he couldn't breathe.

Pearl took her by the shoulders, looked her over, and stared dramatically at her chest. "All I can say is, He-lloooo, Dolly."

After an awkward pause, Ruby burst out laughing. "I got them done last year." The sisters looked at each other, speechless, but Connie and Pearl laughed.

Now she was walking up the steps. "Mama," she said.

His grandmother let go of his hand and began to cry. She clutched her youngest daughter, who said, "I'm sorry about Daddy, I'm so sorry."

Cole wanted more than anything to be invisible, but she'd seen him and he could feel her eyes on him and he looked at her and his jaw tensed. His grandfather was right, she was a whore and she'd given birth to a whore's son.

"Would you look at that pretty hair," she said.

His mother was not weeping and neither was he. They never would. They stood staring at each other and all around them the talking and laughing and crying continued, and the uncles and cousins had come around from the backyard like dogs sensing the excitement, but still it felt as if it was just the two of them, and when she reached out to touch him, he moved out of the way and hurried down the steps. He scrambled into his pickup and didn't look back. He had his keys, his cigarettes. He would go as far he could until he stopped hearing her voice and the voice of his grandfather, calling for her.

PART TWO

CHAPTER 8

H E HEARD VIRGINIA MCGEE before he even stepped into her
room, her labored breathing like a dying motor. Virginia
weighed nearly four hundred pounds and was diabetic and could
not get out of bed. It took two or three aides to turn her, so that
she didn't get bedsores. She used to make jokes about running off
to join the circus, but now she rarely spoke. Her pained breath
sputtered into a wheeze. Cole rested his hand on hers, waiting,
and when the wheezing subsided, he picked up a pink plastic
brush from the nightstand and she murmured her appreciation as
he stroked her long hair. Virginia's hair was shiny and silver and
thick. People said that she'd broke many hearts in her day. Everyone in the nursing home agreed that she had the nicest hair.

Here, nothing had changed. Cole delivered clean towels and
spooned pureed dinners into ancient mouths. The old people depended on him. He bathed them, shook them awake from their
nightmares, listened to their stories. Some of the residents knew
about his granddaddy and told Cole they were sorry. They held
his hands, their cockled skin stretched tightly over brittle bone.
He thanked them. He imagined them as skeletons. They said Now

he is with God. They said Now he is bathed in golden light. They said Now he is watching over Cole from above.

He would rather be near the residents who said little, like Virginia, and avoid those like Mabel Johnson, the old black woman who never forgot anything. Yesterday when he picked up the rest of his grandfather's belongings, he ran into her in the hall, and she said in an ominous voice, "Your granddaddy was right, the end of the world is at hand. I'm ready to be taken up there with the angels, just like him."

Virginia's eyes were only partway open. Cole set the brush aside and didn't bother closing the door, almost as if he wanted to be caught, to bring an end to this. He knew that each week Virginia's daughter brought gifts and left stashes of emergency cash; he opened a dresser drawer, shuffling through granny underwear and thin socks, and found a half-empty bottle of Xanax, which he slipped in his pocket. Another drawer held family pictures, hardtack candy, old Christmas cards. Someone said his name. He looked up, his heart racing.

It was Ellen. She stood in the doorway, looked more startled than he felt.

"Cole," she said softly. "What are you doing?"

He thought about how he looked, squatting, rummaging. But then he saw that she didn't really want to know.

"Virginia wanted to look at pictures." He grabbed a handful and held them close to Virginia's face. "Here's those pictures you wanted," he said loudly.

Virginia smiled, her eyes still half closed. "Thank you," she mumbled.

Ellen looked relieved. She asked Cole if he wanted to take a coffee break. He shook his head. "I'm all right."

"Cole, I'm asking you, take a break with me."

The bottle of Xanax jostled against his thigh and he wondered how much she'd seen. "I guess if you're that insistent."

They went out to the back patio and sat on green plastic chairs.

"I'm sorry I couldn't go to the funeral." Ellen sipped coffee from a foam cup; her eyes peered over the rim.

"It's all right. You had to work."

"Was it a nice service?"

"It was all right."

He smoked quickly, thinking of the drugs, the stolen money, the postcards under his bed. He felt unguarded. "My mom's here," he said. "I haven't seen her since I was a kid."

Ellen raised her eyebrows. "Where's she been?"

"All over. Before this, she was living in Pennsylvania. That's what my aunt said."

"And she just came out of the blue?"

"My aunt Naomi's been in touch with her, but she didn't tell me, can you believe that shit?"

"Wow. What's it like not seeing anyone for that long?"

"I don't know. Weird." He shrugged. "She's at my grandma's, but I ain't gone to see her yet."

The door opened and the newest aide, just a year out of high school, asked if someone could help her. She looked like she was about to burst into tears. Cole started to put out his cigarette, but Ellen motioned for him to stay. "I'll take care of it."

He hadn't meant to tell Ellen. He hadn't talked to anyone about it. He had a million questions for Ruby, but every time he thought of seeing her, he felt sick and angry and scared. His mind buzzed, his stomach fluttered. He wasn't ready. The night of the funeral, he'd driven around the county until he couldn't see straight, the lines in the road blurring, the trees curving around his truck, until he finally ended up at his aunt's. It was one in the morning, but Naomi and Kay were up, sitting at the kitchen table, waiting.

"I was afraid you got in a wreck," Kay had said.

Naomi's eyes were swollen from crying. "Cole, I'm sorry. I should have told you."

He looked at his cousin. "You knew too?"

"I didn't know she'd really come back," Kay said quietly. "I didn't know that."

He felt furious and betrayed as his aunt tried to explain. About a year ago she'd gotten a call from Ruby, but they had talked only a few times. "I didn't want to disappoint you if she didn't show up," Naomi said. "She made me swear not to say anything. She was scared you wouldn't want to see her."

"Well, I don't," he said.

That night, after he had left his aunt's, he didn't go home, worried that Ruby might be waiting for him. Instead he slept in the back of his truck with a couple of ratty blankets thrown over the top of him, shivering but refusing to move into the cab. He'd not slept outside since he was a teenager, when he and Terry Rose used to go up to Rockcamp Point with sleeping bags and a couple of joints, when the moon would shine over them and they were not afraid.

He didn't think about where he was going until he was there. He saw the brothers' pickups, so he parked around the bend and walked up the back way, startling a flock of mourning doves. He crept feline-like up to the open window and stacked two cinder blocks on top of each other to give him a boost. The room was a mess, just the way he remembered it. He saw her tangled in the sheets, bleached hair the same color as his pressed against the pillow like a bunch of dandelions. He felt a catch in his throat. She was alone. He said her name. She rustled, pulled the blankets to her chin.

"Charlotte," he hissed again, the cinder blocks wobbling. He called her several times before she finally opened her eyes. When she saw him, she screamed.

"Charlotte, it's Cole. Shh, it's just me."

She clutched the pillow to her chest.

"God, Cole, what the hell are you doing?" She climbed out of bed wearing nothing but a T-shirt and little black panties, and helped him crawl through the window.

"It's not even six o'clock."

"Well, you know me," he said.

He removed his muddy boots and sat beside her and hoped the brothers didn't come busting through the door. Then he remembered that they slept like rocks. Charlotte eyed him warily and he thought how he must look, unshaven and rumpled and bleary-eyed. She didn't look much better.

"You gonna tell me why you were breaking into my house?"

"I wanted to see you." He hesitated. "You want me to leave?"

"No," she said, her face softening. "I heard about your granddaddy. I'm sorry."

"It's all right."

"You okay?"

"I'm all right."

She fluffed up the pillows behind them and they sat side by side, not touching.

"How's your grandma?"

"Well, she's got my mother to look after her now."

"What?" Her eyes widened. "She's back?"

He nodded.

"That's crazy. You ever seen her before?"

"Once. When I was ten." He lit a cigarette. "She taught me how to shoot pool."

Ruby had taken him to a trucker bar and told him if he was really her son, then he better learn how to play pool. Leaning over him, she had held his hand on the cue stick, her hair falling onto his shoulder. He'd never been around anyone so pretty before and could hardly look at her. When he knocked in a stripe, she whistled, You're a natural, and he blushed with delight. But when they took a break, she seemed distracted, nursing a drink. Then she told him that she was leaving in the morning. His tongue had felt heavy and flat, and after a few false starts, stuttering wildly, he asked her to take him with her. She had looked at him, then laughed: *Lord, it would have to be over Daddy's dead body.* That night they slept on Esther's pullout couch, and his mother promised she'd be back for him one day. *I know he's a crazy son of a bitch, but he treats you all right, don't he?* Cole nestled deeper into her arms, afraid to speak. When he woke the next morning, she was gone.

A door slammed and he jumped, but Charlotte said, "Shh, they're just getting up for work," and she put her hand on his chest and let it stay there like the folded wing of a bird. They listened to the heavy footsteps, the hacking and grumbling, until all three mules were out the door.

"What's your mama like?"

"I don't want to talk about her." He looked at her hard. "How come you ain't left? I thought you'd be gone by now."

"You know how it goes. But things are going to be different. I'm cleaning up." She moved her hand underneath his T-shirt, her fingers light on his skin, and he felt a spark of heat in his belly.

"I got fired," she said.

"Oh shit."

"Terry tried to talk them out of it, but there wasn't much he could do. I'm looking for something else. Put my application in a couple of places. Once I get some money saved, I'm planning on getting out of this shit-hole."

She dropped her cigarette in a half-empty beer bottle, and then he did the same. She leaned over and kissed him, tasting like morning, and he reached for her thighs, her flesh warm and familiar in his hands. The ink on her skin rose like blood, and he felt the tattoos wrap over him like vines, like muscles. But when he stopped to tear open a condom, Charlotte grew distracted. "Maybe we shouldn't," she said.

"Why not?"

Sighing, she pulled him toward her. "Come here, just come here." She opened her legs and dug her nails into his shoulders, but her eyes were closed and the motions she made were half-assed, like she was bored.

"You want me to stop?"

"No, don't stop." She wrapped her legs tighter around him. "Don't stop."

Afterward, they lay next to each other, not touching, staring at the ceiling. The plastic stars dull and cheap-looking in the morning light.

"You're lucky you caught me alone," Charlotte finally said.

"Well, I was wondering." He sat up. "You seeing somebody new?"

"Yeah."

He expected as much, but still, the words cut through him. "Not that old boy you were dancing with at the Eagle?"

"No, God no." She also sat up, drawing her knees to her chest.

"That was fucked up," he said.

"I know, sorry."

"Well, who is it?"

"I ain't telling you."

He grabbed her foot. "Is it a guy?"

Laughing, she kicked his hand away. "Yes, it's a guy."

"You ever been with a girl?"

"Mister Curious. When did you get so talkative?" She smiled playfully. "I've been with a few, nobody you would know." She poked his chest. "What about you?"

"What about me?"

She raised an eyebrow. "Ever been with a guy?"

"Real fucking funny."

"Maybe you should try it, you might like it."

He pounced and pinned her to the mattress, and she was laughing and squealing. He felt her underneath him, the wetness and heat of her. But she twisted and turned, and he let go.

"You got some sick ideas," he said.

She told him not to be so closed-minded. Then she tapped his face, right under his eyes. "You look sad."

"I'm just tired. I haven't gotten much sleep."

She told him to try. He closed his eyes. He smelled her familiar scent and felt her skin next to his. Memories rose up and broke apart and disappeared.

"I thought you couldn't sleep," she said.

Charlotte was looking down at him like he was a fish rising to the surface. He jumped, then glanced at the clock. It was just past ten.

"You need to get laid more often," she said. "But not by me."

He remembered his dream: thousands of black crows soaring in the sky, raindrops the size of pinwheels. "Something bad is on its way."

"You're no prophet, Cole. You never figure anything out until it's over and done with."

"My grandma always said crows were messengers," he started, but Charlotte interrupted.

"You got something to tide me over?"

"I thought you were cleaning up."

"It's a slow process. You got something or not?"

"No."

"Bullshit."

"I'm getting more tomorrow. But I ain't selling to you."

Her eyes narrowed. "Whatever." She pulled on a pair of panties. "I heard that meth can get you off Oxy."

"You need help that bad?"

"I don't need anything." Then she said, "I don't think we should see each other anymore."

"Why not?"

"It's not what I need. Not what you need either."

"What do I need?"

"What you need to do is to go home."

"I'm going, all right?"

"No, honey, I'm serious. What you need to do is go home and see your mama."

Another week went by before Cole followed Charlotte's advice. Naomi had been calling, begging him not to be so stubborn. "She wants to see you," she said. "She came back here for you." He didn't believe her. Though he was no longer angry with his aunt, he still felt afraid to see his mother. His grandmother called only once. "I'm praying for you," was all she said. For the past week he'd been driving by the house, gazing at his mother's car. Today, for the first time, the Camry was not in the driveway. His stomach dropped. He killed the engine. His grandmother came to the door.

"Beginning to wonder if I was going to see you again. I got the notion in my mind that you ran off."

"It wasn't me who ran off."

She looked at him, did not respond. She was wearing a white cardigan, a plain dress with a hemline falling just below the knee, stockings, and rubber-soled brown shoes.

"You going somewhere?"

"Esther's taking me to the beauty parlor. I'm getting a haircut." She raised her eyebrows. "What do you think? You think that's a sin?"

"If I thought that, why would I be wearing my hair this way?"

"Every time I see you it looks more yeller."

But he did not know how to imagine her without long hair. Though she wore it twisted in a bun most of the time, whenever the spirit moved her, she would let it spill out to her hips like silver water. They both knew what the old man would have said about her cutting off her hair.

He followed her down the hallway, running his hands along the weblike cracks in the walls, afraid to ask about her, but when he stepped into the kitchen, he started, knocking against the wall clock. "I didn't know she—," he stammered, finished: "I didn't know you were still here."

His grandmother turned her back on him and began rummaging through the refrigerator, and his mother smiled like they were old friends. She wore ripped-up jeans, a V-neck T-shirt that was stretched tightly over her fake ones. She was barefoot, her feet small and bony, the toenails painted huckleberry blue. A silver ring shone from her second toe.

When she came toward him, he stepped back. "Don't," he warned.

"All right, all right," she said, her voice too loud, excitable. "At least sit down, visit with me. I don't bite, you know."

Cole pulled out a chair, its feet scraping the linoleum.

"How come your car isn't out front?"

"I moved it behind the house." She reached for her cup of coffee, the silver bangles on her wrists clanging. "I've been watching a blue pickup drive by. Figured you wouldn't stop if you saw I was still here. Sorry, it was a mean trick."

"Well, here I am."

She scooted closer, and he stiffened as if he'd been hit with a cold blast of air. Her eyes were bloodshot, and there were tiny wrinkles around her eyes and mouth that had not been there the last time. The last time she was here, she was twenty-seven. His age. Now she was forty-four. Still, he was startled by how much she looked the way he remembered her, the thick dark hair and almond eyes. She was pretty, he'd been right about that.

"You look different," she said.

"A person changes in seventeen years."

"What happened to your hair?"

He shrugged.

Her voice softened. "You're all grown up now."

His grandmother set two plates stacked high with sliced ham, buttered biscuits, and coleslaw in front of them, though they both protested that they weren't hungry. There was the sound of a car. "That'll be Esther."

"Isn't she going to come in?" Cole asked.

"You know Esther, always in a rush."

"I never thought that about her."

"I've got an appointment," she said. "You two visit, get to know each other again."

After she left, Ruby slid a cigarette out of a pack of generics, but Cole said they weren't allowed to smoke inside. It was still his grandfather's house. She looked like she was trying not to laugh. "Then let's go outside."

They sat on the porch steps. It was a cool afternoon, the sky heavy and without color. Ruby offered him a cigarette, but he said he had his own, searching his pockets.

"Just take it," she said. "You think it's poisoned or something?"

He lit the cigarette, and she asked him when he started smoking. "Thirteen."

"I didn't even start that young. Daddy ever find out?"

"No." He shrugged. "I don't know, maybe he knew."

He stared at his scuffed boots. The last time she'd come bearing gifts. Not this time. This time her hands were empty.

"I was just kidding about your hair," she said suddenly. "It's cool." She twirled a strand of own. "I used to have mine bleached. I also had it dyed. Pink, purple. Not when I was living here. I mean, this was about ten years ago. Once I almost got a mohawk." She smiled to herself, remembering a time he would never know.

"I did a lot of stupid things, but I never did get that mohawk. Probably should have. Maybe I should have got one before I came back here. That would have given people something to talk about. Well, something else, anyway."

Cole said nothing. Wanting more space between them. She sat too close, talked too loud.

"Hell, I knew it'd be hard. But I didn't think talking to you would be like this."

He looked at her. Anger shot into his voice. "I don't know what you came back here for."

"Well, you don't have to know, do you?" She closed her eyes for a moment and he saw how tired she looked and then he knew that she came back because she was running from something.

"How long are you staying?"

"Don't know," she said, an edge to her voice, which sounded the way he remembered it, cigarette-hoarse, scratchy. Even though she'd lived all over, she still had a mountain lilt.

"You're staying here?"

"As long as Mama will have me. I think I'm already getting on her nerves, but she'll never say that. I sleep too much, smoke too much, and I'm a slob. But she won't put me out." She smiled. "Don't worry. I'll stay out of your way. I won't get in your space. Everyone wanted to drag you out here to talk with me, but I said, Jesus, give the kid a break. He'll come when he's ready. See? I'm looking out for you."

She wanted to play catch-up, for him to give her the rundown on all twenty-seven years. She asked about his job. Did he have a girlfriend? Had he ever traveled? What did he do when he wasn't working? Cole gave short, closed answers, and all the questions he'd had for her seemed to vanish now that he was sitting next to her. He knew all he needed to.

"I'm on your land," he said.

"Baby, that's yours now."

The word *baby* made something inside of him skip. "Coal company wants to buy it," he said.

"That's what Mama told me."

"I ain't selling."

"Do what you want." She looked off. "This land doesn't mean much to me anymore."

Carelessly, she touched his arm, her fingers resting lightly on his skin, the first time he'd been touched by her since he was ten years old.

"I got to get going."

"Now, Cole, wait," she started.

But he waved without looking back and drove down to his trailer and for a long time he lay on his bed, his heart pounding wildly, until he couldn't stand it anymore.

It was early and the Eagle was dead. Four guys in the back shooting pool. Two brunettes in a booth, faces made up and cigarette smoke lassoing around their heads like their gossipy talk. An old man who worked for drinks mopping the floor. Bad Company on the jukebox. Lacy Cooper behind the bar.

"How you holding up?" She poured him a generous shot.

"All right, I guess."

He'd not seen much of her in the past couple of weeks and the few times that he did, it felt awkward, which he thought had to do with her being at his grandfather's viewing. But now as they talked about their jobs, the high cost of gasoline, the cold snap, the awkwardness fell away. He did not say anything about his mother. He felt like he could have stayed all night by her side, but when it started to get busy, he turned around in his seat, scanning the crowd.

"Hey. Cole, right?"

A guy in 1950s-style glasses was smiling at him. The writer from New York.

"This is a cool place."

Cole lit a cigarette. "Cool how?"

"Um." Michael paused, then looked relieved when Lacy came over. Cole tried not to show his surprise when she leaned across the bar and hugged Michael.

"I'm glad you're back," she said. "How's the writing?"

"It's good. The article will be out next week." He set down a twenty-dollar bill. "I can't get this place out of my head. I really want to write a book."

As Michael and Lacy talked about who Michael should interview, Cole was quiet, his mother crowding his thoughts. He saw her walking through his grandparents' house. His childhood room. Touching his arm. He used to dream about this. One time he and Terry Rose got their hands on a stash of magic mushrooms and they went up to the top of Rockcamp Point and looked out at their homeland and Cole swore he could remember his mother holding him when he was a baby and he'd sat down among the dead leaves and suddenly remembered everything about her, the touch of her hand and how she smelled and how her hot tears fell on his baby face.

"Talk to this one," Lacy said, pointing to Cole. "He's living under the sludge dam too. And a hell of a lot of blasting. It's ruining your grandma's house, isn't it?"

Michael turned to Cole, waiting.

"It's just the same shit everyone's dealing with."

"You want to talk more? Any day this week works for me. And I don't have to record you."

Cole shook his head, then pretended to see a friend. "I gotta go."

Hidden by the now large crowd, he moved to the other end of the bar and drank his beer alone. He could still see Michael out of the corner of his eye, leaning in, nodding at whatever Lacy was saying. He held a small notebook, scribbled in it from time to time. Cole knew these types. His grandmother had told him stories about the newspaper men and the VISTA people coming to the mountains to look at how poor everyone was. One time, when he was about ten, a man came to the door wanting to film his grandfather—he'd heard about the serpent handling. His grandfather asked him if he was a believer, and when he said, "Sort of," the old man told him to come back one day when he wanted to experience the Lord "without that camera."

Loretta Lynn came on the jukebox, singing about growing up in Butcher Holler, having no shoes. Michael would like that. It would go with his book.

After a while, Lacy came over. "What's wrong, you don't like him?"

"It's not that. I just don't trust him."

"He's a nice guy."

"Where is he?"

"Over there." She pointed. "Talking to the Calhouns, you know them? They've got a four-thousand-acre mountaintop removal site behind them. Down by Muddy Ridge."

"Nothing he's gonna be able to do about it."

"He knows a lot about all of this. The laws and all that. Anyway, he's made a few trips out here already, that means something. We need all the help we can get."

"For what?"

"Stop the coal companies from taking over. Everyone's leaving."

"I ain't," he said. "I'm staying."

"You might be the only one."

"My grandma's still lives up there."

"You don't think she'll sell?"

"Nope," he said. "She won't."

Lacy poured a shot of Early Times for a sad-looking man at the other end of the bar. Cole felt a hand on his shoulder. He expected it to be Michael again, but it was Terry Rose. He was lit up, eyes dilated and cheeks red like he'd been running, but he spoke cautiously, the way he might talk to an injured animal.

"Heard about your granddad. I'm sorry, buddy."

Maybe it was the booze, or maybe just the timing, but when Cole looked at Terry Rose, he saw him as the friend he once was and told him to take a seat. Terry shed his Carhartt jacket. His long-sleeved T-shirt, dark jeans, and black Nike sneakers resembled what he used to wear when they were kids. He looked thinner than he had the last time Cole had seen him.

"Darling, we need two bourbons over here, and two more beers," Terry called to Lacy. She looked at Terry, then Cole.

"You're not friends with this asshole, are you?"

Terry slung his arm over Cole's neck. "Me and him go way back, don't we, buddy?"

"I'm sorry for you, Cole," Lacy said.

"You're hilarious. Come on now, how about getting us those shots?" Terry turned to Cole. "Tell me what you been up to."

"Just the same old." Cole lit a cigarette. "How's Kathy? Your kid?"

They held each other's eyes for a second, a hard, flinty gaze. Then Terry said, "Doing good. Everybody's all right."

Lacy brought their drinks over, and Cole tossed back the shot and then looked at Terry. Before Terry could get started talking, he said, "My mom's back."

Terry set down his empty shot glass and Cole waited, thinking, He is the only one, except my kin, who knows me from that far back. "You mean she's here?"

"Came back for the funeral, except she missed it."

"How long is she staying?"

"I don't know."

"That's fucked up. That's like my old man coming back from

the dead. Except that won't ever happen." He shook his head. "Shit, you've had a rough couple of weeks, bro."

The bourbon moved through Cole like light cutting darkness. He and Terry used to take their twelve-gauges and shoot up beer cans and road signs and abandoned houses in the hills. They tried hunting a couple of times. Cole was a good shot, but Terry, although he was crazy about the idea of hunting, didn't know how to be quiet and couldn't hit a target if his life depended on it. Cole didn't care. He had just wanted to be around Terry. They were burning up with boredom and recklessness and hope for something they could not name. They were young then; they had each other.

He felt unguarded. "Remember when we cut open our hands?"

"Stupid kids. Yeah, I remember." Terry grinned. "But blood runs thick, don't it."

Cole said it did. He ordered another round.

"You're gonna be shitfaced," Lacy warned.

Cole laughed and said maybe he already was. Terry said, "Darling, anytime you want to go out, just let me know."

"Yeah, I'll be sure to let your wife know too," she snapped, but Cole saw how she looked at him. Terry had always had luck with girls. They fell for him, he broke their hearts.

Terry said in a low voice, "Cole, buddy, you should get a piece of that. Older chicks, all they want to do is fuck."

"Yeah, well."

"You seen Charlotte lately?"

"No, not really."

"I felt bad that she lost her job," Terry said. "I liked working with her. She's a nice girl. Wild, right?"

"I guess."

They talked about people they'd gone to school with, who was still living in Dove Creek, who'd gone off, who was dead—car accidents, suicides. Just like when they were kids, Terry did most of the talking. He complained about his job, and told Cole that he missed working with his hands. "Remember how good I was at fixing cars? I could have done something like that." Cole recalled him always working on something, rebuilding carburetors or repairing transmissions, but never making much progress. Terry told him that Kathy was the one who'd wanted to move to Kentucky, that she'd been happy when he got the job at the plant and was bringing home a nice paycheck. "The first couple of years after Kathy and me got married, it was real good. But now? Shit. You know that Kathy got saved? Got religious on me. That's about the last thing I need."

Cole remembered the one time he brought Terry Rose to his grandfather's church. Terry sang and praised God and got down on his knees. But later when he and Cole were up at the creek, he told Cole that speaking in tongues was fake, and he laughed about the way the women shook and fell to the ground, mocking them, breathing heavily and crying, "Oh, Jesus, oh," grabbing himself and writhing around. At first it was funny, and true in a way that Cole didn't want to dwell on, but Terry took it too far. Cole told him to knock it off. "Oh Jesus, fuck me, oh, oh, oh," Terry'd said, and Cole had surprised them both when he raised his fist and cracked Terry in the jaw. For a second, Terry had looked stunned, and then he was on top of Cole, and by the time they finally rolled off of each other, Terry had a busted-up mouth and Cole's left eye was swollen shut.

Now Cole felt like the bar was beginning to spin, and he told Terry that he was going out for fresh air. Terry laughed. "Take your time, bro."

Outside, he held his head in his hands and wished everything would stop moving. He took a few deep breaths, the mountain air slowly sobering him. A couple of party boys came over, wanting Special K, which he didn't sell. But he offered them Valium, and they tossed the pills back like peanuts.

When he went back in, the bar was even more crowded, loud and full of drunks. Terry was happy to see him. "Bro, I was beginning to wonder if you took off."

He was smoking cigarette after cigarette and Cole figured he was on speed, but wasn't sure, since Terry always seemed wound up. His wedding band gleamed under the bar light, and he told Cole he was trying to save enough money to take his family on a vacation. "I want that boy to see something," he said. "You know, the ocean or something."

"You never saw it? You never drove down to Texas or anywhere?" Cole asked, knowing he hadn't. "The Gulf of Mexico?"

Terry would not meet his eyes. "No, I never made it."

Then he quickly changed the subject and told Cole about people he'd met when he was in Kentucky, working at the RC factory. "They got some crazies in Kentucky," he said, laughing. "Those old boys, they are *crazy*." He told him about a guy who used to cook up crystal meth in his trailer. "You ever do it?"

"Nah."

"It's pretty wild."

"That's what I've heard."

"Your buddy knows something about crank," Terry said.

"Who?"

"That faggot in Stillwell." He pointed his beer at Cole. "I got him hooked up with some boys down in Bucks County. We're working together, you know?"

Cole did not know. He looked up and saw their reflections in the cracked mirror behind the bar, his own squirrelly face and blond hair, and Terry, curly-headed and dark-complexioned, his eyes puffed up: they were not boys nor friends but some other ghostlike versions of who they'd once been. He did not like the way Terry was talking, like he was trying to trick Cole into something.

"You ever want to go in with me, bro, I can hook you up. Run

a little pill and meth operation. We could get us a trailer somewhere, cook that shit up."

Cole shook his head. "Nah."

"Why not?"

"Just not into it."

For a second he felt Terry's eyes on him and they were full of
hatred, but the moment passed, then Terry was laughing. "Lord,
I'm wasted." He waved Lacy over. "Girl, you sure you can't sneak
out to my truck."

"Man, lay off," Cole said, but Terry didn't listen. "Honey, I got
something you're gonna love."

"Go home to your wife," she said, and this shut him up. He
pushed the beer aside. After a few seconds of silence, he clapped
Cole on the back.

"I gotta hit the road."

"You can't drive," Cole said, wondering if he should take him
home, but he didn't feel sober enough to get behind the wheel
either.

"Hell, I'm all right."

They regarded each other warily like dogs. Something in the air
had shifted. Terry smiled, but his eyes did not.

"Catch you later," he said.

"All right."

Cole watched him head out the door. He still had that same
tough little swagger. Tough, but not mean. He'd never thought of
Terry as mean.

Lacy brought him a glass of 7UP and he thanked her and took
a drink and the fizz tickled his nose. The crowd had thinned out.
Lacy washed glasses, wiped the counters. Cole thought about asking her to come home with him, but then she began to complain
about how she tired she was. She said she was taking tomorrow
off to spend with her kid.

"Hey, sorry about Terry," he said. "He don't mean nothing by it."

"You been friends a long time?"

"I knew him when I was a kid. We ain't tight anymore."

"Well, don't worry, honey. I get that kind of shit all night long. There's nothing special about Terry Rose."

"No, I reckon not." But he remembered Terry holding him by the wrist. He drew the blade of the knife across Cole's skin and they smashed their bleeding palms together. Nothing could hurt them.

CHAPTER 9

THE OLD PEOPLE were dying like flies. The units were cleaned, "terminal cleaning" it was called, the beds stripped and washed down with disinfectant. Cole bagged and labeled their personal items, checking the inventory records and making sure that whatever he'd taken did not show up on the list. The units were restocked, the trash cans lined.

"Isn't it weird how we get used to all of this?" Ellen asked.

Cole nodded. "I need some new friends," he said. "Younger ones."

But he wasn't sure that was what he wanted. He spent most of his time here, working doubles and skipping out on family events. His mother had been back for over a month and he'd seen very little of her, despite all the sudden Sunday dinners and get-togethers at the aunts' houses. These were always awkward, although at least now he was no longer the only outsider in the family; the tension around him had shifted over to her like a swarm of bees. Ruby wearing too much makeup and bursting out of her shirts, the easy center of attention. Everyone was uncomfortable. The aunts didn't know what to make of her—she wasn't the kid sister they remembered. She was loud and edgy and disdainful of their quiet lives. They disapproved, but wouldn't say it, at least not directly. The hardest to watch was the way his grandmother looked at her with so much love and hope, like she believed Ruby had come back to save the family.

Cole fed a woman some kind of brownish slop, which she spit up, and he said he didn't blame her a bit. Then one of the new aides asked him to help her move a patient who was twice her size. Cole hooked up the transfer belt and together they lifted the man into the wheelchair. "Assholes," he yelled, "you assholes." He slapped at the aide and she dug her nails into his fat pale arm.

"Don't be so rough," Cole said.

"I ain't being rough." She glared at him. "He's trying to hit me."

"You would too if you were stuck in this hellhole."

He checked on Wanda Woods, who soon would be joining her beloved son Jamey on the other side. Her breaths were harsh and strained, like somebody was holding a hand over her mouth. Cole pretended to be her son. Stroked her ossified hand.

She whispered, "You're a good boy."

"Some people say I'm pretty bad."

"They can't fool me."

From Wanda's room, a few months ago, he'd stolen a hundred bucks and a trinket ring that wasn't worth much but he liked how shiny it was. She never noticed. Just like Warren Fletcher, half dead himself, had never noticed that his money-sock was missing. Cole only took what they didn't need. He touched Wanda's stiff face, the skin cold and rubbery. Ellen said he was her ray of sunshine.

He stepped outside for a much needed cigarette break and wasn't out there for more than two minutes before Ellen called him back in. "It's Red."

"Christ," he muttered.

A year ago Red Adkins had told entertaining stories about playing the fiddle in honkytonks. All the fights, all the women. He was funny and sharp, and once proved to Cole how athletic he was by standing on his head for five minutes. But now he was addled and confused. This morning he'd refused to eat because he did not have the cash to pay for it. When Cole tried to explain that the food was free (though Red was right, everything was tallied up, even a box of Kleenex), Red yelled, "I don't take welfare," and hurled the tray across the room, food spraying everywhere. Cole was sick of cleaning up after people.

Now Red was in the center of the lounge, cussing, screaming at the baffled residents.

"What's wrong, buddy?" Cole asked. "Just settle down."

When he put his hand on Red's shoulder, the old man cocked back and swung, cracking him in the jaw. Ellen shrieked as Cole stumbled against the TV. He slowly stood, shaking his head until he could see clearly. Red was laughing, "Don't mess with me," but then the director and two other aides rushed over, and Cole walked away, rubbing his jaw, didn't want to see the old man taken down.

"You okay?" Ellen asked.

It was only his jaw but he felt bruised all over, inside and out. She brought him an icepack and he held it to his face until it felt numb. Linda told him to take off early. "You've had a hell of a day."

He spent the rest of the afternoon doing what he did best, filling up his pockets and glove compartment with cash. He scored big with Diane Chapman, a divorcée who looked as straight as a pin but was one of his hardest users. She invited him in like she always did, leading him past her kid who was watching TV, into the kitchen, which was spotless and bright. She handed him the cash and he gave her the Oxy and she smiled like she was on a TV commercial and said, "Thank you." As he pulled out of the driveway, he saw her at the kitchen counter, bent over and snorting.

Next, he headed into Big Bear. When he turned the bend, he slowed down. "What the hell?" Interspersed among the American flags and junked cars and broods of chickens were signs written in black marker and attached to tomato stakes: "Stop Mountaintop Removal" and "Corporate Greed Is Killing Our Children." A group of six marched up the road, carrying the same sorts of signs and chanting, "Save our mountains." He shifted into neutral, waiting for them to pass, and then he saw Lacy's kid.

"Hey," he said. "Hey, Sara Jean."

She stopped and did not return his smile. Then she set down her sign and trotted over. "Y'all want a ride or something?" he asked.

"A ride?" She made a face. "We're having a protest."

Then he noticed what else was different on this Saturday afternoon: nobody outside. Blue October sky, the trees on fire with scarlet and gold, and nobody was out burning trash or tinkering with cars. Doors closed, blinds down. It was a stupid place for a protest—almost everybody in this holler worked for Heritage.

The old woman that he'd seen that day in the diner came over and peered at him through big owl-like eyeglasses. "You know what they're doing ain't right," she said.

Sara Jean handed him a flyer and told him to come to the next meeting. Then they returned to the group, no longer chanting, but walking quietly like a funeral procession. He looked at the paper. "Are you tired of the dust, the trucks, the blasting, the bad water?" There was a date and time and meeting place. Cole crumpled it, tossed it on the floor.

On his day off, Cole stayed home, reading medical books. He'd told Lacy Cooper about wanting to be a nurse, mostly to impress her, and she'd been so enthusiastic that he felt hopeful about it again. Ellen had lent him these books a while ago. He kept them stacked up next to the sofa, along with glossy nursing school brochures, most of which he'd never opened until today. The names of pills and the Latin names for diseases filled his brain as easily as scripture, but getting a degree was something else.

He was reading a chapter on cancer treatments, but couldn't concentrate. The blasting was getting more frequent, a few times a day now, sometimes even at night, and every shot shook the trailer, set his teeth on edge. Forty thousand pounds of ammonium nitrate and fuel oil. He'd seen in the paper that Heritage was requesting to expand the site behind them and take down another mountaintop. He'd been receiving more letters, offers to buy the land. They'd cut back on their original offer, and eventually they would stop making them. They didn't need to buy him out, they had what they wanted. He skimmed the letters, tossed them.

After a while, he set aside the textbook and picked up the pill guide. As he was running through a list of all of his sources' prescriptions, someone knocked. He froze—the cops, a desperate pillhead? Then realized that he had not heard a car. He put the book down and looked out the window.

"Shit."

His mother stood there, hands in her pockets, waiting. Since that day at his grandmother's, he had managed to avoid any one-on-one time with her. He swung open the door.

"What happened to you? You get in a fight?"

"I got sucker-punched by an eighty-six-year-old."

"You kidding? Well, it makes you look tough anyway."

She looked more rested than usual. Color in her cheeks, no circles under her eyes. Hip-hugging jeans. A black-hooded sweatshirt that did not belong to her.

"That's mine," he said.

"I found it over at the house. You don't care, do you?"

"I guess not." It was the first time he'd seen her in a shirt that wasn't showing off her figure.

"Nice place," she said, looking around. "What's all this? You studying for something?" She picked up a brochure. "Nursing school?"

"It's nothing." He took two beers out of the refrigerator and sat at the kitchen table. It was the first time she'd been in his place, and he could sense her soaking everything in.

"You don't care for much decorations, do you?" she said. "You're like Daddy. Sparse house leads to a healthy soul. Is that what you think?"

"I just don't have much use for them," he said coldly.

She sipped her beer. "Well, I've got news."

"What?"

"Esther got me a job at the Pizza Shack." She rolled her eyes. "The Pizza Shack. I guess I've worked in worse places."

"You got Grandma thinking you're going to stay?"

"Well, she'd like for me to get out from under her feet, and I'm getting sick of her harping on me. Don't leave your wet towel on the floor, why do you sleep so much, go to church, blah, blah. I'm starting to feel a little stir-crazy. It'll be good to get out."

"How much longer will you be here?"

"I don't know. A few months, maybe. I don't know. A while."

"You're going to stay at the house with Grandma?"

"Jesus, I just said that didn't I? There or wherever we end up."

"What's that mean?" Cole glared at her. "Don't you talk her into selling."

"I'm not talking her into anything. I told you before I could care less what happens to the land. That's not why I'm here."

"Well, I don't know why you are here."

The quiet between them felt raw and dangerous. Then she said, "It seems like nobody around here wants to know about me. My sisters don't want to hear it. And Mama, well, I think she wants to pretend I've been living in a church for the past twenty years." She smiled, trying too hard. "I could tell you some things."

Cole both wanted and did not want to know. He used to make up stories about her, that she was an actress, a model, a world traveler. But from what she told him, her life was nothing but a sad accumulation of failed relationships and dead-end jobs. Married and divorced twice. Waitress, bartender, cleaning lady, factory worker. She said that she'd lived the high life when she was married to her second husband, who ran various businesses and made his living by gambling. Cole wondered if he'd paid for her plastic surgery. But he did not really want to know.

"I've been all over. Cities, beach towns, and pure shit-holes. The longest I stayed in one place was in Dallas, and the last place I lived was a little crappy town in Pennsylvania. I was a cashier at a liquor store. Jesus, what a mess. Too much drinking and what-all. Every time I got a step ahead, I fell back about twenty."

So Cole had been right. "You came back here 'cause things were getting too hard out there?"

She shrugged. "If that makes it easier for you to understand, baby."

He asked why she never came back until now. "You came back once, that was it."

She looked away. "I don't know. I had a different life. I just couldn't start being a mother. It's weird, you know. You're a man. But you're my baby."

"You never even called me."

"I wrote."

"Till I was fifteen."

"I got married to Don around then. It just seemed better that way." She'd made mistakes, but she was here now, she said, she was trying. "I *did* write to you. Did you get the postcards, or did Daddy burn them up?"

"I got them," he said. "You want them?"

"What?"

Cole went in his room and opened the Christmas tin and came back with a stack of postcards and dropped them on the table. They landed with a soft slap. At first she looked confused, then she picked them up one at a time, studying the pictures, the dates. "You saved them. That's nice. Real nice." She smiled at him. "That makes me feel better."

"You can have them back. They're yours."

"No, they're yours."

He sighed. "Listen, I've got things to do. You should go."

As he stood at the window, she came up behind him and put her hands on his stiff shoulders and he felt like every point of her on him was something hot, sharp. She pressed her lips to the back of his neck, a naked spot of skin, and he squeezed his eyes, did not move until he heard her close the door behind her, and even then he waited, standing there with his arms wrapped around himself. The room felt different now, as if a gust of wind had come through, leaving everything ruffled and confused. The light of the afternoon had abated to something dim, tremulous. He touched the back of his neck, as if he could still feel the heat emanating from the place that she had kissed. He would never tell her, he swore he'd never tell her or anyone his grandfather's last words.

The phone rang. He stared at it stupidly, then picked up on the third ring. "I'll be there," he said. On his way out, he glanced at the nursing books, then slammed the door behind him.

Reese pulled a blanket around his shoulders like a shawl. "Good Lord, were you in a fight?"

"I got clocked by a patient."

"Hazards of the job," Reese said with a grin.

"Hell, I've been punched, bit, slapped. I get cussed at all the time."

"You mean they ain't all sweet like Ruthie?"

"You wouldn't believe what I've seen."

"Like what? Tell me the craziest."

Cole paused. "I've walked in on old grandpas jerking off. The women too. There used to be this lady who tried to get with all the guys. She'd flirt and rub herself on them, and half the time, they didn't know what the hell she was doing."

"Maybe I ought to see if one of those old guys would come over here and give Ruthie some loving." Reese laughed, shook his head with wonder. "Hey, you should have come over last night. It was a kick-ass party. Your ex was here."

The first time Cole and Charlotte had hooked up, they'd been at one of Reese's parties. Kissing on the sofa, drunk and happy. Cole did not ask Reese how she looked now, if she was using.

"What about Terry Rose? You see much of him?"

"Huh? Yeah. I see him from time to time," Reese said.

Whenever Cole ran into Terry, he was revved up, talking non-stop, usually about drugs or ways to make a quick buck. Cole wasn't sure if Terry was selling Reese crank, or if they were mixed up in something together. It was better not to know.

"Hold on," Reese said suddenly. "I got something for you."

He walked through the door that led to Ruthie's side, and a few minutes later returned with a revolver, aiming it at the ceiling.

"Jesus," Cole said.

Reese, laughing, dropped the gun in Cole's lap. "It's for you, man. I'll sell it to you."

"I don't want it."

"Son, you're in a line of business where you need protection."

Cole lifted the revolver. It was small and fit easily in his hand. He had never wanted it to be like this, never wanted his operation to get too big, too dangerous. "You got any pills for me or not?" he asked. "That's what I came over here for."

"That damn Medicaid," Reese said. "They screwed up again."

He was lying, but Cole didn't know if Reese was selling the pills himself or using, or both. He felt annoyed that he'd wasted his time.

"Well, do you need anything? I got some Percs with me."

Reese shook his head. "Nah, me and Ruthie, we're set. But you take that gun, I don't want it lying around." He named a price and Cole said again that he did not want it, but Reese insisted, and Cole finally gave in.

"All right," he said. Stupid waste of money. He handed Reese the cash, which would not stay in his hands for very long. Then he snapped open the cylinder and dumped the bullets into the ashtray, and Reese just shook his head. Cole put the gun in his jacket pocket. "I better be going."

"Stay a while." Reese folded up the bills, stuck them in his pocket. "How's home life? How is it with your mama being back?"

"Like having a stranger in town."

"The two of us, we're similar."

"How's that," Cole said, thinking, No we ain't.

"Both of us are orphans. But at least you got a mama." He paused. "You ever wonder about your daddy? He might could live right around here."

"I always got the idea that she didn't even know who he was. I never thought about him the way I did her." When Cole was a kid, he rarely asked about his father: there was nothing to hook on to, nothing to imagine. But his mother was somebody, flesh and blood.

"I don't know what I would have done without Ruthie," Reese said, sighing. "She saved me from a life of torment."

Cole wondered how he could actually be taking care of her anymore, he seemed like such a junkie. He was hard to talk to, drifting in and out of conversation, jumping from one story to the next, or forgetting halfway through what he was talking about. But he was also a source of information; although Reese rarely left the house, he always knew what was going on in Dove Creek.

During a lull, Cole asked him if he knew Lacy Cooper.

"As in Lacy who married basketball star Denny Cooper?"

"Yeah."

"Why do you want to know?"

"Just wondering."

"Yeah, I know her. We were in the same grade. She was a Willis before she married Denny." Reese smiled dreamily. "God, what a beautiful boy he was."

"You know Denny ran off."

"That's old news, son." Reese raised his eyebrows. "Wait a minute. Are you screwing Lacy?"

"No. I was just wondering about her."

"Well, she's got a kid, you know that, right? And she's strait-laced, always has been. She ain't gonna want to mess with anyone like you."

"I was just wondering," Cole said again.

CHAPTER 10

TAKE A SEAT, birthday boy," Esther said. "I'll go get your mom. She's in the back."

There were a couple of families at the booths, but otherwise the Pizza Shack was empty. Cole sat at the bar and reached for the tin ashtray and looked up at the TV mounted on the wall. Rubble and smoke, U.S. soldiers, people running. Yesterday at the nursing home, when some politician came on the TV, a woman yelled, "That dirty Nixon, he don't care about our boys."

Esther told him that Ruby would be out in a second. "How does it feel to be a year older?" He said it did not feel much different. He asked how she was, and worry lines broke up her forehead. "You hear about Justin?"

"Yeah, Grandma told me."

"I'm worried to death. He needed that job."

"Why'd he get fired? Union talk?" Justin was always complaining that there was no union at Heritage. Every so often at the home the aides grumbled about unionizing, but Cole did not get involved; it didn't seem worth the trouble.

She shook her head. "He'll tell you all about it. You won't believe it."

Ruby sauntered across the room wearing the customary Pizza Shack button-down shirt, which she still managed to make look whorish, pairing it with a little denim skirt. She asked if he wanted any pizza, but he said he wasn't hungry. "Here, at least have a beer." She brought two out from behind the counter and sat next to him on a stool. She was decked out in silver: chain-link bracelets, a necklace with a heart pendant, and a row of hoops in one ear.

"What do you think of this? Embarrassing, huh? This uniform? And I go home every day smelling like pizza."

"It's a job," Cole said.

He hadn't wanted to stop by, but earlier he'd been at his grandmother's and this was what she wanted from him. He hadn't been spending much time over there, and was surprised by the changes, signs of his mother all over the house: flimsy blouses tossed over chairs; high heels in the hallway; and in the bathroom, bottles of perfume, jars of cream and moisturizes, strands of hair clogging the sink. "Grandma, you got to make her clean up around here," Cole had said. "Don't let her get away with this." His grandmother had laughed. "I get after her, but I don't mind, as long as she's home where she belongs." She had baked a chocolate cake for his birthday, and they watched a travel show about Mexico. His grandmother commented, "Ruby told me I should go somewhere. You know what she says, There's more to the world than Dove Creek."

"She would know."

"Well, I wouldn't ever leave home," she said quickly. "I mean, I'd like to visit someplace, but I'd never leave for good."

On his way out the door, she'd stopped him. "Cole, go see her," she said, her fingers digging into his arm. "Do this for me. Spend some time with her."

"Why?" He looked up and saw tears in her eyes. He still couldn't get used to her new hair—short, curly, and fluffed. She looked like a little gray poodle.

"Because she might not stay much longer," she had said. "And because it's the day that she gave birth to you."

Now his mother asked, "Did Mama tell you to come by?"

He started to lie, then nodded.

Ruby laughed, didn't seem bothered. "What are you going to do tonight to celebrate? Wait. I know. The Eagle. Don't worry, I know it's your territory." She adjusted her skirt. "I'm trying to stay out of trouble. Good thing I'm in hicksville, not as many temptations."

"I guess," Cole said.

"Except that I've lived in dinky-ass towns before, and being in the middle of nowhere doesn't stop trouble." Cole still didn't know what she'd been hooked on; whenever she referred to that time in her life, she said, "What all I was on," or, "That trouble I was in."

She went behind the counter and handed him a paper sack. "Happy birthday. Sorry it's not wrapped."

He opened it and took out two nursing books.

"I got them from a bookstore in Charleston. I don't know if I got the right ones or not."

"They're good," he said, barely glancing at the titles. How long did she really plan to stay? His grandfather used to say her name in a tone that was both rage-filled and warbling with sadness. Now he understood why.

At the Eagle, Lacy Cooper drew him a beer and he told her it was his birthday. "Well, shit, happy birthday," she said. "And you're still such a baby compared to me."

"I feel kindly old."

"You do talk like an old man. Must be the company you keep."

Around him everyone seemed happy. Laughter, conversation. He felt apart. Same way he used to feel at his granddaddy's church, surrounded by God's love and yet not in it.

Then the twins came up and clapped him on the back. Justin was with them, already shit-faced. "You hear I lost my job?"

"What happened?"

He rubbed his eyes like he was just waking up. "We was up there at Scrabble Hill and I was bulldozing, knocking down trees, then I saw a tombstone. So I stopped, got out to look, and sure enough, there was a little old cemetery. I told my supervisor. He says, You want a job or don't you? I say, We ain't allowed to tear up cemeteries, and he says, Nobody even knows that's up here. I can't mess with the dead like that, I told him, and he says, You get your ass back on that dozer, or get your walking papers. That was about the end of it."

"That's fucked up," Cole said.

"I don't know what I'm going to do."

"You'll find something else."

"I got a wife and kid. I ain't like you."

Cole didn't even blink. "Well, they're always looking for aides at the home. I'll put in a good word for you."

"Fuck that," Justin said.

Cole just shrugged. He didn't care what his cousins thought anymore. Then Dell said, "Them Heritage boys sure do like their Ritalin, cuz. You should have stepped up."

"They still need any?"

"Nope. It got taken care of."

Cole tried not to dwell on how much extra he could have made. He didn't know why he'd been so worried about selling to family in the first place—was he trying to protect them or himself? A few drinks later, Cole left his cousins and went looking around to see if he could drum up business. By the pool tables, he ran into Terry Rose.

"Hey man."

Terry looked surprised. "Yo, bro, what's up? I haven't seen you in forever." He was twitchy, his eyes dilated. "Want to play doubles, like the old days?"

"All right."

Cole did not tell Terry it was his birthday. When he'd turned sixteen, they had gone up to Rockcamp Point with sleeping bags, a tent. They sat by the fire and got drunk and stoned. He remembered how cold it was, the ground nearly frozen under them, but there was nowhere else that he wanted to be. Now he looked at Terry and pushed all of that out of his head. There was no sense in thinking about the past. He grabbed the cue, started chalking it.

Then a familiar voice said Terry's name, and Cole looked up. Charlotte handed Terry a beer. She saw Cole.

"Hey," she said.

"Haven't seen you in a while." His stomach lurched, and he looked from her to Terry and back to Charlotte again. "You two here together?"

She stared at him like she didn't understand the question, but Terry said, "We just ran into each other. We see each other sometimes, you know, ex-coworkers. Ain't that right?"

"Yup," Charlotte said. Then she smiled and hugged Cole, moving in a nervous-acting, speedy way. He felt how small she was.

"You okay?" he whispered.

"Yeah, I'm good." She giggled. "I'm great."

They drew apart.

"You find a job?" he asked.

"Not yet."

He watched her and Terry closely; the two of them barely looked at each other. "Goddamn," he muttered.

"Hey, bro, we're up," Terry said.

They played against two guys from Bucks County. Cole had forgotten how good Terry was; he ran the table with ease, taking long pulls on his cigarette, chattering away.

They won the first game, lost the next. "We're getting too old," Terry said, grinning. "Let me get the next round."

After he walked off, Cole looked at Charlotte. "You sure you're all right?"

"Why do you care," she snapped.

He just looked at her. Then he said, "I don't."

"Good."

Terry came back with three beers. "Your cousins are up there. Damn, they haven't changed at all. I hated the twins when we were kids."

"They're all right," Cole said.

"Remember that time they were after you, trying to hog-tie you, and I jumped out at them with my brother's muzzleloader? Scared the shit out of them." Terry laughed. "You remember that? I saved your ass, bro."

"I remember."

Cole saw a married couple who liked to party, and he told Terry and Charlotte he'd be back in a minute. The exchange was fast, out in the parking lot near the Dumpster. When he went back in he saw a few people he knew and it took a while to get back to the pool tables. By the time he did, both Charlotte and Terry were gone. He saw no sign of them. He wandered around, telling himself to go home. But something held him there; he wanted to know.

He found them in a corner, pressed against each other, kissing like teenagers.

"Hey."

They both spun around, but it was Terry he was looking at.

He could feel the stutter rise up, and waited until the mangled words straightened themselves out: "How long has this been going on?"

"You two broke up a long time ago."

"What about Kathy?"

Terry's eyes narrowed. "What about her?"

"All right," Cole said. "Whatever."

"Come on, don't act this way," said Charlotte.

He went out the door and the cold air rushed through him. How long had they been fucking? He got in his truck and was about to turn the key when Jody Hampton pulled in next to him, her beater car shooting black smoke.

"I been looking all over for you," she said.

"You know I'm always here on Saturday nights."

She got in and he asked how much she needed and when she told him, he said, "I hope that's not all for you."

She was snorting about six 80s a day, maybe more, and went to three or four different dealers. She looked like a skeleton. Her face was too thin, her mouth pinched. She smelled musty and sour.

She handed him a crumpled bill.

"What's this? Ten bucks?"

"I'll get you the rest tomorrow."

"Where you gonna get it from?"

"I'm seeing my sister, she'll give it to me."

He tried to return the money, but she wouldn't take it. He dropped it with disgust on the dashboard, and she grabbed his hand. "You know me, Cole, you know I'm good for it." She put her hand on his thigh. It felt warm, and surprisingly heavy. "Please." She moved her hand to his crotch and he pushed her away and she began to cry. "Christ," he said. He doled out half of what she'd asked for, and she thanked him and with her fingernail she crushed and snorted and then she tilted her head back and closed her eyes.

"Give me the rest," she said. "Please."

She moved closer to him. He felt like he was outside himself, watching as he opened the bottle and shook out the tablets into her shaky hand and then unbuckled his belt. She unzipped him. He could not look at her. He stared out the window, across the dark parking lot, as she lowered her head. Her mouth was cold. He closed his eyes and held on to the steering wheel as if he were flying down the roads. But he couldn't get hard. He opened his eyes and saw her there and what had been numb inside of him started to ache.

"What's wrong?"

"Go on home," he said. "Just go on."

She pushed her hair out of her eyes. "You sure?"

"Next time, no money, no pills. That's how it works."

He waited in his truck until she drove away. The ten-dollar bill sat on the dash like a discarded tissue. He felt clammy and short of breath. He got out of his truck, and inhaled deeply. He took another deep breath, and then he turned and kicked the front tire. Goddamn it. He wanted different people in his life. A different life. He kicked it again, and this time pain shot through his toes. Goddamn. He didn't want to go home alone. He straightened himself and walked back into the Eagle.

"I thought you left," Lacy said.

"I should, but I'm still here."

"You want another drink?"

He shook his head. "What are you doing later tonight?"

"You mean after I get off of work? I'm going home."

"You want to come over to my place?"

"You drunk?"

"No."

She studied him for a while, then smiled. "I didn't think you would ever ask. I thought I was too old for you."

"No, that wasn't it."

"See how you feel in the morning," she said. "And then if you still want to, you can come over to my place tomorrow."

"Okay."

"Okay."

Smiling, he turned to go, but Terry found him first. "Cole."

"Man, leave me alone."

As he crossed the parking lot, Terry came after him. "Look, she don't mean nothing to me, she's used goods." His grin slowly faded. "Come on, bro."

Cole spit between his teeth. "I don't know what you want me to say."

Terry hesitated. He started to talk, then stopped. He shook his head.

"Nothing. Fuck it. Just, nothing," he said.

Cole turned up the stereo loud, blasting an old Metallica song that he used to listen to back in high school. Suddenly, when he was almost home, he pulled over, tires squealing. The slam of his truck door echoed like a gun shot. He tramped through the moonlit woods along the creek until he reached the swimming hole where he and Terry used to go, and he looked out at the still water, a mist rising above it and a night bird he didn't recognize calling from the woods. It was his birthday. He was one year older. The swimming hole no longer looked the way it used to. It was too shallow, cluttered with rocks and debris. Now he could have walked across it. He thought of Terry laughing, *I saved your ass.* It wasn't true. Terry stood right here on this bank on a spring day and said he was getting married and that was the end of it. Cole looked but could not see through the thick white mist. *Fear them not therefore: for there is nothing covered, that shall not be revealed; and hid, that shall not be known.* Nobody ever saved anybody else. Nobody. And now, not even the dead could save them.

Thorny Creek had a reputation for wildness. There were people here who were related to the families that had been part of the old-time feuds. Ex-cons, a crazy Vietnam vet, and a witch who was said to be over a hundred years old, who rarely stepped foot out of a shack that was overgrown with vines and weeds. Thorny Creek was a place his grandmother had always told him to stay clear of, but Cole had several customers up here and a supplier. It was also where Lacy Cooper lived.

This morning he'd woken up a year older and thinking of Charlotte and Terry with their arms around each other, and he'd picked up the phone and dialed Lacy's number. She told him to come over around six. Sara Jean would be staying with her grandparents.

Now he drove past her modular one-story house, her black pickup parked out front, and continued on to Arie Webb's. Arie lived in a clean, sparkling double-wide near the creek. She used to be a schoolteacher. She'd never married, and now she took care of her sister, Janice, who was blind and diabetic. Arie gave her sister insulin shots and read books to her. Except for her arthritis, Arie was in good health. Cole never had to check to see if she had enough food or if the milk had gone sour. She drove into town once a week to run errands and paid all of her bills on time. She wanted to move to the coast of North Carolina, and saved every penny that Cole paid her.

"You ought to come by more often," she said.

They sat on the loveseat, draped in doilies, while the sister slept in a recliner. The room was neat and uncluttered; books lined the pine shelves, and framed pictures of landscapes—the ocean, snow-capped mountains—hung from the walls. A small TV in the corner of the room was turned off.

"I was just reading to Janice before she dozed off. *The Good Earth*. You ever read that, Cole?"

"You know me. I don't read too much."

"Except the Bible."

He grinned. "That's true."

"Well, that's nothing to be ashamed of." Arie patted his knee. "The Bible is a good source of literature."

Arie was the only old person Cole knew who did not seem at all religious. His grandmother said Arie Webb was a Communist.

Cole didn't know about that, but it was true that she held different views than most of the people around here. Nobody would guess that just by looking at her. She looked grandmotherly and soft. She wore granny eyeglasses and pressed dresses, and her hair was as white as snow.

"You still thinking about nursing school?"

He told her he was not sure.

"Now Cole, if you want to be somebody, you got to get an education. I didn't have the support of my family when I went off to teacher's college. But it gave me a freedom I never would have had otherwise."

"If you were so free," he said, "then why did you come back here?"

"I thought I could change things, help the children who didn't have a chance. And I wanted to come home. These mountains, they got a hold over me."

"Yeah, they'll do that to you."

"But now I want to spend the rest of my days where it's warm and quiet. Nobody will mess with the ocean the way they're doing to the mountains. . . . At least people are trying to stop it. Trying to do right. Organize."

Cole stayed for a while, listening to Arie talk books and politics, but then Janice woke up and stared with her glassy eyes and said she was hungry. It was almost six; Cole said he had to go.

"I got a date."

"Don't be a heartbreaker." Arie gave him the pills and he handed her the cash and she said, "I'll add this to the cookie jar."

At exactly six he pulled in and Lacy held open the door. He stepped into the warmth, rubbing his hands. "Cold out there."

"I'm glad you wanted to come over."

"Hell yes."

He dropped his leather jacket on a chair. The living room was small, tidy. A picture of a baying wolf hung on the wall, and all shapes and colors of candles were arranged on the coffee table and on the top of the TV.

Lacy handed him a beer. She was wearing snug black jeans and a blue sweater and socks with pink balloons on them. A little white cat ran up to him, curled around his ankles.

"That's Snowball, a stray. Somebody dumped it a couple of weeks ago."

She put in an old Aerosmith CD and asked if he liked it and he said he did. Then she sat next him on the sofa, but not so close that they were touching. They smoked and drank and talked.

She pointed to a magazine on the coffee table. "Did you see this?"

"No."

She opened it to a picture of Dove Creek. There was also a picture of Lacy and Sara Jean. Arms around each other, faces grim. On the next page, a picture of a mining site: a gray mass hacked into a forest of green. Michael's name appeared in bold print under the title: "Almost Heaven, Almost Gone."

"Any good?" he asked.

"Yeah, it's good. Take it home with you."

"I'll take your word for it."

"You should read it."

Cole flipped the pages and stopped on a picture of the old woman who'd been up at Big Bear. He tapped the woman's face with his index finger. "I seen her in some kind of protest," he said. "Your kid was there too."

"Yep, that's Blue Tiller."

"Who is she? What's she want?"

"She used to fight for the union, way back. Her daddy was a miner, her husband too. Later, she fought the strip mines. She lives alone, way up there at the head. I never saw her before, but one day she was knocking on doors, trying to get people to come to a meeting. Denny had just taken off." She paused, took a drag on her cigarette. "I guess Blue said the right thing to Sara Jean. At first nobody went to the meetings except the two of them, but now they got a handful of people. She got me to go to a few. You should go."

"I'm pretty busy."

"Well, you should at least talk to Michael when he comes back. Maybe you can be in his book."

Cole laughed, shook his head.

"Why not?"

He drained the rest of his beer. "I don't know," he said. "That's just not me."

The light outside had disappeared, and Lacy lit a few of the candles. She asked if he was hungry, but he said he was not.

"Me either," she said, smiling.

He asked if she wanted another beer, and she said she did. He got two more out of the fridge, and just stood there for a few seconds, happy and nervous. On the refrigerator hung Sara Jean's drawings, and snapshots of her and Lacy. He did not see any of Denny, the ex.

When he walked back in, Lacy was looking at him and he stood in front of her and she grabbed his belt loops and pulled him down, beer spilling, cushions falling, clothes sliding off. They moved from the couch to the floor to the bed, and when he reached over to turn off the light, she stopped him. "Leave it on, I like to look at you." She was naked and freckled and flushed and without a single tattoo. He put his mouth on her neck and she yanked down his briefs and told him what she liked, surprising him with her dirty talk.

With her smell all over him, he stretched out on his back. "You wore me out."

"I could keep going," she said, laughing, her hands wandering.

But eventually, she fell asleep with her head on his chest, and he reached over and switched off the light. He felt the heat of her skin and his breathing slowed and he sunk into his own bones and felt strangely at peace. But halfway through the night he awoke in a cold sweat, his heart pounding. He saw his grandfather, skeletal face and bony hands and prophetic eyes, and he looked at the woman next to him. "Charlotte," he whispered. Then he remembered this was not Charlotte. This was Lacy Cooper. She was a married woman. She was a mother. He traced his fingers lightly along her spine, but her skin felt suddenly strange to him and he climbed out of bed.

The floor creaked under his light steps. He went into the kitchen and looked out the window and tried to remember his dream, but it was already starting to fade into confused images: a raging fire, the nursing home, his grandfather's gnarled fingers reaching into Cole's mouth. He turned on the faucet, splashed water on his face. He looked again at the pictures on the refrigerator, then nosed through a pile of papers on the table. Electric bill, a stack of coupons, a checkbook. The little white cat came up to him and he picked it up and tried to cuddle it, but it grew wild and jumped out of his arms.

He wandered through the house. He went into the living room and sat on the sofa and imagined how they used to be as a family, Lacy and Denny and Sara Jean, here together drinking hot chocolate and watching TV. Then he went in the bathroom and checked the medicine cabinet, but the only drugs he found were children's aspirin and grape cough syrup. He turned down the hall and into the kid's room and looked around at the computer and books and stuffed animals and sport trophies that were her father's. He lay on the bed and stared at the ceiling. He and this kid had something in common, not having a father. But it was different because she'd known her daddy, and Cole had never met his and did not even know his name. He smoked a cigarette, ashing in his cupped hand, and when he felt that the nightmare had finally disappeared from his mind, he returned to the bedroom and crawled in next to Lacy and she murmured something and wrapped around him and he put his hand on her moist thigh and felt as if he were the only one left in this world. What was this thing he searched for? He held on to her and wished her beauty would somehow fill him and later when dawn broke and she was still in his arms, he slipped out of bed without waking her, dressed quickly, and went out the front door into the cold.

CHAPTER 11

CHRISTMASTIME IN THE MOUNTAINS. Plastic reindeer, inflatable Santas, and strings of lights outlining trailer homes and satellite dishes. At the nursing home Christmas music played all day, and Cole couldn't get the lyrics out of his head. "Deck the Halls," "Joy to the World," goddamn "Silver Bells." There were more visitors during the holidays, and this morning, kids from the elementary school went down the halls, chanting "Jingle Bells" and looking scared; the old people stared listlessly and a few smiled and a few cried and still others reached out their crippled hands. Lacy Cooper's kid was among them, and at first she pretended like she didn't see him. He said her name three or four times before she acknowledged him. She was eleven and missed her daddy; she had no use for Cole.

He had been sleeping with Lacy for about two months. Usually, he saw her on the nights that she worked late, when Sara Jean stayed at her grandparents'. They would drink a few beers and talk, then they'd be at each other like teenagers. He no longer ran off in the mornings but lingered over coffee and cigarettes. The sex was good and he could lose himself in it, and for this he was happy. But, truthfully, Lacy made him nervous. She was not like the other women. She was clearheaded and strong and sober. "You're my bad boy," she liked to say, but she did not know. She believed that he would go to nursing school like he'd been talking about, and that he would earn a good living and be a daddy for her kid.

Cole clocked out and went out the back door, but pulled up short when he saw a police cruiser parked next to his truck. He stood there stupidly, an easy target. An opal ring and two hundred bucks and a handful of Valium stuffed in his pockets. He thought of what was in his glove compartment. More pills, a roll of cash, the revolver that Reese had sold him.

The driver door opened and a tall, thick-muscled cop stepped out. He was in full uniform, minus the hat. His hair was cut tight and high.

"Hey," he called sharply.

Cole was not surprised. Yesterday a doctor in Raleigh County was arrested for overprescribing medication; last week, a string of meth labs were busted.

"Buddy, you know if my wife is in there?"

"What?"

"Ellen."

It took him a second, then Cole understood. He sighed with relief. Just as he started to answer him, Ellen walked through the doors.

"I've been wanting you two to meet," she exclaimed. "This is my fiancé, Randy. Randy, this is Cole Freeman."

"Hey," Randy said.

"Hey."

They shook hands. Cole barely reached Randy's shoulders. He noticed the gun resting on his hip. Randy had a wide, empty-looking face and restless eyes.

"You a nurse?"

Embarrassed, Cole shook his head. "No. An aide."

"Well, at least you got a job. Hard to find around here. That's why I went to the police academy. Been a cop two years this Christmas." Randy spit between his front teeth. "Pays all right. Not much action, you know. Domestic violence, drugs, robbery. Not much else."

"Babe, you've been in some rough situations." Ellen bragged to Cole, "He had a gun pulled on him."

"A couple of times," Randy added.

As Ellen looked up at Randy, her face sparkled. Nobody had ever looked at Cole like that, but Randy didn't even seem to notice. He said they had to be going. Cole waited until the cruiser was gone, then he drove over to T-Bone Martin's.

Usually, T-Bone's wife, Patty, answered the door, but this time T-Bone let him in. T-Bone had broad shoulders and a craggy face and thinning silver hair, and it was easy to see him as the bartender he once was. He'd had some kind of cancer, and now was in remission. These days, T-Bone rarely took the painkillers prescribed to him, instead favoring the white mule his son-in-law brewed.

"How you doing, T-Bone?"

"Oh, can't complain."

Cole usually spent at least an hour at T-Bone's. Patty would offer him something to eat, and T-Bone would grill him about who was at the nursing home, his friends and enemies. But today he just stood there looking at Cole through his dark-tinted glasses. Behind him, two TVs were going at once. A basketball game on one, with the sound muted, and on the other, a celebrity gossip show.

"How's Patty?" Cole asked, wondering if T-Bone was going to ask him to sit down.

"She's all right. She's over at her sister's." He shifted his weight. "Look, Cole, I don't have anything for you today."

"You think you'll get it tomorrow?"

"No, I mean, I'm not gonna have anything else for you." T-Bone chewed his bottom lip. "It's just, well, we got a lot of bills," he continued, his voice dropping off.

Cole looked at him, uncomprehending.

"It just seems like it makes more sense for us, financially I mean, to you know, take care of things ourselves."

Then it dawned on him what the old man was saying. For a moment, Cole was speechless.

"Goddamn, T-Bone. You know what you're getting into?"

"I think so." He sounded nervous. "I been mulling it over for some time now."

"Goddamn."

T-Bone gave him a sad little smile, as Cole calculated in his head how much he stood to lose. "I guess that's that," he said.

"We'll see you later," T-Bone called after him.

Cole drove up the block and thought about the nerve of the old man. He was going to cut Cole out, sell directly to the pillheads. He ran through a list of his customers, wondering who T-Bone was stealing from him. He'd been betrayed. But he had to give T-Bone credit, it was a smart move. He'd make twice as much. Cole wondered if Patty was in on it. She was a smart lady—maybe it was her idea. Was this a sign? First, Randy the cop, and now this. He could walk away. It was something he'd been playing over in his mind lately, especially as he spent more time with Lacy. He parked, locked his truck. Told himself, You could let go.

Reese was sitting on the floor, surrounded by boxes of Christmas decorations. He held a cigarette in one hand, an ornament in the other.

"Look at these," he said, showing Cole a set of foam balls adorned with colored pushpins, fabrics, and glitter. "Me and Ruthie used to make them every year. Now I don't know what to do with them."

"Why don't you hang them up?"

"No tree, dumbass."

"So get one."

But Reese dumped the ornaments back into the box, and when Cole asked about Ruthie, he shrugged. "Still dying." Then he said, "You hear about those meth labs? Man, I can't go back to the pen."

"You won't."

"If there's any trouble, the cops are gonna be on my ass. And I'll tell you another thing, I wish I'd never met that little shit friend of yours. He's gonna get us all busted."

"He ain't a friend of mine." Cole had not seen Terry Rose or Charlotte since that night at the Eagle, and did his best not to think about them. But he'd heard the rumors, that they were both on meth, that Terry was a runner, some sort of middleman for a Bucks County outfit.

"I been thinking about getting out of it, quitting all together," Cole said.

"For real?"

"Yup. For real." But now as he said the words aloud, it seemed to him that this would not happen; he was not ready.

Reese sighed. "Man, Ruthie loved Christmas. She loved to decorate. The gaudier, the better." He picked up a tangle of tinsel and stroked it like it was a cat. "And bake, son, did she love to bake. When I was in the pen down in Georgia, she'd send me stuff. At Christmas, look out. Boxes and boxes of cookies. The motherfuckers hated me, all the cookies I was eating. Gained about ten pounds. I didn't give up a single one unless it was for trade. Her sugar cookies went a long way. Worth more than smokes."

Cole was surprised that Ruthie was even still alive. The last time he was here, she was moaning in pain, and Reese had been too speedy to concentrate on what Cole was telling him about how to give oxygen treatments and inject morphine. Cole wasn't sure where the hospital equipment had come from and did not ask, but when he suggested that Reese hire a nurse, he just laughed. "I got you, don't I?"

"Funny how you said you're thinking about getting out of it," Reese said now. "I've been thinking about going clean." He talked about his plan for living a sober life even as he snorted an Oxy; he didn't seem to notice the irony. It had been a couple of months since Reese had sold Ruthie's prescriptions to Cole; now he and Ruthie went through the pills themselves, and sometimes Reese bought extra from Cole.

"She's bad," Reese said, wiping powder from his nose.

Cole followed him upstairs. He was expecting the worst, but still, he was not prepared for this. The room reeked of urine. Ruthie was skin and bones. Cole tilted his head to her chest and heard a rattle. The oxygen tube had slipped from her nostrils and he adjusted it and her eyes rolled back in her head. Her skin was the color of oatmeal. He gently pulled back the blanket and examined her legs and saw the purple bedsores. He faced Reese.

"She needs a hospital."

His face paled. "No. No hospitals."

"She's in a lot of pain."

For a second, Cole was afraid Reese would hit him. The air between them crackled, but then Reese let out a heavy sigh and put his head in his hands.

"I thought by now I would just do it, give her the fuckin' morphine." He looked up at Cole. "But every time, something stops me. I know she wants to go, I know she does."

Cole wanted Reese to look at her—the bedsores and bruises, the brittle skin. He'd been so careful before, turning her and applying lotion and massaging her. It was the drugs. He was too strung out.

"I can't do it, Cole. You do it for me, give her the morphine, give her all of it."

"No way."

"You're a nurse."

"I'm not."

"Jesus, nurse's aide, whatever the fuck. Come on, you do it."

"Take her to a hospital," Cole said.

"No. I won't."

Cole touched Ruthie's brow and she moaned and he remembered how he'd sat with his grandfather. He did not want to be the one who took away her last breath. He was no death angel. He was no nurse either. He was a dealer, and this was his customer, and there was nothing else for him here.

"I'll be by in a week or two."

Reese's face shattered, but he just shrugged. "Cool."

"Call me if you need anything else."

Reese's hands were folded in his lap like he was about to pray. "One day all of this will be behind me and I'll turn over a new leaf. Ain't that what they say?"

Cole pulled the door behind him and walked through Ruthie's musty half of the house, past the faded pictures and peeling wallpaper, the cluttered candy dishes and figurines and stacks of books, and he went out into the cold and stared at the dark sky and wondered if men like himself and Reese and Terry Rose could ever turn over a new leaf. His grandfather used to preach that a person could only be saved if he gave up everything and forgot his past: he had to die in order to be born again.

CHAPTER 12

LACY TURNED ONTO A BACK ROAD that Cole had never been on before. He was not used to being a passenger. Sara Jean sat between them, snapping grape gum.

They were on mining territory. Up ahead were gates, fencing, and a security guard outpost that was empty. Lacy pulled in front of a small pond with a fountain spraying streams of water; the sign next to it said "Heritage Coal: Safety Is Our Way of Life."

"If you were to take a drink out of that fountain, you'd probably be dead by tomorrow morning," Lacy said. As she continued driving, they passed several ponds of green water, then began going up hill.

"You ever get caught?"

"Once or twice. But I just tell them I'm looking for a family cemetery. There isn't anything they can do about that."

"Yeah," Cole said, deciding not to mention Justin's story about bulldozing the graves.

Sara Jean blew a bubble, quickly sucked it back in. "I can't believe you never been up here before."

"Well, I've got other things to do."

She looked at him with her large brown eyes and said nothing. He still felt uncomfortable around her. She was a know-it-all kid.

"Michael came with us. He's putting this in his book. He interviewed Mom and me."

Cole was getting tired of hearing about Michael. He'd seen him a few times at the Wigwam, interviewing people, notebook in hand. He still wanted to talk to Cole about his "situation," but Cole held the details of his life close to his chest like a hand of aces. Or more likely, a bluff.

Lacy followed the curve until they came to a grassy plateau, then killed the engine. Cole looked around, disoriented. "This is a mountain?"

"This is what's left."

Except for a few clusters of scraggly trees and shoots of crown vetch, it was barren, like a golf course that had not been watered in a long time. Lacy told him it had been mined a couple of years ago, and now it was supposedly restored. Cole had seen his share of old strip sites, but this was enormous. He turned in a circle, trying to understand. His granddaddy had told him, *The mountains carry secrets.* This mountain would have reached at least five hundred more feet into the sky, with steep hills, narrow valleys. But the valleys had been filled with what used to be the mountain, so now everything was level, like a hayfield that spanned about a thousand acres.

"After they blow it up, they're supposed to make it look like a mountain again," Sara Jean explained. "But they never do it right."

"Fish and wildlife land they call it," added Lacy. "That's what this is supposed to be."

They could see all around, the little houses and zigzags of roads down below, and miles away, mountains rose to the sky.

"I think we live over in that direction." Lacy pointed. "But I get confused up here now, it's all so different."

Cole walked over to a line of scrubby pines that stood no taller than his shoulders. There were no other trees, no animals, no birds. It was eerily quiet. It looked to him like something he'd seen on TV. A savanna, another country. A trail of gray rocks snaked nearby. "Used to be a stream," Sara Jean said.

"You see the grass? It's hydroseed. Chinese lespedeza. Spray-on grass," Lacy said. "They do that when they have a politician or somebody coming in to take a tour." Her breath turned to smoke when it hit the air. "The trees only live for a few months. They can't survive without topsoil."

"Topsoil takes thousands of years to form." Sara Jean stood in front of Cole with her arms crossed, like a teacher. "Pretty soon the whole state's gonna look like this."

"No, we'll stop it, hon," Lacy said, but Sara Jean did not look convinced. She had anxious eyes, like an old woman's.

The emptiness stretched out like a gigantic canvas, and darkness seemed to rise from the valleys, the thin silver light turning a deep velvety gray. Sara Jean pointed, and Cole followed her outstretched arm to an enormous Christmas tree standing alone on a knob.

She ran over to it and called out triumphantly, "It's not growing. It's just sitting here."

As Cole and Lacy walked toward it, loops of colored lights suddenly blinked on, like hundreds of little eyes. On top glowed a white shining star.

"What the hell?" Cole said.

"They have it on a timer. The electricity is running from one of their power sources." Lacy's voice rose. "You can see it from down below. That's why they put it up here, so it shines all the way into the valleys."

"Well, it is pretty."

Lacy just looked at him. "What?" he asked. "What did I say?"

"It's not gonna look pretty anymore, not after I'm through with it."

"Hey," Cole called after her. She ignored him, heading in the direction of the pickup, and when she came back, he saw the glint of a pistol in her hands. "Where did you get that?"

"I keep it in the glove compartment."

"What in the world for?"

"Protection." She patted Sara Jean on the head. "Baby, cover your ears," she said, and Sara Jean pulled down her knit cap.

"Now what are you gonna do?" Cole chided.

"What do you think I'm going to do."

"Lacy, come on."

Even in the growing darkness, he could still see the details of her face and last night flashed in his head, her hands on his chest, her tongue flicking his nipple.

"Listen, either you just keep on going the way you're going, or one day, something changes," she said. "If you're lucky, you'll have a moment."

"What the hell are you talking about?"

She waved the pistol. "They ruin our land and water, and now they have the nerve to put up a Christmas tree, like they're being good neighbors?"

"Shooting it up ain't gonna to change anything."

"No, but it'll make me happy."

She told them to stand back. She held the gun in both hands, but hesitated. Cole didn't think she would do it. She glanced at him, then at Sara Jean.

"Come on, let's just go," he said.

But she set her eyes on the tree again, raised her arms, and fired off three rounds. The gunshots rang out like a song over the emptiness. Bam, bam, bam. The twinkling lights shattered in the sky like fireworks. Sara Jean was laughing, jumping around. Lacy stood there staring at the gun in her hands, looking as surprised as Cole felt. He waited for what she would do next.

"Okay, let's go," she said, sounding nervous.

"You sure you're ready? You don't want to put a few more holes in it?"

He took the gun from her shaking hands and clicked the safety. Her eyes were wide and scared, but she also looked exhilarated. He could feel her trembling.

"Look at the stars," Sara Jean said.

They all looked up. "I've never seen so many," he said. Nothing stood in the way of the night and the millions of stars glistened like the hearts of the dead. He wrapped his arms around Lacy and said in her ear, "Damn, you are a hell of a good shot," and she said, "Honey, you don't even know the half of it."

He woke up in her bed, blankets tangled around his bare legs. The watery morning light shone through the thin curtains and he looked out the window at the first snow of the season. It made him feel sad. He watched Lacy sleep, and wished he could watch himself sleeping. Maybe he would look like a different person, maybe he would learn something about himself.

He did not belong here. But it was a Sunday morning and he had nowhere else to be. He fit his hand between Lacy's legs, squeezing her thigh. She murmured something and he unwrapped a condom and she lifted her hips. The snow continued to fall, large spinning flakes. She was half awake. She put her hands in his hair, kissed his face. He saw her eyes open, he saw falling snow.

After she fell back to sleep, he got up and padded into the kitchen. He looked outside at his pickup, slowly disappearing under white. The coffeemaker gurgled and wheezed. He felt like an impostor. He didn't know who he was pretending to be.

"Smells good." Lacy walked in, wearing a white bathrobe, and she put her arms around him. "You feel good." She smiled up at him, happy; he did not want to hurt her.

"You hungry?" she asked.

"A little."

"There's not much here, but I'm going shopping today. I promised Sara Jean I'd take her to Walmart. You should come."

The thought of walking around with Lacy at the mega-store where Terry Rose worked was not his idea of a fun Sunday afternoon. "I can't, I've got stuff I have to do."

Lacy turned on the tree lights and they nestled on the sofa and drank coffee and the cat jumped on Cole's lap and curled into a tight ball. The room smelled like pine and all things good.

"This is the first Christmas without Denny. I want to make it nice for Sara Jean." She squeezed his knee. "Why don't you come over on Christmas Eve? We'll make caramel corn, watch movies."

Her eyes were steady and wanting, and he looked away, said he'd try. The cat purred and he scratched behind its ears and stared at the tree and thought about the Christmas lights that Lacy had shattered into millions of pieces. The light that had filled her, the glint in her eye. When he laid out the changes to his life, all of it made sense: Quit dealing. Go to school. Get a better job. Live in a house with a wife and child. Take care of his grandmother. All of this was waiting for him under the tree, and here was Lacy, offering it to him. But thinking about it made his heart beat fast, his mouth turn dry. There was no turning back. He did not love Lacy Cooper. He did not know if he'd ever known love.

He drained his coffee and said he better hit the road, but when he turned to look at her, the disappointment on her face made him pause. He hesitated. "I guess I could get a few things at Walmart."

"Really?"

"Yeah. We'll grab a bite at Pizza Hut or Micky D's, whatever Sara Jean likes."

"Good luck," Lacy said, rolling her eyes. "She's got in her head that she's a vegetarian. I think it's Michael's influence."

"What, you mean he's a vegetarian?"

"Yeah."

"I never heard of a guy being a vegetarian."

"Do you know *any* vegetarians?"

He grinned. "I guess not." Then he said, "Why the hell is he always around?"

"He cares about this place. He's a nice guy, Cole."

"I never said he wasn't."

"Yeah, but you got a look on your face."

"It's a look of hunger. Let's go get Sara Jean, see if we can't tempt her with a Big Mac."

Lacy kissed him, but her eyes were wary. "You're one confusing boy."

"You're mixing me up with somebody else. I'm just a simple Dove Creek boy."

"Oh, honey," she said, shaking her head.

Lacy's parents lived on the north side of Stillwell in a small run-down house, close to the road. They'd lived in the mountains all their lives, but sold their place when the noise from the mining nearly caused her mother to have a nervous breakdown. "I think Mom always wanted to live in town, anyway," Lacy said. "But it broke Daddy. He was a rank-and-file coal miner for thirty years. He's got the dust in his blood."

She wanted Cole to meet them. "It'll only take a couple of minutes." Then the front door opened and a thin, hunched-over man waved at them.

"Dad's seen you now. Anyway, you better come in."

"Shit," Cole muttered, cutting the engine.

It took longer than two minutes, but was not as bad as Cole was expecting. Her father was nice enough, in a silent country sort of way, and her mother offered him jelly-filled doughnuts until finally he took one just to quiet her. He couldn't stop staring at her. She was as big as Virginia McGee at the nursing home, if not bigger, ensconced in a La-Z-Boy, her calves as thick as fence posts, rolls of fat jiggling with the slightest movement. Her hair, cut in a bob, was the same color as Lacy's. Like honey. Her lips were painted pink.

Sara Jean sulked when she realized that Cole was going with them. But when she started to complain, Lacy shot her a look and she shut up. Cole shoved down another doughnut and thanked her mother and shook her father's hand, and then they were out the door.

Sara Jean, in a mood, sat between them, and Cole gave up trying to talk to her and concentrated on the snowy road, the doughnuts sitting like a damp sponge in his stomach. The light snow spread across the brown hillsides like cobwebs. He clicked on the radio and an old AC/DC song came on. It was going to be a long drive.

"Can we turn this?" Sara Jean finally decided to talk.

"What do you want?"

She named a station, and he fiddled with the dial. "What, you like this rap shit?"

"Hip-hop," she corrected him.

"Turn it down," said Lacy. "I can't hear myself think."

At least now the kid seemed happy. Cole looked over at Lacy and told her that her parents seemed nice. "What did you think of my mother?" she asked, eyebrows raised.

"Nice."

"Big?"

He grinned. "Well, yeah."

"She was always on the heavy side, but it wasn't till the last few years that she ballooned out. I tell you, it scares me, I don't want to look like that."

"Girl, I don't think you have anything to worry about."

"You'd have to roll me around everywhere."

For some reason, this struck them, and they couldn't stop laughing. When Cole pulled into the parking lot, wiping his eyes, even Sara Jean was giggling.

But as soon as they walked inside, the mood was crushed by blaring Christmas music, beeping registers. "Hidy, welcome to Walmart," said the greeter, who looked like a senior-citizen Boy Scout, various buttons, like badges for good deeds, pinned to his uniform.

Lacy pulled Cole aside, said she needed to shop for Sara Jean. "Can you take her around? Don't let her spend all of her money."

"She's eleven. Ain't that big enough to be on her own?"

"You going to do this for me or not?"

He felt as if he'd been tricked. Sara Jean didn't like it any better than he did, so he kept his distance and followed her around the store, watching her pick things up and put them back. It was crowded. Kids ran down the aisles, and their mothers screamed at them. Other shoppers blocked the shelves, standing there as if in shock and staring at their lists. A father and son, in matching camouflage jackets, cussed at each other. A little girl squalled. Cole looked over his shoulder. He felt antsy, wondering if Terry was here.

At the jewelry counter, Sara Jean looked small and out of place, her stringy hair falling in her eyes. "You think my mom would like any of this?"

Most of what she had laid out on the counter was gaudy and cheap. He pointed to a pair of silver earrings shaped like feathers. "What about these?"

She nodded. "These are good."

"You got any money?"

"Twenty bucks."

"You plan on buying anything else?"

"Mom said I can just draw pictures and make stuff."

"I've got some extra. Why don't you buy more presents?"

For the first time today, she made eye contact with him. "I don't want Mom to get mad."

"If she does, it'll be at me, not you."

She thought it over for a few seconds, then grinned. "Okay."

Cole pushed the cart and Sara Jean filled it up. Whatever was between them had been knocked out of the way, at least for now. She chattered up a storm. He didn't spend much time with kids, but he couldn't imagine that most of them talked the way she did.

"Blue says if we get enough people together, we can stop it."

"You'll never stop people from mining coal."

She dropped a Magic 8 Ball in the cart; he didn't ask who it was for. "If the sludge dam breaks, there won't be anywhere to go," she said.

"It won't break."

"How do you know?"

"I just do." He patted her head. "You shouldn't worry about all this."

But she had a worried face, like some little animal, a weasel or squirrel. He tried to change subjects and interest her in all the stuff around them. "Your uncle, he's a carpenter, right? Look at this hammer, that would be a nice present."

He pushed the cart to the end of an aisle and turned and realized they'd walked into the gun department. Shotguns, high-powered rifles, and handguns were locked behind Plexiglas cases, and Terry Rose was behind the counter.

Coe started to turn around, but Terry said, "Hey, buddy, hold on."

Cole gripped the cart. A hotness bloomed in his chest. He looked at Sara Jean. "Why don't you go look at the fishing stuff for your grandpa? Right over there."

"He doesn't fish."

"Well maybe you'll find something else for your uncle. I bet he likes to."

Terry asked a woman with a buzz cut to cover for him, and then he stepped out from behind the counter. "What are you doing, bro?"

"Christmas shopping."

"Everything all right?"

"Yup. What about you?"

Terry picked his scabby meth face. "I'm all right. Man, listen, about Charlotte—"

Cole cut him off. "It ain't my business."

Terry bit his lip, looked around. He spoke in a hushed, nervous voice. "I'm telling you, shit has got me spooked. All these busts."

"Yeah, I know."

"I need your help."

"With what?"

"I'm looking for a place to test a couple recipes, you know," he said, talking fast. "I can get everything we need right here, but I need an old trailer, something like that. Maybe those trailers out by you, or the old church?"

"It's all gone. It's Heritage property, not mine."

"We could make some good money." He had that desperate junkie look, which made Cole's stomach turn. "You remember how it was between us. You can't turn your back on that."

"You better take care of yourself," Cole said quietly. "You got a wife. A son."

Then, from behind them, a small voice. "Cole?" Sara Jean said. "I'm finished."

"Who's this?" Terry crouched down. "What's your name, sweetie?"

"Sara Jean Cooper."

He looked up at Cole. "Lacy's kid."

"We gotta go."

"I'm Terry Rose," he told her. "I'm Cole's buddy."

Cole took Sara Jean by the hand.

"Wait a sec." Terry stood up. "I'm going over to Reese's tonight. Why don't you come by?"

Cole hadn't talked to Reese in a couple of weeks, but he looked in the paper every day for Ruthie's obituary. He was afraid to go over there again, did not want to be led back into that room of death.

"I can't, not tonight."

Terry smiled, but it was not real. "Listen, that faggot owes me. He's your friend. Tell him he can't fuck me around like this. I'm not getting fucked over by that cocksucker."

Cole looked down at Sara Jean. She was quiet, but he knew she'd heard every word. Terry stood with his arms crossed over his chest, his face twisted up in anger. He'd turned hard. He never used to be that way. He used to make people laugh. Teachers let him get away with everything, and other kids always wanted to be around him.

"I don't like that guy," Sara Jean said after they were out of earshot.

"You don't even know him."

"I can just tell."

At the front of the store they met up with Lacy, and she looked at Sara Jean's cart. "What's all that?" When Cole told her, she shook her head. "You can't just give her things."

"It's not that much." He handed Sara Jean a few twenties and told her to get in line. He asked Lacy if she'd bought the camera that Sara Jean wanted.

"I'm going to wait till after Christmas when it'll probably go on sale." She paused. "I really don't like this, you giving her money."

"C'mon, it's Christmas. Look, I need to get a few more things. You two get something to eat, and I'll meet you in a half hour."

"Cole—"

But he was already walking away. A sudden image of Terry Rose and Charlotte—smoking crank, kissing, fucking—flashed in his head. He turned into the kitchen section and stared at a display of coffeemakers. Percolators and Mr. Coffees and carafes and espresso machines. He wanted Terry out of his head for good. The shelves and rows and stacks of factory-new, unused objects slowly calmed him. He grabbed one of the fancier Mr. Coffees, thinking maybe his grandmother would like it. He walked up and down the aisles, shopping quickly. When the cart was full, he felt oddly satisfied, and stood in line and paid for everything in cash. He could not give Lacy what she wanted, but he could shower her with gifts. "You're going to make somebody real happy," the cashier agreed.

"What the hell is all this?"

It was Christmas Eve, and he'd come over like she'd wanted him to, to watch movies, eat caramel corn. The three of them, like a family. After Sara Jean had gone to bed, Cole unloaded everything from his truck.

"Stuff for Sara Jean. Look." He showed Lacy the gift tags. "From Santa."

"What did you get her?"

"Stuff. That camera. Some video games." He pushed a few presents toward Lacy. "These are yours. Come on, open them."

They were sitting on the floor in front of the tree. Under the light, Lacy's face looked pink. She wore a red bow on each tit and had promised him that his present be worth waiting for.

"Come on," he said eagerly.

She unwrapped the paper carefully, without tearing it, the same way the old people did at the nursing home. After everything was opened, she stared at the gifts as if she wasn't sure they were for her. A stack of CDs, a sweater, a purse, and an opal ring that had come from Hazel Lewis's top dresser drawer. She wasn't smiling. She didn't seem happy at all.

Cole's grin faltered. "What's wrong?"

"You got Sara Jean a camera after I told you I wasn't getting it for her? *A camera?*"

"She won't know I bought any of it. Tell her that it's from you."

He pointed to the gifts. "But what about all this? You don't like what I got you?"

Lacy examined the ring, turning it over, holding it up. She did not try it on.

"Cole, where did you get this?"

"What do you mean? I bought it."

She arched one eyebrow. "Did you win the goddamn lottery or something?"

He did not like the look in her eyes. "I worked for it," he said evenly. "I've got a job."

"I never heard of a nurse's aide making this much."

It was like she'd spit on him. He stood up slowly. His face on fire, pulsing.

"I don't know what you think you're doing, but it's gonna stop." Lacy was whispering, but the rage in her voice poked through like the teeth in a saw. "It's got to stop right now."

She stripped him bare with her eyes, and everything inside of him buzzed. He wanted to stomp on all the gifts, kick the shit out of the tree. But he grabbed his jacket.

"I'm out of here."

"That's all you're going to say?"

"What else do you want to hear?" Before slamming the door behind him, he added, "Throw it out if you want, I don't give a shit."

He climbed in his truck, punched the steering wheel two or three times. He didn't know why he was trying so hard. Still, he sat there and waited a few more minutes. Maybe she'd come out, knock on the window, ask him back in. But she turned off the outside Christmas lights and everything darkened, like nobody lived there. He punched the wheel again. His hand throbbed. Fuck this. He checked the time. It was not even midnight; he could still make a lot of money. He gunned the engine, tires spitting gravel.

There were people out there who were waiting on him, who needed him.

It was the first time that the house had been decorated, and his grandmother had gone a little wild. Icicles drizzled from every branch. Christmas bows and wreathes cluttered the mantel, the banister, the windows. Garland, tinsel, Santa figurines. Cole and Ruby stared at the glittery tree. It didn't feel like home.

"Everyone will be here soon," Ruby said. "God, I get nervous with these big family things."

"You never seem nervous," Cole said.

"It's my good acting skills." She ran her hands down the front of her jeans as if she was smoothing out wrinkles. "I feel like everybody's waiting for me to mess up or something." She took a deep breath. "Do you have any pot?"

"No." He added, "I might have a Xanax."

She raised her eyebrows. "That'll do," she said, and didn't ask questions.

In the kitchen the windows were steamed up. Pots on every burner. A roast in the oven. Side dishes crowding the table: cornbread dressing, noodles, green bean casserole. His grandmother stood at the stove, stirring.

"You shouldn't have done all of this work," he said.

"It wasn't so much. Ruby helped."

He doubted that. "We could have gone to Aunt Rebecca's."

"I wanted to have it here. It might could be the last one." She gulped 7UP, wiped the fizz off her upper lip. "I been having dreams, Cole. The crows keep coming into my sleep. And I dreamed that the ocean or something raised up and washed us out. I don't have a good feeling, especially with all this rain." She sighed. "Now that Clyde's gone, I just don't know how much longer I'll be around."

"Don't talk like that," he said.

Ruby walked in and lifted a lid from one of the pots. "Is she talking about her dreams again?"

"Don't poke fun." His grandmother looked at him. "One thing I'd like to see before I go is for you to settle down. Find yourself a wife. A good woman, that's what you need."

He sighed as he opened the refrigerator. "Not again."

Ruby laughed.

"Who's your new friend?" his grandmother persisted. "Why didn't you invite her over for Christmas? I'd like to meet her. What is it you said she does?"

The refrigerator was stuffed with covered bowls and dishes, all for today's dinner. He just wanted a glass of damn milk, but couldn't get to the carton. He slammed the door. "My friend is Lacy Cooper. She's got an eleven-year-old kid, and she's still married."

His grandmother's face did not change expression. "I've got to check on them beans," she said finally.

Cole went out the front door and stood on the porch and watched the rain. It fell in thin misty sheets, splattering the yard, rushing through the treetops. Soft, repetitive. A lonesome sound. Everything smelled like damp wood and worms. He looked at the rising creek. The rain always made people nervous around here; too many floods and slides and shredded mountains. He knew that his grandmother was worried about the weather, but he was sick of all the prophecy and dreams roiling in this house. Sick of the old man, lingering. His grandfather had never forgiven Cole for walking out of the church. He was too proud, he accused him, too high and mighty. *You've got to be repentant before you can be saved. You've got to show God your broken heart. You got to get down on your knees. You got to weep.*

Back inside, his grandmother clanged pots and pans, while his mother lounged on the sofa, peaceful. The Xanax, he remembered.

"Is she pissed?"

"She'll survive. There's worse things than dating a married woman."

"Might be over between us, anyways," he said, suddenly missing Charlotte, who was easier to please, in a way. She never would have turned down a gift.

The phone rang and his grandmother picked up in the kitchen. A few minutes later, she stood in the doorway, hands on hips, brow furrowed.

"What's wrong now?" Ruby asked.

"Esther can't get out of her driveway because the creek's too high, and there's flooding around Stillwell. They've all decided to stay home. On Christmas Day."

"More food for us," Ruby joked.

Cole exchanged a glance with his mother, and knew she was as relieved as he was. But he said, "Sorry, Grandma," not sure what he was apologizing for.

"I hope you're hungry," she said sharply. "We've got enough to feed an army."

Instead of eating at the dining room table, they set up TV trays and watched *It's a Wonderful Life*. The angel showing old Jimmy Stewart how miserable everyone's lives would be if he hadn't been born. His mother and grandmother were engrossed. Cole was bored. Still, he didn't want to leave. He didn't know where he'd even go—the bars were closed, the pillheads had stocked up yesterday, and Lacy didn't want to see him. When he couldn't eat another bite, he lay on the floor, wrapping himself up in one of his grandmother's afghans. He breathed in the scent of the Christmas tree and closed his eyes and listened to the voices on the TV and stretched his fingers through the holes in the yarn links, the way he used to do when he was a kid, pretending to be caught in a web and fighting his way out.

CHAPTER 13

"THIS SHIT is humiliating."

Cole was at Lacy's watching an old episode of *America's Funniest Home Videos*. Brides tripping down the aisles, kids dumping bowls of spaghetti on their heads, guys getting nailed in the nuts.

Irritated, she told him to lighten up. "It's funny."

"Yeah, it's funny," Sara Jean agreed. "Lighten up, Cole."

He glanced at the clock. He had customers who were expecting him, but he knew how Lacy would act if he left. Although they had made up after their fight on Christmas and had been seeing more of each other, it didn't feel right. She was suspicious and he was living a double life. The tension put him on edge and made her distant. Now she was sitting next to him but not touching him, her arms crossed over her chest. Cole drummed his fingers on the coffee table.

"I was thinking we could go to the Eagle."

She looked annoyed. "What about Sara Jean?"

"Can't your sister watch her?"

"I work there, Cole. You think I want to go there on my night off?"

On commercial break Sara Jean scooted between them, and in her hands was the camera that had caused the fight. Lacy said she was over it, but it still reminded Cole of what was not right between them.

Sara Jean showed him the digital pictures on the camera's screen, and he had a hard time seeing them. Brown hills, flattened land. "We went up to another reclaimed site with Michael," she explained. "He told me to take pictures of everything. Always document what you see."

"Don't you ever do anything for fun?"

She looked at him with her deep brown eyes. "What do you mean?"

"Fun kid things. You're too wrapped up in this."

She nestled closer and he smelled her clean hair and hesitated and then put his arm around her and looked over. Lacy was watching them with a faint smile, but her eyes were sad. Sara Jean showed him picture after picture, the same blurs of land, and then one of Lacy appeared, a close-up; laughing, her head thrown back, mouth open, eyes squinting. "I want you to print me one of those," he told her. There was one of him too. She pushed the little arrow until she came to it. He was startled.

"When did you take that?"

"The other day."

In the picture he was sleeping. He was stretched out on the couch in a T-shirt and jeans. The sun shone in soft waves on his face; he did not look like anyone that he recognized.

"I'll print you one of these too."

The phone rang, and Sara Jean answered. "It's Michael." Cole shot Lacy a look, but she ignored him and took the phone.

After she hung up, Cole said, "Well?"

"He's coming over. There's a photographer with him. They went up to Stinkweed Hollow. Some old couple let them on their land."

"The Williamses," Cole said.

"You know them?"

"Yeah."

"Then you'll want to see the pictures."

"If I want to see, I'll go up there myself."

"You won't ever go."

The phone rang again. This time it was for Cole. Lacy looked at him strangely. "Work," he lied. "I gave them your number."

He carried the cordless into the kitchen and made plans to meet with his customer. Cole warned him not to call this number again, and the man apologized, sounding desperate. Cole hung up. He watched out the window. Headlights cut through the darkness. The slam of the car doors. Front door opening. Voices. Michael was living here now, temporarily, renting a trailer that Lacy had helped him find.

Cole went back in the living room, wearing his jacket.

"Hey, Cole. How are you?" Michael, in a gray sweater, black jeans, and a light blue scarf, looked like he should be posed on the cover of some kind of fashion magazine. Cole still didn't trust him. He should go back to New York where he belonged.

"I'm all right."

"This is Trip," Michael said. "He's shooting photos for me."

Trip was tall and lean, with red hair and a trimmed beard. Jeans, black leather jacket, boots. "Nice to meet you, man."

Cole was surprised to hear a slight twang. "Where you from?"

"Kentucky. Letcher County. But I've been living in Brooklyn for about twenty years."

Trip was older than Michael, deep creases spreading out from his mouth, his eyes. Silver hoops glistened from each ear. He also wore several rings, but no wedding band.

"You want me to come out and shoot some photos of your place?" Trip stood too close, and even though he still had a country lilt, he talked city-fast. "What's good for you, man? I can come out tomorrow."

"I was telling Trip about where you live," Michael explained. "I'd still love to talk to you more about it, Cole. What it was like living there when you were a kid, and now."

"Actually, I got to get going." Cole wondered how much Lacy had told Michael about him. Abandoned by his mother. Raised by a crazy snake-handling grandfather. "Work," he explained.

Lacy looked at him. "You have to go in now? What in the world for?"

"Another aide called in sick. Sorry," he said, pretending to be disappointed.

He went to kiss her good-bye, but she moved so that he only got her cheek. He told everyone he'd see them later. Through the window he saw Michael in the spot where he'd been sitting, Lacy on one side of him, Sara Jean on the other. Cole released the clutch, and backed out.

He stepped into the smoky darkness of the Eagle and felt more relaxed. He ordered a beer, then saw his customer and followed him into the filthy and dimly lit bathroom. The man thanked him and he said, "No problem." When he walked out, he heard his name and turned.

"I know I said I'd stay out of your way," Ruby said, "but I was feeling kind of crazy. I had to get out."

"It's a free country."

"My son, a man of few words."

She was dolled up, wearing a sleeveless shirt, dark jeans, a thick white belt, and high heels. Lipstick, eye shadow, red nails, and big hoop earrings. A middle-aged man in khakis and a button-down stood behind her, holding a cue stick.

"Steve Nolan," he said.

"This is Cole. My son." Ruby smiled. "Where's your girlfriend?

When do I get to meet her? He's dating an older woman," she told Steve. "She's almost my age."

Cole couldn't tell if Ruby was drunk or just happy to be out of the house, but she was extra talkative. She ran the pool table; Steve Nolan didn't have a chance.

She turned to Cole. "You next?"

He racked and his mother broke; Steve went to get more drinks.

"What do you think? He's a nice guy," she said, answering her own question.

Cole knocked the nine ball into the far corner pocket, but on his next turn, he scratched. The last time they played together, when he was ten, he had loved looking at her, being near her. He had wanted her to take him away.

Steve handed Cole a beer and tried to make small talk while Ruby knocked in one after another. When Steve said he was an engineer for Heritage, Cole looked at his mother, but she just lit a cigarette. "You're up," she said.

Cole hit the eight ball in. "Shit."

"You can't win them all."

"I should go," he said.

"No, don't." She grabbed his hand. "Come on, lighten up."

"Why does everybody keep saying that?"

At the bar, they shot tequila, chased it with beer. "You sure you should be doing this?"

"Baby, drinking is the least of it. You wouldn't even know." Ruby smirked. "Maybe you would."

When he didn't respond, she patted his leg. "Come on, let's just have fun."

As the night went on, they drank more, and she told stories about the places she'd lived and the people she'd known. Cole stopped thinking about how she'd left him for all of that. She made him laugh a few times, and he realized he was enjoying himself. He only wished that the Heritage engineer wasn't hanging around. This guy wasn't one of them. He didn't even live here—he was in town visiting a site that he'd helped design. He laughed at the wrong times, and seemed nervous that his friends hadn't shown up.

While Steve was in the bathroom, Cole said they should ditch him. "He's a nice guy," Ruby said again. "Boring, but nice."

"He's Heritage."

"Your cousins work for Heritage too." She lit a cigarette. "You can't expect me to sit home all the time. It gets lonely."

"Maybe he wants something."

"Yeah, he wants me," she said. "What, is that so hard to believe?"

"You sure he ain't trying to get at Grandma's land?"

"Oh, hell. The land, the land. He doesn't have anything to do with that." She sighed. "Listen, I've got to tell you something. I quit my job."

"So?"

"It wasn't enough to live on. I don't know how you do it," she said. "I mean, maybe I do, but I don't want to know."

She was fishing hard, but Cole gave up nothing. A customer walked in, made eye contact. "I should go," Cole said.

"Wait. Look, when I left Pennsylvania, I was in debt up to my eyeballs. I declared bankruptcy, cut up all my credit cards—"

"I don't have any," he said. "I don't owe anyone anything."

"What I'm saying is I wanted a fresh start, and I'm not going to get that here." She paused. "What I'm trying to say is that I'll be leaving soon." She gave him a weak smile. "I'll come back, visits and all. But living here, well, this just isn't me."

He looked away. He knew this day was coming, but he was surprised how the words hit him, how they scraped down his throat like little pebbles.

"I'm not leaving yet," she added. "A couple of weeks, maybe."

"That's cool."

She looked like she wanted to say more, but Steve came up behind her, draped his pudgy arm around her shoulders. "I'll get the next round," he said, overexcited. "What's your poison?"

Ruby rolled her eyes. "Hey, leave us alone for a minute."

"Huh?" Steve looked confused.

"No, it's cool." Cole grabbed his jacket. "Have fun."

He nodded to his customer, went out to his truck. After the guy left, Cole slid the bills in his pocket, his headlights punching through the dark like fists.

A few weeks later, Ruby was still around. "I thought you would have left by now," he said. He should have known not to believe anything that came out of her mouth.

"I told you, pretty soon. That doesn't mean tomorrow, that means pretty soon. Why, you want me to leave that bad?"

Cole said he didn't care one way or the other, and she blinked, but said nothing. Though he'd never admit it, he was glad that she was still here to keep his grandmother company. Lately, his time felt stretched too thin, between work and dealing and spending time with Lacy, who'd hinted that she wanted something more from him, something that he didn't know if he could give.

This morning he just wanted to get away from it all. Before his shift started, he drove up to Clay's Branch to see Leona Truman. This was one of his favorite places. When he was up here, he didn't worry about anything; it was always easy with Leona.

The wind whipped the thin cords of locust and ash saplings, and when he stepped out of the truck, it snaked down his shirt. Leona's land was untouched by the coal companies; pristine, like a postcard. A mix of field and forest, with winding streams, old cow paths, and rusty barbed-wire fences. Skinny chickens pecked at the dirt yard and the porch was cluttered with milk crates, split firewood, bags of chicken feed. Wind chimes rang out from the trees like fairy music.

Cole knocked and called her name, and after a few minutes, Leona pulled open the squeaky door. "Git in here, boy, stop your hollering."

Leona was hunched and spindly, with short white hair and thick glasses. She'd battled breast cancer and survived, but she was weak and often in pain. He wondered if the cancer had returned. He followed her into the house that was built over seventy years ago by Buddy, her late husband. How had they ever raised five kids in a place this small? The inside was swept clean; potted flowers and plants sat in windowsills, and sun-catchers sparkled in the windows. Leona brought him a glass of milk and a plate of sugar cookies. She sat across from him and talked about the old days, the way she always did, but today she seemed anxious, looking around, tapping her fingernails. She stopped and started, and he wondered if she'd taken her pills.

"You all right?"

"Oh, I'm fine." She thought for a second. "Where was I? Oh, how me and Buddy used to grow just about everything. Corn, beans. All kinds of vegetables." She looked at Cole. "You ever growed a garden?"

"No, can't say I have."

"I worry about you young folks. Used to be family and neighbors helped each other, but nobody wants to work like that anymore. My grandkids, you can forget about them. If you was to take away all these stores and computers, most people today wouldn't know how to survive."

"I guess I'd be one of them," Cole said.

"It all changed so fast, and I'm getting so damn old. Hell, I can't even take a walk in the woods by myself, too weak." Her mouth turned downward. "It's the damn coal company, getting to my kids. Think they're gonna get rich."

Heritage was planning to mine the mountain behind her, and her kids were pressuring her to take their offer. "Don't you want to have a little extra money, they ask. I do all right with what I got. What do I need all that extra money for?" Her eyes blazed. "I ain't ever had money." She paused. "You know what my mother used to say?"

"What?"

"Us poor folk have poor folk ways. But rich people have mean ones."

Cole laughed. "That sounds about right."

"Greed, that's always been our downfall."

"That's what my granddaddy used to say. That and fast women," Cole said, and Leona snorted with delight.

Then she said she had something for him, which was what she always said. Her movements were slow and deliberate; he watched to make sure she didn't fall.

"I don't know why they give me so much," she said, handing him a crumpled sack.

He took the meds and handed her the cash, which she would use for food and bills. Usually, this was his signal to go, but she stood there looking at him, her eyes wide and still, like a fish's.

"You okay?"

"I got to ask you something."

"What's wrong?"

"I heard about that doctor getting arrested a few months back. Now, I believe it's none of the government's business what I do, but I don't want to be doing nothing wrong." She swallowed. "I ain't done nothing wrong, have I?"

"No, no way," he said. "It's your business, like you said. And, Leona. I mean, nobody even knows I come out here."

She looked at him and nodded, but he could not decide if she believed him or not. "It was just on my mind," she said apologetically.

"It's not wrong. Don't worry."

Most of the old people probably knew more than they let on.

Like old T-Bone, cutting him out. He'd never reveal their names, no matter what, but if the cops pressured them, would they turn him in? He didn't think so. These old people were true to their word. They were old-timey, the kind to give you the shirts off their backs. They weren't the ones he had to worry about.

Still, he left her place feeling unsettled. Usually whenever he saw Leona, or any of the old people, he felt better. But now everything felt mixed up. The pills and cash were locked in his glove compartment. What could he do about it now?

When he pulled into the parking lot at work, a text came through on his phone. This was about the only place where he got service. Reese Campbell. Cole looked at the name for a second, then turned off his phone. Ruthie had passed away a couple of weeks ago. When Reese called Cole to tell him, he'd sounded stoned out of his head. He had ended up taking her to the hospital after all, where she died on arrival. He could not give her the extra morphine, he'd told Cole, could not bring himself to carry out her last wish, to die at home. There was no funeral or viewing; she was cremated and he was holding on to the ashes, hoarding them like money, like pills.

"We got a meeting in an hour," Ellen told Cole.

"What about?"

"I don't know. I'm sick of all these meetings. I wish they'd just let us do our job."

Linda passed by, clipboard in hand, and told them there was no time for breaks. Cole slurped down coffee, then walked down the long and familiar hallway.

He felt like he was here all of the time. Linda had been juggling his schedule to compensate for the high turnover rate—new aides were hired and then quit a couple of weeks or months later, fed up with the low pay and the high demands. Or they were fired. One woman had tried to stir things up with union talk. Another was busted for stealing OxyContin, taking entire bottles to feed her habit. Ellen's fiancé had showed up to arrest her, and Cole stood with the others at the window, watching as she was led away in cuffs. He felt sorry for her, but wasn't worried.

In the lounge Mabel Johnson was knitting. "I'm still working on that scarf for you."

"Is that what this is?"

"No, this is gonna be a blanket for one of my grandbabies." She held up a light blue square. "Every year, my family gets bigger and bigger."

"Is that right."

"You're going to have to get married," she told him.

"Me? Why?"

"You've sowed your wild oats. It's time for you to settle. Time for you to figure things out."

He flashed a smile, but her expression did not change—she stared at him with steady, loamy eyes. "I'm late, Mabel," he said, patting her hand.

She stared at him for another moment, then looked down at the yarn in her hands.

The door to the conference room was closed. He was the last one to arrive. There were no more chairs, so he stood in the back, leaning against the wall. The janitor was there, three other aides, Ellen, and Pete Andrews, the head of the home. Pete was short and chubby, and always wore pleated pants and golf shirts. He didn't seem to particularly like the old people, but he had a twangy voice that put them at ease.

"I'm going make this short and sweet, so y'all can get back to work. I called this meeting because we've run into some problems. Real bad problems."

Cole jacked one foot up behind him, glanced around the room. Nobody looked very worried. The janitor, an old man called Jefferson, caught Cole's eye and winked. Pete leaned back in his chair, his hands resting on his stomach.

"As you all know, we had an aide who was stealing meds. Well, there's been more stuff. Belongings. It's been going on for a while, before that woman was ever hired. Watches, jewelry, petty cash. Someone stole three hundred bucks from old Lester. Old crazy Lester, someone took his money, that's what his daughter said."

Cole managed to look bored when Pete turned his eyes on him. "If anyone knows anything, anything at all, I want you to tell me. We won't hold anything against you, just say what you know."

Nobody said a word. Pete got up and paced the room and told them that changes would be implemented. He wanted to be able to trust his staff, he said, but somebody had ruined that. From now on all of the patients' belongings would be locked in a safe; only he and Linda would know the combination. There would be random locker searches and bag searches until all of this blew over.

"I'd hate to think it was any of you. Whoever it is, you better be prepared to lose your job, you better be prepared to go to jail, just like that goddamn pillhead."

They filed out of the room; nobody spoke. Cole picked up a stack of charts and tried to look busy. He felt like people were looking at him, but he wasn't afraid. He felt protected by the old people. They knew things, the old people. Like Mabel Johnson. Even the ones who babbled senselessly, or who screamed at him, or who threw things, hating their own bodies and fearing death. When they looked at him, they saw something deeper.

For the rest of the day, as he checked on patients, he also rummaged through drawers. This might be his last shot. He slipped fifty dollars in his shoe, filched a half-empty bottle of Vicodin. His hands were shaking and he almost returned all of it. But he didn't. He didn't return anything.

After his shift ended, he went out to his truck and checked his phone for messages. There were four calls from Reese, one from

Lacy asking him to pick up a six-pack on his way over, and a short, barely audible message from Charlotte Carson. He had not heard from her since the night he saw her with Terry Rose. The sound of her voice startled him, and he felt a sudden rush of longing. He called her back and it rang eight times. No answer. He hung up, called Lacy. She'd rented a movie for them, she told him, and Sara Jean was at her sister's.

"I'm running late," he said. "I'll be there soon."

At Reese's two pickups were parked in the driveway, the house blazing with light. Cole sat in his truck, the vents kicking out hot air on his face, and watched the house for a while, but nobody went in or out. Now that Ruthie was gone, her prescriptions would be cut off. Maybe Reese didn't care; maybe now he only wanted crank. But he must have needed something, to call so many times. Something felt wrong. Cole tried to call Charlotte again, but now he wasn't getting any service. He turned his truck around. There was a pay phone at the Exxon. He pulled into the parking lot and grabbed a handful of quarters from the collection of change that was piled up in one of the cup-holders. It was blustery and cold, the wind smacking against him. Six rings, then Charlotte picked up.

"God, I'm so glad you called."

"What's going on?"

"Cole, I need to borrow a little. I'll pay you back, I promise."

"Ask Terry Rose."

"That's who it's for." The connection was not good. Charlotte talked fast, her words speedy, wild. Cole only heard bits of what she said. He asked her to repeat herself.

"It ain't for me, it's for Terry. He's afraid to ask you, Cole, but he's in trouble."

Cole was shivering, the phone freezing in his hand. "There's nothing I can do."

"I'm afraid he's gonna do something stupid. He owes people, people owe him."

"Well, then he should tell them to pay up."

"That guy, you know the one."

"Who?"

"That guy, that fag."

"Reese."

"He owes Terry. He owes him."

"I was just about to head over there. Look, I'll talk to him. He's been upset, you know, Ruthie and all. He'll pay up."

"No, don't go over there now."

"Why not?"

The operator cut in, and Cole dropped in more change. "There's something you ain't telling me," he said. "You better tell me."

But she jumped around with her talk, confessing how nervous she was and how she should have gone to New York like she said, until after a while she wasn't making any sense and he'd run out of quarters and the wind was biting his face. He said he had to go, and she began to cry, and though he'd never heard her cry before, he knew she was not crying out of sorrow but that she was strung out and had hit some wall of paranoia, and he gently set the phone on the cradle and zipped up his jacket and got in his truck. He should just drive up the mountain, where Lacy was waiting for him. There would be no trouble. Movie, beer, sex. It was right there in front of him, a shining light.

"Look what the cat dragged in," Reese said. "Goddamn, I was wondering when I'd get to see your face."

"Here I am."

"Check you out, doctor."

Cole entered the smoky room, nodding to the others. He felt stupid and conspicuous in his scrubs, and wished he'd brought along a change of clothes. Three tough-looking country boys and a woman who had the gaunt, collapsed face of a speed freak were passing around a bottle of Rebel Yell. An old Bon Jovi song,

"Wanted Dead or Alive," was playing on the stereo, rock stars who wanted to be cowboys. Reese sat in the rocking chair, cigarette in hand, eyes heavy. He wore jeans and a western shirt with pearl snaps and a cowboy hat. He was barefoot, wiggling his toes.

Cole patted his shoulder. "How are you, man?"

"I told you, you should have done it. You should have helped me out, helped Ruthie. It was bad, man. Real bad."

"Sorry."

"It's over now. Fucking over." He sighed. "Go grab yourself a beer."

Cole navigated his way through the mess of the kitchen. Empty liquor bottles and beer cans sprouted from the counters like kudzu. The refrigerator was bare except for a nearly empty bottle of ketchup and a case of Miller. He wondered when Reese had last eaten. A bitten-into piece of toast on a saucer, a box of saltines. How many kitchens had he been in over the last year that were not stocked? Homes that were not heated. The dark and cold and empty.

He sat next to Reese and lifted the beer to his mouth and listened without interest to the talk; the two younger men, his age, were arguing about some girl they knew, if she lived around here or not, until the third man, who looked old enough to be their father, with a receding hairline and pale blue eyes, told them to shut the fuck up. The woman sat on his lap, and his hand twitched nervously on her knee.

"Settle down there, Everett," Reese said, grinning. "This is Everett," he said to Cole. "That's Laura. And that's Tommy and Wes. This here is Cole."

"You from Dove Creek?" Everett said.

"Yeah. Up at Rockcamp."

"He's all right," Reese said. "Don't worry about old Cole."

Everett stared at him intently, then reached into his jacket and took out a small bag of crank. He used a razor blade to cut up the lines on an old *National Geographic*. When Cole passed, Everett said, "I thought you said he was cool."

"He is. He's cool, man."

Everett looked at Cole suspiciously, then snorted a line. There was nothing worse than hanging out with crankheads. Paranoid and temperamental and stupid. They'd get some crazy idea in their head, and you couldn't convince them otherwise. Cole wished he'd never walked through that door. The woman wanted to know why he was wearing a doctor uniform. When he told her, they all began to laugh. Cole took a long pull on his beer. The one named Tommy, with speedbumps all over his face, said he was sick of this music, and he searched through the pile of CDs. "All your shit sucks," he said, then finally decided on Lynyrd Skynyrd. "Honky-tonk."

"Turn it up," said Wes, a squat, chunky guy sporting a classic mullet. Tommy hit the volume and Laura yelled, "Fuck yeah."

Reese turned to Cole. "I need a new direction in my life."

"I hear you."

"I never knew how much of my time I spent taking care of Ruthie. Now there's all this extra time to kill. I might take off, go somewhere else."

"Where to?"

"Down south, maybe. Somewhere new. Start over. Don't you ever just want to start over?"

"I don't know if I'd know how to."

"I'm sick of spending my time with fuckers like this," Reese said, getting loud. "Stupid fucking rednecks."

"Take it easy," Cole muttered.

But they heard and they glared at Reese, like they'd been waiting for this. "Listen, you piece of shit," said Everett. "Let's get this taken care of."

"I already told you I ain't got it. Terry said he'd give me another day. I'm good for it."

"But Terry owes me. And guess what? I don't want to wait another day." Everett nudged Laura, and she sighed and climbed off his lap. When he stood up, Cole saw that he was much bigger than he'd thought. He was over six foot, his arms bundled with muscle. "Terry Rose should be doing this himself, but he's a pussy," Everett said.

"That's the truth," Reese agreed. He went over to the stereo and took out the Lynyrd Skynyrd and put in some kind of techno music that pounded the walls. Then he began to dance, shaking his hips and fluttering his hands.

"Reese," Cole said.

"How about a little dance?" he asked in a falsetto.

When Reese touched Everett's arm, Everett swung and busted his nose, blood spraying everywhere. Cole jumped up, but the other two grabbed him.

"I ain't got it," Reese whined in a tone that was not unlike the one that Jody Hampton used. Cole had never seen him act like this, his toughness gone, nothing but a junkie.

Wes and Tommy held on to Cole, their fingers digging into his arms, and he stood as still as he could, watching Laura prance around, fingering Ruthie's candy dishes and glass figurines. "What a bunch of shit," she said with disgust.

"Take the stereo," Reese said. "The TV. Whatever."

"I want the goddamn money." Everett looked over at Cole and suddenly seemed to remember that they were not alone. "What the hell are you looking at?"

"Nothing."

"You should've sent him out of here before you started all this," Wes said, his voice right at Cole's ear, tickling.

"Shut up," Everett yelled. Everyone was quiet but the techno music grew faster, wilder, the synthesizer beats like little flashes of light, a man singing "oh yeah" over and over.

"Cole, help me out," Reese said.

"What?"

"Loan me the money."

Everett, as if suddenly bored, turned to his crew. "Let's trash this place."

"Fuck yeah."

They descended on it like a storm, hurling Ruthie's dishes, overturning furniture. They knocked over the stereo and the music stopped. This was Cole's chance to run like hell, but he just stood there, watching.

"Jesus, stop it," Reese said.

Then Cole saw the pistol. It was a .45. Everett pulled it from his waistband. "You think this is some kind of game, you fucking faggot?"

The gun seemed to bring Reese back to who he was, and instead of acting whiny and scared, he glared at Everett, unafraid even as blood gushed from his smashed nose. Cole breathed deeply, trying to gain control over his tongue, his mouth, his words.

"H-h-how—"

Everett turned the gun on him.

"How much does he owe?" he managed to ask.

He told him. "You got that?"

"I can get it."

"Now."

"I got it. I got most of it."

Everett slowly lowered the gun. "If you're lying, I'll kill you."

"I ain't lying."

Everett sent Tommy to follow Cole out to his truck and he unlocked the glove compartment and blocked it from Tommy's view. He was too stupid to look. There sat the revolver. Unloaded. Cole left it and took out a roll of bills.

They went back in, and he handed Everett the money. "It's all I got."

"Where's the rest?"

"That's it."

Everett looked at Reese. "You're lucky, motherfucker."

Tommy and Wes hoisted the TV, while Laura ran around taking random items. They smashed up and knocked over whatever else they put their hands on, plates, glasses, chairs. Everett held the gun on Reese, who did not look away, and Cole stood still and wished for all of this to end. Then, as suddenly as it started, it was over. They stood in the midst of the destruction and looked around them and Everett slid the gun back in his waistband.

"Let's go," he said.

Reese mumbled something.

"What?"

"I said, now you can all go home and suck each other's dicks."

Everett's gigantic fist shot out like a spring and cracked Reese's head back, but Reese didn't go down. He lunged like a wild dog, socking Everett in the eye. When Everett stumbled backward, Reese went for the gun, but the other two grabbed on to him. It was all happening so fast. Cole, hating Reese and hating all of them, pushed his way in and tried to tear Tommy off of Reese.

"You got the money, you got what you came for, just go," he said.

But now he was caught in the mix of limbs. He landed one wild punch, then a pair of hands grabbed him and threw him against the wall. Everett, heaving like a bull, stood inches from his face. Reese had been wrestled to the floor by Tommy and Wes.

Everett pulled the gun out and Cole stared into the barrel and saw only darkness. "You queer too? You a faggot, a cocksucker?"

"No," Cole said, feeling himself tremble. He closed his eyes. Trying to stop his shaking. His voice was locked up, his tongue felt torn. Everything in him was cold. When he opened his eyes, the gun was still pointed at him. "No," he said again. "No I ain't."

His voice was loud but sounded like it was coming from far away.

"Everett, come on." It was the woman, standing in the doorway. "Let him go."

The gun hovered in front of Cole's eyes. He heard Reese's muffled curses, saw him on the floor. Saw the skinny woman, like some apparition in the doorway. Saw Everett's empty eyes, the cords of his neck, a vein in his brow popping out.

He lowered the revolver. "Get the fuck out of here or you're gonna get hurt."

Cole just stood there for a second, hearing the loudness of his own breath. Then he looked again at Reese, bleeding, his arms pinned up behind him. He started to take a step toward him, and Everett got in his face.

"Are you stupid? This is your last chance, asshole."

Now Cole felt like everything was moving in slow motion. He went toward the open door. Toward the cold air. He looked at Reese and didn't know what to do. *I can't save you.* The thought filled him, repeated itself in his mind, calmed him. There was nothing he could do. He slowly backed out of the house. The woman was now outside, slumped on the porch swing, smoking a cigarette. Cole heard shouts, fists. He knew that the neighbors must have heard also but their lights were off; nobody would report this, nobody would help. Reese yelled his name, but Cole kept going.

"Hey," the woman called after him.

"What?"

"They won't kill him or nothing. They're just cranked out."

He didn't know what to do. He found himself in his truck, trying to start the engine, still shaking. He had a gun, but no bullets. Stupid. He didn't know where he was going. Felt like a pussy. What could he do? He couldn't call the cops. He drove around aimlessly, then pulled over at an old cemetery where high-schoolers liked to party. He zipped up his jacket and cupped his hands over his freezing ears, but he could still hear Reese calling for him. The night was dark, no stars, but the sliver of moon reflected a faint light on the leaf-covered ground. Beer cans, plastic flowers, crosses. He felt panicked and confused and angry. He walked over the dead and around the headstones that sprouted from the ground like white and gleaming stumps. He passed by a statue of an angel with folded wings, then went up a little slope to where some of the graves dated back to the 1800s. He couldn't save him, he thought, couldn't even save himself. He sat on the cold ground, leaning against a worn and shoddy-looking headstone, and thought about the bones all around him and underneath him turning to dust.

He finally started to calm down. Now he could feel the ache in his knuckles from the punch he threw, the tenderness of his jaw where someone had clocked him. He felt calmer. Not scared, just sickened. Jesus. He couldn't just sit here. He got up and hurried back to his truck. Dread spreading through him as he turned onto Reese's street. The trucks were gone, the house dark. Cole gently pushed open the door, hesitating. The three-legged cat brushed against him. He flipped the light switch. Broken glass and overturned chairs and splattered blood. He heard a groan.

"Reese?" he said.

He found him in the kitchen, crumpled on the linoleum, near a pan of spilled cat food. A long trail of blood was smeared across the floor from where he'd been dragging himself. Cole turned him over and his face was unrecognizable, blood, flaps of skin, bone. He ripped open Reese's shirt but didn't see a bullet wound; all of the blood was coming from his face. He tried to lift him, and Reese screamed. "My ribs," he said, clutching onto Cole. Then, "No hospitals, man." Cole knew the drill. No cops, no doctors.

He'd been beaten to a pulp, but was still conscious and breathing, and after he took a deep breath, he put his arm around Cole's neck. Cole half dragged him, half carried him into the living room. He moved the broken things from the sofa, then lay Reese down. For the next hour, he wiped blood from his face. He went over to Ruthie's side of the house and searched through over-the-counter and expired pills. Found iodine and peroxide, a couple of Ace bandages. He wrapped ice in a washcloth and placed it on Reese's face, and gave him whiskey and Oxy for the pain. As Reese bit down on the rolled-up *National Geographic* where Everett had cut the speed, Cole struggled to remove his bloody cowboy shirt. Naked chest, tattoos, dark matted hair. Queasy, Cole wrapped the bandage around him and taped him as best he could. When he was through he took the magazine out of his mouth and Reese let out a long sigh, then asked for a cigarette.

"You're gonna get yourself killed," Cole told him.

"How come you left me?"

Cole fumbled with the lighter. Not looking at Reese, he said, "I had to. He had a gun."

"We could have taken them."

"He had a gun," he repeated. He finally got the cigarette lit and transferred it to Reese's bloody mouth.

"You're a good nurse."

"I can't do this," he said. "I can't look after you."

"I gotta get out of this place," Reese mumbled.

"You could have not said anything," Cole said. "You could have shut your fucking trap."

Reese's eyes were black and swollen, his entire face one big cut and bruise, but still Cole could see the trace of a grin. "I ain't afraid of punks like that," he said. "I'll never shut up."

"You're gonna get yourself killed."

Reese started to say something, but the pills and drink overcame him, and like a child, he was suddenly sleeping. Cole looked around at the mess. He was not going to clean it up. He was tired of cleaning up messes. Tired of taking care of people. Tired of sitting next to the dying and the sick and the broken. He switched off the light so he wouldn't have to look at any of it. "He's gonna get himself killed," he said to the dark, then he said, "I'm gonna get myself killed." He wanted someone to sit next to him, to watch over him through the night. He wanted a hand on his brow, someone to hold him. Maybe he could have had that. But he did not know how to start over, he did not know.

CHAPTER 14

R EESE LOOKED EVEN WORSE in the morning light, his face
swollen twice its size and bruised lilac and velvety blue. His
puffy eyes were blackened, nearly sealed shut. He told Cole he
wanted to see what he looked like.

"You sure?"

He said he was. Cole found a broken piece of mirror and held it
up and Reese studied himself. "It's bad," he finally said, "but I've
looked worse."

Cole had to go to work. He showered and tried to clean the
specks of blood off his uniform. He left Reese pain pills, a pack of
cigarettes. "I don't have time to clean up."

"Hell no, you've done enough."

As Cole started out the door, Reese called him back. "I was bad
to her in the end."

"No, you were all right."

"Not in the end." He sighed. "I'm gonna change. I'm not going
to be like this anymore."

"Just rest." Cole locked the door behind him and stepped into
the golden daylight and felt like he was going to be sick.

But he wasn't. He went to work and somehow got through the

day, and afterward, he drove to Lacy's. He had nothing in his
hands to offer her. He rang the bell and after a minute she let him
in. They sat on the sofa, a noticeable space between them. The room
was dimly lit, one weak lamp and a few candles, the flames flickering and throwing shadows across the walls. He wished she'd
turn on more lights so he could see her eyes.

"Where's Sara Jean?"

"Over at Blue's, with Michael."

He told her he was sorry that he didn't come over last night.

"I was waiting for you."

He said that he'd been tied up at work and she stared at him
and saw right through him and said to tell her the truth.

"I was at a friend's. He was in trouble."

"Who?"

"Nobody you know."

"Who?" she said again, her tone sharp.

He picked up one of the candles and watched the flame dance.
"Reese Campbell."

"We went to school together," she said.

He put the candle down and turned and faced her.

"I know who he is," she continued. "Faggot drug dealer."

He was surprised by the meanness in her voice and he shook a
cigarette from the pack and tipped it to the candle. "What about
the faggots you hang out with?"

"Who?"

"Michael."

"Cole, Christ. Michael's not gay."

"Trip is."

"That's not even the point. I'm talking about Reese. The dealer."

"He's not really a dealer."

"Addict, whatever. You're one too, aren't you? A dealer?"

He leaned back into the cushions and felt her waiting. He was
tired of all the pretend. "I don't use," he said.

"What do you deal?"

"Prescriptions, nothing big."

For a long time they were quiet. He did not know what else to say. He reached out his hand and touched her leg. "Turn on that light so I can see you."

The overhead came on and the magic of the candles disappeared. Her eyes were sad and scared, and he was sorry he'd done this to her.

"I'm a mother. I got a kid to worry about. I can't do this," she said.

"I know it."

"You've got a different life than me."

He did not try to tell her that he could change, it seemed too far gone for that. He touched her face with the palm of his hand, and she jumped, as if it were on fire. "It's not your fault. I suspected a long time ago. I liked it, in a way, that you were so different," she said. "But it's not right."

"I don't think you ever really wanted me," he said. "You just want Denny back."

She looked at him with steady eyes. "You're wrong," she said. "I think I could have loved you, but you don't want it. You really don't want it."

For the next three days Cole hid in his trailer, calling in sick to work and turning down the volume on the answering machine. He listened to the blasting and the rumble of the coal trucks; he smoked; he ate stale bread smeared with strawberry jelly. Every day it rained. He did not answer the phone. He opened the safe and the Christmas tin and stared at the cash and the stolen jewelry and heirlooms and postcards. He sorted photographs. One of his mother, one of his grandparents. He pinned them on the wall with thumbtacks. He found a picture of Charlotte; naked and tattooed and smiling seductively. He pinned that one up too. He looked at the one of Lacy laughing and the one of him sleeping like someone innocent and young and the one where he had his arm slung around Terry Rose, and he pinned all of them to the wall next to his bed. On the third day he rose and went into the kitchen and scraped the last of the coffee into a filter and he looked at the nursing books and brochures on the table and he could not stand to look at them anymore. He carried them outside to the trash pit, and standing naked in the cold morning, he lit a match and watched as the pages curled into black snakes and the flames flickered, and then shivering and empty, he went back inside and crawled under the blankets and closed his eyes.

Someone was knocking. He waited, but it didn't stop.

"Cole, you in there?"

He pulled on a pair of Levi's and a musty-smelling flannel shirt and went to the door. His grandmother and mother were standing in the rain.

"What's wrong? Where have you been?" his mother asked.

"Here."

"We tried calling," his grandmother said.

"I haven't been feeling well."

She put her hand on his forehead and said he did feel a little warm. He asked them to sit down, embarrassed by the messiness.

"Tomorrow's the big church meeting," his grandmother said.

He looked at her blankly, then recalled her telling him something about it a few weeks ago. "The one in Bucks County?"

"We'll have to leave bright and early. You're still gonna take me, right?"

He looked at his mother. "Can't you do it?"

"I want you both to come with me."

"She's got her mind made up," Ruby said.

"I'm not feeling well," Cole tried. "I've got a fever."

"All the more reason to go, where the Holy Ghost can work on you. Anyway, I don't think you've taken ill. It's something else." His grandmother said the preacher would be able to look at him and see what plagued him. "It may be that God is trying to tell you something."

His insides felt scraped raw. "Grandma, it's been a long time."

"That don't matter. Listen, I got a good feeling," she said. "I think the Lord is going tell us what to do about the land."

Cole sighed, but said nothing. Come spring, Heritage would begin working on the ridge behind them, taking it down even lower. Lacy had told him that there were more permits in the works. "We'll get it on all sides. They won't stop till they get every last bit," she'd warned, telling him this one night, just after sex. He already missed the sound of her hard-edged voice, a fighting voice.

"I'm gonna pray on it and we're gonna see what God tells us," his grandmother said. "Then everything will be clear."

When Cole stood up, the room curved out of perspective, the floor tilting, and he held on to the chair for balance.

"Good Lord, what's wrong with you?"

He sat down, thinking how he hadn't eaten anything but bread for three days. "I guess I just got up too quick."

"Well, you're coming with us," his grandmother said. "I'll make you something to eat. I want you to be in good shape for tomorrow."

He did not argue. Before he left, he checked his messages. Lacy had not called, but there were messages from Reese and customers and work. He erased them all.

At his grandmother's he ate chicken stew and biscuits, and took a long hot bath. After he was dry and warm, he went into his childhood room and lay in the bed and looked up at the ceiling and felt that he had nothing inside of him and that this was good: he was empty and untouched.

He waited for them outside, sipping steaming coffee from a travel mug, while his pickup idled, spitting out white plumes of exhaust. It would be long trip, two hours at least. His fever was gone, but he still felt shaky. He cracked the front door, yelled that they'd better hurry up. The rain had stopped, but the creek looked swollen. He worried about the roads turning icy.

"Y'all ready?"

"Heavens, I think so," his grandmother said.

"We could have been out of here an hour ago, if Mama wasn't trying to tell me how to dress." Ruby smoothed down the front of her below-the-knee skirt. "If they don't let me in, I'll just find a place that will. Hopefully somewhere where I can shoot a game of pool."

She sat in the middle, her knee jostling the gearshift, and his grandmother sat in the passenger seat. The heat vents blew warm air over their faces, but it was still drafty and Cole wished he would have brought a blanket for his grandmother. He'd tried to block the hole in the floorboard, but a stream of air pushed its way through.

At the halfway point, he pulled over at a Sunoco station and filled up the tank and bought a few candy bars. While his grandmother was in the bathroom, he and his mother smoked furtively like teenagers; his grandmother did not want them smoking on this special day.

"You still seeing that guy?" Cole asked. "The Heritage dude?"

For a second, Ruby looked surprised, as if she had forgotten that he was there. She shook her head. "No, that didn't work out."

"Oh."

"You still seeing that woman?"

"Didn't work out."

"Well, someone else will come along for you." She looked away, distracted. Smoking. Thinking about something. "Listen, Cole," she finally said. "Remember what I told you, about leaving?" She paused. "Well, I'm going to be heading out. Day after tomorrow. This time I mean it, I'm going."

Cole took a long pull on his smoke. "Where you headed? Back to Pennsylvania?"

"No, hell no. I'm not sure yet. I got some friends in Michigan. There's maybe some factory work, I don't know." She looked like she was about to say more, then sighed. "I can't believe I agreed to this. I never thought I'd step foot in a church again."

"Maybe you'll get saved."

"I've already been saved, I sure as hell don't need any more of it." She nudged him. "What about you? You hoping to get saved?"

He flicked the cigarette across the asphalt. "I never even once spoke in tongues, and granddaddy said if you never spoke in tongues, then you ain't carried your faith far enough."

"Damn, that old man messed you up pretty good, didn't he?"

As they got closer to Wildcat Run, Cole's stomach tightened and he let his foot up on the gas. Mountains rose up all around them, and the hollow was dark and cavernous.

"Turn right. Go on. Turn right." His grandmother directed him the rest of the way, sending him on back roads until they reached an overgrown pasture that was already filling up with cars and pickups. Up on the hill, butted against forest, stood a rectangular whitewashed building with a yellow cross painted on the door.

Ruby patted him on the leg. "Come on, backslider."

A crowd of about thirty congregated outside, shivering and blowing on their hands. The women wore dresses, long skirts; not a smudge of makeup touched their plain faces. The men dressed in jeans or khakis, long-sleeved shirts; hair short, faces shaved. Cole touched the ends of his bleached hair, pushed it out of his eyes. The majority were over fifty, but there were a few young families and a string of kids running around. He was surprised to see a black couple. The man saw Cole looking at him and smiled. "Hey brother." Cole returned the greeting.

A guy who could not have been over twenty-five approached Cole. "You're Clyde Freeman's grandson." He clapped him on the back. "When I was just a wee thing, I went to one of your grandpa's services. Brother, he could lay it down." He paused. "I'm sorry to hear he passed on. But you know he's happy now. He's probably up there talking to my daddy."

"Who's that?"

"Carl Cutter," he said, smiling. "I'm Luke Cutter."

Cole remembered hearing that Carl Cutter, an old-time preacher from Pikeville, Kentucky, had died last year. Throat cancer. Their church followed the signs, but did not mess with serpents.

"Sorry about your dad."

Luke took Cole's hand in his own, the warm suede of his glove pressed soft against Cole's bare skin. "I'm glad you're here."

Cole sat with his mother and grandmother toward the back of the church. Now even his grandmother looked out of place, with her short hair. The organist began pounding the keys, and Cole mouthed the words to an old hymn about meeting in the sweet by-and-by. A boy with an electric guitar led them through another song. His grandmother had said she missed loud churches, and Cole knew what she meant. In Charleston, he'd gone once to a church where the minister spoke in a gentle voice and the congregation was polite and quiet. He did not know how people could feel God that way, without the sweat and tears and shouting.

Luke Cutter ran up to the pulpit. He was dressed in jeans and a cowboy shirt with pearly snaps. "I'm so happy to see y'all here," he started, flashing a wide, toothy grin. "Are you all happy?"

"Je-sus!" the old woman in front of Cole called.

"The Holy Ghost is here today. Do you feel the Holy Ghost?"

When Cole was a teenager, he'd wanted so badly to be saved.

He'd think about Jesus, how they pounded nails through his hands, forced him to wear a crown of thorns. He had wanted forgiveness, goodness. The guitarist began strumming, and little kids jumped and danced. The congregation found its rhythm, raising arms and swaying. Cole had forgotten this, those times when his grandfather did not speak of burning but of happiness, when love dripped off of him, a deep and abiding love, which was here in this room, right now.

Preaching, praying, and testifying filled up the first hour and a half, and then they took a break, congregating outside to shake off the heat and sweat. A tent was set up with a couple of card tables and the women had put out thermoses of coffee, doughnuts, and cookies. Cole had never been to a big service like this in the winter—usually, they happened in the summer, revivals or homecomings that drew people from all over. But today was the anniversary of Cutter's father's death; he wanted to be with his people.

"I wish Clyde was here," his grandmother said. "He'd be so happy to see you two." Ruby's face was pale and drawn, and for a second Cole felt sorry for her.

Luke Cutter waved him over. He was standing next to the organist, who held a fat baby in her arms. He introduced them as his wife and daughter, and pointed out three young boys chasing each other, his sons. "We're happy to have you, Brother Cole," the wife said. Her face was smooth and guileless, and he guessed she could not have been a day over twenty-one.

Cutter looked at Cole. "You ever think of following in your grandpa's footsteps?"

"What, preaching? No. I don't have it in me."

It started to snow and the snowflakes caught in Cutter's lashes. "You oughtta come up, do a little testifying."

The snow had rejuvenated the crowd, and Cutter's sermons grew more thunderous, more like the way Cole's grandfather used to preach. People were calling out praises. Cole's grandmother moved past him and walked up the aisle. He swallowed the hotness in his mouth as she lifted her arms. She started by praying softly, then her words began to transform, her mouth spitting garbled and strange syllables that set everyone off in a frenzy.

"Oh, yes, Sister Dorothy, listen to Sister Dorothy," shouted Cutter.

Cole held onto the back of a pew so hard that his fingertips turned a dark pink. He was afraid to look at his grandmother. But when the noises finally stopped, he glanced over. She seemed suddenly exhausted, head drooping, hands limp at her sides.

An old woman led a boy out to the center aisle. He was six or seven. Pale as rice, sickly looking. People placed their hands on him. The first time hands had ever been laid on Cole, he was four years old and his grandfather asked God to heal his tongue, *give him a voice,* and he'd touched Cole on the head and Cole felt something jolt from his grandfather's hand into him and he stumbled back into his grandmother's arms, and then it was not only his grandfather's hands, but the hands of everyone. When the stutter stayed, he knew he must be full of wickedness.

"We are all sinners, all of us," Cutter said. "And I am the biggest sinner of all." He told them how he'd lost his way with women and drink, but God forgave him. "It don't matter how bad you been, you can be good." He seemed to be looking right at Cole. His eyes kind and earnest and truthful. "God will forget everything that you did."

A man about Cole's age stood up. He didn't look like he belonged in church. He wore dirty jeans and a T-shirt with the sleeves pushed up, revealing a faded barbed wire tattoo. "When I was living in Lexington, I strayed." He swallowed. "I did bad things." It was an old story: a person went off to the big city, what his granddaddy called the devil's playground, lived a life of sin, and then came home to repent. But Cole lost his way here in Dove

Creek, at his grandfather's side. He lost God among the mountains and the blue sky and the honeysuckle.

Cutter held out his arms. "Come on up here, son."

"This boy's got demons inside him," Cutter said, and he held the man in his arms, and people shouted, Praise God.

Cole's grandfather had once said the same thing to him. Cole was a few months shy of turning eighteen and his granddaddy called him out in the middle of the service and said it was time for him to be truthful. "We'll get the demons out," he said. "All you have to do is ask for forgiveness."

The man raised his hands in the air, and as Cole watched him, his face began to morph into Reese's. The blood, the bruises. Reese had called for him and Cole had walked away. Fists against flesh. Walked away like a coward. He heard crying now. Heard from somewhere the echo of his granddad's tremulous voice. Heard his own name. He wanted it to stop. Everything was too loud and bright, and he wanted it to stop. He stepped into the aisle. Cutter smiled at him. It was a beautiful smile.

Tears sprang to Luke Cutter's eyes. "I love you, brother."

Nobody had ever looked at Cole with such understanding. He could hear the other man weeping. He could hear Cutter.

"It does not matter what you've done, Cole. You can be new."

He started to walk up the aisle. One foot in front of the other. When he reached the pulpit, he could not speak. His tongue was heavy, everything was heavy. He dropped to his knees and felt the hardness of the floor. He looked up at Cutter, who smiled at him through tears.

"Look at this boy. Too much despair. He needs to be loved."

Cole closed his eyes and felt Cutter's hand on his forehead and he thought about everyone who was gone from his life, his grandfather, Charlotte, Lacy, Terry Rose. Soon his mother would be leaving him too. Just like before. His grandfather had said being saved was like being filled with a golden light. He said after you were saved, God would talk to you. *In a quiet voice,* he said. *You have to be still and the voice will speak to you.*

Cole tried to hear what was beyond Cutter's words, beyond the music, the shouts, the prayers, to hear that voice of God, to hear it inside his heart. He'd had this described to him a hundred times, what it felt like to be consumed by the Holy Spirit, how you couldn't breathe and then suddenly just when you thought you couldn't go any lower, you were lifted. Cutter's hand on his head, the hard floor beneath him. Hadn't he gone low enough? He pressed his hands to his face. Wasn't it time to be lifted up? Everything quieted. He opened his eyes.

Cutter was crouched next to him, his face so close that Cole could see the stubble on his chin. His bright and holy eyes. He whispered, "Pray with me, my brother."

But they were not brothers. Cole pulled his eyes away and looked behind him at the people praying. Strangers. They did not know him. When he stood up, Cutter's hand dropped away. He felt shaky and sick. He stepped back. Cutter said, "Don't go," but Cole turned and walked out of the church, and once he was outside, he kneeled in the snow and pushed his hands into the cold. He rolled over on his back and the snowflakes stung his face. He could stay here forever. Nothing inside of him, not darkness nor light. No small voice talking to him. Nothing.

"Baby, come on, you'll catch a cold."

An angel leaned over him, brushing the snowflakes from his hair and face. For a moment, he didn't know who she was or how she'd found him. Then she helped him stand and led him over to a picnic table. He took the cigarette she offered. They sat for a long time, snow-covered and shivering. He wanted to tell her things. The story of himself. But he didn't even know what that was, or how to tell it, or where to start. He once had a mother who did not want him. A grandfather who thought he was bad and tried to save him. And he once had a brother, or someone who was like a brother but not that exactly.

He said nothing. She held his face in the palm of her hand. "He sure messed you up, didn't he?" she said quietly. "He sure messed you up."

CHAPTER 15

THE NEXT MORNING Cole helped his grandmother sort through his grandfather's things. Throwing out his yellowed toothbrush and gnarly socks and such, and donating the clothes, what wasn't worn through the elbows and knees, to Goodwill. He only had a few personal items worth holding on to: a couple of antique knives and guns that must have belonged to his own grand-dad, a worry rock that he used to carry around, the King James, and a stack of sermons. There wasn't much else. They'd been talking about doing this for months now, but it was only today that his grandmother said she felt ready.

Every so often she went to the window, nervous. Yesterday's snow had turned to rain and the creek was rising. "When it rains like this, all I can do is walk the floor," she murmured.

She had asked for the members of Luke Cutter's church to pray over her family because the coal company was destroying their home, but Luke Cutter told her that the only home she needed to worry about was her home in heaven. She had left shortly after, found Cole and Ruby outside, smoking, watching the snow. They took a box of doughnuts and three cups of coffee for the drive. Last night she had gone to bed without supper and prayed for a long time. She had dreams and visions, but when Cole asked her to describe them, she wouldn't.

Ruby lounged on the sofa, channel surfing. Tomorrow, weather permitting, she would be on her way. She'd been helping sort through the boxes until she came across a red tie that her father used to wear to revivals, and she picked it up and held it out in front of her like an old shed snakeskin. "I don't know what I'm supposed to feel about that man." Cole didn't know either. But looking through his granddaddy's things felt like an ending, and that was what he wanted.

He glanced at the sermons, scrawled in nearly illegible writing on a yellow legal pad. His grandfather's education had stopped at fourteen. Although Cole had never actually seen him read from any sermon in church, he occasionally wrote them out, more a random collection of thoughts, snippets of scripture and hymns than actual sermons. *No more tears. No more sorrow or fear. God promises all of that will go away.* Had tears flowed from his grandfather's eyes? What was his sorrow? His fear? Yesterday Cole had had a chance to be lifted up to God. This was who he was, a small, unsaved man.

"Look at your granddad's watch, still ticking."

His grandmother dropped the watch in the palm of Cole's hand and he lifted it to his ear and heard the tick. He thought of all the spouses and sons and daughters and grandchildren who had searched for some kind of reminder, some memento like this, which he had stolen.

"I don't want it," he said.

"It's a nice watch. I think Rebecca got it for him—"

A loud explosion tore away his grandmother's words. The noise was enormous, not like a blast, but bigger, deeper, echoing down the mountain.

Ruby sat up. "What was that?"

Cole pulled on his boots and went out and stood in the drizzle.

He automatically looked up to see if there were clouds of dust or smoke spraying from behind the ridge where they'd been mining, but nothing looked any different. It wasn't a blast. What *was* that? The rain splattered his face and he pulled up his hood and walked around the house, toward the creek, and when he saw it, he stopped. The creek was black and thick and churning, and spilling over into the yard and into the road. He felt confused by the color and the crazy movement, and he tried to think of what he'd been told by Lacy and Sara Jean. Then a rocking chair came bobbing along, and he felt his stomach drop. He looked back at the house, which suddenly appeared so old and breakable.

"What is it?" His grandmother met him at the door, his mother behind her.

"I don't know. Something happened. The creek is black."

"Should we leave?" Ruby asked.

"I don't know."

"Sons of bitches," she said.

"We should report this," his grandmother started, and then there was a second explosion, this time even louder, causing all of them to jump. Cole looked up and saw a tidal wave of black sludge.

"We got to go, we got to get out of here."

But for a second they just stood there and watched. Twenty feet high, the sludge thundered down the mountain and across the ridge, carrying tree limbs and rocks and furniture and what looked like part of a pickup.

"Come on," Cole yelled.

They scrambled up the hillside behind the house. Cole grabbed his grandmother's arm, pulling on her, as mud slid under their shoes, the ground disappearing beneath them. The black stuff came faster, splashing at the backs of their legs. His grandmother was having a hard time, and Cole pulled her closer, practically lifted her. Just keep moving. Finally they got to a place, about twenty feet up, where they stopped and looked back. His grand-mother murmured about dreams and prophecy and the end, get-ting down on her knees even, but Cole and Ruby stood still, their shock holding them up.

The noise of it was incredible, like thousands of trees falling and freight trains crashing into each other at once. The way a dozer must sound to a terrified squirrel hiding in its nest, while all around it, the earth is split open. The roiling creek spit out trees, boulders, a mangled car. A house trailer rocked along like a boat. Were there people inside of it? A cold sweat broke out across Cole's chest, his hands and face clammy with fear. The trailer smashed into his mother's Camry and there was an explosion of metal and blue sparks. Ruby stood there with her hand over her mouth, speech-less.

"Dear Lord," his grandmother said.

As the wave followed the twists and turns of the creek, eventu-ally the roaring grew farther away, but they could still hear the echoes. It had washed by them, just barely. But anyone who was under it would not survive.

Gathered below them like a gigantic moat, the mix of black water and gunk pooled around his grandmother's house and had completely submerged his mother's car. There were tires, TVs, computers, and mattresses still moving downstream and getting tangled in trees. Cole thought of the lay of the land, the little creeks and streams and hollows and homes. He felt hot, then cold. Lacy Cooper. He drew a sharp breath. Lacy.

"The people up at Thorny Creek," he said. "I got to get up there."

"You can't."

"I got to," he said. "I got to."

But at this moment he couldn't see any way to get down. He sat on the hillside and drew his knees to his chest and felt his heart pounding. Rain fell softly. It trickled down the back of his neck. The sudden quiet felt strange and spooky. He thought he still heard faint echoes, or maybe his ears were just ringing. He tried to comfort himself by thinking of those who lived out of range—Charlotte, Reese, his cousins and aunts and uncles, some of his suppliers. But what about Lacy? What about all of the others?

"We're gonna freeze to death," his mother said.

She had lost her shoes and her sock feet were wet and black. Cole tried to give her his boots, but she wouldn't take them. His grandmother was wearing only a housecoat, and her Keds were useless, cemented in sludge. Cole insisted she put on his sweatshirt; he pretended to be fine in his T-shirt, even as goose bumps prickled his arms.

If they were to learn they were the only survivors, Cole would not be surprised. He closed his eyes, trying to stop the hammering in his head. Rain drizzled from the gray and empty sky. For a long time, nothing was said. Then his grandmother checked her watch, which Cole realized was his grandfather's, the one she'd tried to give to him.

"Why it's not even been forty minutes that we've been up here."

Cole stood up. "It looks like the water's going down."

"No, I don't think so."

"I'm gonna see if there is a way to get out of here."

"Cole, you be careful," his mother called.

He found a branch to help him along and went over toward the trailer that had smashed against his mother's car. As the sludge sank, cold black water rose to his knees. He got as close as he could and looked for any sign of a person, but all he found were swollen books and floating T-shirts and underwear and a bag of potato chips that had risen to the surface. He then maneuvered his way down the hillside, using the branch to measure how deep the water was before he stepped. The front of his grandmother's house was caved in. Piles of splintered boards and shattered glass. He wanted to get them warm clothes, but he could not see any way to enter.

He walked along a high part of the land toward his trailer and was surprised to see it was still standing. His truck was there too. The mix of water and sludge was low enough here that he could wade through it. He grabbed the door handle to his trailer, but it didn't budge, so he went over to his bedroom and smashed the window with a rock. He stripped off his T-shirt and folded it over the sill, and shimmied through. Stomping through the mushy liquid mess in his room, he managed to find a dry sweatshirt, and a few hats and pairs of socks, a pair of boots. Then he pulled the bed out from the wall. The safe was submerged. Fuck. He fished a flashlight out of the closet. It wasn't very deep in the kitchen, at least not yet, and he grabbed a trash bag from under the sink. Back in his room, he crouched, holding the end of the flashlight in his mouth and the bag open with his free hand. He wiped off the lock, but still could barely see the numbers. It took three tries, him cursing and shaking from the cold. The lock popped. As soon as he opened the lid, the lava-like water rushed in, and he worked as fast as he could, grabbing the money and pills and jewelry, and dropping them into the bag. After he emptied the safe, he reached under the bed, nauseated, disgusted. Then his hands pressed upon metal, and he pulled the cookie tin out of the mire.

He carried all of it outside and climbed in the back of his truck and opened the cross-bed toolbox, pushing aside random tools and a fishing pole and tackle that he hadn't used in years. He stuffed the garbage bag and cookie tin inside, and then he studied his truck. The tires were sinking. He got a snow shovel out of the back and started digging. Then he saw his mother and grandmother making their way toward him, arms hooked together, taking slow, careful steps. He gave them hats and socks, and Ruby slipped her feet into his boots, which were gigantic on her. "They'll do," she said, shivering.

Cole got behind the wheel, his grandmother and mother

squeezed in beside him. A half-empty pack of cigarettes lay on the dash. He quickly shook one out, but his hands were shaking so badly he couldn't get the lighter to catch. His mother took it, lit the cigarette for him. He inhaled and exhaled, focusing. Now that he had something to do, the panic began to fade. He concentrated on what he knew. Started the truck. Shifted into four-wheel drive. Steer, shift. The wheels finally spun out. He drove wildly along the hillside, dodging felled trees and boulders. Trailers that had stood vacant for years were now busted up or buried.

"We were lucky," his grandmother said.

At Floyd Mitchell's, Cole left the engine running and sprinted toward the half-sunk shack, calling for Floyd, and finally he came to the door, wild-eyed and wearing a tattered bathrobe.

"It took Sugar," he shouted. "She was outside and the creek washed her away. It took my Sugar." Cole stared at him blankly, then remembered the old crippled dog.

"You got to come with us."

He would not budge. When Cole took his arm, he fought him off, yelling, cursing. "All right, Floyd," he said. "All right."

"It's what he wants," his grandmother said as they drove away, leaving the tiny man alone on his porch.

On their way out, they saw a man trying to dig out his truck with a garden shovel. Cole knew who he was, but had never talked to him before. Glenn Kincaid, a miner. He was a part of all this, but now he looked scared and dirty like the rest of them.

Cole leaned out the window. "You want a ride?"

He stopped and dropped the shovel. His face and hands were blackened like the stereotypical old-timey coal miner. After he climbed in back, Cole drove farther up the hillside, the ground sliding, the truck tilting.

The main road was washed out. He turned sharply to the left and they went along a rough path until he reached a place where the road looked safe. He yanked the emergency brake, then slid open the divider window between the cab and the back, and told Glenn that he was going to Thorny Creek.

He looked at Cole like he was crazy. "Won't be nothing up there."

Cole told Ruby to drive his grandmother and Glenn down to Stillwell, that he was getting out here. But she stubbornly refused, as did his grandmother. Cole asked Glenn if he wanted to get out, but he said, "Hell, just go where you want."

Cole turned the truck up an old logging road that looped toward Thorny Creek, and drove until he could not go any farther.

He looked at his grandmother. "We're going to have to do some walking. I think you should wait here in the truck. Is that all right?"

She stared ahead, not answering. But she didn't make any move to get out, either.

Cole took the snow shovel from the back and led the way, his mother and Glenn behind him. They hiked up the backside of the hollow, over slides and piles of rocks and debris. The rain continued to fall steadily. It took them a good forty minutes, maybe longer. And then they stopped. Cole closed his eyes for a second, trying to remember the layout of the hollow, the little houses that had been up close to the road. Now they were flattened, overturned, or just gone altogether. He opened his eyes and saw a trailer flipped onto its side. Broken furniture and cars and shredded clothing. His knees buckled.

"Lacy," he said. "Everyone . . ."

They trudged along a small ridge, then went down to where the people were scattered on the hillsides and staring at the destruction like they did not know where they were. Some were only half dressed, others had no shoes or socks. The sludge had engulfed the creek, flooded the valley. Cole knew whoever hadn't run up the hillsides was dead.

He looked at Glenn. "Man, you better not say who you work for."

As Cole turned, Glenn grabbed his shoulder, hard. Cole spun around, fist drawn, but then stopped. Glenn didn't want to fight. "Wait, you got to listen," he said, his voice breaking. "It was my job. I needed to make a living, just like anybody."

Cole shook his hand off him, then started down the hill. He scrambled over uprooted trees and rutted-out earth, running over to the people. He looked at their frightened faces and did not see Lacy. He went to where her house used to stand, but it was gone. Just gone.

Then there was a scream. A woman screaming. A man next to her held something in his arms. Cole went closer. It was a child. Smothered in sludge. The man said, "She was a neighbor, she was just a wee little thing." Cole looked at the dead child and felt dizzy and dropped to his knees and the retching came without warning, huge dry heaves. Then a hand on his shoulder. He looked up and saw his mother and she helped him stand.

Some people were digging along the hillsides, using shovels and tree limbs and their own hands. Digging out people, digging out the dead. Cole approached a couple of men and they asked where he was from and he said Rockcamp.

"Is it bad there?"

"It's not like this."

They looked like they could be brothers, one short, one tall. "I reckon it will be a while 'fore they get us any help," the tall one said, wiping rain from his face.

"They might not ever send it," the other said. "Might just think we all got swept away."

The tall man spit. "Probably that's what they want. For us just to be gone."

Cole was afraid to ask, but had to know. "Lacy Cooper, you seen her?"

They shook their heads. "Not yet."

"Someone's over here," an old man yelled.

Cole ran with the brothers. A slimy hand stuck up from under a pickup. He fought down the urge to vomit again. They tried lifting the truck, but it was too heavy. So they dug frantically and finally pulled out a body that didn't even look human any more. Cole turned away, blinking. He thought of the old people. His customers, his friends.

People walked around dazed, searching for their loved ones. Wondering when help would arrive. All of the telephone lines had been destroyed and if anyone happened to have a cell, it didn't matter, there was no signal. Everyone was hungry and cold and scared. They kept finding more people, more bodies. Cole was there when a young boy, clutching a mattress, washed up on shore—his clothes were shredded like wolves had been at him, but at least he was alive. He helped dig out an old man whose legs were broken. He saw a drowned teenager who was tangled up in a mess of cable wires. A woman holding a dead girl walked over to him.

"She went right under," she said, her voice taut. "I tried to hold on to her, but she was swept out of my hands."

Cole had seen plenty of death in the nursing home, the waxy faces and blue skin and puckered mouths. But everyone he'd seen up until now had been old. Now he saw swollen, drowned children. A body hung up in a tree. A man's mouth stuffed with black sludge, eyes matted shut. They laid out the bodies like memorials. They needed help, or everyone was going to go crazy.

"How many people live here?" he asked.

"I'd say a hundred." An old woman nodded. "Yeah. Used to be. Maybe a couple hundred."

Now there were around fifty or so people standing around and coming down from the hillsides. Cole made himself look into every face. He wiped away the sludge and blood from the dead and each time expected to see Sara Jean or Lacy, but each time, it was someone else, nobody he knew, but faces he recognized.

Ruby came over and said she was going back to the truck. "I want to check on Mama." But just as she said that, Cole's grandmother emerged from the path they'd hiked, using a large branch to help her along.

She stopped in front of them. "I couldn't just set up there and do nothing. I don't know what you think of me."

Cole tried to get her to sit down and rest, but she saw an old woman she knew and went to comfort her.

The rain finally stopped and the sun broke through the clouds as if it was a normal day, but what continued to float downstream was incomprehensible. Trailers, sofas, baby dolls, TVs, shoes, cats and dogs, and the dead who'd been dead for years. "The cemetery's washed out," a teenager explained.

Blisters rose on Cole's hands, his back and neck burned. He didn't know how much time had passed. There was just too much water, too much sludge. A woman told Cole, "Them trailers and houses, you could see people trapped in them. I could see faces. I could see them."

Two figures weighed down with gigantic backpacks were walking toward Cole. He'd forgotten that Michael was staying up here. Trip was with him. They looked weary and beaten up.

"Cole," Michael said, grabbing him.

Cole stepped back and asked if they'd seen Lacy.

"No," Michael said. "I was hoping she was with you."

"We'll find her," Trip promised.

They told Cole that they'd had to climb onto the roof of their trailer to escape the rising water. When a mattress floated within reach, they grabbed on to it and used it as a raft, until it was shallow enough to walk.

"The sludge dam up there busted," Michael said. "That's the only explanation."

They unloaded their backpacks. Michael's was stuffed with bottles of water, granola bars. "We grabbed as much as we could," he explained, and started handing out the provisions.

"Saved all of this too, thank God." Trip opened his pack, revealing a couple of cameras, lenses, some kind of recorder, and other equipment that Cole didn't recognize. He took out a camera, but Cole stepped in front of the lens.

"I don't think you ought to be taking pictures of people."

"Are you crazy?" Trip said. "You're crazy."

"This is too important," Michael said. "Really fucking important. Heritage will try to cover this up."

But Cole looked around. Kids crying, a woman hugging herself, men staring helplessly. Bloated bodies on the hillside.

"You can't," he said. "Not right now. It ain't right."

Trip looked at Michael. "What do you want to do?"

"Cole, we've got to document this," Michael said.

"Not like this," he said. "Don't do it."

Michael glared at him. "Fuck," he said, shaking his head. "Shit. You're serious?" His face and hands were clenched, but after a moment, he signaled to Trip, and Trip lowered the camera.

Michael got in Cole's face. There was dirt all over him, and his cheeks were red from the cold. He looked like he'd been crying. "It's a big fucking mistake," he said.

Cole did not say if it was or wasn't. He had to get away from him, from all of them. The sky misted with more rain. He walked farther up the valley, and he searched as well as he could under broken homes and furniture, and then he came upon a foot, and he kneeled down and dug out the body, first with the shovel, then his hands. He was slick all over from the sludge and rain. He saw wrinkled skin and felt thin bones and then he came to a face. He used his shirt to wipe away the muck. The old woman Arie Webb. Who'd been saving her money so that she could move to the coast of North Carolina. When he lifted her, she was light, a sack of bones, but he was tired and worn out and weak, and it was hard work. He carried her like a baby in his arms. Like a bride. He carried her up to the hillside and laid her out next to the others and thought of prayers his grandfather might say. His granddaddy would believe that this was the end, the evening hour was upon them. But there were no angels meeting them in the air, no by-and-by, no heavenly light. Only this cold toxic sludge, these broken people.

The police and rescue teams and the National Guard started arriving between three and four o'clock. There was a helicopter to take away the badly injured, and a few army trucks. They'd cleared a part of the main road, and started transporting people to shelters that had been set up in Stillwell.

"It didn't get hit?"

"Just some flooding," an officer told Cole. "If it had come down a different way, there'd be a few thousand people killed, I expect."

Cole took a few extra people with him; they rode in the back of his pickup. He drove slowly, avoiding fallen trees, scattered boulders. It took nearly two hours to get to Stillwell, and by this time it was dark. His headlights shone over the blackness that marked tree trunks, fence posts, basketball hoops. The town was quiet like a morgue. He pulled into the high school, now designated as an emergency shelter. There were cots set up in the gymnasium. Blankets, bottled water, food, and toiletries. His grandmother clutched his arm. She'd hardly spoken; he wondered if the flood was what she'd seen in her dreams, or if it was worse.

There were at least fifty volunteers, maybe more, and about twice as many victims. A group of women had taken charge; they served bowls of chili and handed out blankets. A dozen or so kids ran around, while the adults talked in low voices and sipped coffee and stared at the TV. There were nurses, cops. Cole recognized many faces, but could not place anyone—it was as if he'd stepped into some community that resembled Dove Creek, but was not it exactly. He saw Ellen's fiancé, Randy, one of the cops.

"I don't know much more than you do," he said. "They ain't saying shit." Then he seemed to take in Cole and his grandmother and mother, and his tone softened. "You all should get something to eat. Rest up."

Cole led his grandmother over to a table and one of the volunteers ladled out chili into a paper bowl. Ruby went out for a cigarette.

"Cole, you should eat something too," his grandmother said, but he could not. He looked around the room. No sign of Lacy or Sara Jean.

"I'm going to walk around," he said.

He made three passes around the gym, then went outside where the smokers convened. A couple of his customers nodded at him. Luke Cutter was there, comforting a young woman. Reese Campbell was there too, talking to an old man who wore a baseball hat that said POW. When Reese saw him, he patted the old man on the back and walked over to Cole.

"I was worried." Reese's face was still slightly swollen and discolored with swirls of fading green, yellow. Just looking at him jolted Cole with shame, a reminder of how he'd left him.

"I'm fine," he assured him. "You ain't seen Lacy Cooper, have you?"

Reese said that he had not. His eyes were deep and blue and stoned.

"How you been holding up?"

Reese shrugged. But then he said in a low voice that he'd not been very good. He'd been sitting in his house for days, unable to sleep and afraid to go out. "I don't have any speed left," he said. He'd been eating pills like candy, whatever was left in Ruthie's medicine cabinet.

"You got to get off of all of it." Cole couldn't believe they were discussing drugs right now, but then yes he could.

"I know it. Hell, I know it. I want to get the fuck out, I can't take it anymore."

"What are you doing down here?"

"I turned on the TV and saw what was going on, and I said, Fuck, Reese, get off your ass, and I came down here to see if there was anything I could do. But there are too many cops, making me nervous." He lowered his voice, "Hey, you got anything on you?"

Cole shook his head.

"Just thought I'd ask."

Then the vet came over. "This is Charlie Paterson," Reese said. "He was up there in Thorny Creek."

"Do you know Lacy Cooper?" Cole asked. "Have you seen her?"

"No sir, no, I haven't."

The man began to tell his story, how he'd seen people wash by. His eyes pooled with tears. He'd said he'd seen things today that were worse than what he'd seen in the war. Cole could not listen to any more. All he could see in his head were the bodies he'd dug out. He started to go, but Luke Cutter came over.

"Brother Cole, you're okay, praise God. How is your mama and grandma?"

"All right." He did not look Cutter in the eyes.

"You a preacher or something?" Reese asked. "You look a little young for that."

"I got called young."

"I guess you're in the right place. People are gonna need a preacher."

"It's terrible what's happened," Luke said softly, tears in his eyes, just like yesterday. "But I want people to know that God is here, He's gonna take care of us."

"Cole, we should go check on Mama." Ruby approached them, her voice tight; she did not return Cutter's hello.

Cole felt Cutter's eyes on them as they walked away, but he didn't look back. He followed his mother, who told him that Cutter's brother worked for Heritage.

"So do my own cousins," he reminded her. "That's what you said before."

More people were filling up the gymnasium. Some were crying, but most just looked dazed.

His grandmother was watching TV. "Twenty they've reported so far," she said angrily. "Twenty people that's been murdered."

Cole said he had to go. He offered to drive them to Esther's, but his grandmother said that was too far. "We can just stay here, can't we, Ruby?"

His mother looked skeptically at the cots. "I guess so."

Cole's heart hurt as he drove over to Lacy's parents' place. He did not see her truck. He cut the lights and the engine and thought about what he would say to them. He went slowly up the steps, and rang the bell.

Nobody answered. But a light was on. He pushed the bell again. This time he heard movement, voices. The door swung open. He felt a gasp escape his throat. He wanted to pick Sara Jean up and crush her against him. But he was calm. He kneeled down.

"You're okay, honey?"

She nodded.

"Your mama?"

The girl stared and Cole wanted to speak but his mouth was too dry and then he saw a shadow and looked up and there she was.

They held each other and he could feel her heart pounding against his own chest.

"I was at work, all this time," she said. "I was at work and Sara Jean was here and we're okay." They drew apart, looked at each other shyly.

"Come in," she said. "Sit down, tell us what happened."

Her parents and her sister and her sister's husband were sitting around watching the news. Sara Jean stood in front of him. "Is our house gone?"

He was the bearer of bad news. He felt their eyes on him and he nodded. Sara Jean's face darkened, Lacy covered her mouth. The sister said, "Ours too. We barely got out of there. We barely did."

"I'm sorry," Cole said.

"What about Snowball?" Sara Jean asked.

"What?"

"Her cat." Lacy looked at her daughter. "I'm sure he's all right, baby. He's a tough cat," she said, but Sara Jean's eyes narrowed with disbelief.

They wanted to know everything. He sat stiffly next to Lacy on the sofa and told them what he'd seen without really describing it, and they told him what they'd heard on the news. The dam above the processing plant had broke and what it was holding back had flooded Dove Creek and all of its little tributaries, but nobody knew how much had spilled or how many people died or how many homes were lost. For a long time nobody said anything else, just stared at the TV. The news ended, and a show about a bunch of rich people living in New York City came on. Cole felt Lacy's hand on his own, and this brought him some comfort. But even sitting there, he felt apart from her and from the others. Maybe he would always be apart.

An hour or so later, she walked him out. She said she was afraid of finding out the names of the dead, but needed to know. She asked him about her neighbors and friends, but he did not have answers. "What about Blue Tiller?"

He just stared.

"You know, the old woman activist. Sara Jean keeps asking me about her, I don't know what to say."

"I don't know either," he said.

She held on to his belt loops and he pressed his mouth against her head, tasted smoke in her hair. "What am I going to do?" she asked. "Where am I going to go?"

"It's going to be all right," he told her. "We'll figure something out."

Then she drew back and lit a cigarette and the toughness that came off of her was too much for him to peel away. He said he'd call her tomorrow. She nodded. It was too much.

He returned to the gym, walking past the smokers. He was surprised to see that Reese was still there. He was still talking with Luke Cutter.

"Hey, Cole, where you staying tonight?"

"Here, I guess."

"Why don't y'all stay at my place?"

"I don't know."

"Come on. I got plenty of room."

"I'll check with my grandma."

"Okay, wait up." Reese turned back to Luke. "Hey, good talking to you, preach." Luke called after him, "I'm here if you need me."

"I don't know what the fuck's come over me," Reese told Cole. "That preacher said some things that made sense. I never listened to a preacher that made sense before."

"Well. None of it makes sense to me."

His grandmother and mother looked at him with dread. His grandmother's face was pinched and pale, and Ruby chewed her bottom lip.

"She's all right," he told them. "They're both all right."

"Thank God," his grandmother said. "Thank God."

He told them the new plans, and they were thankful that they didn't have to spend the night in the crowded gym. On their way out, Cole went over to Michael and Trip. Trip was taking pictures, and Michael had out a notebook and a recorder. He started to defend himself, but Cole said he wasn't here about that.

"It's Lacy."

Relief washed over Michael's face when he told him.

"I was scared," he admitted.

"I told you," Trip said. "I told you she'd be okay."

Under the gym lights, Michael's face was still grimy, and he had blisters on his hands from the digging. Trip didn't look any better. Cole never would have expected them to help the way they did.

Then a heavyset girl, maybe eighteen or nineteen, came over. She wore pink sweats that were splattered with sludge. "You ready for me now?" she asked Michael.

Michael hooked a tiny microphone to her collar. He did not interview her the way they did on the news. He just sat next to her and occasionally jotted down notes and didn't say much, while she described what she'd seen. Cole remembered seeing her up there; he'd watched her wipe blood off a little kid. Now she talked slowly and never once broke down. Her face was steely with anger, like the faces of his mother and grandmother, like the face of Lacy. The women were stronger. His knees had buckled. Michael had had tears in his eyes.

Cole asked Michael if they wanted to go to Reese's, but he and Trip wanted to stay. "The media isn't going to cover this the way they should, you just wait."

"We gotta get up there," Trip said.

Michael looked at Cole. "Could I borrow your truck?"

"I'll take you up there myself. I'll come by in the morning."

"What time?"

"Early," he said, walking away. "Real early."

He pulled in front of Reese's. His mother and grandmother followed Reese inside, and Cole said he'd be in in a minute. Finally alone, he closed his eyes, breathed deeply.

He was exhausted. His eyelids fluttered, but he snapped them open. Wake up, he said. He made himself get out of the truck, and he got the trash bag out of the toolbox. The jewelry and money was all there. Some of the bills were moist, but they could be dried out. He opened the Christmas tin and took out some of the rings and coins that he'd stashed there, and poured out the remaining black water onto the driveway. Disintegrated postcards dribbled out with the mess. He looked up at the starry sky and wondered if he'd be able to forget about the bodies that were lined up on the hillside, and Arie Webb, who'd felt so light in his arms.

He was surprised by how brightly lit and warm Reese's house was. Everything was cleaned up. No blood, no broken glass. Reese was telling a story. His mother was laughing, his grandmother grinned sheepishly. Cole thought Reese was acting awfully queeny, but they didn't seem to mind.

"Man, you look beat. You can sleep in my room," Reese said. "I'll make up the extra bed for the ladies."

"What about you?" his grandmother asked. "We don't want to put you out."

"Don't worry about me, I like the sofa," Reese said. "I sleep there most of the time."

"Thanks," Cole said, meaning it.

He went upstairs and took a hot shower and wished the water would wash everything away. He scrubbed his face and rinsed and spit and looked at the red splotches on his legs and wondered if the rash was something toxic. He went into Reese's room, which was still a mess. The sheets weren't clean, but he was too tired to care. He lay down and his heart thudded. It was dark. The explosions echoed in his head. He could see the sludge caking the dead's eyes, filling their mouths. He felt like he couldn't get his breath and he sat up and switched on the light and the words from one of his granddaddy's favorite verses, old Isaiah 10:3, was loud in his head: *What will you do on that day of reckoning? To whom will you run for help?*

PART THREE

CHAPTER 16

TEN DAYS LATER he drove his mother and grandmother to Rockcamp to see what was left. On the way, they passed by yards where sofas and mattresses and toys and knickknacks were laid out, drying in the sun. As they got farther away from Stillwell they saw heaps of trees, the remains of houses. Blackened craters were cut out of the land, like burnings. Nothing looked like it could be saved. The National Guard and the U.S. Army Corps had just opened up this part of Route 16, but most of the mountain was still closed off to the public and media; only government or Heritage employees had access. In the immediate days after, Cole had tried to volunteer for a recovery team, but the National Guard would not let anyone help who was not called to duty. That hadn't stopped Cole from driving Michael and Trip around, taking back roads and avoiding barricades, and getting out to walk whenever the water was too high or a bridge was washed out, Trip taking pictures or shooting videos, Michael writing notes. Each time they went, Cole was stunned: houses buried, dead horses and cows, mangled cars and appliances flung across the creeks and fields like the shredded pieces of a nightmare, and in the background the incessant noise of bulldozers, backhoes, helicopters.

Whatever the world had looked like on the day that the black water came down, it looked even worse the day after, the wreckage naked and visible under the bright sun, laid out like a demolished city that had been spit up by a black sea.

By now everyone knew what had happened: the dam had begun to leak early in the morning, and at nine twenty-five a.m., the middle part of it collapsed, sending 200 million gallons of toxic sludge down over the ridges and into Dove Creek. Thorny Creek was the hardest hit; more or less wiped out—the wave had been over twenty feet high when it came down on the hollow, zigzagging over the land like a tornado. If it had gone three hundred yards in either direction, it would have killed hundreds more. It flooded streams and creeks all the way to Stillwell, running for eighteen miles, then began to slow, spilling into the Cherokee River. Since the lower part of the dam had not collapsed, they'd been able to head it off so that all two billion gallons had not let loose. Nobody living downstream had been informed, except by word of mouth, neighbor to neighbor. The final count of the dead was sixty-four, but some were still missing, including Lacy's friend Blue Tiller.

The governor talked about the dead being heroes and commemorated them on TV. The president of the United States sent federal aid and talked about passing bills. Heritage had been holding press conferences and meetings, offering condolences and hauling in clean water and promising a thorough cleanup. A man on TV said, "We're investing millions of dollars into this." Cole didn't see how it could ever be the same. The streams and creeks were thick walls of sludge. The wells ruined. The National Guard was delivering bottled drinking water, but people still bathed in what came out of the faucets, those who still had running water. What else could they do? The red splotches on Cole's skin had disappeared, but he heard about others having them too. He did not go to the doctor, did not want to know.

The newspaper and TV people from the state capital and New York and D.C. descended on Dove Creek. Cameras were everywhere. But they couldn't get access to the site and did not seem to grasp the immensity of the destruction. They talked about the dead and the failure of the rescue, but they didn't understand the layout of the land or what the mountaintop removal sites looked like. They were pushy and nosy, demanding stories. Cole watched one of the segments on the national nightly news, but it seemed like all that the newsman talked about was how poor everybody was. His grandmother said, "See how they do us? Anytime we get attention, it's to show how backward we are. Just like in the days of LBJ." Cole had snapped off the TV in disgust.

Though some people had been able to move back into their homes, two thousand were left homeless, including the Freemans. The high school served as a temporary shelter, and people had no choice but to move into the trailer parks that the government had set up on the edges of Stillwell and Zion. His grandmother said she would never move to one of those. For now, she stayed at Rebecca's and his mother was at Naomi's—since the flood, she hadn't said anything else about leaving, and she'd gotten her job back at the Pizza Shack. Cole felt too confined at his aunts', like he was always being watched, so he stayed with Reese, which had its own drawbacks: Reese high on speed and paranoid and drilling Cole with questions about God, swearing again and again that he was going to quit using and start his life over. Luke Cutter's phone number was taped to the refrigerator, and Reese said one day he would call on him, that the preacher would turn him right. But the only person he ever called was Terry Rose, even after he'd sent that crew over to beat the hell out of him. Terry never came to the house when Cole was there, but Cole knew he was around.

He turned onto Rockcamp Road and after about a half mile came to a barricade.

"Now what?" his grandmother asked.

He stopped the truck; up ahead a part of the road was washed out, and uprooted sycamores lay across the land like giant caskets. The creek water was gray and still. "We'll have to walk." He looked at his grandmother. "You sure you want to do this?"

"I need to see it. I need to know what I got left."

They'd brought along a disposable camera, rubber gloves, and flashlights; they were not sure what to expect. Cole had heard how the National Guard was condemning houses, knocking them down with bulldozers and burning them up, sometimes without telling the owners.

He helped his grandmother along, while Ruby, in jeans and leather jacket and hiking boots she'd borrowed from Naomi, raced ahead. They heard the churning of bulldozers and backhoes in the distance. Cole guided his grandmother around the enormous ruts, the broken boards and scraps of furniture.

"You reckon any of this is ours?" she asked.

"I don't know."

Floyd Mitchell's shack had been knocked off its foundation. There was a giant white X spray-painted on the door. The old man had been brought into the nursing home, crying about his dead dog. He'd looked at Cole and did not know he was.

There was also an X on Cole's trailer. When he forced open the door, black greasy water poured out. Gagging from the stench, he stepped inside. He shone his flashlight around, snapped a few pictures. The stench was unbearable, a mix of rot and chemicals, and he covered his mouth and nose with the sleeve of his jacket. The cupboards bulged with sludge, and in the living room the stereo speakers floated like buoys. The water in his bedroom reached halfway up his knee-high rubber boots. He opened drawers and looked at the damp, moldy underwear and T-shirts. The photographs on the wall were also dotted with mildew, and he carefully removed them and slid them in his jacket pocket.

"Ain't much that can be saved," he said.

His grandmother shook her head, lips pursed.

And then, the house. Standing but broken, a giant X scrawled across the door. The footbridge had been washed away, and the lawn was a scar of ripped-up earth. His mother's Camry was sinking, along with the trailer that had smashed into it. Cole sloshed across the waterlogged yard. The front porch was caved in. He tried the back door, but it was jammed. The side door was the only way.

He went back over to his grandmother, who had found a mound of dirt to stand on. "You can't go in there without boots."

"You go in first, then let me borrey yours when you come back out," she said.

While she waited outside, Cole and Ruby went in together, the beams of their flashlights revealing black pockets of water, submerged furniture. They covered their noses and mouths. They walked across the family room, their boots sinking into the wet carpet, and snapped pictures and went upstairs and here everything looked untouched, though still the sickening stench oozed from the walls and floorboards. Cole picked up a photograph of his grandfather and it fell apart in his hands.

They stood in his grandparents' room and golden light shone through the window and Ruby went over to the small oak desk his grandfather had built many years ago and she touched the surface and remembered him and Cole could still see the old man as well, sitting there with a lamp at his side, scribbling, then he recalled how they'd been sorting through his things. Probably all of his writings were gone.

"We better go tell her," he said.

They walked quietly through the house, taking what they could. Cole found his grandfather's King James, damp but intact.

His grandmother stood shivering. "Anything left?" she asked, but didn't wait for their answer. "Give me your boots."

"Be careful," he told her.

Ruby offered to go with her, but she wanted to do it alone. Cole stood in his sock feet on a dry rock while his grandmother stepped into the boots, wobbling at first.

"It's gone," Ruby said to Cole.

"I know it."

Even if the house could be fixed up, the debris cleared away and walls scrubbed clean, the oily black mud would still be there, buried underneath, seeping.

After about fifteen minutes, his grandmother came out and sat down on a rock and pulled off the boots and put her shoes back on without saying a word. He expected her to be crying. It was like that now. Sometimes he'd walk into his aunt's house and find her staring at the TV, crying. It wasn't just her. He'd see people crying at the grocery store or the gas station, or they would just stand there, looking lost. This time, though, his grandmother's eyes were dry.

"You okay?"

She stood up on her own, refusing his hand.

"You and your cousins and uncles are gonna have to haul everything out that's still good," she told him. "It ain't all ruined, but it will be if it sets in this dampness anymore."

"What about the house?" Ruby asked.

She shook her head. "This ain't our home anymore."

"What about the cemetery?"

"I don't want to see that," she said sharply. Then she sucked in her breath and looked at them with a hardness in her eyes. "We're all going to that meeting next week. You understand?"

Cole nodded.

"Ruby?"

"Okay, whatever."

"Good. Now take me out of here. I can't stand it no more."

* * *

It did not look like Cole was getting off work anytime soon, but he didn't mind. It was easier to be here than to be around Reese or his grandmother. Within these walls very little had changed. Though a few of the old people talked about the disaster, many of them did not know about it, or they'd already forgotten. He did not tell the patients or other aides that he'd been up there, that he'd carried the dead.

Linda told him about the newest patient, an old mountain woman who'd been found up in that mess and had just been transferred from the county hospital. "She might seem a little nutso, but don't let her fool you. She's a spitfire."

He glanced at the name on the chart, Beatrice Anne Tiller. The woman was gray and wrinkled, and so thin that her bones jutted out, stretching the skin. "Hey there," he said, but she only stared at him with glassy eyes. He took her blood pressure, temperature, and heart rate before he looked closer and realized who she was. "There are some people that are going to be real happy to see you," he said.

He told Linda he was taking his break. "I'm going over to the Wigwam. You want anything?"

"How about a slice of pecan pie?"

Cole walked quickly up the street, happy that he could finally deliver good news. He'd seen very little of Lacy over the past two weeks, and the few times he had, she was withdrawn, distant. She'd lost friends and neighbors, her home. He did not know what to say to her.

When he walked in, she was behind the counter pouring coffee, her face a mask. It was busy and she did not see him. Cole was not surprised to see Michael there. He was always around now, scribbling in his notebook, talking to people. He'd published another article, and his was the only one that got it right. Michael had friends here now. Stories. He no longer needed Cole's.

When Lacy saw Cole, she asked how he was doing. Her voice was flat; the light had gone out of her eyes.

"Blue Tiller's at the nursing home," he said.

She stared at him like she didn't hear, then, "Oh, thank God." She bit her bottom lip. "I thought for sure she was dead."

"She's pretty weak, but stable. You should come over and see her."

"I will. I'll bring Sara Jean."

"That's great," Michael said. "That's really great."

Lacy smiled. "Best thing I've heard in a while."

She was looking at Michael with a steadiness in her eyes, a twitch of her lips. Cole knew that look. He felt confused. Then he noticed that Michael was smiling at Lacy as if they were the only two in the room.

"I got to get back to work," Cole said.

She glanced at him. "Okay. Thanks again."

"See you later," Michael called out, but Cole didn't answer.

He crossed the street to the nursing home and smashed out his cigarette before he went through the automatic doors. He'd forgotten Linda's pie.

"They were out," he told her.

"Well, that's a first."

He felt too numb to be angry. He worked as if he were in a trance, changing diapers and bedpans. After he spent the hour cleaning up shit and talking with the old people, the numbness began to shake itself off. Lacy and Michael. *Christ.*

When he returned to Blue Tiller's room, she was awake and thirsty. He filled a plastic cup with water and adjusted her so that she was propped up. She breathed heavily. The water dribbled down her chin.

"You need anything else?"

A shadow crossed her face. "My house, my land," she said. "What happened to my dog?"

"You just rest."

"Who are you?"

He told her his name and she said, "Freeman, from Rock-camp?" He said yes, and she said she knew his grandfather. "Holy roller."

"Yep."

"Your mama the one that left?"

"That's her," he said. "She's back."

Someone coughed. He looked up. Sara Jean and Lacy were at the door. "Hey," he said. "Come on in." He looked at Blue. "You got visitors."

Sara Jean got right in her face. "It's Sara Jean," she said loudly.

"I know who it is. I ain't blind."

Cole turned to go, and Lacy, still in the doorway, moved out of the way. Then she said, "Hey, Michael told me what you did up there."

He turned, waiting.

"How you helped those people. How you wouldn't let Trip take their pictures. That was good of you."

He shrugged. "It wasn't anything."

They stood there looking at each other, then at their feet. It felt awkward between them. He did not want to think of Lacy and Michael talking about him.

"You better go in and visit," he said.

"Okay. See you around?"

"Yeah, I'll see you."

Every day there was another funeral in Dove Creek. Cole read the announcements in the paper or saw the signs on church billboards, and although he recognized most of the names—a few people he'd gone to school with, a customer's boy—the only person he knew well was Arie Webb, whose sludge-covered face he saw every night when he tried to drift off to sleep. Her blind sister, Janice, had been moved to an institution up in Charleston. He wondered what had happened to Arie's stash. Just when it seemed like things were quieting down, he heard that his customer Taylor Jones, the Iraq vet, had shot himself. Cole did not go to any of the funerals. Everything was fucked up. Several of his suppliers had been displaced; they had been moved into the nursing home or were living with their kids. Those who had not even been in the path of the flood were also nervous, afraid they would be next. He did not know what to tell them. He went to see them, but the visits were different now. And his customers were even worse, jumpy and paranoid. Everyone in the county was on edge, like they'd just realized that one day they would die.

CHAPTER 17

HE CARRIED IN Blue Tiller's supper tray.
"You should be in the dining hall with the others," he told her. "There's no reason for you to be eating in bed."

"I don't like it out there."

Blue had already gained a couple of pounds. She liked the chocolate Ensure. "I never had that before," she said. "It's good." She was getting stronger, but her breathing would never get any easier; the tiny air sacs inside her lungs were swollen like wood ticks, fat with blood.

"It would be good for you to talk to people."

"I talk to you."

"Yeah, you do." Every day she told him stories. She told him how she and her husband George used be roving picketers, going from one mining site to another, fighting for the union and for blacklung benefits.

"It used to be all about the union, but people don't care about that anymore."

"It's too hard now," Cole said. "They all got busted up."

"When I was a child, the coal companies sent in thugs. With guns. My daddy was an organizer, and one day they broke into our house. Mama got out her shotgun. Made them put back every piece of furniture they overturned. The union was everything. We all came together, black and white."

"You ought to talk to Mabel Johnson. You two could swap stories."

"Mabel," she said. "Yes, she's a good woman. I know her."

"She's here. You could go talk to her. Socialize."

But Blue wasn't listening. "Do you know what we did when they started the strip-mining? We held them off by laying down in front of the bulldozers. A bunch of women. And illiterate men with shotguns. The police was always on the side of the coal companies, and they dragged us away like dogs. But we fought them tooth and nail."

"It's different now," he said.

She shook her head, disappointed. "Boy, tell me when I can get out of here."

"That's not for me to decide. You got to talk to the doctor."

She dipped the spoon into a bowl of applesauce. "There's that meeting tonight."

"You're in no condition for that."

"You going?"

"I guess so." His grandmother had already called twice to remind him.

"I used to wish the sky would crack wide open or the mountains would fall, thought that was the only way to wake people up, get them to see," Blue said. "Well, now we've got that. We've got poison in the water. Still it ain't enough."

"People are scared," he said. "They don't know what to do."

She stared at him with ice-blue eyes. "You still don't know who I am."

"What do you mean?"

"I was there when you was born." Behind all the wrinkles and lines and harsh edges, her face was tender. "I was there."

At first he laughed her off, but the longer he looked at her, the more he thought she was telling the truth. "What are you talking about?"

"You thought you were born in a hospital? You was born at home."

"I guess I never thought about it."

"I remember every baby I delivered. I delivered babies all over Dove Creek. Never had none of my own. But I delivered them, I remember every one." She eyed him. "You were the only one I saw born with the caul."

"What's that?"

"Comes from inside your mother. It covers the face, like a veil. It's a good omen."

"Didn't do me any good." He looked at her hard. Her old hands the first that ever touched him. "So were you there when she ran off?"

She stopped chewing. "Honey, she never run off."

"Hell yes she did."

"Well, yes, she left. But she didn't have much say in the matter."

"What do you mean?"

"Your granddaddy. He couldn't forgive her. He was shamed by her. His daughter getting in trouble like that. It was different back then. He took you out of her arms, then drove her to the bus station."

"What?"

"You didn't know?"

Cole stared ahead at the beige walls. Beeping machines and muffled TVs echoed from other rooms. *Naked I came out of my mother's womb; and naked I shall return thither; the Lord gave and the Lord hath taken away.* He looked again at Blue. She was focused on the food, chewing loudly, smacking her lips. Pork chops, mashed potatoes. He wondered if she was crazy. She noticed him looking at her.

"Well, you turned out all right. Didn't you?"

He forced a laugh. "Hell, I don't think so."

"That's just your granddaddy talking." She pointed the fork at him. "Can't you get me some salt? There's no taste to this."

Later, as he drove over to the high school, dressed in his scrubs, her words continued to ring like tiny bells in his ears. It was a strange feeling, like looking at an old picture of himself that he did not recognize.

Cars and pickups filled the parking lot, like on ball game nights. A group of middle-aged men congregated outside the double doors, and Cole stood there for a while and listened to them talk. One of them had shaky hands; another couldn't stop blinking.

"Did you hear what kind of emergency plan they had in place? Some fool was supposed to stand there with a bullhorn."

"I'll tell you what their emergency plan was—run like hell."

The oldest of the group, a man with a beard and thick wrinkles under his eyes, looked at Cole. "What do you think, son? What do you think of all this?"

He hesitated. "I don't know. Seems pretty bad."

"Ain't nothing pretty about it," the man said. "It's bad. Plain bad."

Cole was surprised by the large turnout. He'd heard Lacy complain about the permit hearings, when only about a dozen would show up, but tonight there were close to three hundred people in the auditorium. Newscasters, cops, men in suits, and the familiar tragedy-stricken faces. He saw a few of his suppliers, a few customers. Near the front was Lacy Cooper, her arm around Sara Jean. Ellen's fiancé was in uniform. Trip with his camera. He saw Michael in the first row, his notebook open. In the back a group of young hippie types, out-of-towners, held signs: "People Not Profits," "Heritage Murderers," "Coal Keeps West Virginia Poor." The room was stuffy; he shucked off his flannel jacket and looked around until he spotted his mother and grandmother.

His grandmother moved her coat and purse from the chair next to her. "I didn't know if you were coming or not."

"I said I'd be here."

Ruby wore a denim skirt and low-cut blouse, her face sparkling with makeup, her hair pinned back.

"What are you all dressed up for?"

"I want to look decent," she said. "In case I get on TV."

The mayor, whose son worked for Heritage, walked to the front. "Folks, we're running a little late. I apologize, I know you're eager to get this show on the road. We'll start in about fifteen minutes." He told them to help themselves to the punch and cookies.

There was a buzz in the room, shifting in seats, moving around. Ruby went out for a cigarette. "I'm on pins and needles," she said.

His grandmother unwrapped a stick of Juicy Fruit and broke it in half. She seemed hopeful. She'd been going to meetings, coming home with pamphlets and books. Cole was not surprised, but the rest of the family did not know what to think; they lived too far away to understand, to have felt that terror in their bones. None of them had shown up tonight. He and Ruby and his grandmother were on a team, the three of them. Whenever they were around others, his grandmother would bring up how Cole had driven them up to Thorny Creek to help out, or she bragged about how he'd cared for his grandfather and stuck by the land, half-truths turning into one story in her head. The rest of the family still thought of him as a fuckup, the same way they thought about his mother.

She offered him a half of the stick of gum and he folded it in his mouth and bit into instant sweetness. "Blue Tiller is over at the nursing home," he said.

"That's what I heard. She's all right?"

"She's pretty weak."

"She almost got your granddaddy to speak at one of them meetings against strip-mining a long time ago. But you know how he was, didn't feel right preaching politics." She snapped her gum. "I wish he would have. Maybe we could have stopped all this."

Cole wiped his sweaty palms on his pants legs. He wasn't sure how to start his question. Maybe he should just skip it. His grandmother was chatty and wound up about the meeting, and he didn't want to ruin her mood. But when she paused to catch her breath, he spoke up. "Blue told me that she delivered me," he said quickly. He stopped and tried to sound more casual, nonchalant. "She delivered me," he said again. "At home."

"That's true."

"That's not all she told me."

She raised her eyebrows. "What else did she say?"

His words came out in a rush: "Granddaddy made Mom leave. That's what she said. It wasn't her choice. Nobody ever told me that before."

For a few seconds, there was no reaction. The smell and taste of the chewing gum reminded him of being a kid. He could see the story in her eyes, but she would not let go. "Honey, he made some mistakes," she said.

"How come Ruby never said anything?"

"Maybe she doesn't want you to think bad of him. It was a long time ago, a hard time."

"Where did he send her?"

"She was supposed to go to Kentucky, to stay with his kin."

"But she didn't go."

She shook her head. "No. She went her own way."

"You never said anything," he accused.

"I don't like to think about all of that." She put her hand on his knee. "I just can't."

A man said they were ready to begin, and people took their seats. Cole felt a lump in his throat. Maybe there was nothing else to say.

His mother was one of the last to return, squeezing in front of people. Cole noticed how men checked her out. She'd been just a kid, he thought. Pretty, and scared. A newborn baby squalling in her arms. He'd always imagined her riding off in a fast car, not driven to the bus station by her father. He chewed his gum fiercely, the flavor already gone. His grandmother's gnarled hand remained on his knee.

A group of men in slacks and button-down shirts sat at a long table in front of the room. They were Heritage men, including the vice president. Cole saw the engineer that had been hitting on his mother at the Eagle, and he hissed, "Look who's up there." Ruby saw him. "That bastard." There were also lawyers and representatives from federal and state government agencies. Plastic bottles of clear drinking water from some mountain spring in the Alps sat before them. The old man behind Cole said, "Vice president, huh? The president too busy?"

"Busy destroying somebody else's mountain," someone else shot back.

The VP thanked them for coming. He was stocky and bullish, with dark hair combed to one side. He told them that there was no denying that this was a terrible disaster, but that Heritage would do its best to clean up and find homes for those who had been dislocated. He assured them that Heritage was a responsible and fair company. He was no outsider. He was born and raised down in Bucks County, he told them, he understood.

"You ruined us," a woman in the audience shouted. "We lost everything."

The VP paused, but when he continued, he sounded calm and clear. He used words like *community*, *restoration*, and *reclamation*. The crowd was not impressed. Glazed eyes, hardened faces. Some were teary-eyed, a few cried. What they'd seen up there had changed them. People trapped in their homes. People hanging from trees. Black poison dribbling out of mouths. The images playing and replaying in their heads. They'd seen and touched and felt the horror, and now they were supposed to continue on with their lives.

Sweat dotted foreheads and necks; women fanned themselves with their hands. The heat was smothering, and Cole wondered why they did not turn down the thermostat, unless this was what they wanted—they were trying to make the crowd uncomfortable, to break them. A few walked out. Sighs of disgust. His grandfather had never lost a crowd like this. The old man had believed in every word he said. But the man who was talking did not appear to believe in anything. His eyes were like mirrors. He dodged questions about the law, about culpability. He used the word *neighbor* again and again.

Lacy Cooper got up and stood at one of the microphones that were set up in the aisles. "Where would you like us to go?"

"Well—"

"Because from the looks of things, you're taking over. And you don't care how you get rid of us." She went on to name the chemicals that were in the sludge, and recited numbers and statistics, and read a list of the company's other violations. She was articulate and smart, and when she finished, the crowd applauded and shouted support.

But after it quieted down, the VP responded in the same even tone. "Ma'am, I know how this must look. But you have to understand, we are terribly shocked and saddened. We will help all of you, each and every one."

"If you want to help, it seems to me you should leave us alone," she said.

The man went on to speak about how Heritage was a part of the community, until the activists in the back began to shout out facts about job rates and the economy: the mining machines had taken the place of hundreds of jobs, and this was one of the poorest parts of the country, even though the coal companies made billions. Then the mayor stepped up to the microphone and said it was time for a break.

"I'm about to roast," Cole's grandmother said.

Cole needed a smoke. He followed Lacy and Sara Jean out, but lost sight of them in the crowded hallway.

"Hey, Cole." Michael held out his hand, and Cole shook it. A hand that had touched Lacy. It was cool, strong.

"I knew it would be bad, but the way this guy is whitewashing everything, hell. They haven't even really apologized yet."

"They won't. We all know that."

"I'm sorry, Cole."

"For what?"

"It's just—well, I know I can just go back to New York. I know it's not the same for me. You're the one that has to live here."

Michael was looking at him kindly, like they were old friends, and Cole didn't know if it was shame or rage he was feeling.

"Nothing to be sorry for." He added quickly, "I need a smoke," and walked away before Michael could say anything else. On his way out, he bumped into Luke Cutter.

"Brother Cole," he said.

They went outside with the smokers. Luke wore a leather jacket and jeans and boots, and did not look like a preacher. Cole took a long drag, felt better when the smoke filled him. Luke's eyes were on him. Deep eyes, Jesus-like eyes.

"I seen the dead up there," Cole said.

Luke said he'd been talking to a woman who lost her children in the flood, but that there was no spite in her, no bitterness. "She's not blaming anybody."

"Seems like she never would have lost her babies if that dam wasn't up there."

"We have to be there for those who lost their family, who lost their homes. We can't be blaming." He squeezed Cole's arm. "We don't need outsiders coming in here to stir things up."

A man came to the door and said the meeting was starting again, and people snuffed out their cigarettes and filed back inside. It was just Cole and Cutter. Their breath bursting in the air. His young, serious face. In church he'd told his story: he'd walked away from his daddy, he'd walked away from God. "But God did not let me go," he'd shouted. "He came looking for me. And now here I am, back in the arms of Jesus." When Cole had left the church, it was the first time, the only time, that he'd stood up to his granddaddy. He had walked away from all that he knew and went down to the swimming hole where Terry Rose was waiting for him.

"I got to get back in there."

Luke looked like there was more he wanted to say, but Cole went inside. He walked down the fluorescent halls and back into the crowded room. The engineer was explaining what had happened, using diagrams and drawings. Cole's mother looked over and mouthed, "He's a liar." He went on for another ten minutes, and Cole thought that his fuming mother was going to jump right out of her seat and slug him. But it was a frail-looking woman in the back who stood up.

"I can't stand to listen to this anymore."

She was little and angular, like a bird, with short brown hair. She stood at a microphone and told her story. When the wall of sludge came down, she and her daughter scrambled for the hills, but the wave took her daughter from her. "Like she was nothing, like she was a piece of wood, or a leaf." Her voice broke. "You sit up there and talk, but you don't understand. It wasn't just our houses. People died. Children. Babies."

The engineer's face was drawn and ash-colored. He looked like a man about to go down. But the vice president was unmoved: "We know we can't bring them back, ma'am, but we can do our best to clean up the mess, to make sure this never happens again."

"It'll happen again. If not that, then some other disaster. The mountains is too torn up," an old-timer said. "They can't hold the rain."

"You got it so we can't even go up there," someone else said. "We can't even get up there to hunt or fish."

"The mountains can't take what you're doing to them," called out his grandmother. Cole looked over, surprised. She was on the edge of her seat. "You've made a mess of everything."

Ruby said, "Keep talking, Mama. Get up there to the microphone."

"Oh, he ain't listening."

She was right. The VP was just repeating everything he'd said during the first half of the meeting. The only one in this room with a voice. He said that it was to be expected that emotions were running high, but that people had to understand that the company was on their side. There was no one to blame, it was just that the snow and rain had accumulated. It was an accident, he said. "It wasn't anything we did. It rained and flooded, and that's an act of God."

The phrase was nothing new to the people in the room, but still, the words cut deep, anger spreading through the crowd like a fever. Cole tried to stay calm. Bit his lip hard. Then he looked up at the man again and before he could think it through, he was out of his seat and walking up the aisle. He stood behind a microphone. Everyone's eyes were on him, and he remembered when teachers called on him and the kids would laugh, *Spit it out, retard*.

"That ain't no act of God." Surprised by the echo of his voice, Cole stepped back.

"Rain and snow are natural occurrences, son."

"G– g–" He stopped, started over. "God didn't make those chemicals." When he touched the microphone, bringing it closer, the movement caused a loud scratching sound. He struggled to spit out another sentence. "God n-never made no sludge dam."

A few called out in support. It was almost like being in church, the people encouraging him, *That's right, tell him!* and he wondered if this was what his grandfather had experienced, if this was what the anointing felt like, a voice running through him, a feeling of wholeness. He took a deep breath—*speak plainly*—and the scripture came out of him like a sudden exhale.

"In Revelations, the Bible talks about who is going to be saved," Cole said. "It says that God *shouldest destroy them which destroy the earth.*"

"What?"

"Well. That's what it says."

The man stared at him uncomprehending, and Cole felt the heat jump from his throat to the back of his neck. *Retard.* He started to go back to his seat and then saw Lacy watching him. She had tried to show him. They had stood together on a flattened mountain and could see for miles, all of the fake green and the gray, like being lost in a gigantic cemetery.

"Wait," Cole said.

Heads turned his way again; the VP stopped talking.

"You've made all of us too scared to stand up for ourselves. Made us think there was nothing we could do. That we just had to accept it." This time Cole ignored the sound of his voice, and didn't get stuck on the words. "You took what was ours," he said. "And now you're just telling lies, just like we've been telling ourselves."

"Now listen, son—"

But the crowd had reached their breaking point. Someone yelled out that they were tired of his bullshit, and others joined in, a cacophony of inconsolable voices. Cole walked up the aisle.

His mother was smiling at him. She was here. His granddaddy had ripped him out of her arms. But she'd come back, and now she was here. He sat down and she leaned over and squeezed his hand. He looked straight ahead, but he left his hand in hers. The mayor stepped up to the microphone. "Folks, we're all hurting," he said. "This is a sad, sad time."

CHAPTER 18

Two months went by. It was early April. Green grass, budding trees. Mayflowers and bird's-foot violets rising up. Yet there were so many reminders, so many places where nothing grew. The National Guard and U.S. Army Corps had vanished, and the media had packed up their cameras and moved on. The government sent in psychologists to talk to people, but most people that Cole knew, himself included, did not speak of what they saw that day or what they still saw at night when they closed their eyes. Cole just wanted everyone to pull themselves together; the high emotions made him edgy. He was renting a little one-story house on the edge of Stillwell with his mother and grandmother. They called it temporary and talked about buying land somewhere else. The house sat up near the road, with other houses crowded on each side of it. They could hear their neighbors' TVs and arguments and their barking dogs, and the noise of cars and trucks.

It was hard to keep track of where everybody had gone. Lacy and Sara Jean had moved into one of the government trailer parks on the other end of Stillwell. Though Cole had not seen Lacy since the night of the town meeting, Sara Jean came to the nursing home almost every day to visit Blue, and he learned from her that Lacy was becoming more involved, that she had started a group called Dove Creek Defense. There were other activists living here now, strangers coming down from Charleston and up from North Carolina, determined to help. Several of Cole's customers had also relocated to the trailer parks, and a few, like Jody Hampton, simply disappeared. Michael had left. He was going away to write his book. He'd stopped by the nursing home on his way out of town; they shook hands, but there wasn't much to say. Michael had wished him good luck, and Cole said thanks, but later thought about it and wasn't sure what Michael was referring to. Cole had not seen Charlotte Carson or Terry Rose. Nor had he seen Reese Campbell, not in the past month. He did not know if he wanted to see him. It was rumored that Reese was off speed and that he had found Jesus.

This morning he woke before sunrise. He made scrambled eggs, toast, a pot of coffee. He ate quickly, standing in the ugly, cramped kitchen. All of the furniture had come with the rental, mismatched pieces from secondhand stores. There were a few of his grandmother's dishes and belongings, but not enough to make the place feel like home.

They'd saved what little they could from the house, but most of it was molded and disintegrated beyond recognition. It had been a sad day. Only Cole and his mother and grandmother had been prepared for the scale of the destruction. Several times his aunts broke down in tears, and even the uncles were red-eyed and sentimental. They wanted to try to repair everything, but Cole's grandmother told them just to haul it away. His cousins were nervous around her, ashamed that they worked for Heritage. Nobody mentioned the cemetery, which had been washed away; they could not bear to think that Clyde Freeman was no longer in the ground. At the end of the day, covered in grime and sludge and dust, they walked away and did not look back.

Heritage had been cleaning up, like they said they would, and every day they moved more equipment up the mountain, sucking sludge out of the waterways, digging it out of the yards. They'd never get it all. By summer things would look all right, but the sludge would still be there, underneath, strangling the roots of the trees and plants. An investigation was under way, but the governor had his hand deep in Heritage's money pot and nobody was expecting much of a result. Instead, people were turning to the courts. There were two hundred citizens involved in a class-action lawsuit. His grandmother and mother were a part of it. He was not. He did not want to be tangled up in any court, did not want to be near the law.

Recently, the law was turning up the heat, probably to take some of the attention off Heritage. More meth labs were busted, a couple of small-time dealers picked up. Cole heard about an old lady in Bucks County who was arrested for selling painkillers and he knew he needed to get out. He could smell it like a slow-burning fire. But he wanted to make one last sweep: buy as much as he could and sell it to the junkies who needed it most, who would buy at a higher price. It was easy to find drugs right now because doctors were filling out prescriptions for nerve pills left and right—he'd actually lost a few of his regulars who suddenly had easy access. Luckily, the government trailer parks were rife with drug use, so almost every week he found a few new customers. He planned to buy as much as he could and then sell everything: then he would be free.

Cole turned onto the narrow road that led to Cazy Creek. Though sycamores leaned toward the sun and the reeds along the stream glistened in purple and gold, black rings stained the tree trunks and the yard was a mess. Still, Elvira Black had told Cole that she wasn't leaving. Elvira was one of his regulars; she always had big stashes of Oxy. She was a sassy, good-natured woman who used the money Cole gave her to pay her bills, including

Internet service. She was always telling him about crazy things she read on the Internet.

He maneuvered his way around the junk on the porch and rapped on the door. When there was no answer, he went in and was engulfed by the stench of rotting garbage. Elvira's little terriers ran up, yipping and jumping at his ankles, flattening their devilish ears. Everywhere he looked were piles of books, jewelry, clothes, pictures, and overstuffed boxes. There was hardly any room to walk. He peeked in the kitchen. A rotting ham sat on the counter, drawing flies. He went down the hall and into the bedroom and hit the light switch. She was crumpled on the floor.

"Elvira," he said. "Elvira, can you hear me?"

He felt her pulse humming in her neck and gently rolled her over. Her eyes were open. She looked frightened, but he told her who he was and her face relaxed. "I been getting these dizzy spells."

"Are you hurt?"

"I don't know."

She put her arms around his neck, and he gently lifted her and lay her on the bed and looked her over. Nothing appeared to be broken or sprained, but there was a large bruise on her hip, a goose egg on her brow.

"The dogs," she said. "What about my dogs?"

"The dogs are okay."

"Two of them drowned," she said angrily. "They got swept away. Two of my dogs."

"Elvira, where's your son? When's the last time he was around?"

She looked perplexed. "I think he's in the pen again. I ain't sure when he was here last . . . I been having these dizzy spells. I can't explain it, I've just been feeling different."

"I'm taking you to the doctor."

"No, no doctor. That's what they want."

"Who?"

"They're trying to steal my house," she said. "They'll get in here if I leave. They've already been in here. They're trying to run me out."

"Nobody's been in here."

"They'll put me in that home. I ain't going into that home."

He told her to rest. "I'm gonna clean up a little."

"Will you feed the dogs?"

He said he would. He draped the moth-eaten blanket over her, and then started with the kitchen. Threw out rotted meat, cleaned out the refrigerator, wiped down the counters with Ajax, washed the dishes, and carried all of the trash bags to the fire pit. He made sure the dogs had food and water. He did not know what to do about Elvira. He stood in the middle of the mess in the living room and decided to leave it as it was. In the medicine cabinet he found OxyContin and Vicodin, and an old bottle of Ritalin, all of which went into his pockets. Then he went back in the kitchen and opened a can of tomato soup and while it was heating up, he sorted through a stack of mail and found her prescriptions and put these in his pocket as well.

He filled a plastic baggie with ice chips and ladled the tomato soup into a bowl. The dogs whined at his feet, and he kicked them away. "You still awake, Elvira?"

"Did you feed the dogs?"

"Yeah, don't worry." He propped her up with pillows and pressed the ice to her forehead. She took a few bites of the soup. "That's good," she said, but would not eat anymore. She was sweating. He gave her the pills she was supposed to take for the day, and two ibuprofen.

"Why do you got all those boxes out there for? You moving or something?"

"I'm packing it up so they don't find it."

"Who?"

"You know who," she snapped.

"For God's sake." He sighed. "Listen, I'm going to town to get you a few things." He showed her the envelope of cash. "I'm taking part of this out for the groceries," he said. "The rest of it I'm putting on your dresser. Don't lose it."

"I won't lose nothing." Then she said, "Did you feed the dogs?"

"Yes," he said. "The damn dogs are fine."

More bottles of pills sat on the counter. These Cole counted out and separated into Elvira's plastic pill box, the compartments divided by the days. She had enough to last the month. Then he stashed the Vicodin, Oxy, and Ritalin in his glove compartment, and he drove to the Pick N Save where he bought bread, milk, jugs of water, toilet paper, tomato soup, crackers, cheese, and baloney. She was sleeping when he returned. He would get social services to check on her, or he'd come back later tonight. He put everything away, then scrawled a note, telling her to make sure she ate something and to take her pills. Before he left, he rummaged through a few of the boxes. Most of it was worthless, but he did score a pair of pearl earrings and a ring.

He spent the rest of the day buying pills from the old folks and taking them to the store to get their prescriptions filled. He told them that he might not be buying from them anymore, and they did not understand. They asked if he was leaving, and he did not know how to answer them. He did not know. He gave them a little more money than usual and said he'd be around to visit.

Leona Truman said, "Well, you won't be seeing me here anymore."

"Why not?" Her little slice of paradise had been spared; it looked no different than usual. But she'd signed the papers. "I had to," she said. She looked scared and ashamed. Cole told her she'd done nothing wrong. He looked at the bottle she handed him. "Is this all you've got?"

"I'm supposed to get more in the mail. Come back in a day or two."

"Okay," he said. "I will."

Next he went to see the Williamses. He told them they needed to think about moving. "Something could happen here too." They said they would rather die in a disaster than leave their land. Tiny hugged him and Lottie kissed his cheeks, and he felt sick about driving away from them. The valley fill looming. Two little figures waving from the porch.

In Zion, he went to a pharmacy known for its negligent pharmacist, and he gave the old man Elvira Black's prescription slips and said he was her grandson. The man did not ask questions. By the time Cole got to work for his three o'clock shift, his glove compartment was stuffed full. He'd been going nonstop since dawn and couldn't believe that now he had to work at least until eleven.

He went to check on a new resident. She was in bed watching TV, the volume insanely loud, and in the chair next to her was a pretty middle-aged woman who introduced herself as her daughter, Lisa. Cole asked if she minded if he turned down the TV, and she laughed. "Please, do."

The woman, Florence, was small and elfin, with only a few wisps of gray hair left on her head. "*General Hospital*," Cole said. "You don't like that old show, do you?"

She grinned, and Lisa explained that her mother's hearing wasn't good. She also had cataracts and could not see very well. "I don't know how much of that show she can actually see or hear, but she'll throw a fit if I turn the channel. She's been watching it from the start."

Cole needed to take her temperature, but Florence wouldn't open her mouth. Lisa said, "Mom, it's okay. Open up." Florence's wrinkled lips finally parted, but when Cole set the thermometer under her tongue, she clamped down and attempted to chew it.

"Mom, it's not to eat. It's a thermometer."

Cole tried again, and the same thing happened. He explained to Florence what he was doing, in loud and simple words. She opened her mouth. He set the thermometer under her tongue. For a second, she was still. Then she began chewing wildly. Cole looked at Lisa, and they burst into laughter. It was the first time he'd laughed in a long time.

He took Florence's blood pressure and pulse without any trouble, then said he'd come back later to get her temperature. As he was leaving, Florence suddenly perked up.

"Now who was that cute little actor?"

Lisa laughed, looking at Cole. "He's your nurse, Mom."

"I've seen him on some TV show before."

"You think she's mixing me up with one of them soap stars?"

Lisa just smiled, and suddenly he felt shy. It had been a while. Maybe that would take the edge off. He was still smiling about it when he ran into Ellen in the hallway.

"What are you so happy about?"

He told her about Florence. She smiled, but it was forced.

"What's wrong?"

"Can we talk later?"

"Sure. You okay?"

"Yeah," she said, but he could tell she was not.

As Cole checked on the residents, he also went through drawers, suitcases, and pants pockets. Even though everything of value was supposed to go into the safe in Pete Andrew's office, the aides often forgot to check things in, and there had never been any locker or bag searches, the way they'd threatened. Still, he didn't find much. Some petty cash, a brooch, a wedding band.

Blue Tiller was sitting up in bed. "Do you know what the land used to look like?" she asked. "Wild strawberries used to grow. My mama would cook them and we'd spread them on thick slabs of bread. They were about the size of buttons. They were so sweet. You ever eat them?"

He shook his head.

"You don't know what you're missing." She looked over the top of the newspaper. "When are you going to help me get out of here, boy?"

Every day she asked him to help her escape. He'd already searched her belongings and knew that she had nothing. She'd come in with only a picture of her dead husband. He wondered if she'd lost everything, or if she'd always had nothing, which seemed more likely.

"There ain't nothing wrong with me," she continued. "They're keeping me in here on purpose. They don't want me going after the coal company."

The old folks' paranoia ate at their minds like salt on slugs. He checked her blood pressure and temperature, wrote the numbers on the chart. She still needed oxygen treatments twice a day. She had no family. No children. She would never leave.

"Did you see this?" She rattled the newspaper. "Coal company says they'll be mining up there at the end of the week. They were supposed to be shut down."

"I ain't looked at the paper yet."

"You ought to read more. You ought to know what's going on."

Then Sara Jean walked in.

"There's my girl," said Blue. She looked at Cole. "She knows what's going on."

"I don't doubt it."

Sara Jean scrambled up on the bed next to Blue. She looked wild. Her hair, as usual, was stringy, falling in her eyes, and she wore jeans that were patched at the knee, a ratty sweatshirt. Her sneakers were muddy, and he told her not to get the bed dirty. She threw the shoes off; her toes poked through the holes in her socks.

"Your mama working at the Wigwam today?"

"Yeah."

"Maybe I should go see her. You think she'd want to see me?"

She shrugged. Then she said, "I got to talk to Blue about something."

"What, you telling secrets?"

"We got things to discuss."

He pointed at Blue. "I better see you tomorrow at game night. You need to get out of that bed."

"I ain't playing games," she said angrily. "I ain't no child."

On break, Cole went to the Wigwam. Lacy stood at the counter, her back to him, her hair pinned up. Her neck was slender, pretty. He'd put his mouth on it many times, but the memory was distant, like a sad song.

"Hey there."

She turned. "Where you been hiding?"

"Nowhere. Just busy. How are you doing?"

She shrugged. "Just trying to hold on."

Her face looked strained, all bones and angles, and there were pale purple rings under her eyes. She was fierce and beautiful. He told her he was sorry for not being around.

"I take care of myself pretty good," she said.

"I know you do."

She asked where he was living, and he told her about the rental. She said that it sounded better than the trailer park. "I can't wait to get out of there."

"Where will you go?"

"I don't know. I'll tell you one thing, I'll never back down from them sons of bitches."

He hesitated. "Hey, you think it would be all right if we got together sometime?"

Finally, she cracked a smile. "I guess it wouldn't hurt."

He said he'd call her later.

"Yeah, well. I won't hold my breath."

The next hour was busy, but when he had a free moment, he peeked in on Blue. She was sleeping, and Sara Jean was packing clothes into a paper bag.

"What are you doing?"

Startled, she dropped Blue's nightgown on the floor. She had her mother's cheekbones, high and sharp. "Nothing," she said, still as a turtle.

"Don't be scared."

"I ain't."

"What are you packing for? Blue planning on leaving?"

"She don't want to stay here," she burst out. "She don't want to and she don't have to."

"She's got to get better. Then she can leave."

"You're lying," she said. "They don't let people out of here."

He looked at the pitiful bag of clothes. "She just can't walk out," he said. "She doesn't even have a car. Unless you're driving. You driving?"

She told him that they had a plan, looking at him with hope, needing him to be someone he was not.

"Who's coming for her?"

"My grandpa," she said. "He's friends with Blue."

"Your mom's old man? Does your mom know about this?"

"Not him. My *other* grandpa. My daddy's dad."

"He lives around here?"

"He lives in the mountains," she explained. "Gundy."

Cole remembered now. Lacy had told him about Denny's dad. Crazy, she'd said.

"Well, tell me when he gets here, I'd like to meet him." He tousled her hair. "You gonna stay here all evening? You want the TV on or something?"

She shook her head.

"Don't tell," she called after him. He said he wouldn't. As far as he could see, there was nothing to tell, except a silly story thought up by an old woman desperate to return to a life that no longer existed. He walked down the hall, passing Larry Potts, twiddling his thumbs, and Hazel Lewis, trying to take off her shirt. He used to imagine setting them free: Where would they go? They'd be more lost out there than they were in here. Like Elvira Black, her life falling apart around her, tossed and shoved into boxes.

Ellen came up to him. "Hey. You have time to talk?"

He shrugged. "Sure."

"Let's go outside."

They went out to the picnic table, sat under the canopy of a red maple. The evening sky held the lightness of spring. A breeze kicked up, Ellen shivered.

"You cold?" he asked.

"I'm all right."

They smoked, and around them crickets sang. She wasn't talking, so he told her about Elvira Black, said she was a friend of his grandmother's. "I'm worried." Ellen told him she would call social services and have them check it out. "Thanks," he said.

He zipped up his jacket; now he was the one shivering. He wondered if she wanted to talk to him about the union. He'd been hearing rumors; it seemed like this time something might happen. He told her he was in, if that was what she wanted to know. "I been thinking it might be all right," he said.

"They'll never get a union in here," she said. "That's just wishful thinking."

"Well, what is it? You can't keep me guessing all night. I've never seen you like this. Something happen at home, or is it work, or what?"

She looked at him. Her face was tense and small; he remembered when she first started working here, how he'd thought about asking her out. That seemed so long ago.

"Cole, I saw you," she said in a low voice.

The air snapped through his jacket. "What?"

"I saw you take stuff. I saw you a few months ago, and I saw you today."

"I don't know what you're talking about."

"Damn it, I saw you. You're the one."

He took a long drag on the cigarette, trying to steady himself. He tilted his head back until he could feel the night over him, the leaves above, the shadows, the smell of a new season. He looked at her. "I'm good to them, Ellen, you know I am."

"That doesn't make it right."

"You know how much I get paid," he said defensively. "I need it. My grandma needs it."

"Bullshit," she said, still talking in a hushed voice, practically spitting the word. "We all need it. It's about trust, Cole. It's about doing good."

"So now what, you're gonna bust me?"

She said nothing. He smoked furiously. He could not even look at her, he felt so much rage. He thought about her giving him the nursing books; she must have known all along that he would never be able to pick up and go away to school, she must have known that he would always be stuck here, stuck in his own skin.

"I'll give it all back," he said finally. "Is that what you want?"

"Listen to me. Linda suspects you. They'll press charges. I heard her talking to Pete."

"You told." He stood up. "You bitch, you told."

"I didn't. I swear I didn't. They've been watching you."

He was shaking, could not see straight. Everything seemed far away, her voice, her face. He held onto the edge of the table until he felt like it would break in his hands.

"There's more," she said quietly.

"I'm waiting."

"Look, I'm not making any kind of assumptions. But shit is going down, Cole. Randy told me, they're gonna be busting people left and right."

"What the hell are you saying?"

She stared him in the eye. "I'm warning you," she said. "I'm telling you for your own good. Those people you hang out with."

"I don't hang out with nobody."

"Look, Randy likes you. But in the next couple of weeks, things are going to happen. I'm warning you." She paused. "I'm sorry."

"Christ." Cole looked at her, waiting for her to take it all back, but she just said, "I should get in there," and she walked through the doors and he was alone.

He stood under the tree and rubbed his fists against his eyes. "Goddamn you," he said. "Stupid fucking asshole, you fucked up, you fucked up." He said this over and over, like it was scripture, and he looked up at the sky, saw nothing, only darkness. He threw down his cigarette and stormed inside. He didn't know what to do. He was lit up with rage. He stared at a resident's chart until the words blurred and jumped around. You can do this, he told himself, Pull it together. He completed his duties in a daze of disbelief and anger. Avoiding Ellen. Avoiding everyone. When his shift was almost over he walked into Blue's room and saw her sitting in a chair with the paper bag on her lap. Sara Jean was gone.

"Well, go on," he said. "Nobody's stopping you."

She scowled. "What's wrong with you?"

He was afraid if he let up for even a second, he would fall apart. He stayed rigid. Clenched teeth, fists. He stared at her, sick and feeble, holding on to that pathetic shopping bag.

"I don't know what you think you're going to do," he said. "It's all over and done with. Nothing can be changed."

"I've lived eighty-five years, and I would not be alive today if there was not change." She looked over his shoulder, and her voice softened. "I knew you'd come."

A gaunt, bearded man stood in the doorway. He was dressed in tattered army fatigues. He looked like he was afraid to go any farther, his anxious eyes darting around the room. But then he walked in, his boots not making a sound.

"I'd kill myself if I was in a place like this," he said, his voice gravelly, ugly.

"That's why I'm getting out."

The man stepped toward Cole. "She don't belong here."

"He'll let me go. He ain't like the rest."

Cole kept his eyes on Blue. He did not want to look at the man again, did not want to see him, but still he smelled him, the sour sweat of him, his wildness.

"I don't know where you're going," Cole said, "but I sure hope to hell you'll be careful."

She said not to worry. Then she reached out her spindly hand and put it on his face and he flinched, but he did not move away, he let the hand stay there and she said, "Don't forget, you was born with the caul over your face. Means you got a gift, you can see things." She left her hand on him for what felt like hours, years, decades, but was only a few seconds, the first hand that had ever touched him, and then she shuffled away with the crazy hill-man. Cole watched them go out the back door. He stood there another few minutes. Then he went to the locker room. He scrawled a note for Ellen, *Don't forget to check on Elvira Black*. He did not say good-bye to anyone. He stripped off his scrubs and changed into jeans and a T-shirt, and then he clocked out for the last time.

CHAPTER 19

THE NEXT DAY Cole drove to a pawnshop on the outskirts of Zion. The one-story cinder-block building, without any windows, sat on the edge of the road, the mountains rising behind it, and next to it was a junkyard, protected by a barbed-wire fence. The hand-painted sign out front said: "Need cash? We buy jewelry, TVs, stereos, guns, brass, copper." Years ago, he and Terry Rose came here with copper wiring they'd ripped out of a few deserted homes, all part of their scheme to make money and get out of Dove Creek.

He rang the bell. After a few minutes an overweight man wearing dirty work pants and a denim jacket with the sleeves cut out opened the door and glared at Cole through a pair of thick eyeglasses. It was the same man who'd bought the wiring from them; now he was probably in his early fifties and he did not look any different, except maybe fatter. He went back to the counter, sat on a well-worn stool. On the wall behind him were shotguns, revolvers, muzzleloaders, and inside the counter, under the glass top, were knives and jewelry. The rest of the store was crowded with dusty TVs, radios, hubcaps, tools, all of it stacked on sagging shelves and pushed up against the walls. The smell of motor oil and old machinery made Cole think of Terry Rose back in high school, always messing with broken-down cars. He spent a couple of years working on an Trans-Am that was supposed to be their getaway car. Cole would drink beer and watch him as he fiddled under the hood, and occasionally Terry would raise his grease-stained face, his eyes bright. "Bro, this baby is gonna take us places." He never did get it running.

"You buying or selling?"

"Selling."

Cole opened the paper bag and laid out all of the goods accumulated over the past year. Rings, brooches, earrings, necklaces, bracelets, watches, a few old pocketknives and antique coins. He had cleaned the objects until they sparkled. Now he looked at the old people's belongings spread out on the smudged countertop, and he remembered each one, who it had belonged to. He picked up a thin gold ring that was so small, it would not even fit on his pinkie. He'd found it in Larry Potts's nightstand drawer, along with a worn photograph of a woman. He'd heard the rumors about Larry's pretty wife, dead by her own hands, how Larry was never the same after. Twiddling his thumbs, words locked up inside of him.

"Some rich lady die and leave you all this?" the man said, smirking.

Cole asked if he could smoke and the man said no, he had asthma. Cole watched him examine each piece. He already knew that he would not pay their worth. He knew but still dreaded to hear him name his price. He glanced up at the guns and knives. He had not told his grandmother or his mother that he'd quit his job. His cousin Kay was the only one who knew. She was home for spring break, and last night when he'd walked in, she was at the kitchen table, talking with Ruby. His grandmother was already in bed. "I been waiting for you," Kay said, and told him that she and her college boyfriend were engaged.

"That's a little fast," he'd said, but then saw the hurt in her eyes, and apologized. "I'm happy for you." They had smoked and talked, and Cole held everything inside; he felt like he could not breathe. Finally, Ruby went in the family room to watch a late-night movie, and once they were alone, Kay asked him what was wrong. He told her about his job. "Don't ask why," he warned. She touched his hand. She said she was sorry. She knew him better than most people, but it was not enough.

"Two hundred."

Cole put his hands on the counter and stared at the man and saw the brown stains on his teeth, the acne scars across his face. "Are you crazy?"

"That's my offer."

"There's gold here, man, you can get that melted down."

The man shrugged.

"Look at this. This is antique. This alone is worth two hundred."

"Take it or leave it."

Cole began to put everything back in the paper sack. His hands were shaking. He'd never started a fistfight, but he felt a blind fury overtaking him. "I'll take this up to Charleston and sell it. Shit, I'll drive to fucking Columbus."

"You'll never make it that far," the man said. "You need a fix. You need the cash."

Cole stopped what he was doing and leaned over the counter and spit his words. "I ain't no junkie."

The man said nothing, but his face twitched and Cole saw that he was nervous.

"Seven hundred," Cole said.

"You're the crazy one." The man took off his glasses and wiped them on the end of his dirty T-shirt. "Two-fifty, that's as high as I'll go."

Cole was calm. He picked up a brooch and showed the man the intricate detail, the tiny rubies inlaid around the edges. He picked up piece after piece, touching them, remembering the people they came from. They went back and forth, until finally the man said $300 and would not budge, and Cole took the cash and counted it twice and then walked out of the windowless building into the startling sunlight, the greasy bills folded up in the front pocket of his jeans, hot against his thigh.

He went to the bank and closed his account. He got two texts from Reese on the way home, but ignored them. The rental house looked uglier everyday. His mother's car was gone; she was at work, baking pizzas. His grandmother would be watching TV, what she did most afternoons. Although she'd been fired up, writing letters to lawyers and government officials, and attending the activist meetings, she also moved slower these days, a new uncertainty in her eyes.

She opened the door. "I seen you pull in." She lowered her voice, "You got someone here to see you."

"Who?"

She said nothing else, but pointed toward the family room. He stood still, considered running. He looked at her and saw her sadness and his stomach fluttered. Would it be Randy or some other cop? All of the pills were stashed in his room, locked up. He was planning on selling everything this weekend. He slowly hung up his jacket. Then he took a deep breath and went in, quick, like diving into a swimming hole without testing the water. He stopped, gasped a little. Scrunched up in the corner of the loveseat, strung out and biting her nails, was Charlotte Carson.

"Hey," he said softly. "Hey girl. How'd you find me?"

She looked up. "I asked around. I didn't know where else to go, Cole."

She began to cry. She leaned against him and felt so small, like there was nothing at all inside her. He wondered what his grandmother had thought when she opened the door to find this orphaned-looking woman standing there. She was pale and skinny, wearing a flimsy hippie dress and raggedy cardigan. Greasy hair, heavy eyes. But his grandmother had invited her inside; that was what mattered. He could hear her now in the kitchen, the clattering of pots and pans.

"It's gonna be all right," he said. "It's gonna be all right."

He combed his fingers through her wild hair, no longer bleached, and when she lifted her head, his shirt collar was wet with her tears.

"It's Terry Rose," she said. "He's gone crazy."

He turned on the TV so that his grandmother would not hear them. "What happened?"

She talked so fast that a few times he stopped her and asked her to slow down. She told him that Terry had gotten involved in a bad crowd, that he'd been running drugs and owed money. He'd also been cooking up his own crank in an empty trailer; he'd stolen a bunch of ingredients from Walmart, right before he was fired. Rubbing alcohol, match boxes, iodine, cold medicine, Coleman's fuel, Red Devil lye.

"But he was using more than he sold, and he wasn't very good at cooking. He was getting all paranoid. Thinking the cops and other dealers were after him."

"What about Kathy?"

"His wife?" She shrugged. "I don't know. She left a couple of times, but he begged her to come back. He'd clean up for a few days, stop seeing me. But he couldn't stay away."

She asked for another cigarette. Her fingertips were stained yellow with nicotine. He handed her the pack, and she shook one out. It was strange to see her in this room, with its pale green carpeting and beige walls, the worn and unfamiliar furniture, yet everything neat and orderly, his grandmother's touch.

"Then what?" Cole asked.

A couple of days ago, she said, they decided to go clean. They were tired and worn out, and wanted their lives back. They locked themselves up in the trailer where they'd been cooking the meth, and at some point, Charlotte finally fell into a deep sleep. When she woke up, Terry was gone. She felt sick and wasted and tired, and she searched the trailer, but there was nothing left, no scraps to snort or smoke. So she hitched a ride over to Terry Rose's. She'd never been there before. It was a nice two-story, the sort of house that belonged to a family, to people who lived good lives. She rang the doorbell again and again, screaming his name, until he came flying down the stairs. She could see his wife beyond him, wide-eyed, scared, but Terry slammed the door behind him. He grabbed Charlotte and dragged her around to the side of the house and asked what in the hell she thought she was doing.

"I said I'd tell his wife everything. I said I'd go to the cops. I didn't know what I was saying. I just wanted him to come back." As soon as the words had left her mouth, Terry pushed her up against the house and held her there by her neck and told her he would kill her. If she ever said anything about him to anyone, he would find her and kill her. She looked at Cole helplessly. "He'll do it. He'll kill me."

"He won't kill you. He wouldn't hurt you."

"You don't know him. He's changed. He's turned mean."

"I've known him a long time. He'd never kill anybody."

She rubbed her eyes like she was seeing double. "I'm just so tired, Cole, I'm so tired, I don't know what to do."

He put an afghan over her and stroked her hair until she fell asleep, then he went into the kitchen where his grandmother was making sandwiches.

"That girl needs some meat on her bones." She dipped a butter knife into a jar of mayonnaise. "You think she'd like a glass of milk?"

"Maybe."

She looked at him. "It's drugs, ain't it?"

He nodded.

"What's she on?"

"Speed."

"You don't do that, do you?"

He told her that he did not.

"Is she going to be all right?"

"I don't know."

He sat at the table and she fixed him a plate with a sandwich, chips, and baked beans. She sat across from him. She was nervous, but wanted to talk.

"Did you hear about Blue Tiller?" she asked. "This morning I went out to get the mail and Betty Colbert was out on her porch and she said that Blue's missing. Nobody knows where she went to."

"Is that right?"

"They want people to keep a lookout for her." She paused. "I don't imagine they'll find her."

"You don't?"

"Blue's been around a long time. They won't stop her, no sir."

Last night still seemed like a dream, the mountain man, Blue's hand on his face, but now his grandmother was telling him that it was real. She was right, they'd never find her. He sat there with his grandmother for a while. He wondered how much she knew about what he did; she was not stupid. She counted on the money that he brought in.

After Charlotte woke up, he brought her the plate his grandmother had fixed and a glass of milk. She thanked him, but could not eat or drink. "I got to get out of here."

"You need a ride?"

"Yeah. I wrecked my car a while ago."

"You want me to take you home?"

"My brothers kicked me out."

"You could stay here."

"No, I got to go. I mean, I need to leave Dove Creek."

He wondered if she'd loved Terry Rose, but it was not a question he could ask. He told her he would help her. She held the glass of milk in her hands like a kid, but did not drink from it. She talked about going clean. She thought she could do it. She'd been so close.

When they decided to go, his grandmother walked them to the door.

"Thank you," Charlotte told her, "thank you so much."

"Oh, it's no trouble, honey. You take care now."

Cole drove Charlotte to Pineyville and waited for her in his pickup while she ran into the brothers' trailer, where she still had some of her things. When she came back, she was carrying a bulging backpack.

"Anybody you need to say good-bye to?"

She shook her head. "There's no one."

He drove her to the bus station in Zion. On the way, she talked more about Terry Rose, how if it was true that the cops were onto him, he would sell all of them down the river the first chance he got. "You know he sent those boys in to beat up Reese Campbell," she said. "He owed Everett, and he told him that Reese was the one, that he owed a lot more than he did. He was behind it."

"I know it."

"He's gonna try to get to you. He'll want something from you. You gotta be careful."

"He won't mess with me."

"He ain't the same boy you knew in high school," she warned.

Cole parked at the bus station and handed her an envelope and told her not to open it until she was inside. She thanked him. There were tears in her eyes.

"Be careful," he said.

"You too."

She leaned over and kissed him, and he grabbed her, held on to her for a few seconds, desperately. Then he let go. The man at the pawn shop had been right all along, it was cash going to a junkie. He hoped she wouldn't spend all of it on drugs, that she'd at least get to wherever it was she was going. He did not stay to watch her board the bus or to find out where she was headed.

There were still a couple more of his suppliers to do business with. First, he drove up to Clay's Branch, to see if Leona's mail order had come in. The place looked as pretty as always. Towering sycamores, bone-white paper birch trees. The blooms of fire pink and wild blue phlox shone like pieces of colored glass from the roadside. It reminded him of home, the way it used to look. He used to walk in the woods beside his grandfather. Sometimes it was easy between them.

There were two pickups parked out front, loaded up with Leona's belongings. Cole thought about turning back, but then cut the engine. Sunlight turned the tops of the trees gold, like they were blooming with hundreds of pears.

"What do you want?"

A man stood in the doorway, glaring at Cole. He looked to be in his late-forties, maybe older. His gut spilled over his waist, and his muscle T and jeans were dirty, like he'd been crawling around in the mud.

"We said we'd have everything out by tomorrow. Can't you wait a goddamn day?"

"I just came to see Leona."

"You ain't with Heritage?"

"Nah, I'm a friend."

The man walked into the yard, regarding him warily. "A friend of my mom's?"

"My grandma is friends with her. Dorothy Freeman. I just came to check on her."

He squinted, then seemed to relax. He took off his cap, wiped the sweat from his brow. "We got her moved into a nice little trailer down in Stillwell. We took her this morning."

"Is she okay?"

"She's fine. My sister's staying with her for a few days." He spit a glob of tobacco. "It's hard for her to give up this place, but there ain't nothing we can do. They're gonna start blasting and everything else. She can't stay here."

The money would probably go to the kids, Cole thought. Leona didn't want it.

"You want me to tell her you stopped by?"

"Nah, it's all right." He wondered what had happened to the mail-order prescriptions, but there was nothing he could do about it now.

"Tell your grandma she can visit her anytime at her new home. She'd like that."

He remembered Leona once saying that she wished she was strong enough to take a walk through the woods. Cole should have taken her. He could have helped her. Let her lean on him. Held on to her arm and led her to the trees. Instead he had just given her money and pocketed her medicine. That was what he did best.

There was just one last old person to see, and then he would be finished. For good. Glassy-eyed geese and plastic rabbits stared at him as he walked up the pathway. Harley McClain came to the door fanning a bundle of Popsicle sticks in his hand.

"Come on in, I got something to show you."

Cole followed him into the living room and looked around at all the houses and churches. "You've been busy."

"You know what they say, idle hands are the devil's tools."

"When I saw you last month, you said you were stuck."

"Well, I was. I was getting a little bit discouraged on it," he admitted. "But then one morning I woke up and it was like I was filled with all this inspiration. I got to work right away, and I tell you, I haven't been able to stop." He did seem more energetic. His eyes were dilated, cheeks ruddy.

"Your doctor got you on something new?"

"Oh yeah. I can't recall." He sorted through a stack of papers, handed them to Cole. He read over them and learned that the old man was now on a high dosage of Zoloft.

Harley gave Cole a paper sack holding bottles of Ambien, Oxy, and Xanax.

"You'll be all right without the pain medicine?"

"Oh, I ain't in any pain." He grinned. "You remember that cathedral I was building?"

"Yeah."

"I finished it."

"Well, let's see."

He led Cole into a back room. It was bare except for a twin bed and the biggest, most elaborately designed Popsicle building that Harley had ever made. It was probably four feet around, with spires and windows and staircases, and stood as high as Cole's waist.

"Jesus, Harley. You ought to enter that in some kind of contest."

He was beaming. He told Cole that he hadn't felt this happy in a long time. He had so many ideas, he told him. Castles, skyscrapers. He wanted to build cities. Maybe an entire world.

"Hell, I believe you can do it, Harley."

"I feel like a new man," he said.

On the way out, Cole drove past the stripped sites and the orange-tinted creek that was littered with an old washer and dryer, a rotting mattress. Devil's Pike had been spared from the spill, but it didn't much matter. The land around here had already been ruined years ago. Harley was living in the middle of this mess and he would always live here, among his little houses and churches and figurines; he would go on pretending everything was fine in his pretty little made-up world. Maybe that was the easiest way to live, but Cole did not think he could do that anymore.

The next day he went over to Reese's. He remembered the dread he used to feel every time he came over here, but it wasn't like that anymore. He knocked, and after a minute, Reese peeked through the living room window, then swung open the door.

"What's this?" Cole took in the emptiness of the room. "Where is everything?"

"Sold it, gave away what I couldn't sell. Even the crippled cat. Gave it to some neighbor kid."

There were still a couple of folding chairs, a dented boombox, and a plastic milk crate that held an ashtray and the King James. Two duffel bags sat by the door. The floor was dusty; on the walls were bright squares where pictures had once hung.

"Pretty soon nobody's gonna be left in the whole goddamn state," Cole said.

"You're staying, ain't you?"

"I don't know. I don't know anymore."

They sat in the folding chairs, and Cole looked Reese over. He thought he looked better than he had ever seen him look. He was sober and his face was full, his skin had color. He wore jeans, a white T-shirt with the sleeves rolled up, and he was barefoot, as usual. He'd cut his hair and it stuck up in little spikes, made him look younger. The bruises on his face had faded, but he was still scarred, he'd always be scarred.

"You sold the house?"

"Yeah. Didn't get much for it, property value's gone down so much. But Ruthie has a lot of antiques, and I'm taking them with me. They'll sell for more somewhere else. Everett and those fuckers were so dumb, they stole the shit that wasn't worth anything, left the antiques behind."

"Where you going?"

"Floridy. Hot weather, the beach. Gonna take Ruthie's ashes and let them loose in the ocean." He sighed. "She never went there, but I know she'd like it. You ever been?"

Cole shook his head. "I used to think about it a lot."

"It ain't for everybody. But I got a cousin down there. He's the religious type."

"So it's true," Cole said.

Reese's eyes were bright. "My life is changed, buddy. It's like now I can see. I've been woken up."

"Was it Cutter?"

"Sure, he helped. He helped me quit drugs and get all the demons out."

There was a long pause, then Cole said, "You ain't given up smoking though."

"No, not yet."

"And drink?"

Reese grinned. "I can't do it all at once. I ain't too good with the cussing neither."

"Just don't start preaching at me. I can't stand it."

"Well, I've done a lot of sinning."

"No testimony either."

Reese laughed. "I'm gonna miss you, son."

Cole reached for another cigarette. He felt rattled. He didn't know what else to say to Reese. Charlotte's words, *He'll sell us all down the river*, came back to him and he asked Reese if he'd seen Terry, and Reese said, "I'm done with him." Reese had also heard the talk.

"I gotta get out of town," he said. "Before the pigs bust me."

"You got anything on you?"

He hesitated. "I better not lie no more, now that I'm born again, right?" He admitted that he had a little bit of speed for the drive, the last thing he ever bought from Terry Rose. "But this is it."

"I could have given you something," Cole said. "You shouldn't buy from him, after what he did."

"It wasn't Terry that beat me up, he didn't have the balls for that. Anyway, he sold it to me for real cheap."

"He still cooking?"

"Nah, I don't think he did that for very long. Wasn't any good at it. Word is he's been skimming from Everett. He's desperate. Fucking desperate." He raised his eyebrows. "He's looking for you."

"For me?"

"Yeah, I told him I hadn't seen you in a long time. Told him I'd heard you was getting out of the business."

"What's he want with me?"

"I don't know, but he wants something. Terry Rose always wants something." Reese sighed, stretched out his long legs. "Bet you never thought this could happen to me, old Reese getting saved."

"I never gave it too much thought."

"I wish Ruthie was still alive. I wish she could see me now."

But Cole recalled Ruthie with her wigs and nail polish; she never would have tolerated Reese getting religion.

"Brothers used to talk about Jesus when I was in the pen. Somebody or another was always preaching. But they never reached me. I was too hard, too lost."

"What did it this time?"

"I don't know exactly, but I'll tell you, when I went to church and heard that Cutter boy speak, something changed." He pointed to the Bible. "I don't understand most of it, but I'm trying. You get it though, don't you? I bet you could tell me a lot of what's in there."

"That's not with me anymore."

He wasn't exactly surprised about Reese finding God. Hadn't he witnessed his grandfather convert the most broken-down sinner? But when Reese started to tell him more, Cole stopped him. "I told you not to start preaching. Anyway, I got to be going."

"I just feel like things are going to be good, like I got a new start." He paused. "I've thought about all the bad things I've done, and I just don't want it anymore. Luke said it's about letting go. I might still feel the desire, but let it go." His eyes were hopeful. "I ain't gonna burn. I ain't gonna be that way no more."

Cole sighed with disgust. "You know, I don't think God much cares."

"What's that?"

"You heard me."

"You never heard of Sodom and Gomorrah?"

"If you'd seen what I did when I was digging the dead people out of that mess," Cole stopped. Then he said, "God don't care about fucking or jerking off or none of it. I just don't believe it. There's bad things, and God don't care if you're fucking your own kind or not."

For a moment, Reese was quiet, then he laughed. "Ain't you a changed man."

"I don't know. That's just what I think."

"All right, buddy."

"All right."

They walked to the door. "I'm glad you stopped by. I'm gonna be gone by daylight."

"How you getting there?"

"Ruthie's Cadillac. Gonna haul a little trailer that Cutter loaned me."

"You won't make it to the county line in that thing."

"Hell I won't. It's only got twenty-five thousand miles on it." He grinned. "But if I get stuck somewhere, I'll call you."

"You do that."

He clapped Cole on the back and told him to take care of himself. There were no teary good-byes, none of that. Cole backed out of the driveway, knew he'd never see Reese Campbell again. He drove through town, past the Wigwam, the nursing home. Everyone was always talking about starting over. He tried to picture Reese walking into Luke Cutter's church, broken, strung out, and mourning the woman he'd loved maybe more than his own mother. Luke had promised him eternal life, forgiveness. Wasn't that what they all wanted? He had no trouble seeing it. He understood. It was the kind of thing that had made his granddaddy's eyes shine, snatching souls up from the flames.

CHAPTER 20

IN THE MORNING COLE, groggy and half awake, brewed coffee and lit a cigarette and opened the newspaper and read that the police had arrested Reese Campbell on his way out of Dove Creek. They were charging him with possession of narcotics and a firearm. Cole folded up the paper. He stared at the cracked coffee mug, the stack of paper napkins. Then he went outside and stood on the porch and felt the warmth of the day rising. Shit, he whispered. A car went by, followed by a speeding coal truck, dust flying.

He went back in, threw the newspaper away. Then he called Lacy. Sara Jean picked up. "She's still sleeping. Want me to wake her up?"

He glanced at the clock. It was only seven. "No, just tell her to call me."

"Did you hear about Blue?" she asked, excited. "She escaped."

"That's what I heard."

After he hung up, he fished the paper out of the trash and read the article again. His mother walked in, yawning. He'd never seen her up before his grandmother.

"Couldn't sleep." She took one of his cigarettes. "Getting to be like you."

The newspaper was spread out flat on the table, Cole holding it down with his palms as if guarding it from a breeze. The article was short, a single paragraph. He stared at it again. His mother asked him what was so interesting, and he told her in a few words. She poured herself a cup of coffee, then came and stood behind him and leaned over his shoulder.

"The guy we stayed with that night?"

"Yeah."

As she read the article, her hair tickled the back of his neck. Then she pulled out a chair, sat next to him. She had been all over this country. She had seen and left behind more than he could ever grasp.

"You think you're gonna stay here for a while?" he asked. "You think you could?"

"Hell, Esther's practically made me a slave at the Pizza Shack." She smiled, but it disappeared. "What about you? You going somewhere?"

"I might."

He met her eyes. They showed no surprise, no worry. The morning light shone through the kitchen windows and over her face and her eyes looked more green than brown and he wondered if his looked the same.

"You running from something?"

"It's not running. It's something I've been thinking about." He hesitated. "Could you say something to Grandma for me? Just to prepare her. . . . I don't know what to tell her."

"You gonna tell me anything about what's going on?"

"Not yet," he said. "I can't. I don't know myself."

For a while, they said nothing else. They finished off the pot of coffee, and Cole got up to brew more. Then his mother asked if he was hungry. He wasn't, but he said yes because she'd never cooked for him before. She moved clumsily around the kitchen. She made toast, eggs, and bacon, and though the meal was slightly burned, he ate every bite.

Hours later, he stood in the afternoon sun, smoking a cigarette, waiting on Lacy. She and Sara Jean were living with Lacy's sister and her husband in a double-wide in Green Hills, one of the government trailer parks. There was nothing to look at except other thin-walled trailers, pushed up close together. No hills, nothing green. None of the trailers had any decorations or flower beds or anything like that because people did not think of them as home. A couple of mongrel dogs chained up outside the trailer next to Lacy's began to bark. From someplace unseen, another dog joined in.

Cole had shown up a half hour ago, driving around the maze to the homes of his customers. He sold the pills for almost double what he usually did; they were pissed, but there was nothing they could do. The places he'd stepped into were cramped and dark, and the noise of TVs traveled from one trailer to the next. He was glad Lacy had not invited him in. He did not want to see any more.

The door slammed and she walked out, wearing tight jeans and a thin black shirt, a red purse slung over her shoulder. "I need to get out of here."

"We could go catch a movie in Zion or something," he said, but she shook her head. "What do you want to do?" he asked.

"I could eat something."

So they went to an all-you-can eat Chinese buffet in Zion. They loaded up their plates and took a booth in the smoking section. It was before five, and the only other customers were a handful of senior citizens.

"You heard about Blue?"

"I saw her before she left," he admitted. "I saw her with him. Denny's dad."

"Gundy." Lacy shook her head. "I just thought he was some crazy recluse."

"Ain't he?"

"Yeah, I guess so."

"Is Blue gonna live with him?"

"As far as I know. But I don't know even where that is. Somewhere up on a mountain. Gundy's been fighting the coal company. Blue said that it was him that shot up the mining offices, busted their power source. Personally, I don't think it's a technique that will get you very far."

"I remember someone shooting up a Christmas tree."

"Well, anyway. You can't talk to him. Or Blue either. They've got their minds set."

"What do you think they'll do?"

"Hold them off as long as they can, until they get caught. Honestly, I don't think Blue will live much longer."

"No, probably not."

"And Gundy'll go down shooting."

Lacy talked about Dove Creek Defense, their plans to meet with congressmen and senators, about the lawsuit. The flood had changed her. She was sharp-tongued and her hands shook slightly, maybe from fear or nervousness. And yet she was also filled with some kind of light, it shone off of her, the way religion had shone off of his granddaddy. She knew more than Cole could ever hope to know about politics and the environment.

She smiled. "I'll shut up for a minute. What about you?"

There was nothing to say. He did not tell her about losing his job, did not tell her about Reese. Instead he pushed aside his plate. He looked at her, how pretty she was. Remembered their early mornings together.

"So Michael left town?"

"You know he did." She set down her fork. "What else do you want to know?"

He ran his finger around the edges of the ashtray. "You and Michael . . . were?"

"You know we were."

"You thought he was gonna stay here and marry you or something?"

"I never thought that. He swept me off my feet for a little while. That doesn't happen much around here."

"No," he said. "I guess it don't."

They did not stay much longer. Neither of them wanted seconds. Cole paid for the meal, Lacy thanked him. "It's nothing," he said.

He started the truck. She was looking out the window, thinking about something. He was about to ask her what she wanted to do when she turned to him, put her hand on his knee.

"I don't want to go home yet."

"Where do you want to go?"

"Let's go there." She pointed across the road.

"There?"

"Why not?"

"Why not," he agreed, and pulled into the parking lot of the dilapidated motel. Lacy waited in the truck while he went in and registered and paid the bill; then he drove around to the back and they walked up the concrete steps to room 11.

"This is pretty bad," he said.

Stained burgundy carpet, fake-wood paneled walls, a rabbit-eared TV. The drapes were pulled shut and the room was like a cave, smelled like cigarette smoke and take-out. A picture of the Last Supper hung over the bed. Cole parted the drapes slightly, and a thin line of light shone through.

"It's worse than I was expecting, but I don't care." Lacy put her arms around his neck, and his blood quickened.

"I get the feeling I'm not gonna see you around anymore," she said.

"I'm here now."

They undressed quickly, both laughing as Cole fell, his jeans caught around his ankles. Lacy pulled them off him, and he yanked off her socks, the last thing to go. When he grabbed on to her, he felt as if everything else in the room had disappeared into these points of light, her fingers and thighs and back, the curve of her stomach and breasts, the angles of her bones.

After, lying face-to-face, he looked at her and wanted to be able to love her. To sweep her off her feet. But he didn't know what to say. Lacy asked for a cigarette, breaking the silence. He reached for the lighter.

"I'll go crazy if I stay in that trailer park another day. Sara Jean will too. I need to figure something out."

"You'll get out of there. You're a fighter."

"I never thought things would get this bad," she said.

He told her things would not always be this hard. She leaned up on her elbow and looked at him. "When I heard about you digging out those people, what you did . . ."

"It wasn't just me. We all did. Anyone would have."

"Something changed in you," she said. "That meeting, where you talked."

"Oh, Lord."

"You were great."

"Hell I was."

"You sure know your scripture, don't you?"

"That's one thing I'm certain of."

She drew loops over his chest, like she was spelling something, but it was no word that he knew. "Tell me what made you want to be a nurse."

"I'm just an aide."

"You know what I mean."

He thought for a second. "It wasn't like I set out to do it, it just happened. I needed a job. Once I got used to it, I guess I kind of liked being around them. Felt like I was doing something." He waited for her to bring up the drugs, but she didn't say anything.

"You shouldn't give it up."

"Well," he said.

Then she rolled over on her back, looking up at the dirty, water-stained ceiling. "You really believe in heaven and hell?"

"I used to," he said. "Sometimes I wonder if we ain't already living in both." He paused, put out his cigarette. "You want me to take you back home?"

"I want to stay. Can you stay?"

"Yeah," he said. "Yeah, I can stay."

She called her sister to tell her that she wasn't coming home tonight, and Cole looked up at the picture of the Last Supper. He used to stare at this picture during his granddaddy's sermons. He wondered if he would have denied Jesus, like Peter, or if he would have turned him in, like old Judas, who'd betrayed him with a kiss. He didn't think so. He believed he would have stuck by him.

She hung up. "It's all settled."

The night was good. They had more sex, they talked. They tried to watch TV but there was too much static. She fell asleep in his arms. He could hear her breathing. After a while, his arm, nestled under her head, began to ache and he slipped it out from under her. He switched on the lamp by the bed and picked up the Gideon Bible from the nightstand and started to read the book of Job, and when he came to the third chapter, twenty-fifth verse, *For the thing which I greatly feared is come upon me, and that which I was afraid of is come unto me*, he stopped and put the book down and turned off the lamp. He felt awake, in a good way. The room was dark, except for the occasional glare of headlights. There was someone coughing in another room. The hum of traffic outside. *You better believe it*, his granddaddy had said, *we are nearing the end*. He moved closer to Lacy and she reached for him.

The afternoon was warm; he drove with the windows down, smelled wild honeysuckle growing along the road. He fiddled with the radio and came upon a religious station and listened to an old-timey preacher, "And Je-sus-ah!—is gonna let you burn, unless you repent-uh, unless you're saved," singing the words the way his granddaddy used to. He'd been out selling pills and he pulled into the Stop-and-Go in Jefferson. He usually did not deal around here, but he knew a few pillheads, friends of Reese's, who were willing to pay more than his regulars. He filled his tank, went in the store and paid for the gas and a package of powdered doughnuts and cigarettes. He ate a doughnut quickly. He felt wired and anxious.

He'd been expecting to hear from him, like Charlotte had warned, but still it had surprised him this morning when his cell had started vibrating on the stand next to the bed. He was still at the motel with Lacy, who was next to him, asleep. He'd checked the number, and though he did not recognize it, he knew exactly who it was. He'd gone across the street to McDonald's and bought egg sandwiches, pancakes, orange juice, and coffee, and called him back.

"Hey."

"Hey man."

He'd not heard Terry's voice for months, but it sounded as familiar to him as his own. He wanted to meet early tonight, around eight. Cole said the Eagle or Wigwam, but Terry wanted to go where there was no one else around. "How about the swimming hole?"

"You been up there?" Cole said. "It's a mess."

"Well, we ain't going swimming. We're just talking."

"I don't even know if we can get to it."

"It's probably our last chance to see it," Terry said.

Cole said okay, but now he felt nervous. His stomach flip-flopping. Everything was turned upside-down. Reese was saved and sitting in a jail cell. Charlotte had disappeared. And where was Terry Rose? He was hunkered down. Was he naming names? Cutting deals? Turning his back on everything?

And here was Cole, still driving around these mountains. He finished three of the doughnuts, tossed the rest. He thought of Lacy last night and this morning, her hands and her mouth and her hair and her hips. Something good to think about. Not all of this worry. A kid on a four-wheeler pulled out in front of him, a "Jesus Saves" bumper sticker slapped on the back.

Up ahead on the left, a car was parked off the road, in a little turn-around spot. A woman sat on the hood. She had clothes and all kinds of junk spread around her and on the ground. He slowed down and when he saw who it was, told himself to keep going. He went about a hundred feet. Then he made a U-turn and pulled in behind her.

"Hey Jody."

He felt sick as he got closer and saw her damaged face. Two or three of her front teeth were missing, and her left eye was swollen and purple, as fat as a night crawler.

"What happened?"

"Oh, just a little scrap," she said.

He asked her how she was doing, but did not need to be told. She'd been beaten and she was too thin and her eyes were chalky. She wore a flimsy dress, grubby sandals.

"You want to buy something?"

He looked around. Ratty sweaters, a beat-up radio, a deck of cards, dented pots and pans. All of her belongings.

"No, I don't need anything," he said.

She asked for a cigarette and he took one for himself, then

handed her one of the packs he'd just bought. "Keep it," he said. Cars and pickups sped past them, sending up waves of dust; nobody stopped, nobody even slowed down.

"I been wondering what happened to you," he said. "Everyone's spread out all over the place now."

"Yeah, my trailer got fucked up, but I wasn't home when it happened." She shrugged. "I moved in with my sister in Zion. For a while, I went to that center there."

"The rehab?"

"Yeah. I was clean for a month." She sucked on the cigarette. "But a couple of weeks ago, everything fell apart. I was living with this guy. He's the one that did this to my face. Knocked my teeth out."

"Jesus. I hope you're not going back to him."

"Hell no," she said, her voice flat, unconvincing. "Hey, you got anything on you? I'll give you all of this, just for an eighty. All of this right here, it's yours."

He looked at her beaten face. "I'm getting out," he said. "I'm done."

"No you ain't." She laughed, showing her battered mouth, the gap where her teeth should have been.

"I am," he said. "I'm not in it anymore. I don't have anything." She put her hand on his crotch and he pushed her away.

"Don't."

"You don't like it?"

"Jody, you should check yourself back in. I'll drive you over there. Right now. I'll do it."

She stared at him and he thought maybe she would say yes, maybe she would thank him, but suddenly she grabbed a frying pan and swung it wildly, nearly smashing his face. "Fuck you," she screamed. "Fuck you."

He jumped out of the way and she flung the pan and it landed at his feet. "Get out of here, get the fuck out."

He got in his truck and hit the gas, watching her grow smaller and smaller in the rearview. She would not sell a single thing. She'd drive around on empty fumes to every dealer around until she found one who'd let her suck him off, then she'd melt into her little piece of heaven. He knew all of that. He drove almost all the way back to Dove Creek. Then he stopped and told himself, *You did this to her, you fucker, you did this.* He turned the truck around. He drove fast around the bends and curves, the sun glaring in his eyes, her broken voice ringing in his ears, but when he got back to the spot, she was gone.

He ate supper with his grandmother and mother, cheeseburgers with grilled onions, boiled potatoes, salad. It was mostly quiet, except for the occasional scraping of forks, the hum of the refrigerator.

Then his grandmother said, "Get you another one. I know how you like them."

"I already had two."

"You can afford anothern."

He reached for a third burger, put it between two slices of white bread and drizzled on ketchup. His grandmother watched him. He took a big bite and she nodded with satisfaction. She sat stooped in her chair. Her fingers were sore-looking, knotted with the beginnings of arthritis.

"Your mama told me you got something you're planning."

He looked from her to his mother. Ruby's eyes told him nothing. She reached for the salad bowl, red flashy nails, jangling bracelets. She asked if he had things figured out.

"I might go up to see Kay for a few days first. I don't know yet."

"You don't have to know," Ruby said. "It's a big country, lots to see."

His grandmother sounded nervous, like she was reciting something she'd been rehearsing all day. "I know you've got to live your own life, I want you to." He wondered what his mother had said to her, how much convincing she had to do. "But I'm scared," she added.

"Mama," Ruby said quietly.

"I won't start." She spooned out more potatoes onto Cole's plate. "Eat up, put some meat on those bones."

It seemed that the conversation was already over. It was that simple, and he was grateful. "Thanks, Grandma," he said.

She looked up at him with teary eyes. "You're welcome."

After supper he took a shower. He stood naked in front of the mirror. This was what other people saw. Not much to look at. He hadn't bleached his hair since before the flood and a few days ago he cut off the last of the blond. Now his hair was brown and choppy. Made him look regular, made him look old. He stared at himself until he looked strange and unfamiliar, the eyes and face of some other man. Then he dressed. Briefs, socks, T-shirt, jeans, hooded sweatshirt. The remaining Oxy went in an Ibuprofen bottle. He'd been able to sell almost everything and planned to stop by the Eagle later tonight to get rid of the last of it. Or maybe Terry Rose would want to buy it. Maybe Cole would need to use the pills as some kind of leverage. All of the cash he'd made from the sales was hidden under his mattress. He wondered how far his truck would take him.

He went into the family room where his mother and grandmother were watching TV and told them he was going out.

"You be careful," they said.

The temperature had dropped, and he was glad for the sweatshirt. He took the revolver out of the glove compartment and checked the cylinder, as if bullets might magically appear. But it was unloaded. He set it on the seat beside him. He did not know what Terry Rose wanted, but he expected the worst.

He switched on the headlights, their beam almost invisible in the silvery twilight. On the way up Dove Mountain, rabbits darted along the side of the road, and deer in a field stared at him. He wondered if they would die from drinking the water. The sludge had wiped out thousands of fish, crawfish, frogs, turtles, ducks. The day he'd been digging out the dead, he had seen a great blue heron with its toothpick legs half-stuck in the sludge, its wings folded and wet with the black lava. There was nothing he could do. There seemed to be no end to it. Even now, in the parts of the creek that had been cleaned out, where the water appeared clear, there was nothing living in it, no chubs or minnows, nothing.

He took a sharp right onto the old logging road. It was a muddy mess, tree limbs and rocks strewn all over. He did not know if he should wait here, or walk down to the swimming hole. Was this a setup? Would the cops show? Or would it be Everett and his crew? His heart raced. He told himself to wait fifteen minutes. Not a second longer. He got out of his truck and looked back at the gun lying on the seat. He hesitated, then grabbed it. He slid it in the waistband of his jeans, his sweatshirt hiding it from view.

He walked the narrow path, ducking under low-hanging branches, stepping around brush and sticker bushes, and he came to the part of the creek that was wide and still, where he and Terry Rose had spent so many of their days fishing, swimming, and getting stoned. He stood at the edge. It was black and lifeless. He picked up a stick and churned it, and when he took it out, it dripped with what looked like oil but was not. Heritage would never clean this up, there was no one left to complain. He sat on a log and felt the gun press into him. He'd not been here for years. He'd stopped fishing, let it all go. But now he recalled a time before Terry Rose, when he used to come here by himself, how safe he felt, the quiet, the shade of the tall sycamores, the smell of the dirt. He'd see deer and herons and coons; he'd felt God all around.

Suddenly there was a blast of music, a pair of headlights

sweeping over the woods. He jumped up, an icy tingling in his gut. The engine stopped, the music cut out. A door slammed, just one. He heard branches breaking, careless movement.

Then, "Hey, bro, you here?"

"Down here."

A minute later, Terry Rose appeared, shoving branches out of his way. The trees blocked out the last of the sunlight, and Cole could not discern his face from here, but he saw how his jeans and flannel shirt hung off him, like a boy dressed in his father's clothes.

"I wasn't sure you'd show up."

"I wasn't sure I would either," Cole admitted.

"How you doing?"

"I'm all right. You?"

"I could use some sleep, you know what I mean." Terry laughed, short and forced. "Ain't got much sleep, lately."

He walked down to where Cole was, and now Cole could see his face and it was thin and pasty. He didn't seem to be cranked out, but Cole didn't know for sure. They studied each other only for a second, then turned their gaze on the swimming hole.

"What a fucking mess." Terry picked up a rock and tossed it and it sunk. "I ain't been up here in a long time."

"I stopped coming up here after that day that I walked out of Granddaddy's church," Cole said, avoiding Terry's eyes. "I thought I'd be leaving for good. Texas, remember? It was stupid, but that's what I thought."

"Well, we were kids."

"Yeah. We were."

Terry flicked his burning cigarette. "You seen Charlotte?"

"She's gone."

"Where'd she go off to?"

"I don't know. But she's gone. Took a bus."

"Kathy left me again, took the boy. This time for good." Terry spit between his teeth. "Shit, I can't stand to look at this anymore. Let's go back up to my truck."

The front end of his pickup was plastered with weeds and branches, as if he'd bulldozed right through the forest. Cole was parked farther down the road; he could not see his truck from here.

"You hear about Reese?" Terry asked.

"Yeah."

"I never should have left Kentucky. They're onto me now."

"Who?"

"The fucking pigs. And fucking Everett. I gotta get out of here." He scratched his face, fidgeted with his sleeves. Maybe he was high, Cole didn't know anymore. All he knew was that he was stupid for agreeing to this.

"So what's going on, man?" Cole pretended to act casual, as if this was normal. "Why are we here?"

Terry stuck a cigarette between his lips. "I heard you might be leaving town."

"Who'd you hear that from?"

"Shit, you know how things are around here."

"I don't know," Cole said. "I might be."

"When?"

"Don't know," he lied. He wished his truck was closer. He just wanted to get out of here. He made himself speak more forcefully.

"Terry. What the fuck are we doing here?"

Terry stared at Cole through a stream of smoke, his face darkening. Now he just looked pissed off. His mouth twitched. The revolver felt heavy, conspicuous, and Cole did not know how quickly he could grab it. The handle of it squeezed into his stomach.

"I need help," Terry said finally. "Money." He talked fast, as if he was just now coming up with the story. He knew someone, not Everett but someone else, who would have a package tonight. If

Cole loaned him the money, then Terry could make the buy. He'd then split the crank into smaller portions and sell it, he knew a lot of people, he said, Cole wouldn't even have to worry about that part of it. He'd pay Cole back, plus cut him a part of the profit. The more Terry talked, the more angry and impatient he sounded, as if he was annoyed that he had to explain any of this to Cole.

When he was finished, Cole hesitated, then said, "You set Reese up."

"No man, no way."

"Bullshit."

"It had nothing to do with me," Terry said.

But Reese had bought his last supply from Terry and was busted on his way out of town. Cole knew he could not show any fear. Not now. He flicked his cigarette and the ember flew in an arc across the night. "You talking to the cops? Or you got something set up with Everett, or what?"

Terry's eyes looked wild, like a trapped animal, but then he took a long drag, regaining his cool. "Jesus, brother. Hell no. Would I do that? Hell no."

"Man, I can't help you."

"I know you've got the money. I know you do."

Cole shook his head.

Terry swore, then took a deep breath. This time he started talking in a friendlier tone. "Listen, buddy, you'll get it all back. You're gonna make money off this, way more than you would selling pills. It will help get you to wherever you're going."

Cole looked away. Could feel Terry's eyes on him. Reese said that Terry had been skimming from Everett, which meant that Everett was probably looking for him. Whatever was going on, Cole did not want to be a part of it. But he didn't know what to do. Should he agree, just to calm Terry down? But then what if he didn't show up with the money? Would Terry come after him? Would he go to his grandmother's house?

"I can't," he said. "I gotta get going."

"No, not yet. Wait." Terry grabbed his arm, and Cole tensed. Maybe Terry was waiting for Everett or the cops to show up, Cole didn't know. It was his own fault for coming out here, for hoping that Terry would still be the kid he used to know.

"Let go of me," he said.

Terry looked confused, then slowly removed his hand. "Goddamn it," he said, sighing, defeated. He looked up, and Cole followed his gaze. He could see the light of the moon through the trees. The sky was clear and sharp.

"We could have met at the Eagle, or anywhere else." Cole felt scared, but he wanted Terry to tell him the truth. "What's the real reason you wanted to come out here?"

"I told you the goddamn reason." Terry's voice was shaking, and he took a step toward Cole. Scrawny-ass tweaker. *Fuck.* Cole thought he could probably take him in a fistfight, maybe. But what if Terry had a knife or a gun? Should he pull the revolver? What good would that do? If Terry had a gun on him, it would be loaded.

He stood too close to Cole. Wound up with anger and paranoia. It seemed like minutes passed, but was probably only seconds. Something rustled behind them and they both turned quickly, but it was just the breeze.

"Jesus. Let's just chill," Terry said. "Okay? Let's just take it easy."

Cole nodded, afraid to speak.

"Good," Terry said, like he was talking to himself. "Good, that's good. Let's just take it easy."

The air was cold now, and Cole wished he'd brought a jacket. He glanced at Terry, a scarecrow. His flannel shirt unbuttoned and blowing in the breeze.

"I know what we need," Terry said, and started over to his truck.

"Wait. What are you doing?"

Terry didn't answer. His footsteps were loud, things crunching under his boots. Cole stiffened. A drumming in his ears. He watched Terry open the passenger door and reach for something. Cole automatically put his hand on the revolver. But when Terry turned, he was holding what looked like a cigarette.

"Got this from a chick I know. This will help chill us out, bro. Like the old days."

Cole just looked at him. His heart still racing, loud in his ears.

"Don't you want to smoke?" Terry took a plastic lighter out of his pocket. "It'll settle my nerves."

"I don't know."

"Jesus, it's just a fucking joint. You can trust me. Okay?" He smiled, but it was forced. "Buddy, I might not see you again."

"What's that mean?"

"You're leaving, ain't you?"

Cole nodded.

"All right then."

Terry lit the joint and took a long drag, then handed it to Cole. He felt Terry's eyes on him, but didn't look at him. More stars were visible now, their light drizzling through the tree tops. Cole inhaled. Just weed. It tasted earthy and sweet.

"You all right?" Terry asked.

"Yeah."

Terry took a long toke. He told Cole he hadn't meant to freak him out.

"I'm fine," Cole said.

Terry talked in spurts as he exhaled. "Man, everything's so fucked up. I wish I'd never started selling." The anger was gone from his voice. "I just need to sell this last package. Then I'm gonna get cleaned up. Gonna change."

Cole didn't reply. Everyone said that, but nobody ever did it. He took the joint again and listened to Terry talk about his fucked-up life. Cole felt hyper-aware of everything around him. The patch of dirt under his feet. The smell of the trees. The cold air on his neck. He didn't know if he was still scared or stoned, or both. Terry talked and talked, and then finally seemed to run out of things to say.

They sat on the tailgate, passed the joint back and forth. The fear didn't disappear completely. It was still inside of Cole, a ball of ice. But at the same time he felt more comfortable. They could have met anywhere, but Terry *wanted* to come back here. Where they spent so much of their time. They could have been seventeen again. Almost. It was quiet between them now, and he remembered that sometimes Terry could be quiet. He would get sad about his dead father, and Cole would think about his absent mother, and they would smoke and not say much because they knew what the other was thinking.

"Man, I miss this. Just chilling out," Terry said. "I just feel like I'm always running. You know?"

The joint burned down to nothing. Cole had not been stoned in a long time; he wondered if he was now. He heard crickets, the trill of a katydid. "Yeah, I know."

Terry stretched out on his back. Like he finally felt at ease. "Man, I feel old. It seems like forever ago that we was kids. Sneaking around, hiding from your granddaddy. He scared the shit out of me."

Cole looked up at a sliver of sky. "Sometimes I miss being scared by him."

"Hell, I think you still are."

The day he left his granddaddy's church, it was an unusually hot spring afternoon, the building sweltering, and church members, about half being the Freeman family, fanning themselves, shouting, Lord, oh yes, thank you Lord. His grandfather had stood at the front, mopping his brow with a handkerchief.

"You think this is hot, it's nothing like the sinner will feel, what Satan's got in store," he said. "God abominates sin. If you've sinned, you've got to ask for forgiveness." He'd paused dramatically.

"Come Judgment Day, you don't want to be left alone. Do you want to go with Satan, to suffer and burn, or do you want to be with the Lord? That's where I'll be. I'll see you there, in the sweet by-and-by."

Sweat had dripped down Cole's back and under his arms and he'd stared at the picture of the Last Supper, at the squares of light that shone around the church, trying to find quiet in the noise. There was a long pause. He had looked up. His grandfather set his eyes on him.

"We got a boy with demons. He's got to be saved."

Suddenly an owl hooted, and Cole jumped.

"Relax, bro. You ain't scared, are you?"

Terry was still stretched out on his back, his arms behind his head and a cigarette between his lips. He hadn't come here to kill Cole, to hurt him. He looked content. Relaxed. Like there was nowhere else to be. Cole looked at him and felt his heart pounding and then he stretched out next to him, the way they used to lay next to each other. Looking up at the sky, talking or not. Nothing to fear. Nowhere else to be. The orange tips of their cigarettes glowed. It was cold. Terry swallowed loudly, but said nothing. They were both so still, so quiet. They used to go camping up on the mountain. How far away the rest of the world had seemed. Back in those days, he would have gone anywhere with Terry Rose. He remembered how it used to be. He remembered what he'd never told anyone, what he'd never forget. Were they fifteen or sixteen? It happened only three or four times. They went camping up on the mountain. They had sleeping bags, they had the woods and the sky and the night animals. It was cold. It was cold and they slept close together. They slept close together and they put their hands on each other and the rest of the world disappeared and it was them and the stars and the ground and the trees and the night animals. It was cold and they held each other close, they pressed their mouths and hands and bodies together. He remembered all of it, the hardness of Terry's lips, the quickness of his hands, the heat of his chest and thighs. How good everything felt. There was no fear, not then. Long ago they'd mixed their blood. They'd held each other.

It was a long time ago. But now they lay side by side. Both tired of running, both tired of feeling stuck. How much did Terry remember? Cole looked at him and the truth was, he saw no trace of the boy he used to be. But Cole moved closer anyway. The fear rose thick on his tongue. There was nothing else to say. It was cold. He was shaking. He closed his eyes and moved over until his head was resting on Terry's chest. Terry said nothing. Did not push Cole away. They held their breaths. Terry's chest was flat and hard, protecting his heart. Cole could hear it, pumping, beating. Then he felt Terry's hand on his shoulder. The touch so light, as if Terry was disappearing into air.

"It's funny how you stop dreaming of things," Terry said. "Remember how I used to want to be a race car driver? And all the plans we made to get the hell out of here."

"That's just how things are," Cole said. "Like you said before, we were kids. But now we're not."

"Yup, now we're old. Old and used up." Terry tried to laugh, but his voice was small and thin. It sounded scared, the way he never used to be.

Cole closed his eyes and lay as still as he could with his head on Terry's chest. Terry's hand, light as a cat's paw, stayed on his shoulder. Both of them quiet. Tense and relaxed, safe and scared.

That day his granddaddy had singled him out, the others in the church had shouted and prayed, and Cole had looked desperately around for his grandmother. He could not find her. Nowhere to hide, no one to turn to. His grandfather was coming toward him, God in his eyes. There was no light, no light at all. His grandfather had put his old knotty hands on Cole's face and said in a voice that only Cole could hear, "Your mother give birth to you, but only God will save you. You can be born again." What was bearing down on Cole was too heavy and he'd suddenly pushed the hands away, then forced his way through the crowd. His grandfather came after him.

"Don't you step out of this church, boy."

He grabbed Cole by the neck of his shirt and told him to repent. "You walk out of this church, you ain't never coming back." Cole twisted out of his grandfather's hands. He almost fell, then steadied himself with one hand against the wall. He and his granddaddy stared at each other. Cole's heart was thumping wildly. He took a step toward the door, and this time the old man didn't stop him. Cole couldn't see anything. Couldn't see his grandmother, or anyone he knew. Just saw shadows, and ahead of him, the bright light of the sun. But once he was outside of the church, he suddenly understood what he'd done, and he started running down the dirt road, through the forest to the swimming hole where Terry Rose would be waiting.

Now he sat up. He was still shaking: his hands, his legs, his whole body. "I gotta go," he said, and scrambled over the side of the truck.

"Wait, Cole." Terry jumped down. "Will you show up with the money?"

"Man—"

"I won't ask you for anything else. Come to the Eagle at midnight. Come with the money, and I'll get us what we need. I'll be able to sell it fast, don't worry about that. And when you leave this shit-hole, you'll be a richer man."

Cole said nothing. Terry said, "Please."

For the second time tonight, Terry put his hand on Cole's shoulder, and then moved it over until he was cupping the back of Cole's neck. A touch of affection, a touch of trust. Terry leaned in close. Cole looked him in the eyes. It was like it used to be. He did not feel afraid.

"Terry Rose, don't fuck me over," he said.

A few minutes later, after Cole agreed to show up, Terry was driving away, music blaring, tearing up little trees as he went.

Cole stood alone in the woods. Swore at himself. Then he walked back to the creek, stepping around little gullies, piles of rock. He stood in the dark. It used to look clear, sunlit. On that day, he'd come running down the path, breathless, and Terry was there, sitting on the bank, drinking a beer.

"You get saved?" he joked.

Then he saw Cole's tears and asked him what was wrong.

"We got to go now," Cole said. "We can't wait, we got to go."

Terry had put his arm around him, led him over to a mossy patch under a weeping willow. Cole, gulping breath, explained that he'd walked out of the church. He'd run away from his grandfather. Terry said everything was going to be all right and Cole believed him, thinking this was it, they would go. They were a month away from graduation and now they were going to leave; everything they'd been talking about was here in this moment: they were going to go to the ocean, get the hell out of Dove Creek. But then Terry, his arm still around Cole, said there was something he'd been wanting to tell him. He sat there with his arm around Cole and said that Kathy was pregnant.

"We're gonna get married." He smiled at Cole. "You see what I mean? I can't go anywhere. Things are different now."

Cole felt as if little needles were pressing into the back of his neck. The air smelled of chemicals, no sounds of birds or night insects. How much money could he make. What did he stand to lose. He stared intently, as if the swimming hole could give him the answer. The gun felt slippery in his hard. He held it away from him and then let it go. It sank into the black toxic water. He hesitated, then did the same thing with the last of the Oxy. He wanted nothing on him. He stuffed his hands in his pockets and stood there and watched the sinking. The sludge would rise up and eat them all. He recalled the words of Moses: "I *am* not eloquent . . . but I *am* slow of speech, and of a slow tongue." And then the Lord promised him that Aaron his brother would be there for him: "I know that he can speak well." He promised Moses, "I will be with thy mouth, and with his mouth." God was with both of them, brothers. But Cole and Terry were not really brothers. He remembered what Charlotte had told him; he'd not forgotten, even with his head rested on Terry's chest, listening to his beating heart, Cole knew the truth: Terry Rose would not go down, and he especially would not go down alone.

When he got back to the house, his grandmother and mother were watching *Law and Order*, eating popcorn. He sat between them on the sofa and watched two cops run down a busy street in New York. He asked what had happened, and his grandmother told him that a store owner had been shot and they thought the killing was linked to the mob.

"I don't know who would want to live there," she said.

On commercial break he told them he would leave early in the morning. His grandmother looked frightened, but did not try to talk him out of it. The show came back on and they did not talk about him going, but it was there, weighing on them, in their movements, their quietness. Then his grandmother said she could not keep her eyes open any longer. She told Cole to make sure he woke her in the morning.

Cole packed very little. A pair of boots, jeans, T-shirts, underwear. An old sleeping bag, a couple of blankets, a jacket. Pictures of his family, pictures of Charlotte and Lacy and Sara Jean and Terry Rose. His granddaddy's King James. It was all he really owned. When he was finished, he slid the money out from under the mattress and divided it into three piles. He took the smallest pile for himself, then put the other two into separate manila envelopes and he wrote names on them with a marker. He did not feel satisfied. It felt like something was missing, a nagging feeling. So he added more money to the pile in his hands. He thought about Terry Rose, talking so fast and desperately, his hand on the back of Cole's neck, Terry leaning in close.

When he walked through the living room, his mother looked up. "You're going out now?"

"Yeah, I'll be back."

But he did not look at her when he said it. He got in his pickup and stared at the numbers glowing from the dash. It was fifteen minutes past eleven. He would be early, but he couldn't stay in the house any longer. He drove through Stillwell. Tomorrow he would be gone from this place. But he could not focus on what this would mean. He felt edgy and nervous, like somebody was tailing him. That ball of ice in his gut returned. He looked for cops, but saw none. He almost stopped and turned around. But he'd told Terry he would be there. Cole was going to give Terry half of what he asked for. Then Cole would leave. He wouldn't wait around for the profit. He would just go. He summoned his nerves and kept driving. But when came around the bend where the Eagle was, there were red and blue flashing lights dancing across the night. He slowed down. The ball of ice melted in his mouth. Cop cars, an ambulance. He pulled in the parking lot, cut his lights and stayed far back from the scene. After a while, someone staggered across the lot. Cole rolled down his window. "What's going on?"

The man stopped, looked up as if he'd been addressed from the sky.

"Over here," Cole said.

He was old and drunk. He came over to Cole's window. "A shoot-out."

"What happened?"

"It was told to me that there was some kind of drug deal. Some-thing went bad wrong. Feds was here. Some big guy was shooting."

"Did anyone get killed?"

"Yes. One of them did. Jerry or Gary or something. The big one was shot in the leg, they arrested him and a couple of others." He took a drink. "Drug dealers, drug addicts. I don't know what's going to become of this country." Then he said, "Son, would you mind giving me a lift?"

Cole stared at him, uncomprehending.

"I'm just down there in Stillwell."

On the way back to town, the man said more about the shoot-out, and when he described the person who was killed, Cole knew for sure. He talked the entire time, going on and on about the state of the world, but Cole stopped listening. He focused on the beam of the headlights. Terry's hand on his neck. His granddaddy's hands, trying to heal him. Blue's hands. She had told him that the mysterious caul that had covered his face was a gift, and he wondered what it was, if it had been wiped away, if it was still with him, if it had blinded him or if it had hidden him. What it was he was supposed to see. After he dropped the old man off, he went back to his grandmother's. His mother was asleep on the couch, the blue light of the television soft on her face. He dropped a blanket over her, turned off the TV. Then he went into his bedroom and sat on the edge of the bed in the dark and waited to feel something.

CHAPTER 21

H<small>E WOKE BEFORE DAYLIGHT</small>, but did not get out of bed
right away. He lay for a few minutes under the blanket, between worlds, remembering last night like a dream. He lifted his
hands close to his face and could smell the outdoors. The house
was quiet and dark. "Get up," he told himself. "Get up." He dressed
and washed his face and brushed his teeth. He looked at his hands
under the bathroom light. They were dirty. He scrubbed them,
cleaning under the nails. Then he made the bed with hospital
corners and looked at his room and it was neat and clean. He carried his few belongings out to the pickup. In the east a faint glimmer of light trembled across the sky. When he went back in, his
mother was brewing coffee.

"You're up early."

"I didn't sleep much," she said. "Might as well be up. Mama
will probably want to drag me off to church." His grandmother
had started going regularly to a different church; she'd not gone
back to Luke Cutter's.

"Maybe you'll get saved," he told her.

"I already been."

It was their joke, and they smiled. But Ruby's quickly faded;

she looked worried. "I feel like there's still so much we need to say to each other."

"I'll be back," he said, and he knew this was true. "There'll be time for that."

He did not tell her about Terry Rose. He couldn't. He did not want to believe it.

When the coffee was done, Ruby poured two cups and they sat at the table and drank it the same way, black, no sugar.

She looked like she wanted to say something.

"What is it?"

"You never ask about your daddy."

"Would I know who he is?"

"No, I guess not. He used to live down in Bucks County. Last I heard he was in South Carolina." She ashed her cigarette. "Joe Milligan. He was good-looking."

"I'll remember his name."

He finished the coffee. She asked if he wanted more, but he said no, he should get going. When she stood, he went over to her and put his arms around her and they held each other. When they pulled apart, they looked embarrassed.

"You stay in touch," she told him.

"Better than you ever did."

She tousled his hair. "You miss him, don't you?"

"Who?" he said, caught off guard.

"Your granddad, who else."

"Oh. Yeah, I miss him. You?"

She nodded. He stopped at the doorway and turned to look at her once more. "He asked for you. On his deathbed, you were the one he wanted."

For a second she looked confused. Then she grinned. "Probably he just wanted me there so he could preach at me." She told him to be careful, he said he would. He went quickly and knocked on his grandmother's door. Her eyes were heavy with sadness.

"Were you sleeping?"

"No, I been praying."

"I'll be all right."

"You listen for Him. He's gonna be talking to you."

He sat with her on the end of the bed and handed her a manila envelope that was stuffed with cash. She felt the weight of it. She'd never refused his money, no matter where it came from.

"I'll be back. You know I will."

He told her that when he came back, he wanted to find her living on a nice plot of land somewhere, far away from the mining.

"Wherever I am, they ain't gonna walk all over me again," she said.

"You'll keep fighting?"

"I will. Will you?"

"I'm gonna start," he promised.

He kissed her cheek, and her old hands clutched onto him.

"Go on," she whispered.

When he started his truck, his mother waved from the porch, but his grandmother was inside, praying. He did not want to be afraid anymore, there was no time for that. No time for feeling helpless. The world was big and uncaring, and he was going into it, like Jonah swimming into the belly of the whale. He heard his grandfather's voice: "You surely are your mother's child."

Light shone from the east as he drove to Green Hills, where everything was still. He pulled in front of Lacy Cooper's and walked up to the trailer and slid the second envelope behind the screen door and left without lingering. He remembered the Christmas presents and hoped that she would take this: it was all that he could give her. Then he drove through Stillwell. He went past everything that was familiar. He passed the Wigwam and the bank and the Laundromat. No cops pulled him over. Everything was quiet. He parked on the street behind the nursing home.

He went in through the side door and stepped into the familiar smell of ammonia, cafeteria food, old bodies. He looked around. Larry Potts twiddling his thumbs. Cole touched his nervous hands, waiting until the thumbs rested. Then he went into the rooms of everyone he knew. He said good-bye, and if they were sleeping, he just looked at them. He thought of all those who had died. Remembered what he'd taken from each of them. He'd not returned any of it, not a single piece, and he wondered if they could forgive him.

He went to see Elvira Black, who'd been moved here against her will. She was sleeping, hooked to oxygen and fluids. He touched her face and her eyes fluttered. He told her good-bye, but she did not wake up.

As he was coming out of her room, he saw an aide bent over Hazel Lewis, trying to get her shirt back on, and he ducked back into the room and waited. When he looked again, the aide was gone, but Hazel was there, grabbing at her shirt.

"It's so dang hot," she said.

He pulled down her shirt and put his arms around her and smelled her moldy, stale smell. She began to cry. He'd never seen this before. "Shh," he said.

"Cole, Cole, Cole," she said.

He said, "That's my name. Don't wear it out."

Then he drew back and she looked at him and said it was so hot, and he said he knew it was, and that he was sorry, but it would not always be this way.

Mabel Johnson was in her rocking chair like she'd been waiting on him. "You're up early," he said.

"Early bird gets the worm."

He asked her how the new aide was treating her, and she said all right. Then he touched her hand and told her he was going.

She told him to get into her dresser. "Go on," she said.

He pulled open the top drawer and took out the blood-red scarf. "I know it's getting warm now, but you take it with you to wherever you're headed." She motioned for him to lean closer, and then she held the scarf up to him. "It'll look right handsome."

He wrapped it around his neck. It was soft, delicate. He had never worn nor owned such a thing. He told her he felt proud to wear it.

She did not like good-byes, she told him. So he kissed her cheek and she called after him, "You be careful."

He turned east and drove up the mountain. As he passed by the Eagle, his fingers curled around the steering wheel. The lot was empty, no signs of last night. The hurt in him was dull and throbbing, and he sucked in his breath, afraid to let go. His knuckles were a spine of white, and he forced himself to loosen his grip on the wheel. He kept driving and turned onto Rockcamp Road. His grandmother had told him to make peace with his grandfather, but what he had to make peace with was bigger than any one man. He drove around the barricade and pulled up on a slope, hiding his truck in a grove of pines. When he got out, he wrapped the scarf around his neck like something to ward off evil spirits.

He did not go near the swimming hole. Last night seemed like a strange and sad memory that hummed inside of him, a dull pain. He did not know if Terry Rose had been setting him up or was just asking for help; he would never know. He felt sorry for Terry, sorry for all of them. Up on the hillside, he looked across the land and saw his empty trailer and his grandparents' house, the blackness still spread over the yard. It still took his breath away, how bad it was. It looked as if something had fallen from the sky, rolled down the mountain, and left a burning gash. The cemetery was washed away, the bones of the dead, lifted up out of the earth. But what did bones matter? Everything turned to dust. Rage jolted his blood.

He cut up through the forest and headed up the mountainside in the direction of where the mining site would be. It would be a long walk. He would have to go all the way around, bypassing the

Heritage gates, and head up the backside of the mountain. He was not in good shape and the cigarettes did not help. He stopped often to catch his breath. Sweat clung to his back, but he did not take off the scarf. He wished he'd brought water. His granddaddy used to walk the mountains and hills like a mountain goat; he would not have tired out like this, not even in his old age.

The forest was threaded with cracks and slips, water pouring out from gashes. Other places were bone-dry. What used to be Little Blue Stream was buried. Everything around here had been named. Dove Creek and all of its offshoots, dozens of fishing holes and hollows and knobs and hills. Sugar Holler, Big Lick, Bony Knob, Red Bird Hill, Garden Hole. All of these names that were a part of him like the scripture itself and now all of it disappearing. He climbed over caves of brush and piles of rocks, the places where snakes liked to hide. His granddaddy used to come up here in the summer to hunt them. Cole did not go with him then, too scared. But now he was not afraid. There were worse things to fear. Last night's swirling ambulance lights. Lifting Arie Webb out of the sludge. He did not want to see, but he kept walking.

He came to a sign that said "No Trespassing, Property of Heritage Energy" and went around it. He had been in these woods a thousand times. He used to come here to kneel in the forest with his hands pressed to the dirt. He used to walk with his granddaddy; he used to walk with Terry Rose. He used to dig for ginseng. He knew the plants and trees and birds. But in the last few years, he'd stopped. Too busy, he'd told himself. But that was not it, it was something else. He was afraid that he'd no longer belonged to this place, no longer deserved it. Now he tried to remember what it used to look like. Light shining through the tops of trees; green moss on stumps; blooming foxglove and little pink azaleas, like teardrops.

It was not the same woods anymore. Not the place where he'd gone 'senging with his grandfather, where he'd camped with Terry

Rose. The mudslides, broken trees, all of it confused him, and after a while he wasn't sure where he was. The machine noises grew louder, beeping, shoveling, whining. He thought of Blue, lying down in front of a dozer.

He stopped by an old sycamore and put his hands on its mottled bark. Saplings stood around his waist and ankles, and the mother trees grew around them, gleaming with new leaves. It was spring; everything returned in the spring. His grandfather had believed in the power of the wilderness. The wilderness called to the old prophets. John the Baptist and Moses and Elijah and Jacob and even Jesus himself. His granddaddy, in times of sorrow or pain, would come up to these woods. He'd pray and fast, and give himself over. He was a believer. He was a good man, but he was not God, he was no angel.

Now he knew where he was. He was getting close to the ridgetop, and if he went up to that dip between the sweetgum and the yellow birch, he would come to the small clearing where he used to watch the sun rise. He had watched it with his granddaddy, who took him up here and told him he'd better listen hard because God had a soft voice. And he watched it with Terry Rose. They camped here and woke up together and smoked cigarettes and drank coffee and watched the sun rise, leaning against each other, quiet, so quiet that Cole thought that maybe that was as close to God as he ever got. Now he went forward, clambering up the slope, leaves and twigs sliding under his feet.

He stopped.

He stopped because the mountain stopped.

The world stopped.

"Jesus," he said, dizzy, faint.

He held on to the limb of the sweetgum and looked out onto the mining site. It was all below him, around him. He'd read the statistics and seen pictures and caught glimpses of the sites from the road, but never had imagined how immense. And he was seeing only a part of it. The land simply dropped off a few hundred feet, and below and across from him, all over, was the mining site, which looked like something from outer space, like an asteroid had hit here, or some kind of government testing site. The raging blood raced up to his head, and he felt like he was going to be sick. What had been forest and mountain was no longer here. Just gray rock and scars, bulldozed earth, and glistening seams of coal. The site was so big that the gigantic bulldozers and the 240-ton dump trucks looked like toys. They moved like bloated insects across the site, over the roads they'd carved out and around the blasting holes, the noise of them drowning out birdsong or any other natural noise. On a remaining hillside, newly felled trees lay like bodies, thousands of them. His granddaddy had taken him to the mountaintop and said God is all things good. Cole wrapped his arms around his chest. He thought of Terry Rose, crumpled in the parking lot of a run-down beer joint, dying in a pool of his own blood. The dead hung up in the trees. Buried in sludge. The bodies laid out on the hillside and all those who cried over them.

He looked at everything so that he would not forget. All of this was up here behind him, and he'd never looked. Too scared, too stubborn. No wonder he could not sleep. His granddaddy always said that bad sleep indicated a guilty conscience. He'd been down there, just a mile down there, counting his money and selling pills and stealing and screwing and making promises, and all the time this was right here, looming over them. *Where the worm dieth not and the fire is not quenched.* He was at the gates of hell. He tried to recall the original contour of the land but could not remember. He closed his eyes and tried hard to see it, but nothing. This was his granddaddy's granddaddy's land, and in a few months, what he now stood upon would be gone.

He opened his eyes. The leaves on the trees around him were coated with ash from the blasting below. He looked out again at the missing mountain and felt dizzy. He slowly got down on the ground. It was too much, the feelings inside him. He lay down on his stomach and pressed his hands into the cool dirt. He'd never felt so alone or small. Dirt on his hands. Blood pumping through him. He tried to think of Bible verses, but there were none. But he heard the words of his grandfather: *I had to lose everything, I had to forget all of it.*

He did not know how a person was born again, how there could be more than one beginning, how a person could walk away from the past. The old people, with all of their stories and memories, they never forgot. What connected the land and the mountains and the living and the dead he did not know. But he lay there in the brokenness and began to say the names of the old people. He said all of their names. He said the names of those in his family. He said the names of those who had held him. He said the names of the dead. He said the names of places. Every creek and mountain and hilltop and family cemetery. He said the names of trees and flowers and creatures. He spoke clearly, talking into the dirt. He named everything; the words came easily.

The machines down below rumbled and groaned, but he listened beyond that noise. He heard a rustling and thought it was the wings of some bird. He rolled over on his back and put his hands on his chest and looked at the star-shaped leaves of the sweetgum and heard his heart pumping blood. His grandfather used to say that God was laying on his heart. From far away he heard the clear high notes of a wood thrush melting away into sadness. He looked up through the last of the treetops and saw a jagged piece of blue sky, it was blue and it was good. And he began to weep, he wept for a long time, wept until he felt too big for his own body. Not heavy but big. Filled. Feeling the ground under him, feeling his own muscle and bone and skin. All around him the wilderness sang, the old people sang and God sang. The memory of the place was deep inside of him. He did not need to look again. He stood up and walked back the way that he had come. Dirt clung to him. He left it on him and got in his truck and rolled down the window, squinting at the bright sun. As he drove down the mountain, the scarf that those old bony woman hands had knitted for him blew wildly in the wind, straggly pieces of yarn dancing like pearls of light around his face.

ACKNOWLEDGMENTS

I'm indebted to many people for helping me get here. Thanks to everyone who made this book possible.

First, a heartfelt thank-you to those friends who encouraged me to write and stuck by me in countless ways, big and small, including: Jenny Abramson, Allison Amend, James Cañón, Sara Greenslit, Michelle Hailey, Paul "Prof" Hendrickson, Rebecca Layton, Elizabeth May, Daisy Rhau, Emily Wallace, and Stephen Wiseman (for driving me around the mountains and hollers, and so much more). I'm grateful to all my friends and family in New York and North Carolina (you know who you are), with a special thanks to my folk crew in Carrboro. Thank you to Yukiko Yamagata, who believed before I did. To my family and parents, with much gratitude to my mother who instilled in me a love of reading. And thank you to José Miguel Cruz, who teaches me about grace and forgiveness everyday, and whose steadfast love and support make me a better person.

Much thanks to my careful readers who saw earlier drafts or chapters: Gregory Brooker, Rosanna Bruno, Michelle Hoover, Emily Jack, and especially Urban Waite. Thank you to Lora Smith, for helping me with crucial details about mining and religion. To J. Pasila for the maps and photographs. Thank you to Terry Lee and *DoubleTake/Points of Entry*. To Matt Bialer for your enthusiasm and unwavering support. An immense thank you to Susan and Jim Lapis, for graciously letting me use their beautiful cabin, where a good portion of this book was written. To my teachers who saw something in my earliest writing and told me to keep going: William J. Cobb, Charlotte Holmes, Alyce Miller, and my first creative writing teacher, Eve Shelnutt. To Sewanee Writers' Conference, especially Randall Kenan, John Casey, and my peers in the workshop—you were the first readers. Thank you to Bread Loaf, and to my brilliant teacher Stacey D'Erasmo and the awesome wait staff.

Immense gratitude to the people of West Virginia, who fight the onslaught of mountaintop removal on a daily basis in order to save their homes and communities. A special thank you to those who shared their personal stories with me and taught me something about courage: Larry Gibson, Maria Gunnoe, Ed Wiley, and especially Bo Webb, who drove me around the mountains, offered me beer and a place to stay, and always had knowledge and a story to share. And in memory of the brave and inspiring Judy Bonds, whose fight for the mountains lit the way and opened so many eyes. Although this book is very much a work of fiction, a variety of films, articles, and books helped me along the way. Those that helped considerably include *Everything in Its Path* by Kai T. Erikson, a vivid picture of the 1972 Buffalo Creek Disaster; the *Foxfire* series edited by Paul F. Gillespie and Eliot Wigginton; *Lost Mountain* by Erik Reece, for powerfully detailing the effects of mountaintop removal; *Our Appalachia* edited by Laurel Shackelford and Bill Weinberg; *The Serpent Handlers* by Fred W. Brown and Jeanne McDonald; and *Serpent-Handling Believers* by Thomas G. Burton. Thanks to the amazing films and radio programs at Appalshop in Whitesburg, Kentucky, with special recognition to filmmaker Robert Salyer.

For giving me space and uninterrupted time to work on this novel, thank you to Djerassi Resident Artists Program, Fundación Valparaíso, the MacDowell Colony, and Virginia Center for the Creative Arts. Thanks also to the residencies that showed support in the early days: Jentel Artist Residency Program, which inspired me to quit my full-time office job and never look back; the New York Mills Regional Cultural Arts Center; the Hall Farm

ACKNOWLEDGMENTS

Center for Arts and Education; and the Constance Saltonstall
Foundation for the Arts.

Thank you to my editor Anton Mueller, champion of this book,
for all of his insights and support, and to everyone at Bloomsbury,
for their generous efforts in taking such good care of *The Evening
Hour*. And, finally, my deepest gratitude to my agent, PJ Mark,
whose suggestions, guidance, and faith made this a better book.
Thank you for sticking by me and for caring.

In loving memory of my grandparents.

A NOTE ON THE AUTHOR

Carter Sickels, a graduate of the M.F.A. program at Pennsylvania State University, was awarded scholarships and residencies to Bread Loaf Writers' Conference, the Sewanee Writers' Conference, the MacDowell Colony, VCCA, the Djerassi Residency, and Fundación Valparaíso. After spending nearly a decade in New York, Carter left the city to earn a master's degree in folklore at the University of North Carolina at Chapel Hill and is now living in the Pacific Northwest.